THE HIGHEST ALTAR

THE HIGHEST ALTAR

THE STORY OF HUMAN SACRIFICE

PATRICK TIERNEY

VIKING

VIKING
Published by the Penguin Group
Viking Penguin, a division of Penguin Books USA Inc.,
40 West 23rd Street, New York, New York 10010, U.S.A.
Penguin Books Ltd, 27 Wrights Lane, London W8 5TZ, England
Penguin Books Australia Ltd, Ringwood, Victoria, Australia
Penguin Books Canada Ltd, 2801 John Street,
Markham, Ontario, Canada L3R 1B4
Penguin Books (N.Z.) Ltd, 182–190 Wairau Road,
Auckland 10, New Zealand

Penguin Books Ltd, Registered Offices:
Harmondsworth, Middlesex, England

First published in 1989 by Viking Penguin,
a division of Penguin Books USA Inc.

1   3   5   7   9   10   8   6   4   2

Grateful acknowledgment is made for permission to reprint an excerpt
from *Darkness at Noon* by Arthur Koestler. Reprinted by permission of
Sterling Lord Literistic, Inc. Copyright 1941 The Macmillan Company.

The illustration of "The Evolution of the Andean Gods" on page 281 is
taken from *El Perú Antiguo,* by Federico Kauffmann Doig (Lima: Ediciones PEISA, 1983).

LIBRARY OF CONGRESS CATALOGING IN PUBLICATION DATA
Tierney, Patrick.
The highest altar.
Bibliography: p.
Includes index.
1. Sacrifice, Human.   2. Indians of South America—
Andes Region—Rites and ceremonies.   I. Title.
GN473.5.T54   1989   393   87-40666
ISBN 0-670-82809-2

Printed in the United States of America · Set in Plantin
Designed by Francesca Belanger
Maps by Robert Gale

THIS BOOK IS DEDICATED
TO JOSÉ LUIS PAINECUR, CLEMENTE LIMACHI,
AND ALL OTHER VICTIMS OF HUMAN SACRIFICE
PAST, PRESENT, AND TO COME.

God put Abraham to the test. . . . God said, "Take your son Isaac, your only son, whom you love, and go to the land of Moriah. There you shall offer him as a sacrifice on one of the hills which I will show you."

—Genesis 22:1–2

God willed that His Son suffer inconceivably cruel and horrible torments; not only that He suffer them but that He die the most shameful and atrocious death of all possible deaths! Oh, how severe is the will of a Father regarding His Son! How strange and terrible it is!

—Saint Jean Eudes

Aggression and human violence have marked the progress of our civilization and appear, indeed, to have grown so during its course that they have become a central problem of the present. . . . Those, however, who turn to religion for salvation from this "so-called evil" of aggression are confronted with murder at the very core of Christianity—the death of God's innocent son; still earlier, the Old Testament covenant could come about only after Abraham had decided to sacrifice his child. Thus, blood and violence lurk fascinatingly at the very heart of religion.

—Walter Burkert, *Homo Necans*

ACKNOWLEDGMENTS

Of the many people I've relied on for help in writing this book, none have been as crucial as the Andean shamans whose rituals I observed. Their personalities are more complex and more impressive than anything I have been able to convey in writing.

I am grateful to my brother, John Tierney, who accompanied me on a climb of a twenty-thousand-foot mountain in northern Chile, sponsored other climbs, encouraged me to write this book, and provided me with excellent editorial advice throughout.

I began high-altitude archaeological explorations thanks to Antonio Beorchia and his Center for Andean Investigations of High Mountains (CIADAM) in San Juan, Argentina. Antonio generously opened his archives to me, shared the results of his many archaeological expeditions, and adopted me into his warm home. Without CIADAM climbers, especially Antonio himself and Johan Reinhard, I could never have attempted Mount Veladero (21,116 feet) in northern Argentina.

Johan Reinhard spent many hours explaining his theory of mountain worship, which provided a unifying set of insights for my Andean research. I am also indebted to Professor Juan Schobinger of the Universidad Nacional de Cuyo, in Mendoza, Argentina, whose Archaeological Institute gave me access to the most recent finds from the high Andes. Mariano Gambier, curator of the Museum of Laja, in San Juan, was equally helpful.

Anthropologist Thomas Zuidema of the University of Illinois influenced me through his analysis of human sacrifice under the Incas. Many other archaeologists, anthropologists, and experts kindly gave me their advice, including Carlos Aldunate, director of the Chilean Museum of Pre-Columbian Art, Santiago, Chile; Mónica Ampuero and Roberto Barcena, of the Universidad Nacional de Cuyo; Angel Cabezas, anthropologist and high-altitude climber; Claudio Canut De Bon, high-altitude archaeologist and my guide to Mount Tórtolas (20,770 feet, northern Chile); Christopher Donnan, director of UCLA's Museum of Cultural History; María Ester Grebe, professor of anthropology at the University of Chile; Bonny Glass-Coffin, doctoral candidate in anthropology at UCLA, who specializes in shamanism and who introduced me to a famous healer in northern Peru; Evan Hadingham, author of *Lines to the Mountain Gods;* Patrick Horne, a paleopathologist from the University of Toronto; Luis Lumbreras, professor of anthropology at the University of San Marcos, Lima; Alberto Medina, professor of anthropology at the University of Chile; Lydia Nakashima, UCLA anthropologist who is an expert on Mapuche dreams; Hans Niemeyer, director of Chile's National Museum of Cultural History; Rita Prochaska, also a UCLA doctoral candidate, who is doing her thesis on Taquile Island, Lake Titicaca; and Enrique Vergara, director of the Archaeological Museum of Trujillo, Peru.

Professor Hyam Maccoby encouraged me throughout my novitiate in Biblical studies. The framework for viewing the sacrificial ideology of both Old and New Testaments is largely borrowed from Maccoby's pioneering research.

My investigation of ongoing human sacrifices wouldn't have been possible without the company of two outstanding translators: Lorenzo Aillapán, who accompanied me on the Mapuche reservations of southern Chile, and Francisco Paca, who traveled with me through the Aymara territory of Lake Titicaca. Both of them risked their own safety and made invaluable contributions as native linguists, diplomats, and interviewers.

Bob Weil, my former editor at *Omni* magazine, first urged me to write this book. My brother, John, introduced me to Kristine Dahl, a superb literary agent. Kristine not only helped organize the material; she found an enthusiastic publisher for the book in just two days. Dan Frank, my editor at Viking Penguin, has brought *The Highest Altar* along with scholarly insight, critical cuts, and unfailing optimism.

Finally, I thank my parents, John and Patricia, for their selfless support, which ranged from proofreading manuscripts to caring for me when I came down with hepatitis after my final trip to Peru. Although this book is dedicated to the victims of human sacrifice, my parents, who worried about my safety for four years, rank highest on my personal list of victims.

CONTENTS

THE HIGHEST ALTAR

PANAMA

VENEZUELA

GUYANA

SURINAM

FRENCH GUIANA

COLOMBIA

E Q U A T O R

Quito ■
ECUADOR

Amazon River

B R A Z I L

∴ Sipán

∴ Chavín

Machu Picchu

Lima ■

P E R U

Cuzco

B O L I V I A

Nazca • LAKE TITICACA

Arequipa ▲ La Paz ■

Misti ▲ ▲ Illimani

Tiahuanaco Altiplano

Esmeralda • Potosí

PACIFIC
OCEAN

PARAGUAY

Licancábur ▲

▲ Quehuar

Llullaillaco ▲

Veladero ▲

o ← LAGUNA BRAVA

Cerro del Toro ▲

San Juan •

Aconcagua ▲

Santiago ■ Cerro El Plomo

A T L A N T I C   O C E A N

Concepción •

LAGO BUDI →

Valdivia •

C H I L E

A R G E N T I N A

URUGUAY

SOUTH AMERICA

0   2   MILES   6   800

LAGO
BUDI

Puerto
Saavedra • R. Budi

Pacific Ocean

0   Miles   30

Falklands I.

■ Capital Cities
▲ Mountains
∴ Ancient Sites

Cape Horn

60°W.

S. Georgia I.

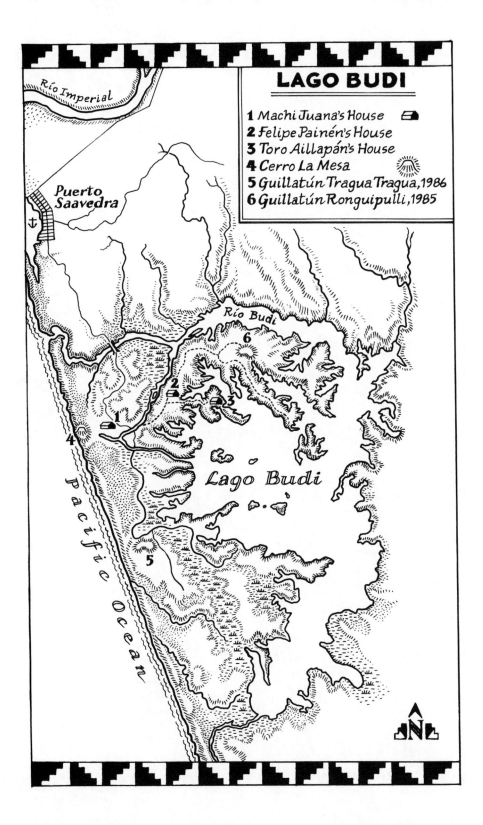

LAGO BUDI

1 Machi Juana's House
2 Felipe Painén's House
3 Toro Aillapán's House
4 Cerro La Mesa
5 Guillatún Tragua Tragua, 1986
6 Guillatún Ronquipulli, 1985

Río Imperial

Puerto Saavedra

Río Budi

Lago Budi

Pacific Ocean

N

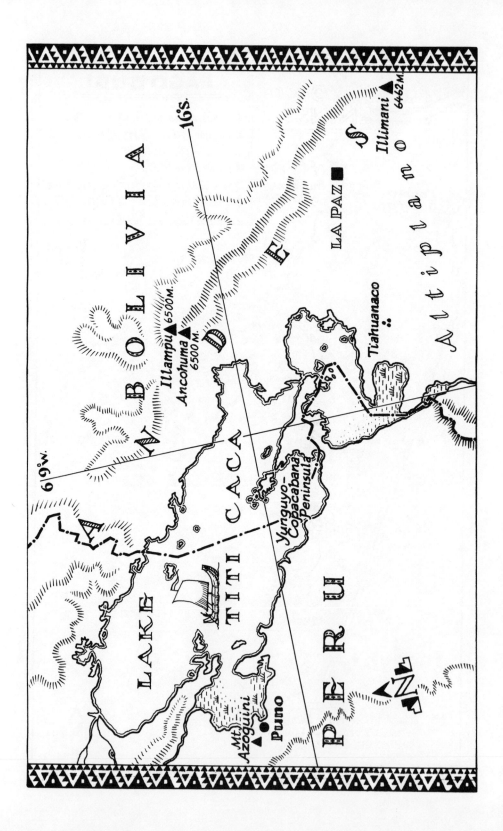

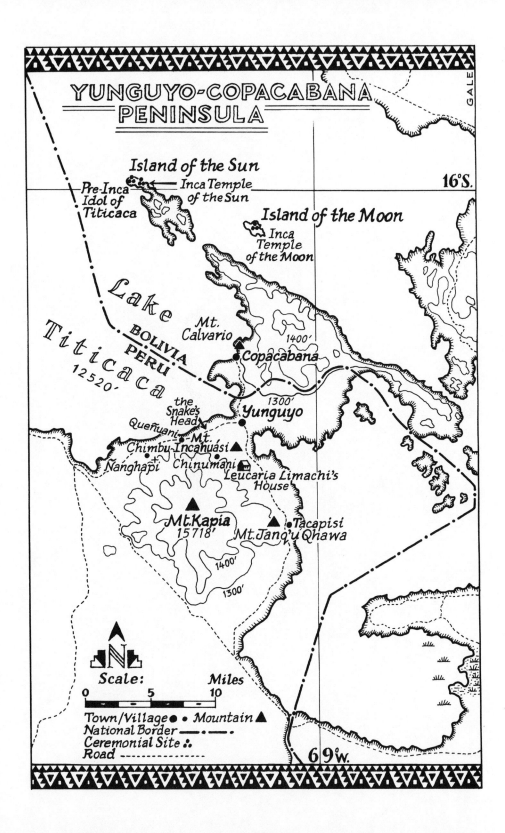

YUNGUYO-COPACABANA PENINSULA

GALE

16°S.

Island of the Sun

Pre-Inca Idol of Titicaca

Inca Temple of the Sun

Island of the Moon

Inca Temple of the Moon

Lake

BOLIVIA
PERU

Titicaca
12520'

Mt. Calvario

1400'

Copacabana

1300'

the Snake's Head

Queñuani

Yunguyo

Ñanghapi

Mt. Chimbu-Incahuási

Chinumani

Leucaria Limachi's House

Mt.Kapia
15718'

Tacapisi

Mt.Janq'u Qhawa

1400'

1300'

N

Scale:
0   5   Miles
                      10

Town/Village ●   ● Mountain ▲
National Border —·—·—
Ceremonial Site ∴
Road -----------

69°w.

PROLOGUE

Police Lieutenant Alfredo González looked out his window on the morning of February 17, 1986, and saw that it was raining again. Torrential rains had been pouring down for a month in the highlands of Peru, filling Lake Titicaca to the brim, and causing it to overflow in Peru's worst flood of the twentieth century. By now Lake Titicaca, which at 12,507 feet above sea level is one of the world's highest lakes, had risen almost six feet above normal, inundating Peru's best farmland—potato and barley fields by Titicaca's reedy shore—and turning thousands of homeless peasants onto the mud-clogged roads in search of safety in the cities. It was one of the biggest disasters to hit the Indian heartlands since the cataclysmic Spanish *conquista* of the sixteenth century.

With so many flood victims desperate for police assistance, Lieutenant González wasn't too surprised to see a small Indian woman with pretty features enter his office in tears. Like many of the Indians living along the southern shores of Lake Titicaca, she didn't speak Spanish fluently. But with the help of a translator she got her message across.

"They murdered my husband last night," Leucaria Limachi said. "They threw his body in the Apacheta."

In spite of the flood, the Indians near the town of Yunguyo had been busy keeping their annual tradition of a three-day Pre-Lenten Carnival. No matter what calamity occurred, the frequent festivals, with their obligatory drunkenness and coca chewing, had to go on. And with them came an obligatory quota of violence. The previous night had been the last day of the carnival. So naturally the victim went drinking with a couple of his cousins. That was the last time anyone saw Clemente Limachi before his body showed up at the place called the Apacheta.

Lieutenant González didn't know what *"apacheta"* meant in the Aymara Indian dialect of southern Peru. But when Leucaria Limachi took him to the spot, located on the skirts of a hill called Mount Santa Bárbara a mile or so outside of Yunguyo, he saw that it was the highest point on a road leading from Yunguyo to the neighboring community of Chinumani. And one look at the body convinced him that this murder wasn't the result of a drunken quarrel.

Clemente Limachi's head had been completely cut off. Both head and torso were deposited inside a curious, hollowed-out rock, as though Limachi had been formally, carefully, executed. This impression was reinforced by the bizarre way in which the victim's entire facial skin had been meticulously scalped off and removed, pushed up above the head, where it hung like a ghoulish mask.

Nor was there any blood near the body. Its absence meant that the murder had taken place somewhere else—and quite far away, since González and his men thoroughly checked the surroundings.

Limachi's body turned up about a quarter mile from where the victim was last seen, drinking with his cousins. Who would drag the body so far and halfway up Mount Santa Bárbara? Hauling the body on a rainy night like February 16, even if it was pulled in an ox cart, just didn't make much sense to González. It would have been far easier to bury him.

The victim's two cousins were arrested. But they revealed only that they'd both drunk a quart of liquor with Clemente Limachi in celebration of the Pre-Lenten Carnival. According to the police report, the two suspects last saw Clemente Limachi "urinating five steps from the door of the house" where they'd enjoyed their revels.

Both cousins were charged with murder on the scantiest of evidence. There was no proof they'd killed Clemente Limachi, nor could the police suggest any good motive. Both of them had gotten along well with the victim. In fact, Limachi was considered an exemplary father and worker. As far as anyone knew, he had no enemies.

But Lieutenant González knew that a lot of things in the Andean altiplano don't make sense to outsiders.

"I'm not from this area originally," González explains. "It's hard to know what to make of all these things." Investigating Limachi's death, he discovered that a young woman was murdered under nearly identical circumstances four years before. Like Limachi's, her body appeared near the Apacheta, along the slopes of Mount Santa Bárbara, with strange disfigurations. When asked if there had been an investigation, González shakes his head quickly. "I wasn't here then. But that murder was never reported. Things aren't the same here as they are in a city. The Indians here, well, they're primitive, almost savages. When I go to investigate something like this, they yell and throw rocks at me. Later they often file protests and accuse the police of torture and human-rights abuses. And it only takes one protest like that for you to lose your job."

There were rumors all over Yunguyo that Clemente Limachi's death had something to do with ancient Indian rituals performed on a mountaintop near the place called the Apacheta. González shrugs his shoulders and suggests that the police keep an eye on that area. But he doesn't know anything about mountaintop rituals. He doesn't even know what *"apacheta"* means.

And it seemed as if he didn't want to know.

🔁 1 🔁

THE UNSPEAKABLE
SACRIFICE

Not wanting to know about human sacrifice is one of the dominant motifs of religious history—almost as dominant as its repeated performance. When the Greek historian Pausanias visited the sanctuary of Zeus atop Mount Lykaion in Arcadia, he heard rumors of secret rituals performed at the peak, rituals instituted by a people whom the Greeks described as "older than the moon." But Pausanias kept the traditions of classical piety by refusing to divulge details about what others called "the unspeakable sacrifice"—the yearly murder, dismemberment, and communal eating of a child at the mountaintop. "I could see no pleasure in delving into this sacrifice," Pausanias wrote. "Let it be as it is and as it was from the beginning."[1]

Pausanias' statement has a liturgical quality. We're accustomed to equating eternity only with divinity, such as the Roman Catholic celebration of the Godhead "as it was in the beginning, is now, and ever shall be, world without end." But Pausanias ascribes eternity to a gruesome blood ritual. And from an anthropological perspective he is close to being correct. Blood sacrifice is the oldest and most universal act of piety. The offering of animals, including the human animal, dates back at least twenty thousand years, and, depending on how you read the scanty archaeological evidence, arguably back to the earliest appearance of humanity.[2] Many religions recount the creation of man through a bloody sacrifice of a God-man—a divinity who is torn apart to sow the seeds of humanity. To paraphrase this crosscultural scripture: "In the beginning there was blood."

Surprisingly, many scientists and religious historians are now describing human evolution in what sound like disturbing echoes of these old creation myths. Advances in Near Eastern, Greek, European megalithic, Andean, and Mesoamerican studies all underscore the importance of human sacrifice in man's social and religious development. Human sacrificial myth and ritual constituted the primitive core for the Panhellenic celebrations at Mount Olympus, Bronze Age ceremonies at Stonehenge, Jewish holidays at the Great Temple on Mount Moriah, and dynastic offerings atop the Mayan pyramids. The broad scope of these inquiries, aided by sociobiological research into the origins of human violence, supports powerful generalizations. "The only prehistoric and historic groups obviously able to assert themselves were those held together by the ritual power to kill," writes classics scholar Walter Burkert in his book *Homo Necans: The Anthropology of Ancient Greek Sacrificial Ritual and Myth*. "Through solidarity and cooperative organization, and by establishing an inviolable order, the sacrificial ritual gave society its form."[3] Blood rituals defined man's development to such a dramatic extent that Burkert suggests *Homo necans*, "man the killer," as a more accurate species name than *Homo sapiens*.

Scholars of pre-Columbian civilizations are making equally radical claims that human sacrifice was an engine of New World cultural evolution. The deciphering of Mayan glyphs, the New World's only writing system, has revolutionized Mesoamerican studies. A thousand years before the Aztecs carried human sacrifice to its bloody zenith, the classic Mayans had already created a sophisticated ritual grammar, with verbs such as "decapitate," "tear the heart out," and "roll down the pyramid steps." Perhaps the most shocking conclusion is that the great Mesoamerican achievements in architecture, art, military organization, and astronomy revolved around the obsessive need for sacrificial victims. "Clearly, from the earliest periods and in every region, human sacrifice was a fundamental element of Mesoamerican culture," writes Arthur Demarest of Vanderbilt University, in summarizing the results of a Harvard Dumbarton Oaks Conference, *Human Sacrifice in Mesoamerica.* "These explorations of the myriad manifestations of Mesoamerican human sacrifice become critical items to those interested in the historical development of New World civilization, and even for those seeking general theories of cultural evolution."[4]

I wasn't aware of the issues at stake when a popular-science magazine gave me what I thought was a bizarre and insignificant assignment: to write about an Inca child sacrificed by being buried alive atop a 17,780-foot-high peak in Chile. In fact, my initial reaction was the same as Pausanias': I could see no pleasure to be gained from delving into this sacrifice. I wondered why the Chileans couldn't have let the Inca child rest in peace beneath the Andean snows where he'd lain for five hundred years.

In Argentina I saw other human-sacrifice victims, one of them buried on a twenty-thousand-foot peak. These frozen children were so lifelike, and the expressions on their faces so peaceful, almost beatific, that touching them seemed to touch a deep chord beyond rational defenses. I also learned that a new breed of mountaineering archaeologist had discovered over a hundred Inca sanctuaries above fifteen thousand feet, complete with a treasure trove of Inca statues and garments. Before long I was addicted to this scientific sport of high-altitude archaeology, as I joined in searching the most desolate regions of the Andes for the world's highest ruins—and for human-sacrifice victims.

Maybe I would have written a book just about these remarkable Inca ruins and mummies—if I hadn't learned that human sacrifice was still continuing in the Andes: in southern Chile, on a Mapuche Indian reservation along the shore of a large lake surrounded by green hills and pine forests. It was a fantastic place, with the South Pacific's huge breakers pounding on the west, and snowcapped volcanoes, rising like perfect pyramids, visible to the east. When I crossed Lago Budi on a wooden raft, I felt that I'd entered Pausanias' Arcadia, the untouched ancestral home of a people older than the moon.

The Mapuches believed powerful creatures lived on every hilltop and in every pool of water; these creatures supposedly waited at night, disguised as vampire birds, to suck your blood. Or they'd emerge from the perennial mists in human shape, then lead you to a cliff where you'd fall on jagged rocks to your death. Of all the fearsome creatures at Lago Budi, however, none was more feared, or assumed more mythical transformations, than the shaman who'd reportedly performed the human sacrifice I'd come to investigate. People warned me to avoid her at all costs. Some people didn't even like to mention her name, which was Machi Juana. Like Moses, she had visions of supernatural fires; like Saint Paul, she had no authority but her spirit. A friend of mine, who accompanied me, said, "I think she may be the most powerful person I've ever met."

Although it was a long time before I met another shaman who impressed me as much as the old sorceress at Lago Budi, I did find an area around Lake Titicaca, in southern Peru, where human sacrifice remains an almost casual, seasonal occurrence. Here, on a peninsula that divides the holiest body of water in the Andes, within sight of the Incas' sacred Island of the Sun, and on top of a 15,780-foot mountain whose stones helped build the two-thousand-year-old shrine of Tiahuanaco, I saw human sacrifice adapting itself to the demands of the cocaine trade.

But the worst was yet to come—the discovery of an ultra-fundamentalist Christian sect in the Andes that performed a human sacrifice on August 18, 1986. This weirdest of events sparked my interest in Biblical human sacrifice. Eventually, my mountain climbing took me to Israel, the home of all our sacrificial hopes.

Academic studies on sacrifice abound. Surprisingly, they've had little impact. Textbooks continue to present the Inca ruins, the Nazca Lines, the Mayan pyramids, and Stonehenge, among others, as pleasant, inoffensive places, where prehistoric peoples might have conducted picnics—in spite of overwhelming evidence to the contrary. College students can still complete courses on world civilization without learning that sacrifice played a vital part in ancient man's economic and political development. When we "cut a deal" we unconsciously echo our ancestors' custom of cutting the throat of an animal victim to seal a contract with blood. Sacrifice was the essence of ancient man's sacred life. Indeed, the very words "sacred" and "sacerdotal" come from "sacrifice." The priest and god were both defined by the act of killing. From Israel to Greece, from the Old World to the New, sacrifice was *the* religious experience.

But you would never guess this if you visited Stonehenge today. Most visitors think the magnificent standing stones belonged to an ancient astronomical observatory. Archaeoastronomers such as Gerald Hawkins, Fred Hoyle, and Alexander Thom popularized notions that Europe's megalith builders were genius stargazers, who used stone circles as giant calculators.

Other evidence, however, lies close at hand—and underfoot. A man shot to death by arrows lies buried at the main entrance of Stonehenge; the Greek geographer Strabo wrote that Druids performed human sacrifice by arrow shooting. And within two miles of Stonehenge there is another circle, built of wooden posts, called Woodhenge. In the center of Woodhenge excavators found a three-and-a-half-year-old girl whose skull had been split "before burial"[5] by an ax. She was killed four thousand years ago, about the same time the giant standing stones at Stonehenge were erected. Apparently she served as a foundation sacrifice for Woodhenge, making her the guardian spirit of the place. At another spot, again, just a mile from Stonehenge, there is a hundred-foot-deep pit, known as the Wilsford Shaft, which contained an ox skull, pottery, and organic remains, suggestive of votive pits known elsewhere. "Sacrificial pits such as this, with a human being lashed to the post, are known on the continent. . . ."[6]

One of the most common features of British stone circles, including Stonehenge, is the presence of cremated human bones. Forensic analysis of bones at fifty Scottish stone circles revealed that there were too few individuals for family burials, and that a disproportionate number were children. "There is a smell of ritual death about all this," concluded archaeologist Aubrey Burl in an article for *Scientific American*.[7] Folk tales about children being burned to death inside these stone circles have survived until modern times, along with the custom of having children leap over bonfires at the harvest, a rite linked to real sacrifices in antiquity. "Stonehenge was not an academy for research into the stars and the nature of the universe," Burl states in his 1987 book, *The Stonehenge People*. "It was a place of death, built by people whose needs and fears were very different from our own."[8]

The same story repeats itself in the fantastic interpretations of the Nazca Lines. For fifty years mathematician Maria Reiche studied these animal drawings and lines, which Peruvian Indians made by displacing shiny desert rocks to make the world's most enormous designs. She concluded the figures and lines are storehouses of calendrical data. This view, widely accepted, has been refuted by computer analysis, which found only chance relations between the lines and heavenly bodies.

But there is a wealth of historical, ethnographic, and archaeological data which links the lines to Andean water and fertility cults. Decapitated heads, used in fertility rites, have been found near the lines; numerous pottery shards reveal trophy heads, some of them drawn so as to appear dripping with blood. "There's no doubt that the people at Nazca had an obsession with decapitation and the cult of the head, which was part of their sacrificial rites," according to British archaeologist Evan Hadingham, author of the recent book *Lines to the Mountain Gods*. "I'm amazed at how many outlandish theories scientists have projected onto the lines."[9]

Anthropologist Johan Reinhard, who has played a role in unlocking the mysteries of Nazca, Tiahuanaco, and Inca high-altitude sites, sees the Nazca Lines fiasco as an example of scientists imposing preconceived notions onto the past. "The man who first saw the Nazca Lines flew over them and said, 'Hey, this is the greatest astronomy book in the world,' without looking at the Andean historical and ethnographic background. It just occurred to him that

this would be a great astronomy book. And he suggested the idea
to Maria Reiche, who, as a mathematician, found it appealing, and
has pursued it ever since."[10]

The Maya were also supposed to be happy stargazers working
from pyramid-observatories. But in 1986 University of Texas
scholar Linda Shele and Yale art historian Mary Ellen Miller published *The Blood of Kings*, a book which argued that the Maya
possessed an almost aesthetic passion for human sacrifice, which
their art portrayed in all its ghastly, gorgeous variety. "Blood was
the mortar of ancient Maya ritual life. . . . Although Maya warfare
fulfilled several needs, the primary ritual role was to provide the
state sacrificial victims, whose blood was then drawn and offered
to the gods."[11] In addition, the Maya had a royal penchant for penis
slashing.

As a whole, these new interpretations mark a major shift in
the way archaeologists view the past. The old fairy tales have been
thrown out, and a grimmer, more realistic appreciation of our ancestors is replacing them. One of the most intriguing issues, however,
is what took scientists so long to come to these conclusions. Some
of the evidence on the Maya, Nazca Lines, and British stone circles
is new. But much of the data has been available for decades.

Why do archaeologists arouse more enthusiasm among peers
by finding ancient scholar-scientists (like themselves) than by investigating leaders who buried children alive? Understandably enough,
scholars tend to see their own specializations mirrored in the past.
Archaeoastronomers see stars everywhere. Others see data-retrieval
systems where head-hunting was the real business. Archaeologists
have appeared too rational to accept the irrational tendencies of the
human past. Yale's Miller noted that scholars "seemed to blind
themselves" to the evidence of ritual killing in Mayan culture. "It's
almost as if people were trying to protect Maya history from itself,"
Miller said in a recent interview with *The New York Times*.[12]

But perhaps we're all really trying to protect ourselves from
the unpleasant truth about our ancestors. Hebrew scholar Hyam
Maccoby, author of *The Sacred Executioner: Human Sacrifice and*

the Legacy of Guilt, says that every culture develops "distancing devices," to hide the facts about its bloody past. "No society is willing to admit fully what happened at its birth."[13]

You might think it's just as well to forget about the past if it's so awful. That's the instinctive reaction—from Pausanias to mainstream anthropology to the Peruvian police officer who doesn't want to know what's happening on the mountain outside his town.

But we, too, have sacrifices going on all around us, on the mountains just outside of town. Our own society has child sacrifice written on our twin foundation stones—the attempted sacrifice of Isaac, son of Abraham, on Mount Moriah, and the sacrifice of Jesus, Son of God, on Mount Calvary. We have a tremendous amount at stake in these sacrifices. There's also an enormous burden of guilt, especially in the sacrifice of Jesus, who died for our sins. Hyam Maccoby claims that Christianity has dealt with its sacrificial guilt by dumping it on the Jews, who have become our culture's continual victims, companions with Jesus on the *via dolorosa* leading from Calvary to the Holocaust. Here, too, we may prefer to be ignorant of our human sacrifices, but the price may be their continuation on a scale larger than anything ever dreamed of by the peasants at Lake Titicaca.

The silence on human sacrifice, however, isn't entirely due to squeamishness or self-deception. In a fundamental sense, science is ill-equipped to deal with the problem of sacrifice. "Sacrifice is the most crucial and fundamental of rites," claims René Girard, author of *Violence and the Sacred.* Yet "it is also one of the most commonplace."[14] And that "commonplace" quality of sacrifice is what makes it so elusive. In addition to the ubiquitous animal and human offerings, prayers are frequently defined as "sacrifices." And what can a scientist make of the Hindu doctrine that a disciplined yogi "sacrifices" breathing and thinking in the mystical union of a meditative trance?[15] Indeed, the *Bhagavad-Gita* teaches that the entire universe is endlessly involved in sacrificing and being sacrificed: "Therefore the all-pervading Brahma is ever established in sacrifice" (ch. 3, v. 15).

Western philosophy has also wrestled with sacrifice and encountered insurmountable odds. In the Age of Enlightenment, Immanuel Kant had attempted, in his system of ethics, to reconcile rational humanism with religious belief. But then Danish philosopher Søren Kierkegaard wrote his masterpiece, *Fear and Trembling*, a dialectical discourse on Abraham's willingness to sacrifice his only son, Isaac. Kierkegaard shows that, no matter how you try to turn Kantian logic on Abraham's decision to kill his son, the program grinds to a halt, unable to get around this "monstrous paradox" of child sacrifice. The end cannot justify the means—and the means are horrible. Without being explicit, the lines of the debate extend invisibly to the even more dreadful sacrifice of Jesus by God the Father. Kierkegaard forces us to conclude that rationality cannot rescue Isaac or Jesus. Something else is needed, Kierkegaard argues, something "which no thought can grasp because faith begins precisely where thinking leaves off."[16] In other words, sacrificial faith begins where philosophy leaves off.

Curiously, Kierkegaard, by stretching reason to the breaking point, reaches the same conclusion Eastern yogis achieve by reducing mental activity to the still point: sacrifice can only be comprehended by a direct experience beyond rational thought.

Rationalists respond that they can simply dispense with sacrifice, and forget about Abraham, Isaac, and company. There is, for instance, the Marxist alternative. But it's curious, at least, that the holiest shrine in the Soviet Union is Lenin's tomb, where people genuflect before the dead leader's embalmed body as though he were an Inca mummy. Moreover, Marxism, like Nazism, adopted many of the ritual trappings of primitive sacrifice in its show trials, with their confessions and expiatory executions. This is the theme of Arthur Koestler's classic, *Darkness at Noon*. "According to what I know of history, I see that mankind could never do without scapegoats," the Stalinist inquisitor tells his victim. "I believe it was at all times an indispensable institution; your friend Ivanov taught me that it was of religious origin. . . . We have the same right to invent useful symbols which the peasants take literally."[17]

The notion that human society can survive without sacrifice remains an unproved hypothesis.

Sacrifice is an enduring enigma. Too subtle to define, too pervasive to ignore, too close to the heart of our culture to observe objectively, and too horrible to accept without flinching, human sacrifice manages to hide from us while making its presence felt everywhere. Like a black hole in space, which destroys all light around it but somehow gives rise to galaxies, sacrifice is a vacuum at the center of culture which somehow spins the web of life. René Girard sees language, kinship, and social organization as derivatives of the "sacrificial crisis" that looms beneath the surface of every culture. Yet even these rippling effects of sacrifice do not reveal its innermost secrets. Sacrifice is also a signpost that points to something other than language, kinship, or social organization. That other is the experience which sacred killing instills in participants. Without this experience we can only partially grasp sacrifice. Even those who've had the experience can't transmit it.

But mystical practices in many religions aim at imparting just such an experience. How many Christian saints have achieved ecstatic union by contemplating and identifying with Christ's agonizing death? One of the key practices in Hindu yoga is called *yoga nidra*—the corpse posture. A disciplined yogi is supposed to experience a deathlike trance in this state of total relaxation. One little-known way in which *yoga nidra* is taught, however, requires the practitioner to visualize his own dismemberment and decapitation. The fertility rites of prehistory are the sublime meditations of today.

My aim in this book is to open the door on the "unspeakable sacrifice" by relating my experiences with the practitioners of human sacrifice themselves. I'm not an anthropologist, having taken just a few courses in the subject at Yale and UCLA. Yet not being a professional has given me an advantage of sorts.

Anthropologists are often worried about their long-term relations with host governments—which are responsible for visas and digging permits. Governments do not like people writing about human sacrifice performed by their subjects, since it gives the impression that the government tolerates barbarous behavior. Peer pressure also plays a role in inhibiting anthropologists. Until recently there's been a kind of gentlemen's agreement that professionals shouldn't focus on nasty, sensational issues that might give Western countries a bad impression of the third-world natives.

But if human sacrifice has been a taboo subject for anthropologists, that's rapidly changing. Although I was at first hesitant and embarrassed about admitting to scientists that I was investigating current human sacrificing, I was taken back by the encouragement they offered. The recent discovery of large-scale human sacrifice at Chavín (800 B.C.), the cradle of Andean civilization, along with similar finds at sites of the brilliant Moche culture (250–750 A.D.), have made sacrifice indisputably relevant across the whole horizon of Andean evolution. As I was told by Enrique Vergara, director of the Archaeological Museum of Trujillo, Peru: "In all of the many studies of human sacrifice that have been published, I don't know of any ethnographic data at all. We need to have a study of human sacrifice as it is done today."

Pursuing human sacrifice entails more occupational hazards than, say, describing Inca settlement patterns. You have to play the unpleasant role of part homicide detective, part Spanish inquisitor. You want the natives to tell you their most intimate secrets, secrets they've pledged not to divulge—and which could incriminate members of the community if learned by authorities. The protagonists who performed the human sacrifice in secret make no secret of the fact that they'd like to sacrifice the prying journalist.

My main interest has always been religion. From the time I was an altar boy in a Roman Catholic church, I was disturbed and attracted by sacrificial motifs. I studied a form of Hinduism under Maharishi Mahesh Yogi. Yogic doctrines seemed to offer an alternative to the violence of the Christian crucifixion. Whenever Maharishi was to speak at our lecture hall, his attendants covered up a large crucifix behind the podium.

But the Hindu deities were not as peaceful as they first appeared. Lord Shiva, the god of death, was adorned with skulls and serpents. Kali, his consort, had ferocious teeth. And as I went on to more advanced studies of Sanskrit and the Vedic texts themselves, I learned that the ancient rituals required the slaughter of birds and beasts of many kinds, often in prodigious quantities, and on hundreds of different occasions. Human victims were required for at least three types of sacrifices—for gaining wealth and immortality, for the fulfillment of vows, and for erecting buildings.[18] The *Rajasuja* frankly states that human sacrifice is the most auspicious ritual, one that turns the victim into the creator god, Prajapati, the Great Victim. But what really surprised me was discovering that human sacrifice had continued on a large scale in India up until the nineteenth century, when the British banned it.[19]

Maharishi claimed that Vedic references to human sacrifice were symbolic. He couldn't face the truth about Vedic violence, because he believed the compilers of the Veda were fully enlightened seers living in a golden age of perfection, just as many others see Abraham and Saint Paul in idealized fashion. Like all of us, he wanted to clean up his ancestors. I believe I've been able to see through these illusions, in part, because I've met our ancestors in the Andes. At least, I've met shamans who are much more like the primitive Vedic seers than Maharishi is. The shamans around Lake Titicaca regard human sacrifice as the most auspicious ritual; the victim becomes a god; the sacrifices are performed in order to obtain wealth and immortality, to fulfill vows, and to lay the foundations of buildings. In short, they have a sacrificial agenda remarkably similar to that of the Vedic *rishis*. Perhaps these Peruvian shamans *are* enlightened. But, if so, they are enlightened in a sense that is not easily comprehended. These Andean seers don't flinch at killing flies or men. And they'd find it pointless to cover up the agony of a crucified victim.

Perhaps the single strongest motive for my long human-sacrifice pilgrimage was my own fascination—with human sacrifice, and with the company of the Andean shamans who performed them. Now that it's over, I think Pausanias was lying when he claimed he could see no pleasure in delving into the child sacrifice on Mount Lykaion.

If we didn't take some delight from human sacrifice, it wouldn't keep popping up in our most popular forms of entertainment. From Aeschylus and Aristotle to Brecht and Ionesco, theater has been obsessed with sacrificial killing, as Mary Karen Dahl showed in a Ph.D. thesis at Stanford University.[20] Two of Steven Spielberg's most successful films, *Indiana Jones and the Temple of Doom* and *The Young Sherlock Holmes,* dealt with human-sacrifice cults.

The enjoyment of sacrificial motifs may be part of a deeply ingrained tendency toward destruction. Psychologist Steven Kull suggests that the insane strategies for nuclear war and other archetypes for Armageddon appeal to religious groups who visualize world destruction as an ultimate, all-purifying, divine sacrifice— "the ritual of world destruction." He traces this ideal of world annihilation to Neolithic warfare, where "the essence of the war was the act of killing as a ritual act."[21]

We carry these sacrificial archetypes with us wherever we go. When U.S. astronaut Alan Bean walked on the moon in 1969 and saw the blue sphere of earth hanging above him, he wondered how a primitive tribe would have reacted to the beautiful sight. "Imagine all the virgins they would have sacrificed to it," he thought. Whether we go to the moon or the movies, to a church in our neighborhood or ancient ruins high in the Andes, we still find sacrificial victims on the altar.

There is an unbridgeable gulf between the analysis and the experience of sacrifice. I found the actual witnessing of an animal sacrifice unpleasant, even frightening. But the victim got into my dreams—as a pile of bones that rebuilt itself into a man; as an animal that turned into Christ and then gave birth to a pool of water. From an anthropological perspective, I can see that these are predictable dreams. They reflect the "structure" of Andean religious rituals: rebirth through death, as the victim's blood turns into the lifegiving flow of water which makes the deserts blossom.

But a part of me feels that the dreams are real and the analysis is illusory.

We feel safe when we talk about structures and models. It's as though we had something very solid under our control. But the essence of sacrifice is surrender, losing control in the excitement and fear of ultimate risk. Blood sacrifice throws out the structure of our everyday thoughts and inhibitions, threatening to swallow up the safety of normal life.

I've felt this in the frenzied screaming surrounding animal sacrifice. When the shamans have finished the kill, there is a double sensation—relief and guilt. There's the infinite relief—"He's dead but I'm still alive." Then there is the guilt—"He died instead of me." And in this mingled guilt and pleasure a sense of incorporation takes place, the commingling of the victim with his killers. "He lives on in me," I feel. I am grateful to the dead victim, so grateful, in fact, that I feel as though he could never die—that I will never let him die. This heartfelt emotion embraces all the participants, and seems, in a moment of drunkenness, like an intimation of immortality. "Some day I will witness my own death—and live."

At that moment you feel an intimate echo of Pausanias' most truthful statement about the unspeakable sacrifice: "Let it be as it is and as it was from the beginning."

◪ 2 ◪

THE INCA CHILD

In February 1954, two miners, searching for a fabled treasure of the Incas, scrambled up a glacier slope to a 17,716-foot peak of Mount Plomo, in the Chilean Andes. They headed straight for a rectangular stone wall, with a heap of rocks in the center. After digging three feet under the heap and prying up a huge slabstone, they uncovered a real archaeological treasure—a young child bedecked in Inca ceremonial regalia. The child's feet were tucked under his black llama-wool tunic, faint protection against the eternal cold above the permafrost line. From the peaceful expression on the child's face, it looked as if it had quietly slept through the centuries.

One of the miners went back to Santiago, Chile's capital, and walked through the columns of the National Museum, where he told anthropologist Grete Mostny that he'd found "a little Inca girl" atop Mount Plomo. The Inca girl had pretty features, showed no signs of decay, and was buried along with several statues. Would the museum like to buy the Inca girl? the miner asked.

This was the strangest news Grete Mostny had ever received in her life. Who'd ever heard of burying someone on an eighteen-thousand-foot peak? Nothing like it was recorded in any other part of the world. If true, it would be the highest burial in history. Building stone walls in such a hostile environment also sounded nearly impossible. Finally, the miner's description of the little girl's lifelike appearance sounded too incredible.

So Grete Mostny called on Alberto Medina, an anthropology student at the University of Chile, to check out the miner's story. Like the miners, Medina had heard legends of an Inca treasure buried under the snows of Mount Plomo. But it's one thing to speculate about Mount Plomo from the city of Santiago, when it looks like a pretty postcard, and quite another to work your way up through the hundred-degree heat of its lower hills to the jagged ice formations of its summit. Medina had tried several times to climb Mount Plomo, assisted by mules, guides, and ample supplies. But each time gale-force winds, snowstorms, and altitude sickness drove him back.

Medina met the miners outside of Santiago. To his surprise, the miners' "little girl" wasn't a girl at all—it was a little boy with delicate features. To this day Alberto Medina goes into a reverie when he remembers his first encounter with the Inca child of Mount Plomo.

"The Inca child was truly beautiful," Medina told me. "He had a huge impact on everyone who saw him. The child's body was soft and flexible, so you could easily move his joints. He had such a peaceful expression on his face, it seemed that he'd only been dead a few hours."

Curled on his side, the child wore a black llama-wool tunic trimmed with red. On his feet were embroidered moccasins. His elaborately plaited, shoulder-length hair was held in place by a headband, and his woolen cap was crowned with black-and-white condor feathers. The Inca child also bore a heavy silver arm bracelet and a silver, H-shaped pectoral adornment, both signs of noble birth. These marks of distinction earned the Inca child the title "Prince of Mount Plomo."

And he was accompanied by princely grave goods. These included two llama figurines, one gold and the other of Ecuadorean spondylus shell; a seven-inch-high silver idol dressed in the gorgeous plumed attire of an Inca princess; five pouches containing locks of hair, teeth, and nail clippings; and a purse decorated with red-and-white flamingo feathers, holding still-aromatic coca leaves.

Although both Alberto Medina and Grete Mostny examined the Inca boy with professional competence, they were limited by the technology of the 1950s. They put the mummy in a freezer, where it rested for nearly three decades, leaving major questions unanswered: How did the Inca boy die? And why did the Incas go to the incredible trouble of building an open-air temple and tomb at nearly eighteen thousand feet above sea level?

Answers to these questions have now been provided by the new science of paleopathology, the study of diseases in ancient man. Paleopathologists use CAT (computerized axial tomography) scanners, X-rays, electron microscopes, and biopsies to examine mummified remains. In 1982 UNESCO gave Canadian paleopathologist Patrick Horne a grant to reopen the investigation of the Inca child of Mount Plomo. Horne, an expert who helped found the International Paleopathology Association in 1973, has studied hundreds of mummies from several continents. But he's never seen anything like the boy from Mount Plomo.

"I was overawed at the preservation of the mummy," Horne told me after completing his study in December 1983. "When I took a tissue sample, it was unlike anything I'd ever seen in a mummy from Egypt or the Atacama Desert [of Chile]. It was still very soft. And the cellular preservation is exquisite. Under the electron microscope it looked like a biopsy of skin you'd see today at any dermatology clinic. There's no doubt this is the best-preserved natural mummy we have."

While using an electron microscope to examine warts on the child's hand (magnifying them 180,000 times), Horne detected the viruses which cause warts, the first viruses ever found in a mummy. Although we don't know the exact date of the Incas' arrival in Chile and Argentina, it took place sometime in the second half of the fifteenth century, under the direction of the Inca conqueror Tupac Yupanqui. Argentine archaeologist Juan Schobinger thinks that the sacrifice of Mount Plomo may have occurred around 1470–1480. Since the Inca boy was probably sacrificed prior to the Spaniards' arrival in Chile in 1536, this discovery helps explode the myth that the Spaniards brought all viruses with them to the New World from the Old.

"Now at least we know that viruses are preserved in tissues five hundred years old," Horne notes. "It's one of the most exciting things I've ever seen."

Short, bearded, and cherubic, Horne is a cheerful exponent of necroscience. He uses words like "beautiful," "incredible," and "spectacular" to describe warts, tumors, and other malignancies. Paleopathologists justify their macabre fascination because pathology patterns can indicate what makes a society tick . . . or stop ticking. For instance, although it's mystifying to the uninitiated, Horne was delighted to discover lice ova in the Inca child's hair. Intraspecies differences between American and Asian lice, he explains, could conceivably confirm man's migration across the Bering Land Bridge.

Horne's UNESCO study aims at conserving the Inca boy. But preserving this unusual mummy would be easier if anyone knew why he was so superbly conserved in the first place. Unlike those of Egyptian mummies, the Inca child's viscera weren't removed. Unlike mummies from the Atacama Desert, he wasn't dehydrated. "It's a difficult question," Horne admits. "People have said for years the child was frozen. But I think it was more like freeze-drying."

Freeze-drying is a laboratory technique whereby fresh tissue is put in an evacuated chamber and all water is sucked out at low temperature. The Incas skillfully anticipated the results of freeze-drying without having the advantage of modern methods. They placed the Inca boy in an earthen cave, covered him with a slab, then covered the slab with successive layers of earth and stones piled five feet high. This tumulus of stone and earth kept the grave's temperature uniform all year round, while air and light, necessary for the growth of bacteria, were practically excluded.

But even freeze-drying would have left the Inca boy rigid— not soft and flexible, as the miners originally found him. "If the child was flexible when they found him, it defies the medical definition of death," Horne claims. "I have no explanation for how the body could have been flexible after five hundred years. Right now you couldn't move one of his joints unless you had a sledgehammer."

Horne says his job is to prevent further deterioration of the Inca boy, not to reopen an ancient murder mystery. But he's already helped solve the puzzle of the Inca child's fate. X-rays and dental-calcification studies show the Inca boy was eight to nine years old. No disease or obvious violence explains his death. Most revealing are the child's hands, clasped together around his knees, with the unprotected left hand blue and swollen from frostbite. His right hand, covered by the left, is not frostbitten, meaning that the boy was still alive when he assumed his huddled position at Mount Plomo's icy summit. Horne's conclusion: the Inca boy froze to death after being buried alive.

The Incas used many methods of sacrifice, including strangling, garrotting, breaking the cervical vertebrae with a stone, tearing out the heart, and burying alive. But freezing to death at high altitude was probably the least painful. It's easy to lose consciousness at eighteen thousand feet above sea level, and children are even more susceptible to passing out than adults. A vomit stain on the Inca boy's clothes hints he was given an unaccustomed drink, probably a strong dose of an alcoholic beverage called *chicha*, before burial. He never awoke to realize his terrible predicament.

"It's a pleasant way to die, to be intoxicated where it's cold, and you simply fall into a coma and don't wake up," Horne says. "The expression on his face, which is very important, is one of great peace. His eyes are closed, very relaxed, and there's no sign of trauma. He's very different from those we've seen buried alive in Denmark, where their faces grimace."

Horne's conclusion challenges the popular assumption that the Incas were America's peaceful empire. Most history books still describe the Inca Empire as a socialist paradise revolving around a harmless and healthy cult of the sun. From the eighteenth century onward, European intellectuals adopted the Inca Empire as an Amerindian El Dorado, and a model of sorts for their own visions of enlightened socialism. Most Spanish chroniclers do write that the Incas succeeded admirably in meeting the basic needs of all their subjects for food, shelter, and clothing. But, by remaking the Incas into a European likeness, writers distorted the central ideology of the Inca state, which, though it seemed to achieve the Marxist dictum of "From each according to his ability and to each according to his need," had nothing to do with Marxist materialism or any Western ideology. Burying a child alive on a glacier-covered mountaintop is a wildly impractical and cruel thing to do from any rational perspective. The discovery of the Inca boy of Mount Plomo is like a face-to-face encounter with a long-dead member of an ancient civilization who seems bent on contradicting our fondest ideas about him and his people.

Historians have either denied that the Incas practiced human sacrifice, or else dismissed it as an unfortunate but peripheral aberration. Yet scholars who've dug deeply into forgotten Spanish chronicles now believe human sacrifice played a crucial role in the social, political, and economic control the Incas exercised over their vast, heterogeneous empire, which stretched from Ecuador to Chile.

The Inca boy of Mount Plomo provided the first archaeological clue to this Inca system of control. Grete Mostny noted that the Inca boy's moccasins, pectoral decoration, and hairstyle—curiously woven into hundreds of tiny braids—all identify him as a member of the Colla tribe, which lived along the shores of Lake Titicaca. But why make a little boy walk two thousand miles from Lake Titicaca, across the grueling Atacama Desert of northern Chile, to sacrifice him on the utmost fringes of the empire?

Abbot Cristóbal de Molina, who spoke to Inca priests in sixteenth-century Cuzco, reported that the Incas sacrificed large numbers of carefully selected children. According to Molina, the Incas preferred ten-year-old children of noble birth who were in good health and of exceptional beauty—a nearly exact description of the Inca child of Mount Plomo. Until the Mount Plomo discovery, many scholars discredited Molina and other chroniclers, whom they suspected of prejudice against the Incas. But if Molina's history is correct, then the Incas weren't just practitioners of child sacrifice. They were also inventors of one of the most spectacular ceremonies in religious history.

Twice a year, at the solstice celebrations of June and December, the empire's best crops, most prized animals, finest clothes, most precious artworks, and most beautiful children were gathered from Ecuador to Chile, from the Pacific to the Amazon, until they converged on Cuzco, the Incas' eleven-thousand-foot-high capital, in four magnificent processions. Each of these processions represented one of the geographical subdivisions of the Inca Empire: Collasuyo to the south, Antisuyo to the north, Cuntisuyo to the east, and Chinchaysuyo to the west. Cuzco was more than a combined Vatican and military headquarters. It was a magical mandala which held the empire together.

Cuzco was a square circle. The city was divided into four quadrants—north, south, east, and west—representing the four provinces of the Inca Empire. Yet Cuzco was also conceived of as a circular hub of the empire, with 328 shrines, or *huacas*, defining its periphery, according to University of Illinois anthropologist Thomas Zuidema. The four quadrants and the 328 *huacas* all took the Temples of the Sun and the Moon as their points of convergence. Inside the sacred precincts of these temples, idols of Viracocha (the Creator) and Illapa (the Thunder God), along with the immense, solid gold effigy of the sun and the silver likeness of the moon dazzled the Spanish conquistadors. And they must have dumbfounded the provincial children awaiting sacrifice.

Together, children and animals were herded into a corral near the Temple of the Sun. At this point the Inca, after a ritual purification that included bathing in a river and publicly confessing his sins, personally inspected the children to make sure none had leprosy or deformities. Once unacceptable sacrifices were weeded out, the remaining children heard talks from the Inca High Priest about the benefits their upcoming sacrifices would bring to the whole empire and to themselves. "From the Incas' point of view, they were doing the children a favor," says anthropologist Johan Reinhard, since the victims were transformed into deities after death. During ten days of festivities in Cuzco prior to sacrifice, the children were already celebrated as semidivine.

At the end of these solemnities the children, accompanied by their mothers, marched in unison around statues of the Incas' major gods—Viracocha, the sun, the thunder god, and the moon. Then the Inca Emperor ordered his priests to "take your share of these sacrifices and offerings to the greatest *huaca* in your lands and sacrifice them there."[1] Priests performed the first sacrifices around the 328 sacred *huacas*, which defined the circle of Cuzco, then spread out in four immense processions going north, south, east, and west, to the farthest edges of the Inca's domain.

At each stop along their way, the priests and representatives of the Incas distributed jars filled with the consecrated blood of sacrificed llamas, which were drunk by adult males in a version of Inca "communion."[2] Children were sacrificed only at the most important spots—often high mountains. Priests uttered a prayer to Viracocha before giving him a human sacrifice: "O Creator who gave life to all, since you said let there be day and night, making the dawn and the light to shine: tell your son the Sun when day breaks to come out in peace and safety, shine on all those who wait for you, let none be sick; keep everyone safe and sound."

The child victims were called *capacochas*, or *capac hucha*, which means "royal sin." As an incarnate deity, the Inca ruler was *the* body politic. If he, or his royal relatives, angered the gods, calamities could destroy the empire. All of the children, animals, and goods dedicated at Cuzco for the solstice celebrations became *ca-*

pacocha sacrifices, payments for the Inca rulers' sins. This entire process of collecting and distributing sacrifices around the Inca domains can be called the "*capacocha* system."

Like the Spanish chroniclers, I've used terms such as the "Inca Empire" and "Inca Emperor." Almost all books about the Incas use these conventions, although they're not entirely appropriate. Several scholars now believe the Incas had a diarchy—dual rulership—not a monarchy.[3] Moreover, the European concept of an empire, based on Roman, Spanish, or British rule, doesn't have much in common with the Inca expansion. The Incas had no writing system to codify laws and facilitate administration; nor did Andean civilization have any tradition of centralized power comparable to that of the European state.

"Andean civilization" refers to the radiating religious, artistic, cultural, and political influences that emerged from several key centers—Chavín (800 B.C.), in northern Peru; Tiahuanaco (A.D. 100 –1100), near Lake Titicaca; and several others, including the final, brief Inca period (1438–1532), which centered on Cuzco. *Chavín, Tiahuanacoid,* and *Inca* refer to these distinctive epochs, as well as to their art and architectural styles. In spite of their differences, all of these cultures possessed a common concern with the worship of mountains and water sources, religious practices that were inseparable from politics, trade, and warfare. In fact, Chavín and Tiahuanaco may have been primarily centers of pilgrimage, a role that Cuzco also played. Of Andean polities, the Inca civilization was the most efficient at military conquest. The Inca territory was the largest, its roads and bridges the best. But it fell apart very quickly when the Spaniards arrived, possibly because the Inca goal of hegemony, called *Tahuantinsuyu* ("the unification of the four regions"), was foreign to Andean peoples. The perfectly ordered Inca Empire of history books was fully achieved only in the reports from Spanish chroniclers, who got their information from Inca bureaucrats in Cuzco.[4]

The "Inca Empire" was by no means so clearly defined, or uniformly administered, as the lines on maps suggest. The Andean world revolved around reciprocity—the exchange of gifts between complex kinship groups. The Incas conquered through a combination of military force and gift giving. Without the proper gifts, the Inca rulers couldn't even be sure of support from their own kinship groups, called *ayllus*. Molina's version of the *capacocha* sacrifices creates the impression of absolute Inca control over the pan-Andean world—and that's exactly what Abbot Molina's Inca informants wanted him to believe. In reality, the vast collection and redistribution of textiles, food, livestock, and child sacrifices which constituted the so-called *capacocha* system reflected the demands of reciprocity on a grand scale, an ancient Andean institution in which the exchange of human-sacrifice victims was possibly the most prized gift of all.

Fortunately, a report written in 1621 by Spanish inquisitor Hernández Príncipe helps complete Molina's version of the *capacocha* system. Hernández Príncipe's account was buried in church archives for three hundred years, and first published in an obscure journal in the 1920s, but went largely unnoticed until 1978, when Thomas Zuidema reconsidered the piece.

Hernández Príncipe was a Catholic priest whose title was *"extirpador de idolatrías"* ("extirpator of idolatries"). Like many such priests, Hernández Príncipe stamped out all vestiges of native beliefs wherever he went. Perhaps Hernández Príncipe and other "extirpators of idolatries" achieved a greater insight into native religion because they gained the confidence of Andean shamans, much as a modern anthropologist would try to do, rather than relying exclusively on sources in Cuzco. Hernández Príncipe had a particularly good informant named Xullca Rique, a converted shaman who helped him get the inside story about human sacrifice in the village of Ocros, Peru. His chronicle provides major clues to unraveling both the enigma of Inca religion and the continuing practice of human sacrifice in the Andes.

Hernández Príncipe learned that the villagers of Ocros worshipped a goddess named Tanta Carhua. But Tanta Carhua hadn't always been a goddess. Her rise to divine status probably occurred two centuries before, around 1430, when her father, an aspiring leader named Caque Poma, decided she would make a good human-sacrifice victim. This proved to be a smart political move on Mr. Poma's part:

> This Caque Poma had the daughter already mentioned, ten years old, beautiful beyond exaggeration. From the moment that she revealed (how beautiful) she was going to be, he had her dedicated as a sacrifice to the Sun. He communicated this to the Inca by going to Cuzco, and from there he brought back the order of obtaining within a few days the seat and chieftainship because of the daughter mentioned. He sent her [to Cuzco] as ordered, and after coming back from this celebration, they feted her as was customary. The old people mention that according to tradition the girl said: "You can finish with me now because I could not be more honored than by the feasts which they celebrated for me in Cuzco." They brought her to this place in Aixa, one league (5 kilometers) from here, to a high mountain, at the end of the lands of the Inca, and with the tomb already made, they lowered her and walled her in alive.[5]

The Inca Emperor rewarded Caque Poma with the chieftainship of Ocros in exchange for the sacrifice of Poma's lovely daughter. This deal was closed by giving Caque Poma a small seat, which the Inca conferred on his local governors throughout the empire as a sign of authority. It's significant that the Inca wanted Tanta Carhua dedicated to the Sun God, from whom the Inca supposedly descended.

People still worshipped Tanta Carhua on Mount Aixa when Hernández Príncipe arrived in Ocros. He was outraged to find devotees in Ocros consulting Tanta Carhua's spirit on subjects as varied as agriculture and personal health. They did this through shamans (called "sorcerers" by Hernández Príncipe) who went into trances and became possessed by the spirit of Tanta Carhua, speaking in falsetto to simulate her. "The old people tell that when they were sick or were in need of help, they came with the sorcerers who, assimilating themselves to Tanta Carhua, answered them as a woman: 'this you have to do. . . .' "

Andean peoples are still fond of this direct communication with God. No amount of persuasion by Catholic missionaries could convince them to give up their mummies and the shamans who spoke to their spirits. The Catholic images of Jesus and Mary were obviously inferior, because they couldn't talk back to their petitioners. They couldn't compete with Tanta Carhua.

But Hernández Príncipe had no intention of letting Tanta Carhua compete for the affections of Ocros's inhabitants. He resolved to find her grave and destroy it. He eventually located Tanta Carhua's hidden grave on Mount Aixa. "I worked almost a whole day," he recounts, "which was on the Triumph of the Cross (the third of May), and three estados deep (about 20 feet), in a hole in the form of a pit, very well leveled off and with a deposit in the form of a cupboard was the capacocha sitting in the native way, with adornments of small pots and jars and of shiny silver pins and ornaments that the Inca had given to her as a bridal gift. She was already decomposed and so was the fine cloth in which she had been dressed when she came to this place."[6]

Like the Inca boy of Mount Plomo, Tanta Carhua was buried alive, dressed in fine clothes, and accompanied by precious objects. The discovery of the Inca boy of Mount Plomo, and the equally remarkable recovery of the story of Tanta Carhua, jointly prove how precisely the *capacocha* sacrifices were carried out.

Tanta Carhua was ten, "beautiful beyond exaggeration," and her father was a local leader. Horne's study confirms that the Inca boy of Mount Plomo was the right age and in good health. He was so pretty the miners thought he was a girl, while his silver jewelry also suggests high social status. Tanta Carhua and the Inca boy of Mount Plomo were perfect victims.

Hernández Príncipe's account of Tanta Carhua both confirms and completes Molina's data. Molina gives an almost unbelievable description of a ceremonial system that prepared hundreds of victims to accept their sacrifices at sacred spots across the continent several times a year; not surprisingly, historians for centuries dismissed Molina's chronicle as a wild exaggeration. But Hernández Príncipe shows exactly how this *capacocha* system worked in the case of one small town in the empire.

Hernández Príncipe's local data support Molina's claim that human sacrifice took at least several hundred victims a year. Ocros sent four boys every four years to Cuzco—one victim a year. Estimates for the total number of children sacrificed vary from several hundred to several thousand per year, depending on the circumstances and the Spanish source. Historian Pierre Duviols concludes that, under the *capacocha* system, "the quantity of natural and cultural products collected was enormous and the number of human victims was very much higher than generally believed."[7]

If the legends about Tanta Carhua can be believed, they tell how effective the Inca festivals were in preparing victims for sacrifice. "You can finish with me now," Tanta Carhua said before being buried alive, "because I could not be more honored than by the feasts which they celebrated for me in Cuzco."

Tanta Carhua achieved celebrity status—and not just in Ocros. According to Hernández Príncipe, the Inca gave orders that "they would have priests that would serve them in their worship that was offered them every year, as this capacocha served as guard and custodian of the whole province."[8] Indeed, we know that the Inca ruler himself later made offerings at Mount Aixa, where Tanta Carhua was buried. Thus she rose from an insignificant child in a second-rate town to a deity of transcendental power for the empire.

Hernández Príncipe's command of detail surpasses that of any previously known chronicler, and in many ways turns conventional wisdom about the Inca Empire on its head. Perhaps the single most radical change in our perception of the Incas is the realization that the imperial sun cult was secondary to the older rituals of mountain worship, with its invariable concomitants of human sacrifice and shamanic divination. For centuries historians have said that the Inca Empire revolved around sun worship. Not surprisingly, Patrick Horne repeated this time-honored formula when he told me that the Inca boy of Mount Plomo was "probably sacrificed to the Sun God." But Hernández Príncipe's detailed inquisition at Ocros calls this conclusion into question.

True, Hernández Príncipe quotes townspeople as saying that Tanta Carhua was "an *aclla* [chosen one] of the sun."[9] But the observant inquisitor then goes on to discredit this testimony thoroughly, proving that Tanta Carhua was dedicated to the sun only in a limited and formal sense. Tanta Carhua's grave was built above an irrigation canal built by her father. Thomas Zuidema believes she was actually sacrificed to assure successful completion of the irrigation canal. Her father was having trouble with the irrigation-canal project, and he went to Cuzco to suggest the sacrifice of his daughter as a means of magically influencing the construction project. Her tomb's position on a prominent mountaintop overlooking both the Inca's granaries and the life-giving irrigation canal made Tanta Carhua the custodian of the town's precious water supply and the protectress of its crops. (The boy of Mount Plomo was also sacrificed near the fount of the Mapocho River, thus connecting him to the water cult as well.)

Tanta Carhua wasn't the only mummified ancestor in Ocros who received offerings and supplications. Hernández Príncipe reported two other kinds of mummies: dead chiefs (headed by Tanta Carhua's father, Caque Poma) and dead shamans (all relatives of Tanta Carhua and Caque Poma). But Tanta Carhua received more attention than any of the other ancestors. She even got better treatment than the mountain deities.

And Tanta Carhua wasn't the only human-sacrifice victim to play such a key role. Hernández Príncipe's data from two of Ocros's neighboring towns reveal that each kinship group, or *ayllu,* used human sacrifice to assuage their internal conflicts or improve their external relations. Thus one *ayllu* offered two child sacrifices to enhance good will between social classes within that group. Another *ayllu* sent four other victims to Cuzco in order to cement better relations with the Inca. A third *ayllu* provided five *capacochas* to several capitals of the empire. Yet another *ayllu* dispatched child sacrifices to Lake Titicaca, Chile, and Lake Yahuarcocha ("the lake of blood"). A group of potters sacrificed children in a couple of pits, to secure good clay.[10]

Thus human sacrifice smoothed relations between classes, created ties between towns, fulfilled obligations to the Inca rulers, and assured a supply of clay. The multiple uses of human sacrifice raise multiple questions. For instance, was human sacrifice an established form of trade in the Andes? Evidence from Chavín now proves that sending offerings of precious objects, animals, and human victims to distant shrines was practiced two thousand years prior to the Incas. Hernández Príncipe's sources told him that *capacochas* went to Lake Titicaca and Chile and did not mention that any of them passed through Cuzco. If Molina's account were the only one we had, we'd assume that Inca priests picked children and sent them around the empire from Cuzco as a matter of imperial policy. But the view from around Ocros is that local leaders decided when and where to perform most sacrifices, and they saw such exchanges as part of their religious and political relations with sacred spots from Ecuador to Chile. We can't tell whether all the victims were formally dedicated in Cuzco or not. But even if all the victims did go to Cuzco, it now appears that the Incas were simply trying to monopolize an established practice. When children like Tanta Carhua were made *acllas* of the Sun God, the sacrifice ostensibly became a gift from the Inca dynasty, thus increasing Inca prestige and attaching the new deity to the imperial pantheon.

Ocros also had a regular human-sacrifice tribute destined for Cuzco—four boys every four years. It's not clear why Tanta Carhua received so much more attention than the other *capacochas*, though it seems related to her role in legitimizing the dynastic claims of her clan to the Ocros chieftainship. Nor do we know whether the other, male *capacochas* were killed in Cuzco or somewhere else. What is clear is that Tanta Carhua's prestige survived long after the Incas and their solar cult had been forgotten.

We now know that sun worship, believed for centuries to have been the centerpiece of the Inca Empire, was a late creation. The

Incas built solar temples at only a few spots—notably Cuzco, the Island of the Sun at Lake Titicaca, and the coastal shrine of Pachacamac. But all of these had been famous places of pilgrimage before they were rededicated to the Sun God during the fifteenth century, less than a hundred years before the Spanish conquest. The Inca's solar reform was an attempt to redirect sacrifice into a new mold consciously, with the aim of heightening the Inca's dynastic influence. Since local tribes were all attached to their individual mountain gods and their ancestral mummies, the Incas had good reason to try to impose a symbol that stood above all the mountains—the sun. But, like the Inca's goal of empire building, the project was only partly successful. "Extirpators of idolatries" mention cults devoted to mummies and mountains far more frequently than sun worship.

In both Mesoamerica and the Andes, human sacrifice played a vital role in polity thousands of years prior to the rise of the Aztec alliance or the Inca dynasty. In both areas, water rites and mountain worship formed the core of the older, pre-Inca and pre-Aztec beliefs. This is shown by the Aztecs' calendar, which opens the year with child sacrifices on mountaintops in honor of the rain gods. The Aztecs, however, reworked the older traditions and created a new theory: the Sun God needed vast amounts of blood to survive, and the Aztec goal was to provide sacrifices in ever-increasing quantities. "In fact, the elaboration of the central solar sacrificial cult was one of the major factors involved in driving the expansion, forming the empire, and giving it its loose-knit structure," according to Arthur Demarest.[11] A new human-sacrifice model motivated the Aztec Empire's militaristic success.

This contrasts with the choices made by the Inca rulers, whose policy of making Cuzco a human-sacrifice hub repartitioned victims all over the empire in a unifying way. In exchange for a sacrifice, Caque Poma got the chieftainship; Ocros got a new canal; and the new goddess, Tanta Carhua, joined the imperial religion. The new leaders and priests in Ocros acquired a stake in the Inca system, while the Incas put their stamp on the local deity. In a real sense, sacrificial victims were the coin of the realm. They were traded over distant areas, and the rules governing these exchanges evolved over hundreds of years. The repercussions of Tanta Carhua's offering went on for centuries at Ocros. People depended on Tanta Carhua for economic success and personal well-being. For two hundred years all of Ocros's leaders descended from Caque Poma, who owed his position to Tanta Carhua's death, while the most influential shamans were also from Caque Poma's lineage. Based on this information, we can safely guess that the Inca boy of Mount Plomo— farther from the great center of Cuzco but buried on a much more spectacular mountain—probably played an equally vital role for all of central Chile. What is irrefutable: the boy of Mount Plomo offers physiological evidence of human sacrifice in the late Inca Empire.

In the ultimate sense, there was no one reason Tanta Carhua (or the Inca boy of Mount Plomo) was sacrificed: it was done to assure a supply of water to the irrigation canal, to provide the sustenance of crops, to get her father promoted, to intercede for the sick with the mountain god . . . Making the Inca Emperor happy by saying she was offered to the Sun God also figured on the list. What's particularly impressive about Hernández Príncipe's report at Ocros is his realization that Tanta Carhua's dedication to the Sun God had little to do with the interests of the local devotees. He saw this as a formality to please the Incas, a formality that local worshippers soon disregarded.[12] Zuidema calls Hernández Príncipe's observation "the strongest and most insightful statement made by any chronicler."

There's something perversely admirable about Hernández Príncipe's single-handed determination. You can just see him sweating away in the May heat at Ocros, finding a carefully concealed grave on a mountaintop, then digging his twenty-foot hole until he finds the body of Tanta Carhua. It's particularly ironic to hear him associate the sacrilegious destruction of someone else's most cherished divinity with "the triumph of the True Cross." Even this most perceptive of Spanish inquisitors couldn't see any relationship between the sacrifice of Tanta Carhua and the triumph of the True Cross.

Yet Hernández Príncipe saw beyond many of the appearances of Inca worship that misled other Europeans, until he finally came close to grasping the core of Andean worship, centuries ahead of modern historians. Throughout my investigation of human sacrifice in the Andes, I returned frequently to the writings of Hernández Príncipe. I've thought a lot about this strange man and his strange mission. In dangerous situations I've conjured up the memory of the old inquisitor, whose fervor rivaled any shaman's devotion to Tanta Carhua or the Inca boy of Mount Plomo.

He is the patron saint of grave-robbers and human-sacrifice detectives.

◪ 3 ◪

THE AMATEURS
TAKE OVER

Bull Mountain (Mount Toro) was supposed to be a virgin peak. The 20,669-foot peak is located in the mountainous desert of northwestern Argentina, amid a tough, barren landscape, with little but scrub grass and cacti, reminiscent of the badlands of the Western United States. Only one attempt had been made to climb it before 1964—and that failed because of a violent snowstorm. But in January 1964 Erico Groch and Antonio Beorchia, members of San Juan's Mercedario Mountaineering Club, conquered the difficult summit. At twenty thousand feet there's less than half the oxygen we have at sea level. The heart and lungs work overtime. Grogginess prevails. Reaction time, both mental and physical, is slow, while emotions are strangely amplified. Just reaching the peak of Bull Mountain gave Groch and Beorchia a tremendous emotional high. So you can imagine their excitement when they discovered a rectangular stone platform, three feet high, thirty-five feet long, and twenty feet wide, about three hundred feet below the peak. Fifteen feet beyond the northwestern corner of the platform they noticed a group of large stones forming a circle three feet in diameter. Suddenly Groch spotted a white sphere in the middle of the circle. "It looks like a skull!" he shouted.

Beorchia began digging as furiously as his numb hands and oxygen-starved body permitted. He soon unearthed the shoulders and knees of a human body. Then Beorchia dug farther and found himself staring into the ghostly-white face of someone who stared back at him through half-opened eyes. Beorchia nearly fainted. His body shook, his teeth chattered, and he couldn't get his mouth to say anything. Antonio Beorchia cried.

"It's an Indian," he finally stammered.

They'd unearthed the body of a muscular young man. Except for a guanaco-wool blanket and loincloth, he was naked. Fighting back their dizziness and pain from altitude sickness, Groch and Beorchia slowly dragged the mummy out of the ground, removed the blanket—and nearly fell over from fright when a mummified mouse dropped out of the blanket's folds. Then they sat the mummy down near the peak of Bull Mountain, which towers in unobstructed splendor over a vast stretch of the Andes. Seated upright, his bleached skull reflecting the brilliant afternoon sun, the mummy looked to Beorchia "like a mythical creature surveying infinite space."

But Beorchia's mountaintop reverie soon gave way to a nasty argument with Groch concerning who had jurisdiction over the mummy. Since they didn't have any means of carrying the mummy down from the mountain, a rescue mission was required. Beorchia wanted the local mountaineering club to be in charge of the second expedition, together with the government of San Juan; Groch felt that outside archaeologists should be brought in, and that, rather than waiting for permission from Argentina's slow-moving governmental bureaucracy, they should act on their own. Unable to agree, they left the mummy on the peak, came down from Bull Mountain, and promptly started working at cross-purposes. Groch went to the local newspaper, owned by Francisco Montes, while Beorchia ran to the provincial government; each backed a separate expedition to retrieve the mummy. Everyone hoped this mummy would attract international attention, making instant heroes of the rescuers.

The race was on.

Groch and the newspapermen got a faster start, with the government forces chasing close behind. After completing a four-day ascent through the parched, frozen wastes of the Argentine Cordillera, the elated newspapermen, accompanied by Swiss-born archaeologist Juan Schobinger of the National University of Cuyo in Mendoza, took possession of the mummy of Bull Mountain. But then the police caught up with them.

"The government opposed our getting the boy on Bull Mountain," Montes recalls in an injured tone. "So they sent the police, armed with guns, to take the mummy from us right there in the high Cordillera. Well, our reporters and mountaineers had guns, too. And we were all ready to kill for that mummy."

Fortunately, no further human sacrifices occurred on Bull Mountain. The police backed down. Later Montes donated his mummy to the government. But the mummy's adventures weren't over yet. Montes set off a furor in San Juan when his newspaper reported that the city of Mendoza wanted to make off with the mummy. "We would start a revolution before letting the people of Mendoza or Buenos Aires take our mummy," he says.

Actually, if it hadn't been for Montes's exuberant patriotism, San Juan might well have lost the mummy to the central government in Buenos Aires, or to Mendoza—or to the United States. "In 1965 the rector of the University of San Juan received an offer of $250,000 from a university in the United States," recalls Mariano Gambier, curator of the Museum of Laja, built near San Juan to house the mummy of Bull Mountain. "There was doubt about what to do, because the university first approached the provincial government with this American offer. The Minister of Housing said, 'Just sell it.' But in the end the government didn't dare sell the mummy, because they were afraid it would have caused a tremendous fight."

Today the mummy of Bull Mountain still looks disconcertingly lifelike as his fine features stare out from a glass refrigerator built in his honor. He's locked in a fetal position, his head resting on one shoulder. As with the child of Mount Plomo, the placid look on his face is most arresting. His Mongoloid features and brown skin identify him as an American Indian, although he's taller (five foot six) than most natives of the Andes. His alpaca-wool clothing is typical of the late Inca Empire (1450–1532). But this wasn't a typical *capacocha,* or royal sacrifice.

Only prepubescent children of noble blood were eligible for the royal solstice sacrifices. The "boy" of Bull Mountain is really an eighteen-year-old young man. The Emperor's *capacocha* sacrifices orchestrated from Cuzco followed a strict protocol exemplified at Mount Plomo: victims were buried dressed in princely finery along with precious idols. By these royal standards, the sacrifice at Bull Mountain was a second-class affair. The young man was hurriedly buried in a shallow pit, unlike the carefully constructed grave for the Inca child of Mount Plomo. No statues were found next to him. Nor do any ornaments hint of royal rank.

What really happened at Bull Mountain?

Scholars are just beginning to realize how widespread and varied human sacrifice was in the Andes, both prior to and during the Inca Empire. In addition to the standard *capacocha* offerings—which claimed several hundred children at each of the solstice ceremonies—the Incas and their subjects also sacrificed children or young adults in cases of drought, plague, earthquakes, famine, war, military victory or defeat, hailstorms, lightning storms, avalanches, to mark the sowing and harvesting of crops, during difficult construction projects, when the Inca Emperor died, when a new emperor assumed power, in case of bad omens, in case of good omens.[1] "The boy of Bull Mountain could have been sacrificed for anything from being a captured enemy warrior to falling victim to a feud with the local shaman," says anthropologist Johan Reinhard.

No one will ever know exactly why the young man at Bull Mountain was sacrificed. But there's no doubt he was sacrificed.

The Incas would never have climbed a twenty-thousand-foot mountain unless they had a special motive. No white man ever climbed Bull Mountain until Groch and Beorchia succeeded in 1964.

Because it's so inaccessible there'd been only one other attempt to climb Bull Mountain.

The well-built Royal Inca Highway, however, did give the Incas better access to the area than today's Argentinians have. But even if the Incas had started from the nearest resting station along the royal road, they'd still have had at least a six-day trek to and from the peak of Bull Mountain—barring accidents or storms, and not including the additional effort of building a twenty-by-thirty-five-foot rectangular stone platform and a ceremonial stone circle and burying a body. Bull Mountain deserved these seemingly insane attentions because, like Mount Plomo in Chile, where the Inca child was sacrificed, its snowcapped peak rises above the surrounding mountains. Everything about Bull Mountain's ceremonial status suggests that the Incas considered this mountain the chief *huaca*, or magical controller, of a wide Andean region.

And everything about the young man at Bull Mountain suggests he was specially chosen as a human sacrifice. "He wasn't one of the masses, but someone selected by criteria of beauty and good health," says Juan Schobinger. The victim's superior height, handsome face, and muscular strength met the Incas' requirements of physical excellence. His uncallused hands and feet show he wasn't an agricultural worker or a miner. Schobinger says the mummy's grave goods, including an alpaca-wool cap with soft gray tassels, and two delicately woven ponchos with embroidered red fringes, belonged to "a well-dressed Andean man." Many think he was from the Incas' elite warrior caste. Others guess that he may have been a captured enemy. One Spanish chronicler reported that the Incas sacrificed enemy warriors after making the victim sing, dance, and recite an acceptance speech to those who were about to kill him.[2]

The Incas liked their victims to die happily, because they saw them as *chasqui*, ambassadors to the gods. An angry, unwilling ambassador wouldn't represent the Incas' interests very well. And the gods might not even receive an ugly ambassador. The Incas saw human sacrifice as a better way of communicating with the gods than simple prayer, which the gods often ignored. It was the Incas' ultimate messenger service.

An exhaustive medical exam confirmed the theory that the young man at Bull Mountain was intentionally killed. Doctors detected no disease that could explain his death. There's been considerable debate about whether or not markings on the mummy's neck indicate strangulation. Antonio Beorchia believes they do, because in one of his later explorations he found a noose used by Andean natives to strangle sacrificial animals. "When I placed the noose around the neck of the mummy from Bull Mountain, it fit perfectly in the deeply marked grooves you can see there."

"I've been working with police homicides for twenty years," says Dr. Carlos De Cicco, an associate professor of medicine at the National University of Cuyo in Mendoza. "If you strangle a person with rope, wire, or leather for as long as ten or twelve hours, you still don't see any permanent marks on the cadaver, except for a few bloodstains. So where does this profound groove around the neck of the Bull Mountain mummy come from? I was never convinced by it. How long would they have had to strangle him? Until the rope froze in place over a period of days, I think. In that case, where's the rope? The fact is that they never found a noose buried along with the boy from Bull Mountain. The markings around his neck were too oblique to be made by a noose."

According to De Cicco, if the boy on Bull Mountain had been strangled to death, and if the noose had been left in place long enough to make the marks around the mummy's neck, then its face would show signs of cyanosis—a bloated, bluish-colored disfiguration caused by oxygen deprivation to the blood. "There'd be a stamp of horror on the face, like the bog men who were strangled in Denmark," he observes. And since the face is very peaceful, prolonged strangulation seems unlikely.

"In my opinion, the position of the young man's feet at Bull Mountain is the decisive thing," De Cicco concluded. "His feet are perfectly crossed, one on top of the other. You would have great trouble arranging a body like that. This means they were actively, voluntarily placed one on top of the other, just as the boy of Mount Plomo placed one hand on top of the other to keep warm. So at Bull Mountain you have a voluntary case of self-sacrifice, with the victim consenting to freeze to death."

In this case the victim almost certainly arrived at Bull Mountain on his own two feet, since carrying a 130-pound body on such an arduous ascent would have been grossly inconvenient. Bloodstains on the mummy's face, upper chest, and woolen poncho hint of a severe blow to knock the victim unconscious, though not severe enough to kill him. At twenty thousand feet above sea level, temperatures rarely rise above zero degrees Fahrenheit, and even the warmest months see twenty degrees below zero. Schobinger is convinced that the young man was somehow put in a stupor before being stripped naked and buried in the freezing ground. He died almost instantly.

The mummy on Bull Mountain alerted scientists that the sacrifice on Mount Plomo was more than a local idiosyncrasy. And the almost simultaneous discovery of the skeleton of an adolescent girl, buried along with three female statues and Inca pottery next to an artificial platform at Mount Pichu Pichu, an 18,471-foot peak near the city of Arequipa, in southern Peru, confirmed it. Pichu Pichu is twelve hundred miles from Mount Plomo.

No other culture had ever built anything above eighteen thousand feet. Europeans hadn't even scaled twenty-two-thousand-foot mountains until the middle of the nineteenth century, which is why the Spanish inquisitors, like Hernández Príncipe, left these lofty ceremonial sites undisturbed. Juan Schobinger started calling them "high-altitude sanctuaries," and he coined the term "high-altitude archaeology" to define the study of these unique ruins. But it was Antonio Beorchia, one of the two mountain climbers who originally dug up the boy on Bull Mountain, who turned these sporadic finds into a new discipline.

"The discovery of the boys from Mount Plomo and Bull Mountain didn't go any further because archaeologists weren't mountain climbers and couldn't reach the sites," Beorchia says. By combining amateur sport and amateur science, Antonio Beorchia became the first professional high-altitude investigator. In 1972 he climbed Mount Mercedario, about seventy-five miles north of Mount Plomo. Mercedario's 22,300-foot peak is the fifth highest in the Andes. About two thousand feet below the summit, Beorchia and Gino Job found three stone circles, so small and simple they'd been overlooked by previous climbers. Beorchia and Job went through the agonizing ordeal of digging in the center of the stone circles for several hours. They found bits of burned wood, flamingo feathers, and plants as they got farther down. Finally, Beorchia recovered two female statues, a llama figure, and a bag of coca leaves. They might as well have been stamped "Made in Cuzco by Inca Artisans." "I was so excited when I went back to my tent at eighteen thousand feet that I couldn't sleep that night," Beorchia remembers. "That's when it occurred to me to assemble a team of climbers dedicated to archaeological work."

Antonio Beorchia started the Center for Andean Investigations of High Mountains (Centro de Investigaciones Andinas de Alta Montaña, henceforth referred to as CIADAM). He directed the ascents of CIADAM's thirty climbers toward mountains with possible archaeological remains. As more and more high-altitude ruins were found, the pieces of this Andean puzzle started fitting together.

Most of the Inca peak sanctuaries were built on mountains near the Royal Inca Highway, a well-designed road that constituted the spinal cord of the Inca Empire. And these ceremonial centers— open-air temples built of dry-stone walls—usually crowned dominant snowcapped peaks like Mount Plomo and Bull Mountain. Furthermore, these outstanding mountains often had complexes of corrals and lodgings—called *tambos*—near their bases, which the Incas used for resting or food storage. Finally, local legends about buried treasures and Indians dancing on snowcapped peaks frequently recalled the Incas' high-mountain ceremonies.

By focusing on high mountains near the Royal Inca Highway, especially those close to way stations, and by paying attention to local legends, CIADAM accelerated its discoveries. Today CIADAM has documented 120 mountains with archaeological remains, eighty of them built above 17,000 feet. Compared with Machu Picchu's superb architecture, these peak platforms and open-air temples are simple. But reaching the summit of majestic snowcapped peaks like Mount Plomo and Bull Mountain is anything but simple. And building walls up to twenty-two thousand feet above sea level is incredible. "This is one of the greatest achievements we know of in the human past," says anthropologist Johan Reinhard, who has discovered more than thirty of the high-altitude sites. "No other culture in history ever built anything at these heights. Europeans thought it was a great achievement in the mid-nineteenth century when they simply reached such altitudes."

Beorchia claims that the Incas' chain of high-altitude sanctuaries is a greater achievement than the famed Royal Inca Highway, the Incas' social organization, or their military conquests. His book, *El enigma de los santuarios indígenas de alta montaña*, is an impressive catalogue of over a hundred Inca ruins. Even a partial roster of the Incas' mountaintop sites is enough to convince one of an achievement whose cultural and religious significance is beyond dispute:

Mount Llullaillaco (22,100 feet; altiplano of northern Chile and Argentina). Llullaillaco is one of the highest mountains in the Western Hemisphere, but it also has one of the most complete and best-built Inca adoratories. Austrian climber Mathias Rebitsch surveyed two high-walled stone shelters at the summit which constitute the world's highest archaeological site. These stone huts, built side by side, are thirteen feet wide, twenty-six feet long, six feet high, and with walls almost three feet thick. Nearby, there's a large ceremonial platform, twenty-two by forty feet, where Rebitsch found burned grass, ceramic fragments, and a finely decorated multicolored cloth, all buried as offerings. There is also a ton of firewood at the peak.

Rebitsch found three more stone buildings four hundred feet below the peak structures. These once had straw roofs, supported by large wooden beams, one of them thirteen feet long. The three-foot-thick outer wall is filled in with grass and sand, making it better protection against the constant wind. Remains of fruits, maize, and utilitarian ceramics suggested to Rebitsch that "people stayed for some time at this intermediary camp on the ascent route."[3] Amazingly enough, one building served as a llama corral, judging from the amount of llama dung found there. The Incas used llamas and other camelids to carry firewood and food. These sacred animals are still sacrificed on high mountains today, and their blood played a major role in the *capacocha* ceremonies.

Antonio Beorchia discovered a still unsolved mystery at Llullaillaco—sixteen skeletons haphazardly buried under a slabstone at an altitude of 16,400 feet. One was a child or adolescent, the rest adults. No one is sure if they were sacrificial victims, a work crew that froze to death, or simply people who died while crossing the Atacama Desert on one of the Inca roads nearby.

Volcán Quehuar (20,430 feet; Salta Province, northwestern Argentina). "We'd heard local people talk about a blond boy frozen in ice on the peak of Quehuar, surrounded by a treasure of gold and silver," Beorchia recalls. "We knew the Royal Highway of the Incas went nearby and we had a theory most high-altitude sanctuaries were near this Inca road. Also, the snow-covered Quehuar dominates the salt flats of the high plateau near Bolivia, where it presides over the altiplano like an immense, beautiful pyramid."

So, in 1974, Beorchia mounted an expedition to Quehuar, fully expecting to encounter ruins at the summit. But even the rumors failed to prepare him for what he calls the most impressive of all high-altitude ruins—ruins that Beorchia claims must have taken months of work by hundreds of people. There are walls six feet high and three feet thick, and a staircase leading to an elevated platform with a small tower, unbelievable achievements at 20,100 feet above sea level. Inside the tower, a child was frozen in ice, just as the legend said. "The child's head had already been torn off by treasure hunters," Antonio says disappointedly. "He was wrapped in an Inca shawl, but was frozen so solid we couldn't move the rest of the body."

In 1981 Beorchia and Johan Reinhard struggled through four-foot-deep snow when they tried to remove the mummy from the ice block. But by this time the treasure hunters had also come and the child was gone—except for some vertebrae, an ear, and pieces of cranium embedded in a wall. The salvaged remains belonged to a fourteen- or fifteen-year-old adolescent, though medical analysis couldn't determine the youth's sex. "The ear was soft, flexible, and perfectly preserved when it thawed out," Johan Reinhard says. "It would have been at least as well conserved as the Inca child of Mount Plomo."

But the treasure hunters didn't receive much reward for their efforts, either. The mummy's vertebrae and ear could only have been impelled into the wall by a terrific explosion. So the local miners must have miscalculated when they tried to loosen the ice-rock with dynamite.

Even so, Quehuar provides clues about Inca human-sacrifice cults. The "tower" where the child was found appears to be a miniature *chullpa*, or burial tower. Enormous *chullpas* can still be seen near Lake Titicaca, and human-sacrifice victims were buried alive in them until the time of the Spanish conquest. The much smaller *chullpa* on Quehuar seems to have served a similar function, as shown by a niche in the outer wall exactly opposite the mummy. This niche was probably used to make offerings to the deified *capacocha* victim of Mount Quehuar, just as the people of Ocros made offerings of food and drink to the mummy of Tanta Carhua on Mount Aixa.

■　■　■

Mount Esmeralda (2,969 feet; coast of northern Chile). A Chilean construction company was putting a road over the top of Mount Esmeralda (the Emerald Mountain) when they came to some rather crude-looking stone walls. They didn't let these stop them. Once again dynamite was produced, and when the smoke cleared the workers found themselves in the company of two girls, a couple of statues, and a treasure trove of Inca textiles and ceramics, some of them considerably the worse for their encounter with explosives. The two girls had their feet blown away.

"Here we confront the most important high-altitude sanctuary with respect to human sacrifice," asserts Beorchia. "Paradoxically, it's also the lowest of all, just three thousand feet above sea level, and the only one which presents two sacrifices together."

The victims were both female, one about eighteen or twenty years old, the other about nine. The older girl is slightly better dressed, in red-and-yellow-dyed clothes indicative of the nobility, whereas the child appears to be of a lower caste. Perhaps the older girl was the principal sacrifice, the young child a servant who was meant to keep her company in the next world. When an Inca ruler or important nobleman died, his favorite wives and servants were killed and buried with him. One Spaniard wrote that "in order to strangle them they made them first drunk and they say that they opened their mouth to blow pulverized coca in it and that they were placed as mummies next to him."[4]

A study from the Museum of Iquique, where the mummies are kept, concludes from neck lacerations that the two girls were strangled. Interestingly, the older girl was "seated cross-legged, Buddha-style, the arms resting in a relaxed way over the thighs, head hanging down on the chest. . . . It can be supposed that the subject was sacrificed in this seated position and without offering resistance, because of probably being drugged or in a semiconscious state."[5] This coincides with Hernández Príncipe's finding Tanta Carhua "sitting in the native way" in her tomb at Ocros.

This site is significant because:

1. Mount Esmeralda proves that the Incas didn't necessarily consider altitude to be the only criterion in choosing sanctuaries. Mountains near the ocean were worshipped for their power to control rain, which the Incas believed originated in the sea. The connection between ocean water and Mount Esmeralda is very clear, since three spondylus shells were found buried along with the girls. Andean shamans still use these special shells, which come from the tropical shores of northern Peru and Ecuador, when they pour water on the ground at mountain peaks to invoke storm gods.

2. The fine clothes buried along with the girls were probably woven by the Virgins of the Sun in Cuzco, who were in charge of making ceremonial clothes for both Inca royalty and human sacrifices. The list of textiles buried at Mount Esmeralda corresponds almost perfectly with Spanish descriptions of the ceremonial finery worn by sacrificial victims.[6] In particular, the girls' colorful headdresses—used as an official form of tribal identification in the Inca Empire—match those of Inca noblewomen, suggesting that both victims were from Cuzco.

3. The girls at Mount Esmeralda were sacrificed along with a vast collection of grave goods—104 pieces in all. Included are ten bags of coca leaves; a potato starch used for prolonged, ritual chewing of coca leaves; a tubular container for hallucinogens; two anthropomorphic statues, one of silver, one of spondylus shell; two squashes filled with seashell ashes; nineteen ceramic pieces with seeds and ground-up plants inside them. These objects link the sacrifices at Mount Esmeralda with rain magic to ensure the agricultural cycle, and with drug-induced trances.[7]

In short, Mount Esmeralda was a royal Inca sacrifice, but one that, like the cult of Tanta Carhua described by Hernández Príncipe, had more to do with water rituals than with the Sun God.

Mount Aconcagua (22,830 feet; central Argentina). Five Argentine climbers slipped out of their tents at sunrise on January 8, 1985.

They put ice cleats on their boots, then began their assault on Mount Aconcagua, the highest peak in the Western Hemisphere.

These five men were attempting a virtually unexplored approach, with no shelters in case of severe storms. They reached a slippery, glacier-filled canyon that took them two hours to inch up. At the end of the glacier they came to a twenty-six-foot-high rock wall. Using ropes, they gingerly made their way to a ridge above the cliff, and noticed something strange: grass.

No grass could possibly grow at 17,220 feet above sea level. Then they realized they were standing near a couple of crumbling semicircular walls. Who could have built a camp at this spot? When they dug around the "grass" they encountered feathers and what looked like a shirt. The shirt fabric was so clean and bright it appeared newly made. Deciding this was just the disposal site of a recent camp, they kept climbing.

But not for long. A wicked windstorm hit about three hours later. The group leader, Gabriel Cabrera, wanted to continue; the other four insisted on heading back. Finally, Cabrera went on alone. That proved an almost fatal mistake, since he contracted snow blindness in the blizzard and barely groped his way back to the base camp. Meanwhile, the others took the opportunity to dig around the feathers and shirt, and discovered a human skull.

At this point, the climbers behaved admirably. They covered up the skull and returned to the city of Mendoza. Then, accompanied by archaeologist Juan Schobinger and other academics from the National University of Cuyo, three of the original climbers and one new addition returned to the same spot. They worked carefully for two days, until they dug out a small child completely wrapped in a many-layered bundle of clothes. Beneath the child they found six statues, three male figures and three camelids. The three human statues wore colorful woolen outfits, including shoulder bags filled with coca leaves. All were crowned with yellow-orange headdresses, in the fashion of nobility from the Inca Empire.

This sanctuary on Mount Aconcagua is the best example of Inca mountaineering skills. The steep glacier leading to the burial site at Aconcagua is more difficult than the route to any other Inca sanctuary. "There's no way that we could have climbed up that glacier without crampons," says Juan Carlos Pierobón, referring to the special ice cleats used by mountaineers. "I see only three possible explanations. The first is that the Incas found another route. The second is that there was no ice in that canyon five hundred years ago. And the third is that the Incas were much better mountain climbers than we are." He reflects for a moment before adding, "I think the third explanation is the most likely."

In many ways the mummy of Mount Aconcagua also proved the most difficult to study. Juan Schobinger's Institute of Archaeology and Ethnology at the National University of Cuyo assembled a team of international experts to examine the mummy, which was wrapped in a bundle of textiles, with only the top of the skull showing. With infinite patience and ingenuity, Judy Palma of the Museo Chileno de Arte Precolombiano of Santiago, Chile, removed the multiple layers—starting with a delicate cape of rose-colored flamingo feathers, and continuing through several Andean shawls and blankets and many other pieces of clothing. "It was very hard to do, because the low temperatures required for preserving the mummy also made the textiles stick together," she said. She found a hairdryer the best tool for warming and softening the ancient clothes. Finally, in August 1986, surrounded by several doctors and archaeologists, all anxiously waiting in white coats, amid the shine of floodlights and the whine of her trusty hairdryer, Judy Palma brought her child out of its egg-shaped funeral wrappings and into the world. It turned out to be a little boy covered with vomit and excrement.

The excrement and vomit were colored bright red. Subsequent analysis by archaeologist Roberto Bárcena proved that the child had swallowed a red vegetable-dye pigment twenty-four hours before his death. "The vomit and fecal deposits are all on top of the boy's shawls," says Dr. Carlos De Cicco. "These are fundamental data showing he was alive when they wrapped him in the complex funeral bundle. They also mean that he was carefully prepared, having eaten special, sacred foods before dying."

When I spoke with him, Dr. De Cicco had just received a CAT scan of the child's skull. "The boy was in good health but he has many traumatic wounds. He has multiple fractures of the skull. We think they are definitely intentional fractures. And there's a strange disarticulation in the child's left ribs, caused by a great, sustained pressure, beyond anything produced by burial. His pelvis is broken, on the right side of his body. I would tentatively conclude that the boy resisted the pressure being brought against him with his pelvis. He was finally killed with a blow, or blows, to the head."

Although we know how the boys of Mount Plomo, Aconcagua, and Bull Mountain died, the question still arises: Why did they die? There were many motives for human sacrifice and for the other rituals of mountain worship. Juan Schobinger believes the children on Mount Plomo, Bull Mountain, and Aconcagua were all immolated to celebrate the Inca conquests in Chile and Argentina, territories which constituted the southernmost reaches of their empire. But this political motive for the sacrifices, however plausible, still leaves the problem of why the Incas were so obsessed with snow-capped peaks that they built a chain of sanctuaries. Johan Reinhard provides a compelling explanation:

> We've seen that mountains were considered extremely important for a variety of reasons. In many places they are considered sites where the spirits of the dead live, and frequently they were identified with the original ancestors of the people. The gods of the mountains were the guardians of crops and herds. They demonstrated their powers by causing sicknesses and storms which killed men and animals and destroyed crops. At times mountains were adored, because they contained minerals. Occasionally they may have been used to pay homage to the sun and for signaling, as previous hypotheses have suggested. Many of these beliefs and prac-

tices were undoubtedly combined one with another, but it was the concept of fertility, with water as the principal element, which has been found underlying the majority of beliefs related to mountains.[8]

In the arid Andean ecosystem, water is crucial for survival. Irrigation is essential and depends on mountain reservoirs. "Central to Andean ideology is its concern with water," wrote Thomas Zuidema.

> The mountains on the horizon were organized into an ever-expanding geographic hierarchy of more potent sources of water. The horizon became a political concept to the state which wanted to assure the availability of water. Snowcapped mountains, especially those along the coast, and mountain lakes, were considered as the sources of rivers of more immediate concern, and the water of the former was believed to be derived from the ocean that surrounded and supported the known earth. Even military and economic expansion were seen in terms of this ideology.[9]

The Incas' chain of high-altitude sanctuaries is impressive proof of this ideology. The Incas didn't invent the idea of building altars on mountaintops and offering sacrifices there. But if the Incas elaborated on ancient beliefs, they did a more efficient job of it than any other Andean civilization. In their drive to take control of new territories, the Incas faced the same problems as the Spaniards: how to impose a centralized government on peoples who are used to direct communication with their own ancestor-gods through shamans. Here the Incas proved far more original than the Spaniards. Instead of killing off every vestige of native worship, the Incas simply carried images of local deities back to Cuzco, where they held the gods hostage. "But since mountain deities were the most powerful Andean gods, the Incas faced a problem," Johan Reinhard points out. "How could they carry the mountains back to Cuzco?"

They solved that problem by making their own presence felt on the peaks of the highest mountains throughout the empire. Reinhard believes that, by building a hundred adoratories along the spinal column of their empire, the Incas usurped and surpassed the local mountain cults. As they established physical control over snowcapped peaks, the Incas also gained political, psychological, and religious control over subjects terrified of the mountain gods.

☑ 4 ☑

HUNTING FOR
MUMMIES

Mount Veladero is located in a remote, almost unexplored, and particularly brutal part of the Argentine desert highlands. When Antonio Beorchia glimpsed Veladero from a distance, he said, "What a lovely mountain! There's got to be an Inca sanctuary up there."

Ten years later, in January 1986, the University of San Juan and CIADAM jointly sponsored the tough trip to Veladero. "This is not a tourist outing," Antonio Beorchia warned me in a letter. "The desert climate is extremely bad, the mule riding is hard, and the actual climbing involves suffering. We'll be far from any help and everyone will have to pitch in for survival."

The weather in the Argentine highlands is enough to make most people wish they were dead. In the first place, it's a fourteen-thousand-foot-high desert where solar radiation is so intense you feel that any exposed skin is being fried in oil. It's always cold and the wind never lets up, making a constant whine that goes through you like the sound of a dentist's drill. "The sky is clear one minute and ten minutes later it's snowing so hard you can't see more than one meter in front of you," our muleteer-guide told me.

The biggest problem in the high desert is drinking water—

there isn't any to speak of. All the lakes near Mount Veladero are contaminated by salt, including the Laguna Brava (the Fierce Lake), whose brackish-white waters extend for about twelve miles in a basin surrounded by high mountains. After making our first camp at fourteen thousand feet, on a rise overlooking the Laguna Brava, we had to send the mules on a special trip every day to fill our plastic containers from a tiny trickle over a mile from our camp. And even this water had a delicious taste of borax and salt which made one want to throw up.

My head hurt terribly and I felt like a stranger inside my own body, with my heart beating ninety times a minute (instead of my usual sixty), as I got acclimatized to fourteen thousand feet. At this altitude you have to do everything with painstaking care to avoid exhaustion and sickness. But I forced myself to follow Antonio Beorchia to 14,700-foot hills near our camp, after putting on many layers of down vests and woolen underwear, getting into heavy boots, wearing a ski mask and winter gloves. It was like being an astronaut inside a cumbersome suit, moving at slow motion, in that lifeless, almost lunar landscape of pure volcanic rock. We were reaching the fringes of the biosphere.

Fortunately, we had a great luxury for our first campsite—a bell-shaped shelter that looked like a stone version of the Mongolian yurt. Antonio told me it was built in the 1860s by Russian Cossacks, directed by Italian architects, during the time when the Argentine government was promoting the cattle trade to Chile. We spent three nights here, acclimatizing. Beorchia had a hunch that the cattle route was the same one used by the Incas for their Royal Highway. So on our second day he set out to search for Inca ruins by the lake.

As I struggled behind Beorchia, in a painful, dimwitted state of consciousness, I heard him give an elated shout.

"Here's the *tambo, muchachos!*"

In fact, we found a large *tambo* (the name for a resting stop along the Royal Inca Highway) on the lakeshore. It consisted of twenty rectangular enclosures, about ten feet by ten feet each, built of dry-stone walls three feet thick and five feet high. "But why would the Incas build a big resting stop here?" I asked Antonio. "They didn't have any cattle to trade. And this is a miserable place to rest."

"We think of these highlands as completely desolate," Antonio said. "But remember, the Incas were a highland people, expertly acclimatized, who made a living from their llama and vicuña flocks. According to the Spanish chronicles, these flocks were the exclusive property of the Inca Emperor. Once or twice a year his subjects all over the highlands performed giant roundups of his flocks. In a place like this, several thousand men would form a circle maybe sixty miles in diameter, and gradually make their way to a central point, beating drums to frighten the llama herds ahead of them. When they finally trapped all the animals, the llamas were counted and fleeced and some of the adult males were killed. But it was forbidden, under pain of death, to kill any females."

The Incas considered the llamas sacred animals—property of the mountain gods, in fact. They also believed that the safety of their Royal Highway, its *tambos,* and all construction projects depended on the good will of the gods. And Antonio soon found proof of this.

Beorchia discovered a rectangular platform and three stone circles facing the lake, with pieces of Inca pottery inside the stone circles. "This is where the Inca priests offered sacrifices," Beorchia explained. He then lifted up a phallus-shaped stone about fifteen inches high which stood there. "I've found this same ceremonial rectangle, with these same phallic stones, at many mountaintop sanctuaries," he said. "But this is the first time I've ever seen one by a lake. It's very curious."

The Incas worshipped highland lakes—especially Lake Titicaca, the place where creation began. The Laguna Brava is one of the Andes' biggest lakes. "It wouldn't surprise me if the Laguna Brava turned out to be a very important ceremonial place for the Incas," Juan Schobinger predicted. "It might be a regional Titicaca."

Andean natives sacrifice llamas every year at the Island of the

Sun at Lake Titicaca. The main recipients of their offerings, however, are not the lake or the sun but Mount Illimani and Mount Illampu, two snow-covered peaks over twenty thousand feet high. One of our climbers, Mario Muñoz, soon found small hilltop ruins which suggested something similar might have gone on at the Laguna Brava.

"From here we can see many things," Antonio said after we'd made the climb to Mario's ruins. "In the first place, this hilltop is aligned with the ceremonial platform by the lake. We can also see Mount Veladero, Mount Bonete, Mount Morado, and the White Mountain [all snow-covered peaks over seventeen thousand feet high]. It's probable that on days like the solstices the Incas made offerings to the lake of metal objects and animals from that platform, while similar offerings were made from all these mountaintops. The smoke rising from all these sacrifices could be seen at the same time, a kind of communion."

As we surveyed minor ruins on surrounding hilltops, I was caught between conflicting emotions. Compared with Machu Picchu, these ruins were nothing at all. But my body hurt so much, as I slowly pulled myself behind Beorchia, that I had to admire the Incas' mountaineering stamina. If I was feeling this much pain gasping my way up a fifteen-thousand-foot *hill*, I marveled that the Incas could build high walls, elevated platforms, and staircases up to twenty-two thousand feet.

And there was a sense of religious respect which began to seep into me in that unearthly silence of the altiplano. I could sense the extraordinary solemnity the Incas' ceremonies would have had at a place like the Laguna Brava, with its ghostly-white waters, where the only sounds I heard were eerie cries from pink-feathered flamingos and the monotonous clicking of rust-colored volcanic rocks under our boots. Piles of centuries-old wood testified to former bonfires, which must have lit up the Andean night, creating a chain of fire encompassing every hill and mountain around the lake—a chain that spread as far north as Cuzco and as far south as Mount Plomo.

The Incas believed that the Laguna Brava and its surrounding snow-covered peaks had magical power to make water flow to the Troya River and other streams that give tenuous life to the fragile Andean ecosystem. It didn't matter that the Laguna Brava is salty and doesn't feed any streams at all. For the Incas, the *idea* of a large highland lake, salty or not, was an irresistible source of water magic. Our concept "water" doesn't begin to convey the many meanings it had for them, although the Christian mystical notion of "living water" comes closer than most anthropological definitions. And when you look at the magical transformation irrigated water makes for people who eke out a living in the Andean deserts, you realize that water is life.

When the Incas built their *tambo* and sanctuary by the Laguna Brava, and on the surrounding mountains, they must have made a great impression on the natives around Jague. But if there also turned out to be ruins on Mount Veladero, mammoth and white in the distance, it would have overawed the locals, who even today are fearful of Mount Veladero, which they consider dangerous to approach and impossible to climb.

I, too, was beginning to think climbing Mount Veladero was impossible—at least for me. By the end of our second day at fourteen thousand feet, I was more miserable than I can remember ever being in my life. My head ached terribly. I was desperate for water but I couldn't bring myself to drink more than a tiny bit of our borax blend at one time. And the thought of eating also turned my stomach.

"You have to eat," Antonio yelled at me. "You haven't eaten anything in two days. Tomorrow we have a rough day on mule to the base camp at the foot of Veladero. And the day after we have an even rougher time climbing to the peak."

Fortunately, my headache vanished just before I went to sleep that night. It seemed almost miraculous—my body apparently went through some kind of adjustment, and I suddenly felt elated and fantastically relieved to have gotten over the most painful experience of my life. The next day I was fine, except for some nervousness whenever my mule reared up because of the high, piercing winds. We made the twenty-two-mile trip to the foot of Mount Veladero in five hours. As we put up our tents, Antonio's altimeter showed that our new base camp was 15,584 feet above sea level. According to our Argentine map, Mount Veladero was 17,550 feet high. "This is a very small mountain," Antonio said. "We'll have no trouble."

Antonio had brought his Rosary with him, as he always did on expeditions. We all prayed that night, hoping we'd be able to work some modern weather magic. The next day Antonio was delighted with the results: Perfect weather. No wind. No clouds.

"You're bringing us good luck, *gringo*," Antonio said. "Today we're going to find a virgin sanctuary on this beautiful mountain. There's got to be something here. And if there isn't, we'll just have to build it ourselves."

With his big white beard and long silver hair, supporting himself on a climbing staff, Beorchia looked like Moses going up Mount Sinai—except that he was wearing his wife's absurd white hat. Although he was fifty-two, Beorchia outclimbed me and the others in our party, and had to wait for us to catch him.

Our climb grew increasingly strenuous. At 17,500 feet, there was still no sign of the peak. "It can't be far now," Antonio said. We climbed for another hour to eighteen thousand feet. By this time I was utterly exhausted, and fell behind Antonio, a Franciscan lay brother named Siro, and a young climbing instructor named Yuyi. A little below me I could see Yuyi's fiancée, Patricia, struggling up the mountain. I had a strange conversation with her there at eighteen thousand feet, where she told me that she was going to make the peak even if it killed her. We climbed together for a while. Then she got too tired, so I carried her backpack. But she finally threw herself on the ground, grabbing her heart and screaming, "I'm going to die. My heart is giving out." She started retching.

I didn't know what the hell to do. This was my first climb and I felt groggy. Our two expedition leaders, Antonio and Yuyi, were far above us, intent on seeing which of them would reach the peak first. All I knew was that Patricia had collapsed on me and was screaming about her imminent death. I started yelling for help and waving frantically to Antonio, Yuyi, and Siro. Finally, I dropped my backpack and Patricia's, and started running after them.

Now, if there's one thing you don't want to do at eighteen thousand feet, it's start running. But I was scared and furious at the same time. When I finally caught Siro, I yelled at him, "Why didn't you come down? Patricia has collapsed and I need your help to carry her back to the base camp."

"No, *che*," he said. "People always get sick climbing mountains. She'll be all right."

Sure enough, we turned around to see Patricia lifting herself off the ground and proceeding onward with another climber. But by now I felt that *I* was dying.

"It's just a little farther," Siro said. "You see that peak there? That's it. Blood's going to pour out of our noses and our asses, but we're going to make it."

We stopped every three steps to rest, and in the end I made it to the peak on my hands and knees. But when we got to the peak we saw that . . . it wasn't the peak. Veladero's bell-shaped, glacier-covered summit was hundreds of yards above the huge plateau we'd reached.

"I can't make it," I said.

Siro agreed to go back, and so did another climber, Gabriel, who came right behind us. It was now 5:00 P.M. We'd been climbing for nine hours. Since we needed at least three hours to get back to base camp, it was obviously crazy to keep climbing. I didn't make any of these rational observations, however, because I was slipping into intermittent unconsciousness. I fell repeatedly; I didn't want to go on. Fortunately, Siro forced me to go on, and finally he and Gabriel supported me from both sides.

"Leave me alone now," I said, when we were a few hundred yards from base camp. "I want to walk in on my own." They left me alone. And the next thing I remember is having Gabriel wake me: "You can't go to sleep here, Patricio. You'll freeze to death."

I had fallen unconscious on the ground.

I was so weak that, even after I reached my tent, Gabriel and Siro had to help me get my boots and clothes off. It would have been humiliating, but I quickly passed out and didn't notice anything until, at 2:00 A.M., I heard Siro shouting next to me. "They're not back!" he kept repeating. "Antonio, Yuyi, and five other climbers never made it back to the camp."

None of the seven had sleeping bags or bivouac equipment— so they were just out sleeping, God only knew where. I was still too spaced out to worry much about it, or to rejoice when, one by one, six of the seven straggled back to camp. But when I got up at 7:00 A.M., Antonio was still missing.

Siro and Gabriel were the only other climbers awake. Gabriel was crying. "What if Antonio fell and broke a leg?" he asked. "He could be anywhere." He and Siro started searching.

I didn't feel up to searching. Instead, I went to break some ice in the nearest stream and proceeded to wash my face and hands. The sun was bright, and in the protected ravine it actually became pleasant. I felt happy enough just to be alive.

Then Antonio appeared. Actually, it looked like a slow-motion version of Antonio, limping down the canyon where I was washing myself. He shook his head sadly. "That was a very bad mountain, *che*," he said. "It fooled us like little children. Do you know how high it is? The altimeter marked 20,768 feet at the peak. That plateau you reached was almost twenty thousand feet. It took Yuyi and me four hours to reach the peak from that plateau. It was pitch dark by the time we started down, so I spent the night huddled up, shivering like mad."

"I was already writing you an eloquent obituary," I said.

"No, *che*," Antonio answered. "Bad weed never dies."

Antonio was carrying several pieces of wood. Since there are no trees for dozens of yards near Veladero, I knew he must have found an Inca site. Then he produced a lovely little jar. "We found a virgin sanctuary at the peak," he said proudly. He drew a plan of the sanctuary in my notebook—a platform, two feet high, thirty feet long, and twenty feet wide, and a stone circle beyond the northeast corner of the platform. "The most interesting thing were two slabstones, weighing about 440 pounds each, placed at two diagonal corners of the platform. They were so heavy we couldn't move them alone. That's when we needed you, *gringo*."

I said we had to rest a day, then mount another expedition to the peak. But Antonio just shook his head. "I don't think you'll have any customers, *gringo*."

Antonio was right. No one wanted to go back up. "That's a very bad mountain, with too many volcanic rocks sliding everywhere," Gabriel said. The seven who had slept exposed on the mountain responded like zombies. They didn't want to do *anything*.

When I thought of how hard the mule trip to Veladero had been, and how rewarding it is to find a virgin sanctuary, the idea of leaving the site seemed absurd. But that's what we did.

"You're lucky to all be getting out of this alive," our muleteer, Alejandro, said. "The weather here isn't normally so good. Last year an Italian expedition tried to reach the peak and the weather looked good—then two feet of snow fell. If that had happened last night, you would have lost several people. The idea of seven climbers sleeping outside of the camp is crazy—you never let that happen. Someone is in charge of all the climbers; everyone goes together; before it gets dark, you go back to camp. These are the rules for survival. And you people ignored all of the rules. You've been saved only by barbarous good luck [*una barbaridad de buena suerte*]."

After the trip to Veladero, I wanted to take advantage of my high-altitude acclimatization and complete a successful ascent to an Inca sanctuary while summer (December to March) still lasted. I chose Mount Tortolas (20,775 feet), in northern Chile, an extinct volcano whose pyramid-straight peak and multicolored spires of metal-rich rocks make it one of the loveliest mountains I'd ever seen. The Incas may have thought so as well. They built a large altar-platform at the peak, where they buried three statues, a dog, and several mice as sacrifices. Since only 20 percent of Tortolas's peak platform has been excavated, everyone wonders what else is hidden there.

Getting to Tortolas's summit proved embarrassingly easy. My eldest brother, John, and I, along with Chilean geologist Claudio Canut De Bon and his son, Claudio Jr., rode splendidly acclimatized mules to twenty thousand feet, and walked the rest of the way. My brother and I were a bit disappointed by the Inca platform—just a rectangle three feet high, twenty-six feet long, and thirteen feet wide, made with simple stone walls and gravel fill. Once there, Canut De Bon showed us how he had excavated the platform years before, and where a female statue had been unearthed. While we talked, Canut De Bon found a large seashell in the rubble. But our attention was diverted from this find when Claudio Jr. suddenly passed out. We put snow on the twenty-year-old's face, talked to him, tried opening his eyes . . . to no avail. His father and I pulled him over volcanic rocks as best we could (to the sound of his expensive clothes' ripping), stopping every thirty seconds to rest, while my brother John summoned the mules to young Claudio's rescue. For me, this crisis put the Inca building effort in better perspective. By one estimate, the Incas moved more than ninety tons of gravel atop Tortolas to erect their altar-platform. Just dragging a 150-pound climber *downhill* left us dizzy from exhaustion. Although Claudio Sr., John, and I counted this as one of the worst experiences we could remember, Claudio Jr. was very serene the next day. He couldn't remember a thing. "In fact, if you had sacrificed me up at that Inca altar, I wouldn't even have known the difference," he said.

I had better luck on several other mountains around Tortolas, where I found minor, undocumented Inca remains—a circular platform, a stone rectangle, and firewood at one 15,800-foot peak; just a stone circle at a 17,100-foot site. Each of these mountains with Inca ceremonial structures had a river flowing by it, and a clear line of sight to Mount Tortolas from the summit. From these top-of-the-world platforms I began sensing the Incas' sacred geography. The highest mountain, Tortolas, had the best-built summit ruins. Lower peaks were clearly secondary, both in altitude and ceremonial remains. There seemed to be a strict hierarchy, with sight lines connecting the lower mountains around Tortolas like the spokes of a wheel around a hub.

With this mountaineering experience, I felt encouraged to try Veladero again. Back in Argentina, I was surprised at how excited Antonio Beorchia became when I mentioned Canut De Bon's find of a seashell on top of Mount Tortolas.

"That seashell you guys found on Mount Tortolas is one of the most important finds to date," Beorchia said. "There's been a long debate over whether the Incas performed rain rituals at these high-altitude sanctuaries. The Spanish chronicles say that seashells full of water were taken from the ocean to high mountains, for rain offerings. But until now the only proof of this was at Mount Esmeralda, where seashells were placed as decorations on the breasts of one of the sacrificed girls buried there. Mount Esmeralda is only three thousand feet high, and it's right by the ocean, so it could be argued that those seashells were unconnected with the really high mountains inland. But now you've found a big shell at the ceremonial *explazo* of Mount Tortolas, proving that rain offerings were made at a major Inca sanctuary over eighteen thousand feet high, and 125 miles inland. That's a great thing."

On February 10, 1987, I headed back to Mount Veladero, with Beorchia himself and Mario Muñoz. Mario, a phys-ed teacher and long-distance runner, had impressed me with his excellent conditioning on our previous trip to Veladero, when he zoomed like a jet up a seventeen-thousand-foot mountain by the Laguna Brava. I was in good shape myself, having spent over thirty days above ten thousand feet in the previous two months. But none of the mountains I'd climbed this season were as high as Veladero.

Our expedition started smoothly this time. We met our muleteers, Alejandro Pinto and Jorge Barrera, and went up the Bonete River to the valley of Las Ciénagas Grandes, where we spent our first night. The second day it started to rain around noon, when we were at an elevation of 10,500 feet; the rain turned to hail a little higher up; the hail turned into a full-fledged snowstorm by the time we reached 13,100 feet. Alejandro wanted to pitch camp immediately, but Antonio insisted we keep going.

Though I was content to suffer my way to the next refuge, Antonio was alert to arrowheads and Inca ruins. He spotted an Inca resting station, with some twenty stone structures, which we had overlooked on our previous trip. "Hey, *che,* this proves the Incas used exactly the same route chosen by the cattle drivers in the nineteenth century," he said enthusiastically. By this time, however, all I could manage was a polite nod. I was tired of these little ruins—I just wanted to get to the slabstones at the peak.

We decided to stop at the Refuge of the Dead Mules, by a small salt lake of the same name, some nine miles from the Laguna Brava. About four inches of snow had already fallen, so Antonio suggested that we attempt a mountain by the shores of the Laguna Brava before going to Veladero. "The weather is bad," he said. "And both Mario and I can use the extra acclimatization."

The next morning we headed for a virgin peak named Mount Pilar, listed as 5,032 meters (16,509 feet) high by the Argentine Military Geographic Society.[1] We'd no sooner reached the site of our base camp at 14,764 feet when it started to snow again. We got another four inches of snow in short order. "This weather has to improve," Antonio said. "I've never seen more than three days of bad weather in a row in all the years I've been in the Cordillera."

Although the bad weather continued the next day, we made the peak of Mount Pilar with no difficulty. Once we reached the summit, however, snow started to come down heavily. We quickly searched the mountaintop, and I was fortunate to stumble across a big pile of wood in the snow. Since there are no wood piles on seventeen-thousand-foot virgin peaks, we knew this was not a virgin peak—the Incas had been here before us.

A closer inspection revealed a small J-shaped platform. But it was impossible to work well in the snow, which was over a foot high in places. We just took pictures and made rough sketches of the platform.

Back at our camp, we waited anxiously for the arrival of our mules, scheduled for 1:00 P.M. But as the afternoon wore on, it became clear that something was wrong. We couldn't see the Laguna Brava, which was covered by an ocean of clouds. Mount Veladero stood above the clouds, completely white now, and so bright in the afternoon sun that my eyes hurt to look at it, even with sunglasses.

"It looks like Veladero is floating in the clouds," Antonio said. "There's far more snow on the mountain this year. Last year we had a clear line of ascent without going over snow. We don't have that luxury now. And if much more snow falls, we'll have trouble even finding the slabstones at the peak."

But it didn't look as though we would be going anywhere without the mules. We feared the mules had bolted during the continued storm.

The next morning we still saw no sign of our beloved mules. To my surprise, Antonio gave marching orders anyway. We took down the tent and stored it, along with our heaviest supplies, under a plastic tarp. Then, with our sleeping bags and a minimum of rations, we headed for the stone refuge of the Laguna Brava on foot.

"Shouldn't we leave a note for Alejandro saying we've gone to the Laguna Brava?" I asked.

"We could leave a note," Antonio laughed, "but I'm afraid Alejandro wouldn't be able to read it. I saw him struggling with some letters, and I don't think literacy is his strong suit. We'll have to make some kind of a sign, like the Spanish missionaries made for the Indians." Beorchia drew a picture of our tent, then made an arrow pointing to the refuge by a big lake. Antonio added a touch of genius to his missionary picture by putting claws on the lake. "That way Alejandro will know it's the Laguna Brava"— which means "the Fierce Lake." "A lake with claws has to be fierce."

I felt rather fierce and self-sufficient myself as we set out with our loaded backpacks, free of the mules at last. But the feeling was soon replaced by aching all over my back and shoulders. Fortunately, we'd only walked a few miles when I spotted the mules in the distance. After we finally rendezvoused, Alejandro explained that the animals had run off, just as we'd suspected. He and Jorge had spent the previous day chasing them all the way back to the Ciénagas Grandes Valley.

Alejandro certainly wasn't his jaunty, confident self. He looked tired and nervous. By this time it was starting to hail again. So the muleteers continued up to our camp, where they picked up the equipment we'd left behind, while we kept going to the Laguna Brava. We walked more than fifteen miles that day, most of it along the shores of the Laguna Brava, which was surrounded by snow which seemed to blend into its white waters. The mountains around the lake looked serene and lovely under their snow mantle. When the clouds parted, we could see the great Veladero reflected in the Laguna Brava. As the mountain and the lake merged, the austere desert changed into a Swiss wonderland.

We marveled at how freakish the weather had turned. After all, we were in the southern reaches of the Atacama Desert, the driest piece of real estate in the world. Annual precipitation at the Laguna Brava, according to park rangers, is on the order of three to four inches. Several of the world's largest observatories are located in this part of South America precisely because of the stable weather and transparent skies. But we were now in our fourth consecutive day of snowfall, and the threatening black clouds kept billowing through, whirling in fantastic formations, as though we were at the height of India's monsoon season.

"The weather has gone crazy," Pinto said, when he and Jorge finally caught up with us at the Inca *tambo* by the Laguna Brava. "Normally it snows for a day or two, then a wind comes and clears the skies, leaving the horizon clean. But this shows no sign of letting up."

The next day we simply waited by the Laguna Brava, hoping the storm would let up. It died down and some snow around the lake melted, but rain, mixed with hail and snow, kept falling from time to time. I wondered how the pink flamingos could survive with all the snow and ice. But they managed a delicate balancing act, standing on one long leg at a time, hiding their graceful necks under their feathers for warmth, then pecking under snow and salt water for food. Whenever we approached, they flurried up in flocks of hundreds, a pink haze beating against the stone-cold air.

I woke at 5:00 A.M. on the sixth day of our storm and went out to look at the weather. Alejandro was already up, saddling the horses and mules for our trip to Mount Veladero.

"You think the storm is over?" I asked him.

"This is the worst weather I've ever seeen," he answered, looking at the dark clouds that ringed the great salt lake. "So you really can't say what will happen; my past experience doesn't seem to mean anything now. Still, I think you've got to try the mountain today. I can't believe the bad weather will continue. It can't go on forever."

Alejandro's hope for better weather seemed to come true. The clouds thinned and the sun came out on our six-hour ride to Mount Veladero. By the time we reached our previous camp at 15,580 feet, the mules were plodding through snow. We paused to let the animals rest, then continued up the canyon to a height of 16,730 feet, at which point the mules were slipping and falling. The snow was too deep for them to go on. Just as we dismounted to set up camp, the clouds closed in on us.

"You'd better put your tent up in a hurry," Alejandro said nervously. "A storm is coming. And it looks like the worst one yet."

Snow started falling, for what seemed like the umpteenth time, long before the tent was up. I felt that the mountain had led us into a perfect trap.

Several more inches of snow fell in short order. Antonio was unhappy. He started reflecting on our experiences over the past week. "In all my years of climbing, I've never had any mountain make me suffer as much as this Veladero. The worst I've had was two or three days of bad weather, always followed by thirty days of clear skies. But we're heading into our seventh day of storms. If we get more than ten inches of snow tonight, we're not going to be able to climb the mountain with our packs."

Our plan was to reach a protected plateau at 19,350 feet, about 1,500 feet below the summit, where we would pitch our final camp. Under normal circumstances, we'd have climbed to the summit from our 16,730-foot-high base camp. But we needed plenty of time to excavate the peak altar. Thus a higher camp was essential, both for reaching the summit in the early-morning hours and for having a quick fallback shelter if we worked late.

In spite of the atrocious weather, we remained optimistic. When you're sealed up in a tent for days with two other guys, rapport is vital. We talked about our lives, our goals—their families, my experiences in spiritual communities. We often argued about religion, since Antonio is a chest-pounding Roman Catholic while I still have something of the Hindu missionary in me.

As night fell, Antonio and I went outside the tent, where we found the snow still falling. We were in the middle of a cloud, with practically no visibility. Suddenly we felt a buzzing all around us; my beard and hair crawled with electrical static, while our metal objects began making a boiling sound.

"A damn electrical storm," Antonio said. "This is terrible. I feel like I have ants all over me."

For some reason, Antonio suffered more acutely than either Mario or myself. He jerked and scratched as though he were being bitten by thousands of insects. Back inside the tent, he felt better. But whenever he tried to sit up, the static attacked him again. "This had better stop," he said from his enforced prone position, "or I'm not going to be able to climb anywhere tomorrow."

Now lightning and thunder started sounding all around us. They seemed simultaneous, and although we couldn't see the lightning in the middle of our cloud, we could *feel* it hitting nearby. This was one of the strangest sensations any of us had ever experienced: we heard a sizzling sound starting near us, then go whizzing across the snow, like a drop of oil streaking on a hot skillet. The snow was alive with electricity.

All in all, we were withstanding the stress of our storm pretty well. But after Mario went to sleep, I noticed that Antonio was having trouble breathing. Then I noticed that *I* was having trouble breathing, and that my heart was racing too fast for comfort. I spent a couple of miserable hours trying to regulate my breathing by sitting up and turning over, but without much success. Finally, I went outside and performed a little Tai Chi, rhythmic Chinese dance movements, while snow fell gently all around me. Everything was overwhelmingly white, perfectly still, except for my movements and the occasional crackle of electricity. When I closed my eyes, I seemed to disappear into the cloud. I could dimly hear distant thunder, though it sounded unreal, like a punch into a pillow. The dense fog was a down blanket which muffled the storm, and made me feel oddly secure. After that, I fell sound asleep inside the tent.

Morning came, enveloped in clouds and absolute quiet. Ten inches of new snow had fallen overnight. This was the upper limit of what we could walk through with our backpacks. We left at 9:45 A.M., to trudge through snow up to our knees and, in some places, up to our waists. I'd never climbed at this altitude with a forty-pound pack before, and the snow added a huge amount of effort to our painstaking progress. Mario and I took turns as pathbreaker, the exhausting job of being the first one to step in the fresh snow. My pulse and breathing rates rose insanely, even though we advanced slowly, resting every ten or twelve steps.

"Mountain climbers are obviously not rational creatures," Antonio observed as we stopped to rest. "Every time I get up to the mountain, I could kick myself in the rear end for subjecting myself to this pain."

But the payoff was the view: the clouds had cleared, forming a backdrop to Mount Bonete, almost twenty miles to the west of us. The whole highland world was empty except for us. There wasn't an animal track, or a condor, or a plant, for as far as we could see. Everything for dozens of miles was white and splendidly bright. I thought this must be the poor man's approximation to the celestial vision. But the vision had its dangers. We had to be very careful not to take our sunglasses off, even for the shortest time, since snow blindness at this altitude can come in a matter of minutes.

There was another danger, which worried Antonio even more. "We should not separate more than fifty yards for any reason," he ordered. "From now on, the three of us are one person. Because, if a strong wind suddenly picks up, all this fresh snow will go flying so fast we won't be able to see each other."

At the time this advice sounded unnecessary. The sun was beating down on us, and, under the weight of our winter gear, we were sweating profusely from the heat and exertion. In short order we took off all our winter clothes except our climbing boots, snow pants, gloves, and sunglasses. We drank all our water and were desperate for more, so we stooped to lick little deposits of water in rocks along the way. By now the snow was getting mushier, making our advance more treacherous. I sank deeper into the snow as pathbreaker. Several times I slipped off rocks and fell down completely. We'd reached 18,050 feet, at 3:00 P.M., when a snow started falling. "Where can this be coming from?" I thought, since the sky was still clear. In fact, the snow shone in rainbow colors for a few pleasant moments. But the visual enjoyment ended in a hurry as the wind became a gale and the snow turned into a blizzard. Antonio called for me to stop. When I turned around, I could hardly see him a few feet away. And my own fresh tracks were already being covered with snow.

We huddled behind some rocks on a nearby ridge, rapidly putting on heavier clothing. It was freezing cold. We had to put up my tent as best we could, even though we had a sharp cliff to the south of us, and the wind was howling from the north, buffeting us at every step. Mario had to get inside the tent to keep it from blowing away. But when Antonio and I returned with heavy rocks for our tent ties, we had the weird vision of Mario, spread in star formation inside the tent, being blown, tent and all, toward the waiting precipice. We caught him in time, but it was a shocking realization that we'd gone from a hot summer day to an Antarctic gale in the space of ten minutes.

"This is a great tent," Antonio said, once we were inside it. "We'd be dead without this tent, even with all our clothes and equipment. This wind is coming at well over sixty miles per hour. It's called 'the white wind,' and it's the most dangerous thing that can happen to a climber. First a heavy snow falls. Then the wind blows the snow and blinds you. You try to sit out the storm, but after you sit in this wind for a little while, you start freezing. It seems easier to just fall asleep and forget about everything. That's how many people freeze to death in the Andes."

The tent was flapping like a stadium flag, and the acoustic effect was like being inside a drum. But my new high-altitude tent *was* great. Its geodesic design broke the wind with mathematical precision. After all, it had been tested and retested under the worst conditions at above nineteen thousand feet on Mount McKinley. We had nothing to fear, I thought as I went to sleep, feeling oddly comforted by the resounding noise of my sturdy tent.

The next morning we suited up for the final assault on the peak, figuring that from where we were it was approximately two thousand feet. But when we took a few steps outside the tent, we realized we could make no headway against the wind. In fact, we could hardly stand up. And we couldn't see anything if we tried to walk uphill into the wind, since the snow was still flying so fast and thick that it completely covered our sunglasses, and every attempt to clean them off seemed to get more moisture on the glasses, moisture that quickly froze to ice.

This was a world as different from our usual one as a zero-gravity spacecraft. All of a sudden, heavy objects began to fly— when I left my backpack on the ground for a moment, the wind started whisking it away. Then I lost my footing as I pursued it, and it seemed, for a moment, that the wind would whisk me over the cliff, too. I've been in very cold weather in Antarctica and the

Soviet Union, but I've never experienced anything remotely approaching the power of Veladero's storm.

Even the smallest tasks were now enormous undertakings. To relieve yourself involved suiting up completely, stepping into the inferno gale, and urinating away from the wind. Unfortunately, the storm turned your urine into a whirlwind that wet you all over. But the cold was so intense that, in the few seconds you took getting back to the tent, the urine was frozen on your suit.

The wind and the cold worsened during that second day at 18,050 feet. About 10:00 A.M. Antonio noticed something ominous. "It looks like your tent is loosening," he said. "The aluminum tent poles are starting to give way."

We forced ourselves outside to try to shore up the tent. By making a tremendous effort, we dug big rocks out of the now-frozen snow, and added them to new pull-lines. We also took our walking sticks, jammed them into the snow, and tied lines to them, too. But these measures only postponed the creeping collapse of our tent, which had apparently met its match on Mount Veladero. By evening we were huddled together in a tent reduced to a third of its normal size; as the night wore on, we feared it might go altogether.

The collapsing tent posed a special problem when it came to melting water, the only thing we were doing as far as food was concerned. Three times a day we melted enough snow to make a quart of water, then divided it up jealously among us. Dehydration is the enemy at high altitude. In theory, you should drink large amounts to combat it. In practice, no one does, because of the time and discomfort involved in melting snow. For us the problem became critical at the end of our second day of the "white-wind" storm, because the tent had fallen down on top of us, and the flames from our little stove were scant inches from the flammable tent material. I still felt no discomfort from the altitude. But my throat was dry and I was suffering from the lack of water.

As night wore on, the storm reached incredible intensity. The sound of the wind beating at the tent was a perpetual, deafening roar. We couldn't communicate at all, except by making gestures, or cupping our hands and shouting, full force, into each other's ears. The tent was collapsing to such an extent that we all had to start leaning against it with our bodies.

Antonio looked very grim. "I don't want to sound overly dramatic," he managed to shout into my ear. "But we could freeze to death in minutes if the tent rips. We have to all put on our boots and all our climbing clothes, so that when the tent goes we get out of here and start down the mountain as fast as possible."

We sat like that for a long time, shivering and afraid, feeling the increasing pressure of the tent coming down on top of us. I was grateful for the company of my two friends, and especially grateful for Antonio's experienced leadership. I also thanked God that I hadn't attempted Veladero on my own.

My prayers for survival that night alternated with other prayers, for God to help us find a mummy at the peak. We still hadn't given up hope for our mummy. We were all suited up, so if the wind died down we'd be ready to jump out and climb to the peak in two or three hours. At least that's what we told ourselves. Looking back at it now, I'm amazed we still entertained such a dream. With all that snow on the peak, and frozen snow at that, we wouldn't have found those slabstones in the few hours at our disposal even if the weather had suddenly turned perfect.

But the weather did not turn perfect. The wind did soften enough so that our tent survived the night, but it was still next to impossible to see what you were doing walking into the white wind. Walking downhill, away from the wind, was much easier. And that's what our sad little party did the next morning: we quickly packed our gear, and got out at 10:00 A.M. Our only losses were the plastic tarp under my tent, which the wind carried off as though it were a magic carpet, and the tent poles, which were twisted wrecks.

We stumbled down the mountain, with the wind at our backs. When we reached 16,400 feet, the weather wasn't so bad. At 15,750 feet we sat down next to some meltwater, ate frozen peaches, and enjoyed the sunshine, with only some wispy signs of blowing snow high on the mountain to hint that the storm factory was still in full operation.

We met our muleteers an hour later. They were right on schedule, but they looked as miserable as I felt. Alejandro's normally robust face had fallen into a basement of despair. His eyes were bleary red.

"We had a foot of snow at the Laguna Brava," he said. "Jorge and I suffered from snow blindness, because we didn't have sunglasses with us." A couple of mules had also gone lame, hurt from slips in the snow.

After we made it back to the Laguna Brava, and I took a bath in freezing meltwater, I felt better. Veladero looked radiant in the distance, while the Laguna Brava grew softer, more seductive, and less fierce with each new layer of snow.

It was hard to believe that I'd started climbing on Veladero just a year earlier, with ridiculously bad equipment—old shoes; a cheap, torn, lightweight jacket; a lousy sleeping bag. . . . My lack of preparation, plus the gross miscalculation of the mountain's height, could easily have proved fatal in a sudden storm like the one we'd experienced at 18,050 feet. And when I thought about Antonio, along with six others, spending the night outside our tents . . . As Alejandro had put it, we'd been blessed with "barbarous good luck." The most perplexing question remained: How did the Incas cope with such violent storms without modern equipment?

☒ 5 ☒

THE PEACEFUL
MOUNTAIN

In spite of our disastrous experience Johan Reinhard was optimistic about the chances of excavating Mount Veladero. Reinhard, who's climbed more Andean peaks and discovered more Inca sites than any other high-altitude archaeologist, told me that he would be willing to try Veladero.

I met Johan Reinhard in San Juan on March 13, 1988. He had just returned from his most successful expedition ever. On Volcán Copiapó (19,921 feet) he and five other climbers found three Inca statues during a twelve-day excavating marathon. After such a long time at nearly twenty thousand feet, Reinhard looked about as gaunt as a human being this side of starvation can look. Yet he was anxious to keep climbing in order to take advantage of his acclimatization, and seemed ill at ease in the city of San Juan. "Don't worry," Johan kept telling me, "soon we'll be back in the mountains."

He didn't realize that's why I was worried.

Reinhard struck me as being uniquely adapted to high altitude. About six feet tall and sinewy, he's been described as a machine for climbing mountains. He's something of an ascetic, with simple tastes in food and clothes, and has a recluse's dislike of crowds. Reinhard is also one of the most doggedly determined people I've ever met. At forty-four, he's conquered many of the major peaks of the Alps, Himalayas, and Andes. At the same time, his hands-on research is changing the terms of archaeological discussion in the Andes.

If there's anyone who can claim to be a real-life Indiana Jones, it's Johan Reinhard. Born in a small Illinois town, he went on to get a Ph.D. in anthropology from the University of Vienna on the subject of Nepalese shamanism. While in South Asia, he discovered two nearly extinct tribes, translated a Nepali treatise on the Yeti (the Nepalese Abominable Snow Man), was a member of a Mount Everest expedition, and was one of the first men to cross the Great Indian Desert by camel. In the Andes he's discovered more than thirty high-altitude Inca sites and surveyed twenty more. As an expert in underwater archaeology, he also dived the crater lake of Volcán Licancábur (19,200 feet), where he found a new species of crustacean. The Licancábur dive was five thousand feet higher than any previous attempt, setting a world record that still stands. Johan's achievement goes beyond the specialized field of Inca high-altitude sites. He's written articles offering fundamental reinterpretations of Chavín (800 B.C.–200 B.C.), Tiahuanaco (A.D. 100–1100), and the Nazca Lines, all based on underlying concepts of mountain-water fertility cults. His theories have aroused both enthusiasm and controversy.

When I asked Reinhard how he got started on his risky career, he told me about a near-fatal experience which changed his life. "I was a teenager working for a railroad company, putting up telegraph lines in a rural area," he recalled. "I climbed up an old pole to unravel wires around the insulator, and, after I'd untied the last wires, the rotted-out base of the pole snapped, and the pole started falling. The pole was heavy and it was coming down right on top of me, so I knew I was going to be smashed. It's true what people say about your life passing before your eyes when you think you're going to die. It seemed like everything was in slow motion, as I saw, very vividly, experiences going back to my childhood, many of which I'd forgotten. At the last moment, the telegraph pole caught another line, and came up a couple of feet short of the ground. I got up from under the pole sweating and shaking. Because of that I realized something that a lot of people never really confront—you're going to be very dead someday. And from that moment on, I decided to live my life the way I wanted to, not the way other people wanted me to."

"I've climbed over one hundred five-thousand-meter [16,400-foot] peaks in the Andes," Johan told me as we rendezvoused with Alejandro Pinto and a younger brother of his by the Bonete River Dam. "There were only two that I didn't make on the first try. In one case, I was on a ridge a few meters from the peak when a freakish electrical storm hit; a current was established all along the ridge, about three feet off the ground. I've never experienced anything like it—I had to crawl on the ground, staying under the electrical current that was flowing. Whenever I tried to get up, the electricity shook my whole body. The other time I missed the peak was during a dense fog when I was on a narrow ridge with razor-sharp rocks. That time my partner and I just didn't want to lose a good rope on those rocks, so we turned back.

"The reason I've had such great success is that I prepare each climb very carefully. If the mules get us anywhere near Veladero, I'll consider the mountain done. But what I can't promise you is that we'll be able to find anything. The ground may be so frozen there's nothing we can do. I've seen axes break on frozen ground at high altitude. At Copiapó six men spent eight days to find three statues. You and I alone would have to spend a month on Veladero to do anything like that. And for all practical purposes, that's impossible."

Reviewing Antonio's map of Veladero's peak structures, and his one black-and-white photograph, Johan was not too excited about the slabstones that had excited Antonio with hopes of finding a mummy. "I've seen a lot of slabstones on a lot of mountains," he said, "but so far I haven't found anything underneath them."

To break through the hard, frozen ground on Veladero's summit, we'd brought several tools, including Antonio's *saca-momias* (mummy finder), which weighed several pounds, and a full-sized pick, weighing nearly ten pounds. Reinhard had a backpack several times larger than mine for hauling all this stuff. A small refrigerator would probably have fit inside it.

Once we'd made our camp by the Laguna Brava, Johan walked around, studying Veladero in the last light of the day. "It's not a living being," he remarked, "but it has moods, changes. It also has strengths and weaknesses. It's a question of finding its weaknesses, picking the right approach."

"Are you planning an ascent route?" I asked.

"Yes. Several. I think this mountain can be climbed from any direction. I'm not optimistic about finding anything, however. With so much snow, the ground will probably be frozen solid. It takes a long time to work under those conditions. And we won't have much time at the peak."

The next day we had a better look at Veladero. In the morning light, the amount of snow didn't look quite as daunting. "We caught the afternoon glare yesterday," Johan said. "A lot of that snow may be a recent dusting. There's still hope."

We rode for four hours with all our ten animals. Then, by a snow-fed pond about six miles from Veladero, Pinto and his brother unloaded most of the mules. Pinto, Johan, and I continued on with two cargo mules, leaving Alejandro's brother to make camp on his own.

Alejandro agreed to try to take us to 16,400 feet, where he had dropped Antonio, Mario, and me the year before. But he shook his head when we reached 15,420 feet and we saw teeming rows of *penitentes*—wind-sculpted snow formations that look like kneeling pilgrims—blocking the way. "This is as far as we go," he announced.

With promises of a bigger fee, considerable prodding, and some shouting, I convinced Alejandro to go on. He wasn't happy about taking the animals through the snow, in and out of bogs. The amazing thing was how the rocky volcanic ground could become so porous and treacherous when soaked with water. Fortunately, our mares were in excellent spirits. Mine actually picked up speed and tried to take the lead. Within an hour, working our way around and through several snowfields, we reached our goal: 16,730 feet. Johan and I both hugged Alejandro.

As we rapidly set up camp, I began to appreciate Johan's climbing strategy. "We have a few hours of light left," he said. "It's nearly four. But we can climb up for a couple of hours, carrying some of the gear we'll need to reach our second camp tomorrow. That will lighten the load tomorrow morning. And it will get us better acclimatized. You should always climb high and sleep low."

We'd been up since 5:00 A.M., taken down one camp at fourteen thousand feet, ridden seven hours on mules, put up another camp at seventeen thousand feet, all as a prelude to the real work—climbing to over eighteen thousand feet with supplies. Marathon runners talk about hitting "the wall" after fifteen or twenty miles, but I hit the wall after only a hundred yards. Every step after that was painful. And the physical pain was compounded by my sense of inferiority at watching Johan move on ahead at twice my speed. I had to stop and rest every ten steps or so, while Johan kept plodding methodically along. It was lonely climbing like this, without anyone to talk to, and I missed Antonio's comradely banter. But the success of the expedition depended upon Johan's getting those heavy picks halfway to the high camp, which we'd planned to put at twenty thousand feet. Otherwise I'd have to carry a heavier load the next day. And, judging from the way I felt at seventeen thousand feet with my twenty-pound pack, that wasn't a good idea. After I left a movie camera, an archaeological hammer, and some food supplies around eighteen thousand feet, I felt that I couldn't take much more weight.

I slept well at our 16,730-foot camp, where we'd erected my yellow-gray geodesic tent. Since Johan had a smaller and lighter tent, we left mine standing and got off to an early start. This time my pack was more than twice as heavy as the previous day's. Johan guessed that I was carrying around forty pounds, while he lugged perhaps eighty pounds. In spite of the huge difference in weight, he was soon out of sight.

The morning was bright and cold, with a brisk twelve-to-fifteen-mile-per-hour wind. By the time I reached the 18,370-foot camp where I'd been with Antonio the year before, the wind was blowing harder, whipping snow into my face. Occasional snow flurries made me nervous, but it was nothing like the previous year's storm.

I moved slower and slower up the mountain, trudging through snowfields that crunched under my feet. My attention got absorbed in the solitary sound of my plodding footsteps. Whenever I stepped on a volcanic rock, I heard a barren *clink* sound, followed by other *clinks* as the rock nudged others. The sound of stepping on snow was more like the grating rasp of Styrofoam. Eventually, I stopped thinking about anything but the rhythmic stress of my feet against the snow and stones. But then the sounds of my footsteps began to echo. Several times I was startled to think that someone was walking next to me. I turned quickly once. Then again. By the third time I realized I was having a mild hallucination, common enough at high altitude, of an invisible companion. I knew my "invisible companion" was in my head, a natural response of a lonely person in a friendless landscape. But it was still disconcerting.

Finally, I made it up the main slope to a broad, flatter area, where we planned to camp before the final ascent. I could see the summit clearly now. Then I realized this was where I'd been two years before, on my first climb, when I'd given up to exhaustion. I was almost ready to give up again when I saw Johan coming toward me.

"I put up the tent around that ridge there," he said, pointing to a rise a couple of hundred yards away. "You'll reach it in a few minutes. Now I'm going to drop down and get that pick. After you've rested, start building stone walls around the tent. When you finish that, start collecting snow to melt."

Then Johan was gone, like a fleeting apparition. Although

Reinhard had said it would take me a few minutes to reach the tent, I spent nearly an hour going that last little stretch. It was an eternity of drudgery, just moving my legs up and down in the snow. I collapsed inside the tent, where all I could hear for half an hour was the frantic gasping of my breath and the flapping of the tent.

It was a good thing Johan had given me a couple of jobs to do. The sense of duty brought me around, and got me busy collecting rocks and snow. The wind grew more cutting, and snow was flying around wickedly now. Still, I was able to build up some shelter around the corners of the tent, and I stuffed a plastic bag full of hard snow.

When Johan got back, we finished building the walls around the tent. Then each of us went inside, where Johan began melting snow. This was a job that lasted a couple of hours, and I was immensely relieved that Johan took care of it while I rested.

"Nothing much happened today," Johan said matter-of-factly. For me, it had been the most strenuous day of my life. For Johan, who'd carried twice as much twice as far, it was nothing much. Well, Johan admitted he'd had a couple of bad moments.

"The wind was so bad I had to turn my back to it a couple of times on the way back," he said. "I've experienced one of the worst windstorms in my life not far from here, on Mount Bonete, in 1986. You have to be very careful where you put your tent. The wind just pours down the side of the mountain where you guys camped last year—you were right in the middle of a wind funnel. Of course, when you're caught in an unexpected storm, like you and Antonio were, you don't have much choice about where to pitch a tent."

Our current campsite wasn't ideal, either. The winds were ripping around our protective rocks, piling up snowdrifts against the tent wall. We kept pushing the snow back, but this was a difficult job. Opening the tent flap for just a few seconds could inundate us with a covering of snow, a dangerous risk when warmth depends on dry sleeping bags and clothes. The wind kept howling and churning snow all night long, making every decision about going outside a major policy choice. "To urinate or not to urinate" became the

Hamlet-like obsession in the nightlong insomnia and lethargy of my high-altitude misery.

It was tempting to think that the most grueling part of our climb was over. But Johan dissuaded me of this when we made our final preparations early the next morning, March 21. "Every hundred meters from now makes a big difference," he said. "We have between four and five hundred meters [1,310–1,640 feet] to the peak. But that may feel as big as the jump from fifty-one hundred to fifty-nine hundred [16,730–19,350 feet] we made today." Johan's altimeter was marking around 19,520 feet, though he explained that altimeters were often unreliable at this height. "Still, I'd say the map's reading of 6,436 meters [21,120 feet] is about right for Veladero. If we leave here between eight and nine, we should be at the peak by ten or eleven. With all this snow, however, I'm pretty sure the ground will be frozen solid. We also have to hope the wind dies down, or it's going to be hell working on the summit."

After laboriously melting enough snow to fill our canteens, we slowly pulled on multiple layers of clothing. Finally, around 8:30 A.M., I clumsily put on my boots and stepped outside to give Johan more room.

The windstorm had died. The weather on the mountain changed from intense turbulence to complete quiet in the time it took me to put on my clothes. All around me the snow was blazing in the sun—there wasn't a cloud to be seen or a breath of wind to be felt. It seemed to be our lucky day.

"We don't have any liquor to offer to the mountain," Johan said. "That's bad."

That startled me. "You make offerings to the mountain before you climb?" I asked.

"Yes, usually liquor and some sweets. It's a habit I've picked up from witnessing shamanic rituals. After all, we're going to a shrine that was sacred to the Incas. I think making a traditional offering to the mountain is a sign of respect."

Johan climbed ahead of me, carrying the ten-pound pick and the rest of his mule load. I struggled behind, too brutalized by the effort of plunging through the fresh, soft, knee-deep snow even to feel embarrassed anymore by Johan's superiority. Actually, Johan performed another service for me by going ahead: following in his footsteps eased my ascent. Still, falling into the snow over and over again, pulling myself out and panting so wildly it seemed to come from someone else, going on, falling in once more, was a long agon. The only merciful thing about it was that my brain kind of shut down, everything turned into a blur, and afterward the climb became as hard to remember as it had been hard to accomplish. This is the one benefit of having millions of brain cells killed off by lack of oxygen.

Occasionally I had a desire just to lie down and rest in the snow. But that thought triggered a switch that made one thing as clear as the snow crystals sparkling all around me: "If you lie down to rest in this snow, you'll freeze to death before Johan ever finds you."

I made the peak at 1:30 P.M., five hours after setting out. Johan was already digging away with his chain-gang pick, but he stopped long enough to give me a hug.

"Congratulations!" he said. "Son-of-a-bitch of a mountain!"

Johan had reached the peak at 11:30 A.M., which made it a surprisingly long time for him, and proof of the difficult going. By the time I arrived, Johan had dug a big hole in the northeastern corner of the peak platform. Although I'd seen Antonio's drawings and photos of the Inca structure, it was not what I expected. The pictures don't really capture the strangeness of encountering a carefully built double-stone wall, along with a nicely leveled-off platform, sitting in the middle of an arctic wilderness. Simply the fact that the stones were so evenly placed seemed miraculous, considering that I could hardly walk a straight line. It was the only human presence in that inhuman place.

Of course, there was nothing to this Inca altar in another sense—just a stone rectangle a yard high in places, filled in with gravel, an empty space carved out of nowhere by a few rocks. Yet it had lasted five hundred years in spite of unimaginable winds, snowstorms, and time allied to perpetual cold. This walled-in space shocked me, for being both so insignificant and so endless in its projections.

The oddest thing about the platform was that it wasn't covered by snow, in contrast to the rest of the summit. The platform was at the very peak, so it received the fiercest winds, which swept it constantly clean. But the best news Johan gave me was that the ground wasn't frozen. He held up some little feathers. "These feathers look like they belong to an idol," he said. "I found them here in the northeastern corner, along with lots of grass and bits of wood and a thread. The corners are where you normally expect to find offerings, and the eastern corners are often the best places to look."

With the hope of finding an Inca statue, I felt immediately energized. While Johan swung the heavy pick, I scooped up dirt with a small pot, then sifted it. After a few minutes Johan gave a happy exclamation and pulled out a red thread.

"I find it hard to believe that, with the feather and the thread, there's no idol here," Johan said. "Unless someone's already been here and stolen it."

I kept panning and finding grass and wood, the most common items at many peak sanctuaries. But the grass and other ritual objects became scarcer and scarcer. Finally, we reached bedrock, below the level of the wall itself. Nothing.

Next we turned to the famous slabstones in the northwestern corner, where Yuyi had pulled out a tuft of grass. It took a horrendous effort by both of us even to budge the rock, which must have weighed a few hundred pounds. But, using the pick as a lever and building up rocks underneath, we gradually lifted the boulder and wrenched it a couple of feet. As we began digging, grass and wood appeared once more, proof that the Incas had moved the slabstone to bury these offerings beneath it.

But we reached bedrock with no statues or mummies to show for it. We were getting discouraged.

Clearly, our hopes of just moving the slabstones and locating a mummy had been mistaken. For the first time I understood how difficult a real excavation at twenty-one thousand feet is. The offerings showed that the Incas had buried things around the platform. But where could the statues be? *Were* there any statues?

"We should keep digging as long as possible," Johan said. "To do this correctly would take half a dozen people a week, but we have to take advantage of the weather and the fact that we've gone through a lot to get here. Besides, with all the publicity this mountain has received in the Argentine newspapers, if we don't find what's here some treasure hunter will."

"Do you think we can dig under the other slabstone?"

The other slabstone was in the southeastern corner of the platform. On closer inspection, however, it appeared to be a part of the landscape, so huge there was no question of budging it with our primitive methods.

"I think Antonio was mistaken about the second slabstone," Johan said. "It's natural."

The other spot Antonio had asked us to excavate was a stone circle where he'd found the ceramic jar. This would have been our next choice, but the circle was completely covered by snow. We couldn't locate it precisely, and clearing the whole area would have taken too much time. So we were reduced to a guessing game— picking a place in the large ceremonial quadrangle and hoping to get lucky. Johan chose a rock in the center of the platform, which he dug around. I helped him, though without much hope of finding anything.

"You work better than most people I've seen at this altitude," Johan told me.

"I have more incentive," I said, although the incentive was rapidly dying for both of us. At five o'clock we quit digging and sifting. After some quick photos, Johan started down the mountain. He decided to skid down the solid snow and ice mass of the mountain's southern face, but he advised me not to follow him. "There might be some nasty holes in the snow," he warned. I rewalked our former route, and reached the base camp as darkness set in.

"I rarely excavate sites, out of respect for laws which regulate archaeological digs. Veladero is an exception because, with all the publicity Antonio has given it, some treasure hunter would have sacked the place before long," Johan told me inside our tent. "What we did today was the third or fourth most complete excavation I've ever done at high altitude. We dug in all the logical places. Unfortunately, the Incas didn't always bury their idols in the most logical places. We came very close in the northeastern corner, where we found the feathers and the red thread. When I found that second piece of thread, I was sure that an Inca idol was going to come up with it. I really don't understand why there was no statue. There are other places I would have liked to dig. But with the shortage of time you're forced into committing one mistake or another. Everything should be dug wider and deeper.

"You may feel disappointed at not finding a statue here, but it took me eight years to really find anything significant. And that came after days of digging with a large team at a site where the Austrian climber Rebitsch had previously worked. We found Rebitsch's old pick, and we joked that all we might discover at the bottom of the platform would be his old cigarette papers. Well, when one of the Swiss found the first statue, I heard a yell: 'Oh, no. Plastic. Oh, God.' My first thought was that someone else had already dug down to bedrock. I came over and saw the guy holding a tiny llama figurine made out of spondylus shell. When I told them it was Inca, they thought I was joking. It was so bright and pink they were sure it was plastic. They weren't too impressed. For the Incas, spondylus shell, brought from Ecuador, was more valuable than gold. But people don't much care about figurines today unless they're made of gold and silver."

In all his years of climbing, Reinhard has discoverd no mummies, and only one precious-metal statue—a silver female figurine which he unearthed at the end of the Volcán Copiapó excavation, scant days before our Veladero climb. "We'd been digging for days at Copiapó and we'd literally reached rock bottom," he recalled as we talked together in our tent. "I was at the summit, and the Swiss gave out another yell: 'There are feathers and gold.' So I went down. I could see a statue, but it was wedged in and frozen solid. To dislodge it, I tried pouring hot tea into a plastic bag and placed it against the frozen ground to try to thaw it out—a new archaeological technique, which unfortunately didn't work. A knife couldn't dig out the frozen ground, either. Eventually, I pounded around it with an ice ax, which freed it. All of a sudden, I held in my hand an Inca idol. I felt a mixture of respect and awe. I was also thinking that after eight long years I finally held a beautiful object. But mainly I felt a desire not to have that moment die in the clamor of photos and everything. I just held the statue for a little while, thinking this was something that had meant a lot to the Incas and which now meant a lot to me."

We spent an unpleasant night at 19,360 feet, but by the end of the next day returned to the more ample tent at the more comfortable altitude of seventeen thousand feet. We both relaxed. "You have to have some residue of good feeling now that you've finally made this peak," Johan remarked. "I consider what we've done to be a good start on Veladero. Do you remember when I told you years ago that these high-altitude structures were one of mankind's greatest achievements? A lot of people might regard that as an exaggeration. But I think just one climb up a mountain like Veladero would change their minds. It's one thing to put a pyramid up on the plains. It's something else to struggle up here to sixty-four hundred meters [21,000 feet] and build walls."

"How long do you think it took them to build this sanctuary?" I asked.

"Not long. I think ten men could have built the walls in one day. The north wall was nicely built and looked like it had two rows of rocks with fill in between. I don't know how long it would have taken to collect gravel for the fill, which can be trouble. Mind you, I don't think they did it all in one day, with all the offerings going on. For the fill, they'd have two or three guys digging and the rest carrying up the gravel in circular trays they used. But all the while a priest and his assistant would be making offerings."

"What did the wood and grass we found all over the platform represent?"

"Wherever you find wood, it means they were making burnt offerings—usually of incense, though it could have been textiles. They'd invoke the gods—Inti [the Sun], the mountain gods, Pacha Mama [the Earth Mother], local gods, local mountains for sure. It's hard to imagine any site where a variety of deities weren't invoked for a variety of reasons. The reasons included health, safe travel up and down the mountain, for their herds, and even for the Inca ruler."

"Were the Incas the ones who built this platform?" I wondered.

"We don't know if the workers were Incas. But I would think that at least the priest and his assistant would have to be Incas. Somebody had to have expert learning in the rites. Because doing them wrong is worse than not doing them at all. You see how hard it is for us to just get up there. The Incas would only go through that much trouble because the rituals must have been extremely important to them, and therefore the celebrant had to be someone more than just a local shaman."

The next day faithful Alejandro came as scheduled, and we returned to the Laguna Brava. I started feeling nostalgic that night, as I walked alone around the Inca ruins by the ghostly lake. A single, bright star or planet shone over Veladero—a special accent mark in our sacred geography. Then a crescent moon came out, illuminating the Inca *tambo*'s stone walls and the mules milling around them. A bell, dangling around the neck of our single stallion, jingled with a light wind. The Fierce Lake was tame tonight. No waves, no disturbances in its murky, salt-white waters. I gingerly made my way through swampy ground, over clumps of tough highland grass, until I found a path heading toward the ceremonial platform by the shore. It was fun to imagine that Inca priests had taken the same path.

I sat down and looked across the lake at Mount Pilar, where Antonio, Mario, and I had found an Inca platform. For the Incas, this whole area was sacred space, circumscribed by invisible connections. From this Inca *explazo* priests had probably offered alcohol, incense, and llamas to the lake and mountains. I could appreciate why the Incas came to this spot to give something back to the earth and water. By contrast, it seemed to me that I'd been too preoccupied with taking something away—a mummy, a statue, or a trophy.

On our trip back to Las Ciénagas Grandes, I asked Johan why he'd made an offering to Veladero the day we climbed the peak.

"I find that offering a piece of candy to the mountain settles my mind and gives me a different perspective," he said. "Normally, I'm always thinking about alternate routes, possible shifts in weather, equipment. And that's why I'm successful. I'm always monitoring time and terrain. But this is also one of my faults. And I find that the offering to a mountain gets me out of this maximizing mode. It's like a technique of meditation which works because it affects your attitude for the rest of the day, outside of meditation. I recommend this kind of respect toward nature to Western climbers, because it gets you out of the adversarial relationship with the mountain."

As the weather warmed, and drinkable water started flowing around us, we laughed together at our anticlimactic conclusion to the great battle with what Antonio, in one of his newspaper articles, had called "The Rebellious Mountain."

Riding through the Bonete River Valley, I started thinking about the Inca priests who'd climbed these mountains for a living. "I wonder if the Inca priests enjoyed their jobs," I said.

"It's interesting to think about those Inca priests," Johan mused. "Imagine if there were only a couple of guys like us and they were climbing all these peaks to perform ceremonies."

"But could two guys have built these sanctuaries by themselves?"

"No. They'd need a team of workers. But once the temples were built, the worship depended on the priests. I'd assume that Veladero had to be worshipped every year. The Incas had a rule that every *huaca* [sacred place] had to be fed every year. If the *huacas* were fed, then they would in turn feed human beings. It didn't have to be anything important, just some booze, incense, and prayers. But doing that for this Cordillera would have kept a couple of priests pretty busy. It wouldn't have been such a bad life, though. They probably traveled twenty kilometers [twelve miles] per day, with a couple of assistants and llamas to carry wood. They were probably just like us, thinking, 'Boy, I can't wait till we get this mountain over with.' "

"They must have had a lot of prestige," I suggested.

"Oh, yeah." Johan laughed. "The Inca priests were the ones who had been to the land of the gods."

As we met the first shepherds along the Bonete River, we were also greeted with a reverence and respect usually reserved for priests. They could hardly believe we'd climbed Mount Veladero. I could hardly believe it myself. And in this shared sense of wonder, it occurred to me that the mystique attached to the Inca priests had been caused by a simple misunderstanding. The people down below assumed we looked so happy because we'd been to the land of the gods. What they didn't guess was that, after the sustained sense starvation of the high mountains, these first green desert shrubs, thatched huts, and skinny shepherds all looked like glowing apparitions from the land of the gods. Those Inca priests knew where the land of the gods wasn't.

⊡ 6 ⊡

THE SORCERESS AT LAGO BUDI

Southern Chile, 1983–84

Everyone was afraid of the sorceress at Lago Budi.

The Mapuche Indians at her reservation in southern Chile avoided her. They had a taboo against even mentioning her name. No outsiders had spoken to the sorceress, a Mapuche Indian shaman, or *machi,* since she'd been accused of sacrificing a five-year-old boy to the ocean, following an earthquake and a tidal wave that destroyed most of the Indian reservation at Lago Budi in 1960. The sorceress so intimidated witnesses at her trial that nothing was ever proved against her. Nor did the authorities get any real information about the child's disappearance—just a story about a child drowning while collecting firewood.

I heard about the sacrifice at Lago Budi from Alberto Medina, the anthropologist who'd first looked at the beautiful face of the Inca child of Mount Plomo. Medina was particularly intrigued by Spanish accounts of child sacrifice among the Mapuche Indians of southern Chile, following a terrible earthquake in 1575.

He had traveled to the town of Puerto Saavedra in southern Chile—the odd rubble that was left of Puerto Saavedra, since what hadn't fallen with the earthquake had been flattened by a series of tidal waves—and while he was having lunch with the mayor, a police sergeant arrived saying that he'd been forced to arrest two men who'd sacrificed a child by order of a *machi*.

Without investigating further, Medina returned to Santiago and broke the news to the press. Unfortunately for him, the Mapuche community mobilized in response. "At first the Mapuches admitted this was a custom of theirs," Medina recalls. "But later they denied it, at the urging of university professors. Then they hired lawyers for the self-confessed sacrificers, who convinced the confessed killers to rescind their declarations."

Judge Jorge Osses, who presided over the trial of the *machi*, was impressed enough by the sorceress's power that he warned me to be careful in approaching her. "There are all kinds of *machis*," he explained. "Some of them cure people. Others use black magic to do evil." Most, Osses felt, do a little of both. If the judge took this shaman so seriously, it wasn't surprising that my Indian guide, Lorenzo Aillapán, was scared stiff of her. As a boy, Lorenzo had seen mysterious lights flare up around the *machi*'s house at night, spirit sparks that crackled and burned but left the sorceress unharmed.

"It's important to find out whether this *machi* is a healer or a witch," Lorenzo explained nervously. "If she's a healer, she has the gift for casting out demons, diagnosing illnesses, and finding herbal medicines. But if she's a black-magician, people secretly pay her to trap souls and make their enemies sick."

The Mapuche Indians were the only Amerindian group to defeat the Spaniards, in a prolonged, all-out 150-year war. The Mapuches' unceasing defense of their lands forced the Spaniards to create the New World's first standing army and caused King Philip II, whose troops had defeated the Italians, French, Turks, and Dutch, to complain that Chile, his poorest colony, was consuming his best soldiers. After Spanish forts and cities had been burned down again and again in Mapuche territory, the Spaniards finally pulled out and signed a formal treaty with the Mapuches, respecting their borders. But even before the Spaniards arrived in the New World, the Incas suffered the most decisive defeat in imperial expansion when they tried to penetrate Mapuche country. The Incas apparently gave the Mapuches the name Araucanos, which means "The People of War."

Lago Budi had been the heartland of the Mapuche resistance to foreign domination, and it remained a tough territory for any outsider to gain acceptance in.

At the banks of Lago Budi a wooden ferry, powered by our pulling, took us to the far shore. Once across, we realized we were on an island, surrounded by the horseshoe of Lago Budi on three sides, and the rough South Pacific on the fourth. On a clear day seven snowcapped volcanoes of the Andes are visible from the coastal hills. But today a persistent drizzle made millions of small splashes in the lake, and fell on us in larger drops as we passed under pine trees. Frogs croaked from tall grasses and a rare species of black-necked swan skimmed the lake, vanishing into patches of fog.

The *machi* lived in a thatched-roof hut, or *ruca*, above an isolated little lagoon. As we climbed toward the *ruca*, I slipped and fell in a patch of red mud. Suddenly geese honked, hens squawked, and dogs barked. The *machi* didn't need a doorbell.

A man stuck his head out of the hut and exchanged long, melodious greetings in Mapuche with Lorenzo. Finally, the man called inside the hut and a woman came out. She walked barefoot and wore a red shirt, a light-blue sweater, and a navy-blue dress, along with a maroon bandana around her head. She was short, heavyset, but had broad shoulders and long arms and looked very strong.

"Hello and goodbye," Machi Juana said. She made a disdainful motion, turned around, and stomped back into her *ruca*. We quickly presented gifts of flour, candles, and maté to the *machi*'s husband, who pleaded with his wife to come out again. When she did come out, she showed no pleasure at our gifts. Instead, she announced: "I am prophesying an earthquake within two years that will be worse than the one in 1960. It's possible you'll all die."

I was beginning to see why Machi Juana didn't get many visitors. The earthquake that struck southern Chile in 1960 measured a stunning 9.5 on the Richter scale—by far the worst earthquake recorded in the twentieth century. I told Machi Juana I lived in northern Chile, so I didn't expect her prophecy to affect me.

"The earthquake will strike hardest farther north," she answered.

I countered by saying that I'd escape the earthquake or tidal wave in my car.

"You can't escape when the earth shakes everywhere at once," she insisted. "And when the sea rose in 1960, it rushed in faster than your car—faster than a bird."

Machi Juana claimed she could hear underground rumblings to foretell earthquakes by placing a pipelike wind instrument, called a *trutruca*, against the ground and listening through the mouthpiece. Thus she converted the *trutruca* into a primitive sound-amplifier. When I asked her if her mother had taught her this strange technique, she indignantly replied that only God can teach a *machi* her magical skills.

Speaking partly in Mapuche, partly in Spanish, Machi Juana explained that God began visiting her when she was a little girl lying in bed, so sick her family thought she would die. "I saw a light, a candle, a brilliance," she remembers. "I also saw a fire inside the *ruca* that wasn't made by wood. God made it."

"But some human being must have taught you your magic and healing arts," I said.

"Only my spirit taught me," she answered.

I'd approached the *machi* with fear and trepidation, expecting to find a black-magician with a homicide in her past. Yet here the old lady was, preaching to me like a prophet of Israel to the Philistines, in a "Do-you-understand-me?" tone.

I felt absurdly out of touch with the *machi*'s feeling world of magic and healing, which made it difficult to even choose questions which made sense to her. I asked her if there was any way to avoid the terrible earthquake she was predicting.

"Earthquakes are punishments for people's sins," Machi Juana said. "The sacrifices of animals can alleviate earthquakes and postpone earthquakes if they're offered every four years. But now people's sins are too great to pay for with normal sacrifices."

"Could you perform some special sacrifice?" I wondered.

"My grandmother told me that in the old days the Mapuches were saved from earthquakes and tidal waves by climbing a special mountain called the Tren Tren," she said. "When the sea rose, the mountain rose, too. The hill grew and grew until it reached the sky, so none of the Mapuches were drowned. But how long ago was that? Maybe a thousand years. When we went to pray at the Tren Tren after the tidal wave of 1960, the hill didn't rise like it was supposed to. Not at all."

I quickly asked if human sacrifices had ever been performed on this hill, the Tren Tren. Instantly, the *machi*, her husband, and her adult daughter all stiffened. "No," they said in a chorus. "Only animals." Machi Juana quickly excused herself, explaining that she had "an appointment with my potato plants."

The court summary from the trial of 1960 concluded that the five-year-old boy, José Luis Painecur, had been thrown into the ocean. Yet Machi Juana now informed us that she and the rest of the Mapuches went to pray at a sacred hill following the earthquake and tidal wave. The *machi* had hoped this hill would have the property of growing faster than the rising water. Something went wrong. The traditional animal sacrifices didn't work, and the hill didn't rise.

"You raised the subject of human sacrifice too quickly," Lorenzo Aillapán said as we left. "A Mapuche meeting with strangers always follows a strict protocol. After talking for several hours, taking a cup of maté together, then we might have hinted something."

I was beginning to realize I'd entered another, older world with many mystifying protocols—a word where *machis* even made appointments with their potatoes, as though the potatoes were living beings. Potatoes *are* living beings, but when the *machi* mentioned her appointment with the potato crop, she seemed to treat them as if they were intelligent creatures capable of calling her to account if she showed up late. I was infected by a strange sense that other intelligences operated tangibly close to us in this Mapuche world— perhaps those "spirit sparks" Lorenzo had (I thought) imagined near the *machi*'s *ruca*. I wasn't sure what was happening.

Maybe I was getting in touch with my spirit.

Maybe the Mapuches were deliberately confusing me.

Maybe both.

It was raining again when I returned to Lago Budi. This time storm winds from the South Pacific whipped the continuous downpour in so many directions that it seemed to be raining up as well as down, soaking my raincoat from underneath and rendering it useless. My car was no good in the endless quagmire of mud, so I walked the twenty miles a day to interview the two men, Juan Pañán and José Vargas, tried for murdering Vargas's five-year-old grandson. Although they initially confessed to hurling the little boy into the ocean in order to pacify the angry water gods, they later retracted their testimony, and were freed after only two years in jail. Some people complained they got off too easily. But the judge ruled that they had acted without free will, "compelled by an irresistible psychic force" of ancient custom.[1]

This doctrine of "irresistible psychic force" was first applied to a religiously motivated Mapuche homicide in Chilean jurisprudence in 1953, when a Chilean court exonerated a twenty-seven-year-old Mapuche woman named Juana Catrilaf for murdering her grandmother. Juana Catrilaf was controlled by a force greater than her own reason, the court ruled, because she believed her grandmother, a *machi* with a penchant for black magic, was responsible for killing Catrilaf's twenty-one-day-old baby—through the agency of a malevolent spirit shaped like a red dog. In addition, the young woman suffered from epilepsy, which she attributed to her grandmother's use of invisible arrows against her. Catrilaf's conviction reflected the widely shared Mapuche fear that *machis*, aided by evil dwarfs and disembodied souls, make magical stones enter their victims' bodies. And Juana Catrilaf found convincing proof for this theory when she hit her grandmother over the head with a large stick—and saw one of these magical stones fall out of the old lady's mouth. After cutting her dead grandmother's forehead with the same stone, young Catrilaf sucked some of the deceased's blood, noting, as she did so, that a spirit of fire, like a devil, left her own body. Following this experience, according to the court transcript, the girl "felt much better and all the Indians are content."[2]

When I spoke to Judge Osses, he agreed that the doctrine of irresistible force applied to the two men who admitted killing José Luis Painecur. But he felt the really irresistible force was not the earthquake and tidal wave, but their fear of Machi Juana Namuncura,* who must have ordered the boy's death. "Some kind of ancient blood ritual must have taken place when they sacrificed the boy," Osses said. "But we could never get them to talk about it, or even to admit that the *machi* had anything to do with the sacrifice."

On the way to talk with Juan Pañán, Lorenzo Aillapán showed me Cerro Mesa, a small hill, only about fifty feet high, overlooking the ocean. This was the same hill Machi Juana had climbed to pray and take refuge upon during the earthquakes and tidal waves of 1960, hoping in vain that the hill would rise higher than the in-rushing ocean. I was told by an old man near Lago Budi that the human race was born on a hill like this one. At the beginning of history, he said, there was a great flood, which destroyed all people, except one couple and their only son, who took refuge on a mountain by the ocean. This mountain, called Tren Tren, grew until it surpassed all other mountains, carrying the progenitors of the Mapuche tribe to safety above the flood. But the mountain performed its miracle only after the Mapuche Adam and Eve had sacrificed their son to the rising waters. Humanity was saved by child sacrifice.

Cerro Mesa owed its name to its pronounced flat top. "Cerro

---

* The spelling of Namuncura, like that of other Mapuche names and words, is an imperfect approximation of the Mapuche pronunciation.

Mesa means 'Table Hill,' " Lorenzo told me. Through veils of mist it looked like a natural altar.

Juan Pañán looked the part of a matinee villain when he received us out of the downpour in his *ruca*. His blind right eye was either closed or wandered aimlessly as he sullenly sat through the interview. I told Pañán I'd read the police report from 1960 about José Luis Painecur's death, including a summary of his original confession—where he admitted to having thrown the little boy into the ocean.

"What can I tell you?" he answered. "The ocean rose. That's all. You think the water can't attack you, too? The water attacks everyone—but you can't attack the water. We climbed the hill [Cerro Mesa] near here. That's how we were saved. The water took our fences, posts, wire, a hundred sacks of potatoes. It even took our house. Where could we sleep? We had nothing—nothing to eat, no seeds to plant for the next season. If it wasn't for that hill, the ocean would have killed us, too, and taken us who knows where. And the water rose until it was only three meters from the top of the hill."

In Mapuche, Pañán confides to Lorenzo: "I will tell the truth to God but not to any man."

Like Pañán, everyone who remembered the earthquake and tidal waves spoke in fearful tones. The quake broke buildings as if they were matchsticks, ripped big rivers miles from their old courses, sank hundreds of square miles of land below sea level, and sent a dozen volcanoes into tumultuous eruption. Japanese seismologists who inspected the total destruction of the town of Puerto Saavedra said it was as though Japan's three most powerful earthquakes of the twentieth century had been released simultaneously in southern Chile. The earth creaked and groaned from hundreds of aftershocks per hour—a convulsive agony that drove survivors out of their minds with fear. And then the ocean rushed in.

First the ocean pulled back, stranding boats like toys, exposing miles of ocean bed and the refuse of centuries. Then, after an ominous silence, the ocean began boiling like an angry pot as it roared inland swallowing trees, houses, horses, and people, all of which tumbled head over heels into the tidal wave's wake. It was in a mood of desperation, thinking that the world was literally about to end unless their prayers produced a miracle, that Machi Juana and her followers went to Cerro Mesa.

"Right after the earthquakes I heard comments that those people at Cerro Mesa had made a dance and a sacrifice," a middle-aged woman said. " 'What sacrifice might that be?' I wondered. So I pricked up my ears to listen, because I was young and wanted to learn. And they said it was the sacrifice of a boy, a little shepherd. One woman cried and said, 'They did a bad thing.' But another one said, 'If they hadn't done that sacrifice, the ocean would have ended everything. Because they did that sacrifice, the sea calmed down.' And some said it was good, because the ancestors sacrificed like that, while others said it was bad. Anyway, little by little the sea calmed down. Whether it was because of the sacrifice of the boy or not I don't know."

One young man reacted violently when queried on the human sacrifice of 1960.

"It rubs me the wrong way to have a *gringo* come here and ask about that," he said, bristling. "Maybe someday they'll make a movie out of that sacrifice and you'll make a lot of money. But it won't help us poor Mapuches. And if you have to ask about that thing go and ask the one who did it, José Vargas. He's the one who knows how he did it and why he did it. Now he's an Evangelical Christian. Ask him if he has God's forgiveness."

That question worries José Vargas these days. His original name, the one that appears on the court summary from 1962, is Juan José Painecur, grandfather of the victim, José Luis Painecur. His decision to adopt a Spanish surname reflects his new lifestyle. By Mapuche standards Vargas is a prosperous man who lives in a well-built house instead of the traditional *ruca*. He was glad to see Lorenzo, a fellow Evangelical. Vargas invited us into another wooden building, which turned out to be a Christian temple, complete with long benches and a four-foot-high altar covered with a

white cloth. A large Bible sat on top of the altar. Underneath it a
sign read: GOD IS LOVE AND CONSUMING FIRE.

Before I could say anything, Vargas burst into tears, telling us
how lonely he was and how happy he felt to have the company of
fellow Christians. He supported his sincere feelings with some rambling, hard-to-understand verses from Scripture. Vargas's tearful
welcome ended abruptly, however, when he learned why I was
visiting him.

"This is a great calumny people raised against me—that I was
the owner of my grandson, that I killed him," Vargas said. "And
because of that gossip I went to jail. But, you know, the mouth
says many things. There was a blindman here who testified in court
that I killed my grandson with an ax. But, thank God, I'm still
alive today, and that blindman is dead. You know that Christ says
the evildoers have to be cut down. And that man died."

Whether God had forgiven him or not, Vargas hadn't forgiven
his accusers.

Vargas claimed his grandson had been swept away by the ocean
while collecting firewood by the coast, about a mile from their farm.
Yet, when asked whether his grandson wasn't really a shepherd, as
I'd been told, Vargas answered testily, "That lazy boy didn't take
care of sheep. He was too lazy to do anything."

Here Lorenzo pointed out that collecting firewood is more
difficult than watching sheep, which is why chopping firewood is
assigned to ten-year-olds, not five-year-olds like the deceased José
Luis Painecur. But even older boys stay as close to home as possible
when they gather firewood, because of the effort involved in carrying
the wood once it's cut. Lorenzo thought it extremely unlikely that
a lazy, good-for-nothing five-year-old would collect firewood along
the coast far from home.

"I feel you're lying to me," I told Vargas.

"Possibly," he said. "Very possibly."

There was no point in continuing. Juan Pañán might be willing to tell God the truth about the sacrifice, but I suspected God
would need a celestial inquisition to pry the truth from José Var-

gas. It was beyond my skills, at any rate. On my way out I asked Vargas if he kept in touch with his daughter, the mother of the sacrificed boy.

"She's as capricious as ever," he said. "She's living with people near here who aren't even her relatives."

I asked how he and his daughter Rosa got along, under the circumstances.

"I don't know her heart," he answered quietly. "She comes sometimes. But I don't know whether she loves me or not."

I found Rosa Painecur living in the *ruca* of some friends, taking care of their five children. A gentle lady with a soft voice and a distracted air, she clearly remembered the events leading to her son's disappearance.

"My father told me to leave the house and find work," she said. "He told me he would take care of my son and nothing would happen to him. I went to the city of Concepción, where I worked as a maid, and four months later the tidal wave came. I never saw my son again."

"What happened?" I asked.

"They ate my son," she said. "They killed him." By now she was speaking so softly I could hardly hear her. Then she broke down and cried soundlessly. When she recovered she continued: "The *machi* said, 'Kill him.' That's what the old woman said—'Do it.' And the rest believed her."

"But where was your son?" I asked.

"He was at my father's house."

"And your father brought the boy to the *machi?*"

"No," she answered. "The *machi* sent for the boy. And what could my father say? The *machi* demanded the boy because he didn't have a father or a mother. After all, I wasn't there. And the *machi* promised that if they sacrificed my boy the ocean would stop rising. That's what the old ones said—a little orphan without father or mother had to be killed so the ocean wouldn't come in. I don't understand that too well."

"The little boy was frightened, because they say he wouldn't

come out of his grandfather's house," said María Trangol, mother
of the children cared for by Rosa Painecur. "So his grandfather
and the *machi* sent another man to bring the boy by force to Cerro
Mesa, over there by the ocean, where the *machi* and his grandfather
and a lot of people were waiting. Before he died, they say, the little
boy asked his grandfather for forgiveness. He told his grandfather
he wouldn't be lazy anymore in watching the sheep. 'I'll be good,
Papa,' he said. 'Please don't kill me.'

"But since his grandfather had already turned him over to the
power of the *machi*, they just took him and did it. They say the
boy cried an awful lot for help, because they killed him by cutting
off his arms and legs. While he was still asking his grandfather for
forgiveness, they started chopping the little boy's arms and legs and
throwing them, piece by piece, into the ocean. 'Let's start cutting
and throwing him into the ocean,' they said to each other. I think
they finally threw the rest of the boy into the ocean, too. What else
could they do? Bury half of him?"

Rosa has never recovered or remarried. Today, at forty-eight
years of age and with no children to support her, her prospects in
the impoverished Mapuche culture are depressing indeed. "They
killed the only son she had," said María Trangol. Maybe that's why
Rosa Painecur is so affectionate with Trangol's children. They all
clung to Rosa when I took a farewell picture. It was the only time
Rosa smiled.

By this time I was heartily sick of the gruesome human sacrifice
and utterly soaked from the storm. It was also getting dark, and I
was getting nervous. All day long Lorenzo and I had seen drunken
Mapuches stumbling or lying on the road, oblivious of the rain.
Many of them had received their paychecks from the public-works
company the day before, and though they make only twenty dollars
a month, many of them immediately invested it in liquor. A social
worker named Manuel Pérez told us to get off the reservation before
night. He pointed to the charred ruins of a medical post that drunken Mapuches had burned down the year before. Although Pérez
is one of the Mapuches' best local advocates he says a group of

intoxicated men once tried to club him to death. Fights and murders go along with the liquor. I didn't need any encouragement to leave Lago Budi.

There was one intriguing piece left to the puzzle: several Mapuches told me that the communal decision to sacrifice José Luis Painecur was inspired by a divine message that Machi Juana received in a dream. Could we get the formidable old lady to talk?

Lorenzo said our only hope was to enlist the *machi*'s ceremonial partner. Every Mapuche shaman works in conjunction with an orator, or *weutufe*, who helps the *machi* enter a trance state. The *weutufe* also acts as a *machi*'s interpreter when she's possessed by her "spirit" and makes prophetic speeches. Fortunately, Machi Juana's *weutufe*, Felipe Painén, agreed to accompany us to ask her about the human sacrifice of 1960.

We decided our best strategy for approaching Machi Juana was for me to pretend that I was desperately sick and in need of her assistance. Machi Juana, like all Mapuche shamans, diagnosed illnesses from her patient's urine sample, so I was obliged to empty my bladder into a bottle. Then, after falling several times on the way up to Machi Juana's *ruca*, soaked and splattered with mud, still clinging to my warm bottle of urine, I waited in the rain for Felipe and Machi Juana to reach an agreement.

"For all his diplomacy, Felipe is having a hard time with the *machi*," Lorenzo Aillapán said in a worried tone. When Felipe finally came down, he said the *machi* would see me, but the rain made a urine analysis impossible. "The *machi* needs sunlight to see the sickness in your urine," he explained. "She didn't want to see you at all. But she said it's the duty of a *machi* to care for all the sick people who come to her, even if they are *huincas*."

Huinca is the Mapuches' term for all white people, meaning "one who steals land." In spite of the disparaging term, I thought Machi Juana's sentiments were worthy of the Hippocratic Oath. Machi Juana ushered us into her cold, damp *ruca*.

Felipe and Machi Juana conferred in Mapuche. The *machi* put on an elaborate silver ornament that covered her chest, draped her black-and-green shawl over her shoulders, and took hold of her ceremonial drum. The drum's circular face was divided by red paint into four quadrants, symbolizing the four cardinal directions. Then Machi Juana turned her chair and sat facing east. Outside the wind kept driving, but inside the *machi* began rhythmically beating her drum.

At first the beat was hardly faster than a heartbeat. Then the pace picked up, and the *machi*'s accompanying chant turned intense. She worked herself into a feverish state—sweat trickled down her face and her breathing became labored. Felipe Painén kept exclaiming, interjecting, apparently encouraging the *machi* into ecstasy. The drumming and chanting grew so wild the *machi* began hyperventilating to keep it up. Then she stopped dead.

No one spoke. The *machi* sat perfectly erect, looking rigid as a stone statue. She appeared hardly to breathe. I was taken aback by her performance.

Felipe Painén broke the silence. "Is he from Germany?" he asked Lorenzo about me. "No," Lorenzo answered, "he's from Pennsylvania, the United States." Felipe communicated this to the *machi*, because I could hear them both muttering their own version of PEN-SIL-BA-NIA while they conferred in Mapuche. Did her magic work differently for Germans than for Americans? Then Machi Juana began drumming again, and even my thoughts kept quiet.

I don't remember much about this lapse of time, except that it was pleasant and strangely warm inside the unheated *ruca*. Maybe the warmth came from the closeness of half a dozen bodies. But there was something else—a loving, maternal feeling from the *machi* which became a kind of radiance. The tempo was less intense this time, so I was able to enjoy the harmonious sounds of the Mapuche language. Occasionally I heard curious and increasingly abstract renditions of PEN-SIL-BA-NIA. In the end I was startled out of my reverie by the chanting of a long OOOMMMM—a sacred sound of the Mapuches that ends most prayers, similar to the Sanskrit OM of Hinduism.

"What's going on?" I demanded of Lorenzo.

"The *machi* created a bridge between you and her," he answered. "With this bridge you'll now be able to receive her spirit."

Apparently, from the *machi*'s point of view, my pretended sickness was real enough—I was walking around without my spirit. To remedy this, she kindly arranged a sort of spiritual transfusion, sharing her own spirit with me until I got in touch with my own.

But why did I keep hearing PEN-SIL-BA-NIA?

"They prayed to God to protect you from dangers and evil spirits on your way home to Pennsylvania," Lorenzo explained. "They asked God to take care of your health and your family's."

As we left the *ruca*, I felt touched, but bewildered and defeated again. What had happened to Felipe's agreement to ask the *machi* about her dream and the sacrifice of 1960?

"Felipe was afraid to ask the *machi* about the sacrifice," Lorenzo said. "Even though Felipe has the gift of persuasion, he didn't dare raise the subject. The *machi* is too strong."

⊡ 7 ⊡

THE DEVIL AND
THE DEEP BLUE SEA

When I first met her, in October 1983, Machi Juana Namuncura prophesied a terrible earthquake "within two years." Five months later, in March 1984, Chile suffered its worst seismic disaster since 1960. The massive old house where I lived in Viña del Mar, Chile, shook so badly no one could stand up—walls cracked, windows broke, ceilings fell, and furniture rearranged itself surrealistically. Our upper-middle-class neighborhood went berserk, with people and their expensive pets screaming, barking, fighting, and clawing one another to get to safety. For the next two weeks the ground rocked constantly, with over ten thousand seismic movements above grade 1 on the Richter scale.

So I returned to Lago Budi, where I congratulated the sorceress on the parts of her prophecy that had come true. Hysteria was sweeping Chile at this time, because seismologists warned that another major quake could come at any moment. But Machi Juana said it was out of the question.

"I see a white horse with reins," she said, as though that settled the matter. When pressed to explain, she added, "A white horse means there will be good weather when it comes in a vision. And the reins mean the horse can be controlled. So the earth will only shake a little." Here Machi Juana imitated the gentle, up-and-down movements of a rider on a tame horse. The *machi* also ruled out a tidal wave. "If we were going to have a tidal wave, I would hear a continuous underground bell ringing very clearly," she said. "But now it's quiet."

I asked Machi Juana to perform the urine analysis for me that the rain had forestalled at our last meeting. As far as I was concerned, this was a polite charade—a way of gaining the *machi*'s confidence by posing as a "patient." My health was fine, although I felt tired from the long trip to Lago Budi and my eyes hurt because I'd been reading without my glasses.

Machi Juana led us through a thicket to a circular precinct I'd never seen before. We were outdoors, yet surrounded by trees and bushes in a natural enclosure. In the center of the circle we saw a five-foot-high tree trunk. It was a greenish-colored *boldo* tree, whose aromatic leaves are used by *machis* for medicinal teas. There were three niches, or steps, that went upward from the ground. I realized the *machi* finally trusted Lorenzo and me enough to let us meet her sacred totem pole, or *rehue*.

"The *rehue* is what gives the *machi* all her power," whispered Lorenzo Aillapán.

Machi Juana took a bottle with my urine and placed it on a table in front of the *rehue*. Then she sat down, also facing the totem pole, and started drumming. I didn't feel any heightened awareness this time, and the *machi* seemed to chant in perfunctory fashion. I got the impression this was a low-key affair—a routine medical exam.

Next Machi Juana lit a cigarette. Without inhaling, she blew smoke from the cigarette onto my urine. She watched the smoke swirl around the yellow urine.

"I don't see any blue spots, so he's not going to die," Machi Juana said. A blue spot, she explained, means an approaching funeral. "He has no serious sicknesses. But there's a cloud in his head. There's pain around his eyes, and he can't see very well. It might be tiredness from his trip. He also has bad circulation of the blood and disturbing dreams."

My own doctor had done a urinalysis for me before my visit to Machi Juana. He'd given me a similar bill of health, but without the details added by the *machi*. I supposed guessing that I was tired and had bad circulation (who doesn't?) and disturbing dreams (yes, from time to time) were pretty generic items in the urine-divinatory business. But her ability to localize a pain in the area of my eyes was intriguingly accurate. I asked her how she did it. But this question seemed to make no sense to Machi Juana, and just led to an awkward silence.

In spite of Machi Juana's having created a bridge to help me receive her spirit at our last meeting, we remained worlds apart. The *machi* excused herself, and we had no choice but to abandon the sacred precinct of the *rehue*. Again we'd gotten no closer to the subject of human sacrifice.

"Felipe Painén was afraid to raise the question of human sacrifice with Machi Juana because she's such a powerful personality," Lorenzo said. "But I know another, strong *machi* who might be able to speak with her on equal terms."

So we went off to see Machi Mariano, who Lorenzo said was the chief healer of a wide area outside of Puerto Saavedra. The mayor of Puerto Saavedra lent us a municipal jeep to approach Mariano's house, located on a difficult road with steep hills and mud slides. Our chauffeur drove straight up to Machi Mariano while he was leading a pair of snorting oxen. But the jets of steam pouring out from the oxen's nostrils proved less dangerous than Machi Mariano's dragon fire.

"Get this jeep away from my oxen!" Machi Mariano screamed, his face red with anger. "What do you mean by driving your jeep so close to my oxen and frightening them? You people at the mayor's office think you are the great chiefs. But you're only the chiefs at your municipal offices. Out here in the countryside we Mapuches are the chiefs. This is *our* country and we command here!"

I offered profuse apologies. But Machi Mariano refused to acknowledge he'd even heard me. He walked off in a huge huff, with Lorenzo trailing after him, trying to smooth things over. By now I knew that *machis* have a license to throw temper tantrums. Since Mapuche shamans are supposed to receive their "spirit" on many occasions, rapid changes in their moods are expected—even behavior that seems neurotic and childish by our standards can be proof of their spirit possession. Their role as healers requires them to act out their feelings without the inhibitions that normal adults develop. I'd seen Machi Juana rage one moment and turn perfectly sweet the next. I was hoping Mariano would prove equally adaptable. And, sure enough, Machi Mariano soon invited me into his house with an affectionate hug. "I got a little angry," he said with a laugh.

Mariano told us how he'd become a healer. "I fought against being a *machi*," he said in a high-pitched, almost feminine voice. "There were many *machis* in my family and they were always poor. I didn't want to be like that, so I worked my land and progressed until I owned some cattle. Things went well for me until my oldest son died." Tears filled his eyes, and he had trouble continuing. "When my son died, half of me died with him. I was more dead than alive, paralyzed. Then, when I was in my greatest pain, I had a dream where I spoke with beautiful young men and women. They told me I had to become a new kind of *machi*. They said I had to keep working my farm, but I also had to start healing the sick."

Machi Mariano preaches improved farming methods to the Mapuches in his area while inveighing against excessive drinking, a combination that closely parallels the proselytizing efforts of Protestant Evangelicals. Lorenzo said Mariano's abstemious life-style commanded respect in the Mapuche community. If he couldn't get Machi Juana to talk, we feared no one could. We devised a plan.

Through Felipe Painén, Machi Juana's ceremonial partner, we would invite Machi Juana to travel with us to the city of Temuco, sixty miles from Lago Budi. The ostensible purpose for the trip was to buy Felipe Painén a bronze trumpet, a crucial instrument in the Mapuche rain ceremony, called a *guillatún*. But the real reason was to get Machi Juana out of her protected *ruca*, away from her family, to a place where Felipe, Lorenzo, Mariano, and I could ask about the sacrifice of 1960.

Things started to go wrong from the moment Machi Juana climbed in my car. When I turned on the heater, Machi Juana objected. I turned the heater down, but Machi Juana demanded it be turned off completely. "Hot air is bad," she said, as she rolled her window down all the way, letting in the freezing winter air.

Nor did Machi Juana like the city of Temuco, with its population of two hundred thousand and its noisy traffic. "Crazy place," she muttered. "Only crazy people live here, married to the machines." And when we couldn't find the exact bronze trumpet required for the magical purposes of the *guillatún* ceremony, Machi Juana proclaimed with ominous finality: *"Mal viaje,"* which, translated, became the universal "Bad trip."

I tried to redeem the trip by buying new shoes for everyone. This inspired Felipe Painén to ask for all kinds of other presents— flashlights, flour, and boots. Machi Juana nagged me for everything Felipe wanted, as well as some jewelry. I felt obliged to comply, like a conscripted Santa Claus tugged by tyrannical children. But I resented having to buy their affections. They saw me as simply a *gringo* money machine.

I wasn't feeling too friendly toward my Mapuche friends when I invited them to eat in a small restaurant. This was supposed to be the scene of our decisive tête-à-tête. By now I'd spent a hundred dollars on gifts, more than enough, I thought, to buy the cooperation of Felipe, Mariano, and Lorenzo in pressuring Machi Juana to talk about the sacrifice of 1960. We had the old lady alone in a private room, exactly where we wanted her.

"We are all very grateful to our foreign friend, Don Patricio," Felipe Painén began. He went on for some time, talking about my past visits, and very slowly leading up to the purchases of the day, all proof that I was a fine person and worthy of their confidence. Since Mapuches give long, formal speeches on all possible occasions, I resigned myself to listening to similar orations from Mariano and Lorenzo. But when it came time for Machi Juana to add her thanks—an absolute obligation in the intricate rules of Mapuche decorum—she didn't say anything, which worried me. There was an uncomfortable pause, and Felipe took up the baton again.

"So," he said slowly, "now that our friend has helped us out with new shoes and flashlights and flour, we would like to help him by answering some questions, particularly about our religion. Don Patricio is interested in why some mountains are sacred. Perhaps you could tell us about that, Machi Juana, since you are the eldest and most knowledgeable person here, and a great healer known throughout the country."

But Machi Juana just sat there, her eyes half closed and her mouth half open, completely oblivious of the carefully sequenced small talk we'd planned to lead up to the subject of human sacrifice. She didn't say a word.

"Yes, it's an important question," Lorenzo added lamely, after another uncomfortable pause, "why some mountains are believed to rise toward heaven during earthquakes and tidal waves. How are these mountains, known as Tren Tren, distinguished from other mountains? Did you learn about these special, magical mountains from your parents or grandparents, Machi Juana?"

Again, no answer.

"Machi Juana," I said, desperately, "I'd like to know about the traditions concerning Cerro Mesa, where you went during the earthquake of 1960 to avoid the rising waters. Could you tell me about Cerro Mesa?"

"*Uhh?*" Machi Juana grunted at me uncomprehendingly, like someone who has received a query in an alien language from an alien life form. Then she just closed her eyes completely and sort of dozed off.

Yes, we had the old lady exactly where we wanted her. Unfortunately, she'd just surprised us with her best feat of magic yet.

She disappeared.

Or, to use the language of Mapuche shamanism, her "spirit" left her. The sometimes angry, sometimes joking, but always domineering personality of Machi Juana just walked out on us. It was like watching the star puppet in a show go limp when the puppet master drops the strings. In her vacuous state there was no chance to interrogate Machi Juana about her role in the sacrifice of 1960.

We left Temuco and returned to Lago Budi in defeat. The next day Lorenzo, Mariano, and I paid another visit to Machi Juana at her *ruca*. We knew that on her home grounds, supported by her totem-pole *rehue* and her family, Machi Juana would be awfully formidable.

I gave the usual gifts of maté and candles, expected of foreigners making visits to Mapuches, and heard the usual exhausting, ritual exchanges about the weather, crops, everyone's health, and the myriad evil spirits wandering around in the atmosphere. Finally, Machi Mariano got down to business. He gave a tremendously moving speech about what a wonderful person I was, urging Machi Juana to tell me everything I wanted to know about Mapuche traditions.

This time Machi Juana didn't keep silent, as she had in Temuco. In fact, she immediately agreed that I was a wonderful person, but for reasons that worried me more than her previous silence.

"He is a good *gringo*," Machi Juana agreed. "Why, just last night I dreamed he's going to build me a new house much better than this dirty old *ruca*. He's a very good *gringo* to build a poor old lady a new house." At this point Machi Juana went on to tell us about all her woes, including the fact that her grown daughter had just gone to Santiago, leaving her alone with her fourteen-year-old granddaughter and her aged husband. "And when my granddaughter gets married, I'll have no one in the world," she said, as she broke down and sobbed.

"You'll still have your husband," I said quickly, anxious to shift the responsibility for building this marvelous new house away from the *machi*'s dream-*gringo* and onto her flesh-and-blood husband. But here Machi Juana gave her husband the most contemptuous glance, as though he wasn't worth the amount of soap it would take to clean him (which would be a considerable amount). Actually, Machi Juana's husband is an ebullient, eighty-year-old man, very well preserved—the problem is that he's been well preserved in a strong alcohol solution. The *machi* wasn't counting on him.

"There's no one to protect me," she cried. "One of my neighbors shot a gun at me. Why? Because they say I'm a witch. And do you know why they say that? Because I get up early, at seven every morning, and offer my prayers at the foot of my *rehue* tree, outside, in the open air. That's how a *machi* serves her God well. But people say I put spells on them. They won't even let an old woman say her prayers."

Now Machi Juana burst uncontrollably into tears.

Although everyone feared her sorcery, Machi Juana was also afraid of everyone. *Machis* may exercise intimidating psychological control over Mapuche communities, but they are also the most frequent victims of haphazard violence. Whenever a deformed child is born, or someone dies an unexpected death, black magic is suspected. One *machi* often accuses a rival healer of being responsible for the misfortune, an accusation that typically leads to feuds. The celebrated court case of the twenty-seven-year-old woman who killed her *machi* grandmother in Valdivia wasn't so exceptional; a male *machi* named Kinturay was murdered near Lago Budi in the community of Ronguipulli not long before the earthquake of 1960. Now I wondered if that old *machi*, murdered by her granddaughter in Valdivia, might not have been like Machi Juana: a poor woman in her seventies, living alone with an alcoholic husband, an easy scapegoat for natural calamities.

Or was Machi Juana really a shrewd performer playing on my feelings and consciously diverting me from the purpose of my interview? Now she whined about being abandoned by her daughter; but when I had first met Machi Juana, she had begged me to take her daughter off her hands, because the *machi* had too many mouths to feed. It wasn't my fault the old *machi* lived with cats, dogs, hens, and vermin inside a smoke-filled *ruca* that could pose as a model for disease propagation. I regretted she had no one to defend her. But I didn't plan to spend this final interview defending myself against Machi Juana's divine vision ordering me to build her a new house. I decided the wily old woman was outwitting the dumb *gringo* again. So I dropped all pretense of Mapuche decorum and launched into my list of questions.

"Did your grandparents ever tell you they sacrificed illegitimate children to avoid earthquakes?" I asked.

"My father told me that happened a long time ago," the *machi* answered. "Longer than a century ago. Maybe longer than a thousand years. I don't know about that."

"I've spoken with Rosa Painecur, María Trangol, and many others," I said carefully. "They all frankly tell me that a little boy was sacrificed here in 1960, after the great earthquake and tidal wave."

"That's an old story," Machi Juana protested. "That boy was looking for firewood and disappeared. Some people lied. They said, 'The *machi* did the work of Satan and killed that boy.' Because of that they put me in jail. For a whole month the police didn't feed me in jail, so that I'd confess. But finally the Chileans released me, because it was a mistake."

So this was my reward for cultivating the *machi* so painstakingly over eighteen months—hearing the same old tape recording about the boy who had vanished while collecting firewood.

"I know this subject brings bad memories for you," I said. "But I'm not working for the police or the Chileans. I'm only asking you about this because I've written about how human sacrifices happen in all parts of the world." Here I showed Machi Juana a copy of *Omni* magazine with a picture of the sacrificed Inca child of Mount Plomo.

"You see this boy?" I asked. "The Incas sacrificed him a little north of here."

Machi Juana looked at the Inca child's peaceful face with interest. "Pretty boy," she said. "Only bad people would do this to such a kid."

"I don't want to hear that old story about the boy who disappeared while looking for firewood," I interrupted her. "And I don't want to hear about how José Luis Painecur died on Cerro Mesa, if that embarrasses you. I already know about that from many people. But what I *do* want to know is the truth about your dream in which God told you to perform the sacrifice on Cerro Mesa."

"What can I do?" Machi Juana asked innocently. "I've told you the truth. I didn't do anything bad at Cerro Mesa."

"If you'll tell me the truth, I'll pay you five thousand pesos," I said, putting a nice, new, five-thousand-peso bill, worth twenty-five dollars, in front of her. I could see she wanted those five thousand pesos.

"What will he do if I tell him the truth?" Machi Juana asked Lorenzo Aillapán in Mapuche. Lorenzo answered, also in Mapuche, that I would publish it far away from Chile, in Pennsylvania of the United States.

"Will he pay me the five thousand pesos before or after I tell him what really happened?" Machi Juana asked. When Lorenzo confirmed that I would pay first, she seemed ready to talk. But her husband motioned harshly for her to be quiet. "If you tell him, they'll come in an airplane and take you away to the United States," the *machi*'s granddaughter interjected.

Her husband's opposition and the threat of the airplane silenced Machi Juana. "I trust you," she told me. "But not enough to talk about that thing."

I felt miserable when we left the *ruca*. But Lorenzo was oddly elated.

"If you had just offered her another thousand pesos, I think she would have talked," he said, delivering an imaginary punch through the air. "She really wants the money, in spite of what her family says. My guess is that she'll approach me to leave you a message without her family's knowing about it. A strong personality like the *machi* won't let her family stand in her way."

We were never very good at predicting Machi Juana's next move. In fact, the *machi* did leave her family and traveled on her own to give me a message—but it wasn't about human sacrifice.

"Tell that *gringo* never to visit me again!" she raged at Felipe Painén, after walking uphill in the rain for a mile and a half to his *ruca*. She fiercely upbraided him for acting as my intermediary. "And tell those others who came along with the *gringo* not to visit me anymore, either."

A *machi*'s anger works weird riptides in a Mapuche community, as I learned when I visited Machi Mariano three months after our disastrous interview with Machi Juana. Mariano's wife came out of his house in tears. "I have very bad news," she said. "The day before yesterday our eldest son was arrested for murder. Mariano is taking his clothes to jail." Their son was accused of beating another young man to death in a drunken brawl.

I accompanied Machi Mariano to the jail in Nuevo Imperial where his son, Pedro Horacio Pailecura, was detained. Although Pedro had been declared "incommunicado," a device common in Latin countries, where law permits a suspect to be held without any outside contact for as long as a judge decrees, the police decided to let us see him after I showed them my foreign press card. The jail was crowded with prisoners and visitors, but we finally found our way to Pedro, a short, athletic-looking young man, twenty years old, who was very depressed.

"The police say you've signed a confession admitting you killed the other boy," Mariano said.

"Sure, I signed it," Pedro answered. "But only after they stripped me and made me get in a tub of cold water. They threatened to drown me if I didn't. They also pulled out some electrical wires and told me they were going to electrocute me. I got scared and signed."

Following this interview, I complained to the Homicide Department in Temuco about Pedro's treatment. The department chief, Hugo Saldés, was polite but noncommittal. "I'll send a team out to investigate the allegations," he told me. "But you have to understand that the number of homicides on the Mapuche reservations is very high, and we have our hands full. This boy was killed on October 12, the Columbus Day weekend. It was apparently a football game at which everyone was drinking. Almost every holiday, when a group of Mapuches get together to play football, or a communal ceremony, there is heavy drinking and violence.

"One of the great Spanish poets, Alonso Ercilla, described the Mapuche Indians as 'gallant, valiant, and bellicose.' They're not bellicose early in the morning. But in the evening, after working, they're accustomed to drinking home-brewed *chicha* [fermented apple cider]. And after a little bit of drinking they have a tradition of fighting with long wooden poles. In many of the murders we investigate the cranium is completely smashed in by repeated blows from long sticks."

When Mariano and I returned from the jail, I was amazed to hear him blame Machi Juana for his son's arrest. "She's an agent of evil, a *calcu*," he fumed, using the Mapuche word for witches who command the souls of the dead on sinister missions. It wasn't clear to me, at first, what Machi Juana, who lived fifteen miles away, had to do with the brutal killing for which his son was arrested. But Mariano saw the whole episode as the inevitable result of Machi Juana's black magic.

"When we were at her *ruca*, I felt an enormously strong force behind her," he said. "It was a great force of evil, the most powerful I've ever felt. The next day I found that my *cultrún* was ripped open." Mariano now displayed his *cultrún*, or sacred drum, which plays such a key role for the shaman when entering a trance state. His tough cowhide drum was torn down the middle, right where the four marked quadrants join. Since the Mapuches believe the *cultrún* is a miniature of all creation, with the four quadrants representing the four cardinal directions, its ripping open following a meeting with Machi Juana was a disturbing and portentous event—as if a statue of Jesus or a saint fell from its niche and broke without apparent reason. Mariano was sure, however, that he knew the reason for his damaged *cultrún:* Machi Juana had hexed him. And this hex had brought bad luck to his son, whose act of homicide was inexorably ordered by Machi Juana's demon-assistants.

"She can bring bad luck to anyone who visits her," Mariano warned me. "It's not safe for you to go there any more."

I wasn't planning to go anywhere near Machi Juana—not after her stormy message to Felipe Painén warning me to keep away from her, and especially not after the weird murder Mariano now blamed on her. Word about both these altercations spread quickly through the Mapuche grapevine, and people around Lago Budi were upset at me for arousing Machi Juana's wrath. She'd always been considered a taboo individual, powerful, unpredictable, and best left alone. It wasn't long ago at Lago Budi that an accusation like Mariano's against a fellow *machi* would have provoked a blood feud between rival Mapuche clans. I was rocking the boat.

Instead of visiting Machi Juana, I accepted Felipe Painén's invitation to Lago Budi's spring *guillatún* ceremony. When I picked up Lorenzo Aillapán at Puerto Saavedra, though, I was surprised to find him unhealthy and emaciated. He told me he'd lost his job, and anyone could see he wasn't eating well. Lorenzo didn't actually blame Machi Juana for his bad fortune, but I got the impression he connected our setback with her to his own reverses. He advised me to stay clear of Machi Juana at the *guillatún* ceremony.

The old wooden ferry at Lago Budi was being repaired, so we took a tiny, leaky boat to the far shore of the lake. We enjoyed the warm spring weather when the sun sneaked out from behind a herd of big fluffy clouds. I thought it only rained here. Hundreds of thorn trees sent out a delicious fragrance from their golden flowers, while eucalyptus trees showed snowy blooms.

Although the weather was pleasant, Lorenzo explained that

this year's *guillatún* was to request more rain. "It's been a dry year," he said. The green potato plants, standing in endless rows on unirrigated hillsides, weren't maturing well.

The *guillatún* ceremony took place at a grassy field on the highest mountaintop of the peninsula of Ronguipulli. A fifteen-foot-high *rehue*, or totem pole, with ladderlike steps rising to a huge, carved head, dominated the field. About fifteen hundred Mapuches surrounded the totem pole in a big, loose circle. Many men rode horses, and almost every family had an ox cart, with primitive wooden wheels, where meat and potatoes were cooked. Although the *guillatún*'s traditional purpose is to affirm the cosmic unity of people, plants, and animals, the main purpose for most Mapuche males was to get stone drunk. Every rider carried a bottle, and every bottle quickly emptied—only to be replaced by another bottle.

Machi Juana was the only rider without a bottle. She was also the only female rider on the field. Machi Juana sat absolutely still, wrapped in a blue cape, on a handsome palomino at the highest point of the clearing. Apart from everyone else, she seemed like a ghost from the Mapuche past.

"She looks good, powerful," Lorenzo said approvingly. "She's a relic from the high Mapuche tradition. Everything else around here is mediocre."

Lorenzo explained that each year the *guillatún* is hosted by a different subcommunity at Lago Budi. Each community, in turn, has two chiefs, who play prominent roles at the *guillatún*. One is the hereditary, or political, chief, called the *lonco;* the other is the ritual expert, or *ngenpín*, who officiates at the sacrifices. Lorenzo pointed out the current political chief: a grossly fat man dressed in a suit coat, derby hat, and sunglasses. He drank heavily and showed scant interest in the ceremony.

The *ngenpín*, or ritual supervisor, was a barefooted *machi* named Retruhuili. He was supposed to animate the spectators into dancing around the *rehue*. A group of some two hundred devotees, mostly women, did gather around the *rehue*. The women went barefoot, though they dressed in red-blue-and-green costumes that lent them a gypsy quality. Everyone held a branch of the green-leafed maqui tree, except for a few who carried black-and-white banners at the end of wooden poles. The banners were a coded message to the nature spirits watching the proceedings. Black means rain; white means clear skies. So the Mapuches were requesting a moderate amount of rain. Banners and maqui branches waved up and down as they joined in chanting of OM! OM! OM! Lorenzo thought it best for us, too, to get our maqui branches and chant with the rest of the devotees. He seemed a bit concerned about Retruhuili's reaction if we didn't.

"Retruhuili is a nickname that means 'Long Fingernails,' " Lorenzo told me. "Since the devil is supposed to have long nails, that nickname really means 'Big Devil.' "

We marched around the *rehue*, chanting, jumping, and waving our branches, for what seemed an interminably long time. The Mapuche music, produced by drums, whistles, the wind instruments called *trutrucas*, and trumpets, sounded about as good as a grade-school band—before the lessons begin. I found the noise monotonous, melancholy, and, frankly, horrid.

When the music and dancing were sufficiently intense to satisfy the presiding *machis*, we divided into two groups. One group kept dancing in circles around the *rehue*, while the rest of us remained, always OM-ing and jumping, in front of a makeshift altar—the *mesa*, they called it. Suddenly the men on horseback took time out from drinking and began galloping in circles around us all, while the five participating *machis* made offerings of grain and wine at the altar. The *machis* bowed up and down at a furious pace, praying in rapid-fire, machine-gun fashion. "We are offering you grain, God," they repeated. "Give us more grain. We are offering you wine. Give us more wine."

The most solemn moment came when two sheep, one white, the other black (to match the rain magic of the banners), were brought to the altar. Ceremonial assistants turned the sheep upside down, holding them by their tied feet. Then a *machi* plunged a knife into each sheep's neck. Blood spurted out in torrents, which the *machis* carefully collected in a wooden receptacle. The assistants held the sheep's hind feet up higher, shaking the creatures to make the blood run out faster. Aside from a few muted bleats, the sheep died quietly—without arguing, as little José Luis Painecur had done.

By now devotees were filing up to dip their green branches in the hot, red blood, which they all sprinkled toward the *rehue*. I approached to take pictures, only to have Retruhuili see my camera and clamor for me to go away. I retreated nervously into the crowd, but Retruhuili angrily chased after me with his long, wooden pole. "Get away from here or I'll hit you over the head with this stick," he shouted. "I'm not fooling around."

From Retruhuili's reeking breath and bloodshot eyes I could see he was not fooling around. And since the homicide chief in Temuco had just warned me that hitting people over the head with wooden sticks is the preferred method of murder at Lago Budi— one that occurs with particular frequency when the Mapuches get drunk on ceremonial occasions—I tried to escape as quickly as possible. But by this time I was surrounded by furious Mapuches all screaming that my pictures, which they believe rob people's souls, were profaning the sacred climax of their rain ceremony—a serious offense during a dry year. The grotesquely fat *guillatún* chief added his inebriated voice to the commotion, protesting that I didn't have his permission to photograph anything. I was scared enough when I saw Machi Juana get down ominously from her palomino horse and begin ambling over toward the angry beehive swarming around me.

Machi Juana walked barefoot into the middle of the irate crowd. "I have remembered you, *gringo*," she said, giving me a big hug. And, turning to the *guillatún* leaders, she announced, "He's my friend."

"What's this *gringo huevón* ["overgrown testicle," a common Spanish insult] doing here at our *guillatún?*" Retruhuili demanded.

"The *guillatún* is for all of God's children," Machi Juana said. "Even the *gringos*."

"Oh, so he's your friend," Retruhuili said, as though this revelation were finally sinking in. He and the other leaders went back to their prayers.

They let me take all the pictures I wanted after Machi Juana's unexpected endorsement. In fact, the Mapuches treated me as if I were the local mayor. When the *guillatún* ended, the leaders respectfully approached to consult me about their problems, including their need for increased police protection. "Today we requested two policemen to keep order at the *guillatún*," one leader said. "But they haven't come. When the police don't come, we have bad fighting. In a couple of hours, when the young men are more drunk, the problems will start." Lorenzo and I prudently ducked out before the fighting started.

Machi Juana's performance that afternoon had been very strange. The last time I'd spoken to her at her *ruca*, Machi Juana had said she trusted me, but not enough to talk about the human sacrifice at Cerro Mesa. Then she turned around, denounced me in no uncertain terms to Lorenzo, and sent the message that she never wanted to see me again. Now she rescued me from the Mapuche mob when I least anticipated any help from her.

Every time I tried to ask her about the human sacrifice, she used a different evasion tactic: she would either suddenly go into a trance, or sob about her neighbor's trying to kill her, or bring up a dream requiring me to build her a house. Did her neighbor *really* try to shoot her? Were her trances genuine? Did she actually have a dream about my building her a house? I had no idea. And I couldn't begin to imagine how she'd receive me if I visted her again. But I was curious to find out. I decided to go alone, since Lorenzo was uneasy about visiting Machi Juana following her interdict against us.

It was raining when I returned to Machi Juana's *ruca* the next day. As I walked the few miles from the lake, I met Mapuches who told me that yesterday's *guillatún* had brought the rain, and I didn't argue with them. I could see the breakers of the South Pacific crashing in front of Cerro Mesa, which appeared, then disappeared again, in the swirling mists. A hundred yards from Machi Juana's house, the medical post, burned down by drunken rioters two years before, stood resurrected in clean, efficient, hospital white. When I reached the *machi*'s *ruca*, it occurred to me that it was two years to the day since I'd first met her. As usual, Machi Juana's contentious little dogs were waiting to bark at me.

I called out the Mapuche greeting, "*Mari Mari*," which means "May you be ten times fortunate." One of Machi Juana's sons, whom I'd met the day before at the *guillatún* ceremony, returned the salutation. "I want to see my friend Juana Namuncura," I said. He went inside the old *ruca*, and Machi Juana soon came out alone.

"Come inside and have some maté," she said in a friendly way.

I was surprised to find Machi Juana's husband stretched out on a bed, with three of their sons around him. The old man shook my hand affectionately, but his face was blanched with pain. "His stomach is frozen up," Machi Juana explained. "That happened because he caught a bad air when he was a little boy." I thought it more likely her husband's liver had given out because he'd done too much drinking, although I kept my theory to myself. "A month ago he wanted to die," Machi Juana said. "But I got angry and yelled at him. 'You can't die yet,' I told him. And he got better."

Machi Juana's unorthodox treatment met with opposition from the efficient men up the road at the new medical post. They wanted to hospitalize her husband, but when they arrived on the scene, Machi Juana indignantly drove them away.

"I told them if they tried to take my husband I'd hit them on the head with a stick," Machi Juana explained, "just like that man yesterday at the *guillatún* wanted to hit you with a stick." Machi Juana picked up a stick and demonstrated her technique. The men from the dispensary must have been as impressed as I was, because they returned with the police to take charge of her husband. "But I told the police that if they took my husband to the hospital he would die in two days," she said. "All the sick people together just make each other sicker." Finally, the police let Machi Juana keep her husband.

Machi Juana's sons were proud, both of the way their mother had defended her right to treat their father, and of how she'd rescued me from Retruhuili at the *guillatún* ceremony. The *machi* explained that hitting people with sticks was an old tradition at the *guillatún*.

"In the old days there was a guard with a stick who defended the *guillatún* field," she said. "He wouldn't let any *huincas* come near. And if any Mapuche came wearing shoes, he hit them and said, 'Take off your shoes.' " Machi Juana again demonstrated by hitting me on the leg with her stick. "But yesterday most of the Mapuches wore shoes. They say the old ones are ignorant to go barefoot. In bare feet one goes better with God."

I told Machi Juana that Moses and other Old Testament figures also went barefoot when they spoke with God. "That Moses must have known what he was doing," she said approvingly. "Did he live to be an old man?" She looked pleased when I answered that, according to the Bible, Moses lived to be 120 years old. "You see?" Machi Juana said. "That one knew what he was doing."

Machi Juana led me out to look at her potato crop, planted on a hillside plot next to her *ruca*. "It's been too dry this year," she said. "It's a good thing the *guillatún* made the rain come, so now the plants are happier."

We walked together through a dense thicket into a small clearing, where Machi Juana's semiconcealed *rehue* stood. I considered it an honor to be taken to her private sanctum alone, a sign she had more confidence in me. Her small, unadorned *rehue* totem looked naturally graceful compared with the brightly painted, fifteen-foot-high monstrosity I'd seen at the *guillatún* ceremony. I was surprised when Machi Juana apologized for her unpretentious tree. "Mine is ugly," she said, "not like that big *rehue* you saw yesterday."

I was alone with Machi Juana for the first time. And for the first time I realized how tiny Machi Juana is—four feet ten inches or five feet at the most. She'd always appeared much bigger and stronger.

Much to my surprise, Machi Juana said that her small *rehue* was small in appearance only—it had an inner life of its own. At times, when she prayed, the *rehue* grew until it grew thousands of rungs high, stretching up into the sky. By beating her drum and singing her prayer songs, Machi Juana learned to climb this *rehue* ladder to a beautiful land with grass and flowers and rich farmlands. She described one of her visions of this Mapuche paradise. "I saw this was God's country," she said. "God was sitting there, man and woman—married, they were sitting together." The Father-Mother gods (which Machi Juana spoke of sometimes as singular, sometimes as plural) were handsomely dressed, with ribbons around their foreheads, and their hands folded on their chests in a position of prayer. Machi Juana was amazed at the immense riches surrounding the couple. "God has so much silver and gold," she said, shaking her head. "So much money. And many wives, too."

She called this divine couple Une Fuche and Une Kuche ("the First Man and the First Woman"). They controlled the world and everything in it. They were the ones who sent earthquakes when people sinned, and it was to them that sacrifices had to be offered. The earthquake of 1960, Machi Juana said, occurred because the Mapuches had fallen away from the true practice of religion—they'd become as bad as the white people. "The earth was sick, like a person who is sick down to his bones."

"When the earth quakes it's because a huge serpent, Cai Cai Filu, which lives in the ocean, comes out and shakes its tail," she said. "That's a real devil. But the Mapuches have a friend, Tren Tren, which lives in mountains by the ocean. When Cai Cai Filu attacks and makes the waters rise, then Tren Tren makes the mountain go up above the waters."

I was confused about Tren Tren. Machi Juana said this creature was a bit like a serpent and a bit like a horse. But Tren Tren lived in a mountain that, like her *rehue*, was capable of rising to the heavens. The reason Cerro Mesa, a Tren Tren, did not rise in 1960 was that people's sins had exceeded the amount that could be achieved by normal sacrifices. One of the worst sins, in Machi Juana's view, was that many Mapuches had stopped attending the annual *guillatún*, with its sheep offerings.

Machi Juana's visions sounded as ornate, and confused, as a medieval illustration of the Apocalypse. A monstrous demon-snake was devouring a good snake. But the good snake was somehow a horse, although it was also a mountain, just as the bad snake was also the ocean. And all of these transubstantiations were decreed by a male-female god (even though the male god seemed to have more than one wife).

Machi Juana's version of the battle between Cai Cai Filu and Tren Tren coincided with one I'd heard from Felipe Painén. During the critical flood and earthquakes of May 1960, Felipe executed animal sacrifices at another hilltop not far from Cerro Mesa. "I took a little piglet and chopped it up, piece by piece," Felipe said. "Normally you sacrifice an animal by cutting its throat. But when the ocean rises, you have to kill it piece by piece, throwing each piece into the water. That's because the serpent Cai Cai Filu is hungry for blood. It comes out of the ocean searching for food. Only after getting blood will it go back into the depths and leave the world alone."

The pig sacrifice parallels José Luis Painecur's. Both were chopped up, piece by piece, in an exceptionally brutal ritual designed to assuage the lust of a predatory monster, who hungers for blood.

Knowing this helped me to appreciate the dilemma Machi Juana found herself in during the catastrophe of 1960. Cai Cai Filu had to be fed, and it was her job to do it. I found an eighty-five-year-old shaman, Machi Rosa, who was frank about the problem. "There used to be fewer earthquakes and tidal waves in the old days, when they sacrificed orphans," she said. "But today a *machi* can't sacrifice orphans. And you know why? Because if she does they'll come and put her in jail." Machi Rosa laughed. From her standpoint, there was no existential agonizing about child sacrifice—child sacrifice was the unquestioned solution to the dilemma of living with Cai Cai Filu. Nor did Machi Juana have scruples about what she did. "For great illnesses, great medicine is required," she told the police in 1960.

But even if Machi Juana had killed an innocent orphan, she'd also protected me from Retruhuili at some danger to herself. She also surprised me by revealing the magical inner life of her *rehue* without pestering me for money or other favors. So I told Machi Juana that I'd build her the new wooden house she wanted—as a sign of friendship.

I was aware that in building this *ruca* I was fulfilling another one of Machi Juana's prophetic dreams. In spite of my investigation I still didn't know if Machi Juana's decent batting average with her dreams was due to her being a healer or a black-magician. But I liked the old lady anyway. And I realized that, from her point of view, Machi Juana hadn't been lying when she said, "I didn't do anything bad at Cerro Mesa."

⊡ 8 ⊡

THE HOUSE THAT
GRINGO BUILT

When I finally came back to Lago Budi in September 1986, I went with Lorenzo to visit Felipe Painén. "This time you'll have a good chance to observe our *guillatún* ceremony," Felipe told me, "because in December I am ordering a *guillatún* for this whole area. Last year my community was a guest at the *guillatún* where Retruhuili threw you out. But this year we are the hosts and I am the chief." Felipe promised to make me "an honored guest" at his community's *guillatún,* so I wouldn't have trouble taking pictures. He also told me that Machi Juana was impatiently awaiting her new house. She'd visited Felipe twice, both times inquiring when I would come to build her house.

"I dreamed that Patricio was measuring the ground for my new house," she told Felipe.

"But he hasn't sent word that he's coming," Felipe answered.

"It doesn't matter," Machi Juana said. "In my dream the house was finished."

We found Machi Juana not far from the raft crossing at Lago Budi. She was limping along the road, barefoot, carrying a bag of vegetables to barter.

"I fell from my horse and hurt my leg," she confessed. "I'm getting old."

"Why are you going barefoot?" I asked. "What happened to the shoes I bought you in Temuco?"

"I had a break-in at my *ruca*," she said. "Thieves stole my chickens, shoes, the food on my table, the flour I had stored away, even my grain mill. They didn't leave anything. It was a nephew of mine."

The complete story, according to Machi Juana's neighbors, was that Machi Juana and her husband had traveled to Puerto Saavedra to pick up their Social Security checks, which they promptly invested in a big jug of wine. As they crossed Lago Budi by raft, one of their nephews—a man in his twenties—noticed they were pretty drunk. He followed close behind and, after the old couple was out cold in their *ruca*, crept in and stole everything but the sheets on their bed. Ironically, they'd given this nephew a piece of land next to theirs so he could build a home for himself and the *machi's* teenage granddaughter—whom this same nephew had gotten pregnant. After receiving the land, however, the nephew refused to marry the fifteen-year-old girl. He just moved in by himself, busily using his new house as a base for livestock rustling. Since I noticed that Machi Juana's granddaughter was pregnant again, I guessed their nephew had used his strategic position for other purposes as well. What I couldn't figure out was what had happened to her granddaughter's first baby, which was nowhere to be seen.

We sat down around an open fire, getting the latest gossip, while Machi Juana chased away her numerous dogs and cats with a stick and occasional shouts. She complained that some foreigners were trying to force her to sell her land. "There's a big woman from Easter Island with a *gringo* husband who keeps trying to buy me out," she said. One of Machi Juana's sons, Julio, called this woman "the Spider Queen," because she reportedly wanted to turn the little lagoon in front of the *machi's ruca* into a breeding land for big spiders, a delicacy for export. "I told her I don't have much land, so if I sold this place I wouldn't have anywhere to live," Machi Juana said.

Technically, no one can buy Mapuche land—not even another Mapuche. Their reservations are divided up according to inheritance, but until the last few years Mapuches did not receive land titles, only "effective possession" of their properties. This meant Mapuches couldn't mortgage their lands, or sell them to outsiders. The current government, however, is giving land deeds to the Mapuches as part of its effort to reduce government intervention in the economy. There are good aspects to these reforms, both with regard to the Chilean economy as a whole and for the Mapuches, but one of the immediate effects has been to foster fights over land ownership. Restrictions still apply on selling land within Mapuche reservations to outsiders, but the Spider Queen from Easter Island was apparently circumventing these rules by renting land for long periods with automatic renewal clauses. In fact, her goal, as she later told me, was to get enough grazing land for four thousand sheep—an idea so preposterous among the crowded, small-plot holdings of Lago Budi that it would be like planning to put up a little dairy farm in Manhattan.

Mapuches clutch their ten-to-twenty-acre farms with incredible tenacity. Machi Juana, as she passed around maté for us to drink, explained that she was involved in a land dispute of her own. "My father owned a lot of land, and I should have received a big inheritance. But one of my sons, Bombero, stole it by not telling me when the time came to transfer the property." She paused to take a sip of maté. "I love that son a lot," she said, shaking her head thoughtfully, "almost as much as a dog."

We next discussed what kind of house Machi Juana wanted. I'd originally preferred buying her a prefabricated wooden house for about five hundred dollars—a price that included installation. Obviously, this was a modest "house," but it was far better than the run-down *ruca* where Machi Juana lived. Lorenzo, however, felt that Machi Juana really wanted a traditional *ruca*, with a thatched roof and wooden beams artfully tied together with hundreds of knots. "In her dream the *machi* saw you building her a *ruca*, not a wooden house in the style of the *huincas*," Lorenzo said. "A *ruca* will resist the rain better than a wooden house, and it's much warmer because of the thatched roof."

Machi Juana agreed.

According to Lorenzo, building a *ruca* follows an ancient ritual that begins with *mingaco*, communal labor to assist with the new dwelling, and ends with a *rucán*, a celebration that consecrates the building with sacrifices and prayers. So erecting a *ruca* would not only make Machi Juana happier than an impersonal prefab unit, but would also involve the Mapuche community in a labor of love. "You'll see the great Mapuche tradition of communal sharing," Lorenzo said. "That's something that capitalism doesn't have."

Unfortunately, the Mapuche community didn't seem as well instructed on the great Mapuche tradition of *mingaco* as Lorenzo. "Nobody wants to help with the *mingaco*," Machi Juana's son Julio announced a couple of days later. "People say this isn't a Mapuche *ruca*. It's a *huinca* house."

"Didn't you tell them we're going to build your mother a traditional *ruca*, including all the ceremonies?" I asked.

"Even if it was a Mapuche *ruca* being built by a Mapuche, they'd make some other excuse not to help," Julio said. "People don't help each other anymore. They ask, 'How much are you going to pay for the oxen to move the timber? And how much are you going to pay for the timber?' Then you have to give everyone ten liters of wine and fifteen pieces of meat. And since the workers all start drinking the wine early, the timber isn't cut right, and the house ends up crooked. The whole thing turns out more expensive than paying cash."

I ended up paying cash for carpenters, timber, oxen, men to cut rushes for the thatched roof . . . and everything else we needed. Even Machi Juana was loath to cooperate with the *mingaco* ideal.

By tradition, the person whose house is being built has to feed the laborers. But Machi Juana announced that she was not feeding anyone. "I don't have any potatoes," she said, although we could see row upon row of potatoes ripening in her fields, being picked for her own use.

I drove my jeep all over Lago Budi, ferrying supplies and workmen, as we progressed from clearing the ground to digging holes to cutting trees and dragging the trunks up Machi Juana's hill on ox carts. One of the odd parts in all this was Julio's repeated request that all our proceedings be kept secret. When the municipal truck brought a huge load of rushes, Julio demanded that the workers immediately get them away from the road and hide the rushes on Machi Juana's hill. "Someone might want to burn them," he said.

"Why would anyone want to burn these rushes?" I asked incredulously.

"*Nunca falta la envidia*," he said. ("Envy is never absent.")

Within two weeks the wooden frame for the house was finished, the rushes had dried out, and thatching for the roof and walls was ready to begin. So I was amazed to arrive one morning to find construction stopped and everyone looking sullen.

"Julio's angry," the chief carpenter told me. "He's convinced Machi Juana that this is a bad house."

Soon Julio came out and started protesting against the style of the *ruca* in a muddy torrent of mixed Mapuche and Spanish.

"All the neighbors are laughing at us," he claimed. "They say, 'The *gringo* has so much money, but he's just building you a straw hut. He should build your mother a good *gringo* house, with wooden walls and a zinc roof.' "

"I thought the neighbors were all up in arms precisely because we were *not* building a traditional *ruca*," I countered. "Isn't that why they said they wouldn't help with the *mingaco*—because this is a *huinca* house?" But nothing could reconcile Julio to the horror of building his mother the same kind of *ruca* in which the Mapuches had lived for centuries.

"If the neighbors are laughing," I said to Julio in a loud, angry tone, "it's because of what you always warn me about: *Nunca falta la envidia*. They're envious of you, and they want to make you mad, so that the construction will stop and your mother won't get her house. That won't do your mother any good, but it will make your neighbors really laugh at you."

Julio just kept up his belligerent style, so I finally told him to shut up or quit. He decided to quit, which made me very happy. But Machi Juana looked forlorn. "The neighbors are laughing," she repeated. "They say our patron is very cheap."

The neighbors are laughing! I marched off with this mantra ringing in my ears. Of all the evil spirits, sea monsters, witches, and acts of black magic that threaten the Mapuche soul, this is the worst: *The neighbors are laughing!* The neighbors laughed if you built a *gringo*-style house—or if you didn't. They laughed if you sent your kids to school—or if you didn't. They laughed if you went for treatment at the new medical post—or if you didn't. Behind this laughter lies a deadly serious opposition to any change or intrusion on the reservation. The neighbors not only laughed at the first school built near Machi Juana's; they burned it down. They not only laughed at the first medical post; they burned it down. And if I wasn't careful, Julio warned me, they'd burn Machi Juana's building materials. *The neighbors are laughing!*

We were worried.

I was forced to compromise with Julio. We agreed to change the house plan, making the walls out of wood and keeping dried rushes for the thatched roof. This didn't make anyone happy, but it avoided a complete breakdown in our relationship, which was always on shaky ground. Julio, and Machi Juana's family in general, distrusted me. If I spoke alone with Machi Juana, Julio got mad. If I took Machi Juana for a ride in my jeep, her husband got mad.

Their suspicions were more than shared by the community at large. Juan Pañán, the one-eyed man arrested for his role in the sacrifice of 1960, sent word that I was a police officer and that Machi Juana, and everyone else connected with the case, would soon be arrested and sent to jail. Another group of people decided that I was the *gringo* husband of the Easter Island Spider Queen—making me the Spider King. According to this theory, I was really building the house near Machi Juana's as an outpost for my spider-export empire, which would start flourishing in the marshlands directly in front of the house. Still others thought I was a communist agitator, since the police had questioned some visiting *gringos* about their political views. One man warned that I was going to do a film about the sacrifice of 1960, and I fervently hoped this prophecy would come true. A few suspected I was trying to corner the market on the budding potato crop, and they tried to speak to me in conspiratorial whispers about the prices they could get me for potatoes . . . in *large quantities*. In short, I'd become, like Saint Paul, "all things to all people."

Machi Juana had an additional demand: I, the stupid, despised *gringo*, was obliged to pay, not only for the completion of Machi Juana's house, but for a big celebration to inaugurate the dream-*ruca*. I had to buy a sheep and lots of food for all the Mapuches, who I knew didn't want me around. I was quite resentful, but was pleased that I'd get to experience a traditional Mapuche *rucán* ceremony.

Machi Juana's family, however, refused to help with the cooking or preparations when the day for the celebration finally came. Her husband, who was particularly angry, just got more drunk than usual and lay down behind the house. This boycotting caused hours of delay, and set the guests on edge. One young man threatened to get a stick and start a fight if he wasn't fed.

Two policemen rode into the midst of our celebration on beautiful horses. They explained they'd come to see a woman named Juana Namuncura.

"That's me," Machi Juana said.

"We came to verify your whereabouts because your eldest son

has declared you dead in an inheritance petition," they said. This was the son, called El Bombero "The Fireman," who Machi Juana had once said was trying to steal her inheritance—the son she loved "almost as much as a dog." Once Machi Juana's status among the living was established, the police rode off.

After dancing in a circle around the house for a while, we all settled down to listen to Felipe Painén give a speech thanking me and Machi Juana for the celebration. Then Lorenzo gave a performance imitating birds around Lago Budi, a Mapuche art. At the very end Machi Juana came with her drum. She played her drum with great feeling and intensity and sang a song, dedicated, much to my surprise, to me:

> My own people had forgotten about me,
> They didn't honor me as a healer;
> I was badly treated here among my own people,
> But then a foreigner came and honored me.
> Why is it that a foreigner honors a *machi* more than
>   the Mapuches?
> These foreign friends are good and kind;
> I think this young man has come to me from
>   heaven,
> Like a son of God.

In spite of my multifaceted personality—Spider King, communist agitator, horror filmmaker, undercover police agent, potato baron—I hadn't expected anyone to call me "a son of God." But I was about to get an even more unexpected promotion, thanks to Toro Aillapán's sense of irony.

Toro Aillapán, the principal tribal chief at Lago Budi, is the only surviving son of Lorenzo's grandfather, who had five wives and enough land really to qualify for the title *lonco*, or "leader." Toro's stature is greatly reduced compared with his father's, but he remains the owner of over a hundred acres of land, making him the wealthiest Mapuche man around Lago Budi. "You'll see that something of the great line of Mapuche warriors still survives in Toro," Lorenzo said. "He's impressive."

Lorenzo and I drove about six miles from Machi Juana's property, out to a lovely, pine-covered peninsula, where Toro's house stood on a promontory overlooking the resplendent blue waters of Lago Budi. From this vantage point we could appreciate Lago Budi's immense U-shape, as it curved out of sight to both the left and right of us. The lake was dotted with craggy islands, also pine-covered, and we watched tiny rowboats precariously negotiating the big choppy waves between them. Lorenzo, like most Mapuches who grew up on the lakeshore, can handle a small boat with professional ease, including rectangular dugout canoes that are too awkward for anyone but a native.

"I was born here," Lorenzo said. "The chief's house has always been here. I've hesitated in taking you here because, well, Toro is special and . . . difficult. If he accepts you and supports us, it will make things much easier. But that will require all our diplomacy." This was Lorenzo's decorous way of warning me not to lose my cool, as I had with Julio.

Although Toro is Lorenzo's uncle, they're very different in appearance and personality. Lorenzo is short, slight, unfailingly correct in pronunciation and protocol. Toro is an immense man with a vast, squat nose—he looks very much like the bull his sobriquet suggests. In addition, he has the biggest, bushiest eyebrows I've ever seen. It's hard to take a picture of him because his eyebrows cloud out his face. He greeted us gruffly, wearing a straw hat and leaning on a wooden cane; except for the cane he didn't look eighty years old. He grunted occasionally, deep, mournful sounds rising from his fat belly, like territorial sounds the big bullfrogs make along Lago Budi's shores.

"My father lived to be 135 years old and he made me chief before he died," Toro said. "He had five wives, and lots of land and animals. I was the son of his fourth wife. My father could remember the time when there was nothing but mountain lions over there at Puerto Saavedra. He never even saw a Catholic priest until he went to Buenos Aires. Those were the days of the *malones*, the battles with spears and horses. My father had to escape to Argentina after battles here with the *huincas*, when they were trying to steal our land. The Mapuches fought as best they could against the guns of the Chilean army. In the old days the Mapuches were good for fighting—one Mapuche could smash twenty *huincas*. But in those days the Mapuches were tremendous, colossal; now we're just chickens, that's all."

Toro's wife came out and offered us some wine, which I refused.

"Are you some kind of a priest?" Toro asked.

"No," I said, "I'm not associated with any religious group, but I am studying the Mapuche religion. That's why I am spending so much time here. And I'll be attending the *guillatún* in December at Felipe Painén's invitation."

"Are you sure you're not a priest?" Toro asked again. "You look like some kind of a priest with that beard of yours. Why don't you drink wine? Perhaps you don't like to drink in public, but when you're hidden in your room you pull out your bottle, eh? Yes, I think if we treat you well, we can get you accustomed to this wine. Anyway, this wine is another *huinca* invention. The Mapuches only made *mudai* [a fermented drink made from maize, with a low alcohol content]. You're the ones who destroyed the *guillatún* ceremonies by selling wine—selling fights among the Mapuches."

At this point Toro began a general broadside against the *huincas*, particularly Evangelicals, whom he blamed for dividing the Mapuches into opposing factions. "The Evangelicals from the United States have ruined everything," he said. "These *huincas* have beards, but they don't have anything else of value."

"Are you a Bahai?" Toro asked, still trying to figure out whom I was affiliated with.

"No," I said.

"The other day the Bahais came here to invite me to a service. 'It will be very good,' they said. But how could it possibly be any good? I told them I'd go to their service only if they gave me a young girl as a gift. That's how a man increases himself!"

Since I didn't have a young girl for Chief Toro, I didn't think I was going to make much progress. But Toro insisted on knowing my real mission in life.

"Are you a communist?" he asked.

"No," I said, "I'm just interested in Mapuche customs. I don't have anything to do with the communists."

"Yes, you have something of a communist in you," Toro said slyly. Here he got up and pointed to his hefty left buttock. "On this side you're a communist," he said. Then he pointed to his right buttock. "On this side you're a capitalist. But no matter which side you use, you're always making more money."

Lorenzo tried turning the conversation to more pleasant subjects. He spotted an expertly made linseed rope on the wall. "That's an example of Mapuche craftsmanship," Lorenzo said. "People sow linseed just to gather more fiber for baskets and ropes. I used to know how to do it, but it's a lot of work: you have to make the cords extremely fine. Linseed fiber makes the best fishing nets, too."

"Yes, and if you make a rope by twisting the cords to the left, instead of to the right as you normally do, you can use it to defeat the *huitranalwe*," Toro's twenty-year-old grandson added.

Now, the *huitranalwe* is a touchy subject at Lago Budi. *Huitran* means "skeleton," and *alwe* means "ghost." So *huitranalwe* is a ghostly skeleton, and people report visions of this skeleton flying around. But the *huitranalwe* can also turn itself into one of several species of birds native to Lago Budi, and in this form it visits people at night to suck their blood. The *huitranalwe* can likewise appear as a rich foreigner, and in that form it can help a person to become rich, if pressed into service through the proper prayers and sacrifices. It's believed that most wealthy people secretly possess a *huitranalwe* who's responsible for their success. But this success is precarious, since the *huitranalwe* is always waiting for a chance to kill its owner, like a resentful genie anxious to thwart its master.

Machi Juana once joked that I must own a *huitranalwe*, because I have too much money. Most Mapuches, however, don't joke about *huitranalwes*. Toro Aillapán didn't take the matter lightly, and his whole manner changed once this subject came up. He looked nervous and ill at ease. In fact, he claimed to have had a close encounter with a *huitranalwe*.

"I remember one evening, just as the sun was going down, I came back to my house with a couple of horses," Toro said. "And right outside by that big tree I saw a rich cowboy, dressed with silver spurs and a white tie. He just leaned against the tree and smiled at me, showing his golden teeth. He was very tall, about as tall as you are, *gringo*. He called out to me. But the horses panicked and started running. I just took off after them and didn't answer a word to the *huitranalwe*."

Toro didn't say another word to us, either, and I sensed he was deeply upset by this *huitranalwe* business. Toro's family mentioned that he had to make a trip to the city of Nuevo Imperial the next day, and I offered to take him in my jeep. His family was enthusiastic about this idea. But Toro was silent.

"I think I'll just cross the lake in my boat like I always do," he said. As I left I shook Toro's hand, and I was surprised to notice that he was trembling. Toro looked at me in a fixed fashion. "*Huitranalwe, huitranalwe*," he repeated.

"It's too bad that whole thing about the *huitranalwe* came up," Lorenzo said, when we were in the jeep. "Toro associated you with the *huitranalwe* because you're tall, a foreigner, and have a lot of money, and he thinks you somehow resemble the spirit he saw years ago. I was trying to change the subject to handicrafts when this thing about the linseed rope being good to catch *huitranalwes* got us into a very dangerous area. It was just bad luck."

We didn't realize how bad our luck had turned until we visited Felipe Painén the next day. Felipe was normally nice and even-tempered. But for the first time he greeted us in an angry way.

"Let me tell you something, Cousin Lorenzo, Friend Patricio," he began. "I hear that you have been to see Toro Aillapán. That was a very bad thing for you to do. Now, on this reservation I am the chief, and I've invited you to the *guillatún*. But you should ask me before talking to someone like Toro. I could have warned you that he's a very bad person—a devil, always causing trouble. If you had told me that you were headed for Toro Aillapán's house, I would have cut you off at the pass."

Social relations on a Mapuche reservation are far too subtle for the average *gringo*. I was confused about who was chief of what. When Lorenzo first introduced me to Felipe Painén, he told me that Felipe was Machi Juana's *weutufe*, an orator who helps her enter a shamanic trance. But now I was learning that Felipe was actually the main organizer of the *guillatún* ceremony for a large section of Lago Budi. In this category, known as *ngenpín*, or cere-monial chief, he outranked Machi Juana and everyone else, although Toro Aillapán, as *lonco*, had other prerogatives. The position of *ngenpín* depends on eloquence, while the position of *lonco* is hered-itary. Felipe is the most important *ngenpín*, Toro Aillapán the prin-cipal *lonco*. It turned out that the *loncos* and *ngenpíns* were usually fighting over turf, and we had gotten mixed up in it. But I wasn't sure how.

Felipe explained that he'd met Toro Aillapán the day before, just after we'd had our unfortunate meeting with Toro.

"What is this damn *gringo* doing at the *guillatún* ceremony?" Toro had demanded of Felipe.

"There is only one God and everyone is welcome to pray at the *guillatún*," Felipe answered. "I'm the chief of the *guillatún*, and I've invited him to attend."

"Maybe you *were* the chief of the *guillatún*," Toro answered. "But this *gringo* announced to me that he is the new *ngenpín*. He says that he's going to hold the white flag on the *guillatún* field, ordering the Mapuches around, telling them how to pray. The Santo Padre (Holy Father) says he's the great *guillatún* chief."

This was all I needed: Toro Aillapán accusing me of usurping the most sacred ceremonial functions at the annual fertility rite at Lago Budi, making me the great pretender to the religious chiefdom.

"Patricio didn't mention anything about being *ngenpín*," Lorenzo said. "Toro just made that up to cause trouble. We were having a good conversation with my uncle, when someone raised the subject of *huitranalwes*. Toro immediately changed with that— he became pale and frightened. He remembered having seen a *huitranalwe* one evening, at dusk, when he was young, and he associated the *huitranalwe* with Patricio, because he saw some similarity in their height and appearance, and perhaps because Patricio, like the *huitranalwe*, is rich. But Toro didn't dare say anything to us about that, because by the time we left he was terrified. He just repeated, '*Huitranalwe, huitranalwe.*' "

At this Felipe and his son, who'd been busy planting potatoes, dropped their hoes and laughed hysterically.

"I think I should dress up like that *huitranalwe* Toro saw years ago, with silver spurs and a white tie," I said. "And wait for Toro at dusk by his house. 'So, Toro,' I'll say to him in an angry tone, 'I hear you've been spreading lies about me.' "

"No, you'd kill him, " Felipe's son said. "He'd die of fright."

Killing Toro Aillapán was one of the nasty thoughts that crossed my mind in the next few days, as word reached us that Toro had expanded his campaign against me. Toro sent his *werquén*, or deputy chief, to give Felipe Painén the following formal message: "I will not go to this year's *guillatún* ceremony as long as the *gringo* Holy Father is going to preside as *ngenpín* over all the Mapuches."

Toro's insistent term for me of "Holy Father" echoed the Pope's title, something that seemed deliberate, given the great publicity that Pope John Paul II's upcoming visit to Chile was then receiving. And since the papers reported that the Holy Father planned to meet with the Mapuches, Toro's name for me aimed at linking me with the Catholic Church and intrusion in the Mapuche culture. All in all, the old chief had concocted a powerful myth appealing to the starkest nightmares of the Mapuches: he was telling the whole reservation that a *gringo* Holy Father planned to seize their last independent function, the *guillatún* ceremony. The fact that this *gringo* Holy Father was also, in Toro's mind, a surrogate *huitranalwe,* a ghostly demon, made the nightmare strangely perfect. It was as though all the Mapuche fears of outsiders had been incarnated in the *ngenpín gringo* Holy Father—namely, me.

9

HOUNDING
THE HOLY FATHER

The initial preparations for the *guillatún* ceremony were held on the hilltop of Tragua Tragua in November. This hilltop was a sacred clearing of virgin land, with a *rehue* tree in the center. Christian Evangelists had put up a cross on top of the *rehue*, but a couple of men quickly took it down and replaced it with white banners. Felipe also carried a long pole with a white banner attached—this was the famous prayer flag Toro Aillapán accused me of trying to usurp. Next Felipe started dancing with a group of six *machis* and about fifty representatives from twenty-two communities around Lago Budi. The *machis* were wrapped in black-and-green blankets, and in their hair all the women wore colorful streamers—red, green, blue, and white—which blew in the wind. As the women danced up and down, and swayed from side to side, they looked like flowers waving on the hilltop.

Machi Juana arrived late and in flamboyant style. She burst into the circle around Felipe and started shaking everyone's hand in a disruptive fashion. Yet from here on in, if anyone else broke the carefully ordered ranks, Machi Juana ambled over and let whoever it was know about it. The dancing went on for three hours.

Finally, Felipe addressed the gathering. He began with an

inspired singsong praise to Nechén, the supreme Godhead; sometimes he would also cry out to Lafquén Ullmén, which means "The Rich Man of the Sea," another term for God. After these praises, Felipe spoke about the relation between Nechén and the devil. In Felipe's view, the Evangelicals who put up the crucifix were working for the devil, since the devil wanted to desecrate the holy grounds of the *guillatún* hilltop. Well, this was to be expected, because the *guillatún* was a sacrificial offering for all humanity, and the devil didn't like this one bit. So the Mapuches would just have to put up a new *rehue* to combat the Christians. There followed a brief assignment of tasks to prepare for the fifteen-hundred-odd people who would attend the *guillatún* in December, concluded by a prolonged and piercing OOOOOOOOOMMMMMMMMMMMMMMMM.

As the participants dispersed, so did the threatening rainclouds that had been hanging over us. Since the purpose of this year's *guillatún* was to request clear skies for the harvest, this was taken as a good omen. "Our white banners signal God to give us clean, cloudless skies," Bartolo Aillapán, the *ngenpín* of another community, told me. "And it happened right away. This hill has great power to control rainfall. And when we have the *guillatún* in December, we'll get the support from the people along the coast. They have an even more powerful hill, next to the ocean. The hills next to the ocean, like Piedra Alta and Cerro Mesa, have the greatest power, because everything comes from the ocean—animals, rain, everything."

"Hills generally have power over water," Machi Juana agreed. "That's because the hills trap the water, dividing it and directing it one way or another, yet always toward the ocean. So the ocean owns all the water, and the hills are connected to the ocean. You have to be careful with the ocean. About a hundred years ago there was a fifteen-year-old boy named Juan Manquián, who was wading and fooling around in the ocean water near Piedra Alta [a hill known as "The High Rock"]. There's a little waterfall that empties into the ocean at that place, and Juan Manquián started laughing at the waterfall. 'You look like a girl who's pissing,' he told the waterfall.

That made the ocean angry. Then the ocean punished Juan Manquián by making his feet stick in place."

No matter how hard the boy tried, Machi Juana continued,
he couldn't escape from the water. All of Manquián's friends came
and tried to pull him out; they even got oxen to pull. But nothing
helped. All the Mapuches around here prayed to the ocean in a
great *guillatún* to free Juan Manquián, offering the ocean animals
to release the boy. In the end, however, Manquián told his friends
to leave him alone. "I belong here," he said. "Now I belong to the
ocean, and the ocean belongs to me." So Juan Manquián turned
into a stone, which can still be seen on the coast.

By this metamorphosis, a young boy became the ocean god.
Some call him "the Minister of the Sea." In this position Juan
Manquián is extraordinarily powerful, because, in the religious
framework at Lago Budi, everything comes from the Rich Man of
the Ocean: fish, mules, tractors, rainwater, and crops.

Felipe Painén's son explained that waterfalls, streams, and
pools of fresh water are intimately connected with each of the sacred
hilltops where the *guillatún* ceremonies are held. "Every *guillatún*
has its own well with its own power to pray for water," he said.
"Every Tren Tren mountain has a powerful spring of water at its
foot. This spring is called Trayenko. During a dry year the *machis*
dig at that Trayenko. They make a canal and see if water flows in
it. If water fills the canal, then rain will come. The spirit of water
and the spirit of the hill are collaborating to request water."

Each one of these Tren Tren mountains has its own "spirit,"
as does the water source at the foot of the mountain. The general
name for the mountain spirit is Ñenmapu, the general name of the
water spirit Ñenco. But these spirits are known in a more secret
fashion by the locals. "Everyone who worships at the Tren Tren
knows the name of the spirit of the mountain," Felipe's son said.
"But it's difficult for others to know it."

I learned the names of some particular mountain and water
spirits. The majority of the mountain spirits were serpents—Felipe
said that Cai Cai Filu, the monster that had threatened to destroy

the world in the earthquake of 1960, was the owner of his *guillatún* hilltop. This was true of another high mountain as well, although there Cai Cai Filu was said to have the face and claws of a wildcat. In addition, I was told that every sacred hill used for the *guillatún* ceremony has the spirits of one or two little children as its protectors. Supposedly, *machis* see these children and talk with them.

Water spirits are varied. I found two waterfalls that people worshipped by sacrificing bulls to the spirit of the waters. "The spirit of the waterfall is a bull because it makes a roaring sound," one man said. "During a dry year you have to sacrifice a bull to the waters so that it will go and fight with the bull spirit and make water come." Another reputedly powerful water spirit dwells in a pond called "The Girl's Water." Supposedly, people have had visions of a young girl combing her hair in the water, and she watches over it. And there was another famous pool called "The Cat's Water."

"The Cat's Water is very powerful for bringing rain," Felipe Painén said. "In 1944 there was a severe drought here. So the Mapuches and the Catholics made a bet on who could get God to bring the rains. They got together on a hill near The Cat's Water. First a priest named Father Luis said his Mass and prayed. Nothing happened—the sky stayed perfectly clear and dry. Then an old *machi* named Juan Cheuquecoy came out in his bare feet, dressed in his blanket. After he prayed, the sky turned black and you could hear Manquián's cat start purring. Whenever it's going to rain, you hear Manquián's cat purring: *lullull*. That's why the cat is called Lul Lul. Then it rained very hard."

I wanted to know the name of the spirit on Cerro Mesa. "The spirit of Cerro Mesa is Machi Juana's spirit," Felipe said excitedly. "It's very strong. Cerro Mesa has a direct view of Volcán Llaima. And there's a vision of a blue sun around the volcano that you can see from Cerro Mesa. Most people can't see it, but if you're able to see the blue sun, you can see the path straight to the volcano."

This was a revelation. When Machi Juana had told me that she was taught by her "spirit," I thought she meant some sort of universal, abstract spirit. But Felipe was now saying that Machi Juana's spirit is the same power that controls Cerro Mesa, where the boy was sacrificed in 1960 under such horrific circumstances. I already knew that the power of Cerro Mesa is closely tied to the ocean god, Manquián. Bartolo Aillapán had said that hills by the ocean are the most influential rainmakers because of their proximity to the sea god—an idea that is exactly paralleled among Inca subjects in Peru, who ascribed supremacy to coastal mountains.

The fact that one of the Incas' most important deities—by some accounts *the* most important deity—was Viracocha (whose name means "Foam of the Sea") suggests that they, like the Mapuches, came close to regarding the ocean as the ultimate controller of wealth and rain. During droughts at Nazca, for example, a man goes to the ocean and brings foamy water to a hilltop, where he makes a water offering.

But what I found even more intriguing was the invisible line of force that supposedly tied Cerro Mesa to the magnificent snowcapped Volcán Llaima (11,152 feet), visible some one hundred miles to the northeast of Lago Budi. In high-altitude archaeology I'd seen that small hills can be connected with snowcapped peaks. This had been the key to Johan Reinhard's reinterpretation of the Nazca Lines. Cerro Blanco, the major mountain deity at Nazca today, is "married" to three other peaks—one at the coast, one in a range that gives rise to Nazca rivers, and one snowcapped mountain eighty-seven miles distant.[1] In the northern Andes it's very important to have sight lines from one sacred peak to another. I'd seen these hierarchical relationships between lesser mountains, with lesser ruins, which circle more impressive peaks like Tortolas and Veladero, with correspondingly better-built sanctuaries. But nothing I'd read about the Mapuches even hinted at similar beliefs.

Felipe gave me this information like someone who was leaking a secret. In fact, the name of a *machi*'s spirit is one of a Mapuche shaman's best-guarded professional confidences. To find out more about the spirit of *machis*, and mountains, I went with Lorenzo to visit Machi Claudina Deumacán, one of the most respected healers in the area. Machi Claudina greeted us warily at first. She explained she was still frightened because several men had broken in during the night to steal her animals.

"Are you the *gringo* everyone says is going to be the chief of the *guillatún?*" she asked me.

Word was certainly getting around—Machi Claudina lived some twelve miles from Toro Aillapán, and the first thing she wanted to know was how I'd gotten promoted to *ngenpín* so quickly. "It's a great surprise to all of us that a *gringo* can hold such an honor," she said.

Yes, I answered, it was a great surprise to me, too.

Claudina had been trained by an older female *machi* from the age of twelve to fourteen. This is the traditional way of becoming a healer. It is also very expensive for a Mapuche—Claudina's father had to pay three sheep, one cow, and one horse for her apprenticeship. Claudina was extremely knowledgeable about local customs.

"Not all *machis* have the same spirit," Claudina said. "Some *machis* work at night, with the bodies of the dead, so no one will see them. They have a special *rehue*, which looks like a monkey, with glass eyes and hair. But they don't let anyone else see it. They bring the dead back to life, and they turn the dead into spirits, called *huitranalwes* who go about only at night.

"There are other dangerous spirits, too, such as the *anchimallén*, which are little creatures of fire. Some *machis* have the spirit of the *anchimallén*, which can sometimes do good by getting evil out of people. Others have the spirit of a snake. Whatever spirit a *machi* has, first she has to see it in a vision. That spirit teaches the *machi* and accompanies her in her prayers. And the *machi* can order that spirit around just like a messenger.

"Other *machis* have the spirits from the snowcapped volcanoes. Those spirits from the volcanoes are called *pillanes*. The *pillanes* are like saints, they don't have any sins. People in the mountains close to the volcanoes say they see a little girl who was sacrificed there on the peak. They say she was good and pure, and for that reason they sacrificed her, putting her heart into the volcano's mouth."

I asked Claudina if she knew anything about the sacrifice of José Luis Painecur in 1960, and if it had anything to do with the *pillanes* of the volcanoes.

"That little boy who died in 1960 at Cerro Mesa is another saint," she said. "And now his spirit is united with that hill where he died. Cerro Mesa is important because it's united with the ocean and the volcano at the same time. It's well known that the sacrifice of that little boy was made invoking the *pillanes*. And that wasn't only at Cerro Mesa. Many sacrifices to the *pillanes* took place all over during the earthquakes of 1960. Machi Clara Huenchillán had two children whose heads were cut off and taken to the *pillán*." My eyes must have really bulged when she told me this last piece of information, because Claudina quickly added, "You won't go and say anything to her, will you? Please don't go and visit her or talk to her about that."

It was a thirty-five-mile trip to Machi Clara Huenchillán's *ruca* near Puerto Domínguez. Her *rehue* was adorned with dozens of fresh flowers, and it stood in a clearing with an exceptional view of both Volcán Llaima and Volcán Villarrica, geometrically perfect snowcapped peaks that stood out on an almost cloudless day. She started talking about Jesus and Mary, and the unity of Mapuche religion with Christianity. "I've been receiving a lot of guests from the city since I converted to Catholicism," she said. "The nuns told me that *gringos* like you should pay a lot of money to hear me talk."

"Do you ever have visions of the *pillanes*?" I asked her, after paying her some money.

"No, the *pillanes* are evil spirits on the volcano," she answered. "I just work with Almighty God, no other spirits."

After a certain amount of prodding, Clara admitted that at the time of the earthquake in 1960 she had dreamed that a *pillán* came and cut off the heads of two of her little boys (she had twelve children in all). "Later the two boys died on the same day," she said. "All that happens because there are many witches. And if people don't kill each other with sticks, they do it with the devil."

When Lorenzo and I were alone, I asked him what he made of all this. "I think there was some human hand in the death of those two children," he said. A Chilean social worker at Lago Budi had told me that sacrifices similar to that of Cerro Mesa had probably occurred all down the coast, according to information she'd received from a local chief. It's also possible, however, that the children died of natural causes, and Machi Clara blamed it on the *pillán* posthumously.

Whatever the truth of the matter, the death of Clara's two children was brought up by Machi Claudina Deumacán as an example of a sacrifice to the *pillán*, the spirit that dwells in the snowcapped volcanoes. Both Machi Clara and Machi Claudina spoke of good spirits on the volcano which can be invoked. And Claudina had some notion that a little girl sacrificed on a volcano was still worshipped as a saint by Mapuches in the mountain country—a concept remarkably similar to the cult that grew up around Tanta Carhua after her sacrifice at Ocros. In fact, there is considerable evidence of such cults. A Chilean ethnographer, Mayo Calvo, discovered a legend surrounding a young girl named Millaray, who was supposedly sacrificed long ago to the *pillán* of Volcán Villarrica. Interestingly, Millaray was supposedly buried on Cerro Challupén, a hill which stands facing the volcano along the shores of the large Lake Villarrica. So there's another case of a congruence between a human sacrifice, a low hill by a large body of water, and a snowcapped volcano. Machi Claudina maintained that traditional veneration of the little boy sacrificed at Cerro Mesa—whom she called "a little saint"—was interrupted by the police proceedings and the conflicts it created. But offerings of bread, meat, and a fermented drink were deposited around Millaray's grave on Cerro Challupén after her death, much as food offerings were given to Tanta Carhua, and other special mummies, in the northern Andes.[2]

All of this confirmed my feeling that Mapuche religious beliefs, in spite of external appearances that made them look radically different from the practices in the northern Andes, had similar underpinnings.

But if the ceremonial system at Lago Budi was getting clearer to me, the specific responsibility for the sacrifice of 1960 was getting murkier. Everyone from Judge Osses to Rosa Painecur, the mother of the victim, said that Machi Juana was the protagonist who gave the orders for the cruel sacrifice, based on a dream-revelation. Unfortunately, this simple story began looking increasingly suspect to me, because I now knew that decisionmaking power at ceremonial occasions, such as the *guillatún*, is in male hands.

Of course, a strong person like Machi Juana could buck the system—as she had at the previous year's *guillatún* when she ignored the presiding *ngenpín*, Retruhuili. But, even so, Machi Juana had no authority to decide what kind of sacrifice would be made at the *guillatún*. That was always in the hands of the *ngenpín*, who carefully consulted the hereditary land chief on major issues. It seemed inconceivable that Machi Juana could have given the order for a child sacrifice.

Lorenzo began to do some sleuthing on his own, visiting family members and close friends, promising them complete anonymity if they would tell him the real story. And what he heard was surprising indeed: Machi Juana didn't have the dream to sacrifice a boy in 1960. It was Domingo Manquián, the dominant *ngenpín*, who dreamed of the sacrifice and gave the order.

"Manquián was the other protagonist of the child sacrifice of 1960," Lorenzo said. "The *machi* couldn't have done it without his approval, since the *ngenpín* is always the final authority at sacred events. And Domingo Manquián was a true *ngenpín* in the ancient tradition—an immensely inspired man. I was a disciple of his when I was young. When he talks, you listen."

We found Domingo Manquián working in a potato patch near his home, not far from Felipe Painén's house. He stood next to his hoe barefoot and ankle-deep in the red, clayish earth, wearing only gray pants and a shirt. Dressed in our heavy winter coats, we thought the old man very hardy to withstand the cold, wet weather in such light clothes. We gave him gifts of maté and candles, which Manquián handed to his four-year-old grandson. One of Manquián's granddaughters warned us that her grandfather was over eighty years old and hard of hearing. But his voice was still O.K.

"I am the spirit of God calling for water when there is no water," he declaimed in a loud voice. "When I pray, God listens and sends rains to all these south lands."

I was startled by his speaking of God in the first person, an eloquent style also used by Old Testament prophets. But in this case there seemed to be a confusion, or simply a fusion, between Manquián the man and Manquián the ocean god. Domingo Manquián perfectly described the magical role of the ocean god Manquián—causing rain to pour down on the unirrigated Mapuche farmlands was the deity's chief function.

After this compelling introduction, Domingo Manquián dropped his role as the oracle of the ocean god, and slipped into his human self. Here the message got more garbled. He objected to Lorenzo, his former student, asking him about the sacrifice of 1960. "What are you mixed up with this for?" he asked disapprovingly. Manquián had converted to Christian fundamentalism in the late sixties, whereupon he destroyed his shamanic drum and gave up his role as *ngenpín*. His interpretation of the sacrifice of 1960 was now mixed up with Christ and the devil.

"When the ocean rose in 1960, it was pure devil," Manquián remembered. "Jesus has his people. But the devil also has his people. Before the ocean rose with the earthquake, I saw a horse that galloped furiously (a sign that the earth was about to shake). I warned the people. I told the people I wanted them to dance, to do the *guillatún* prayers to ward off the evil. But they didn't listen. Then a month later the earthquake came and the sky was covered. The people got together and cried to me for help. But it was too late."

The old man gestured wildly when he recalled the tragedy of 1960—how the water suddenly rose and swept away houses with chickens and geese still squawking inside. "So the people took a little boy, a boy a little bigger than this one here," he said, pointing to his four-year-old grandson sitting next to a potato bag. "They stripped him naked and they cut the boy. There was blood, blood—blood everywhere." At this point Manquián covered his eyes with a look of horror. "I wasn't there," he said. "I didn't see it.

"That was a great sin," Manquián concluded. "The man who cut the boy died afterward. And the woman who collected the blood also died. God punished them."

Whether Manquián actually participated in the sacrifice or not, he'd apparently been consulted by the desperate leaders of Lago Budi right after the earthquake and tidal waves. And, whatever he had told them, he certainly seemed to feel guilty about the outcome—far guiltier than Machi Juana seems to feel. "He may have been the intellectual author of the sacrifice," Lorenzo observed. If so, his account of the death of the man who was responsible for killing little José Luis Painecur was curiously self-descriptive. Because the ceremonial chief of 1960 was dead—the confused if still-eloquent Christian convert in front of us was only remotely related to his former self.

But the lady who collected the blood was alive and kicking. Machi Juana was surprisingly resourceful and resilient. She'd survived the human sacrifice intact, endured the hatred and fear of her community for years, and proved capable of getting a house out of a *gringo* for a dream that may not have been hers at all. And, as I was about to learn, I still didn't know anything about Machi Juana Namuncura.

My best informants at Lago Budi turned out to be neighbors of Machi Juana, Rosario and Senovio Opazo. But when I first approached them, in 1984, I got only perfunctory denials about the sacrifice of José Luis Painecur at Cerro Mesa. Later, in 1985, they refused to let me in, because, as they explained, one of their neighbors had recently been murdered and thrown into a ditch by a stranger who stopped by and asked for a drink. "You shouldn't go walking around here alone carrying that big camera," they told me. "There are people around here who would murder you just for that camera."

Finally, toward the end of 1986, after several more visits, they started opening up about Machi Juana. Machi Juana claimed she had learned to be a *machi* from her own spirit, in a series of visions and childhood revelations. But that's not the story I got from her neighbors.

"One time, when Juana Namuncura was already a grown woman in her forties, she became sick to the point of death," Rosario said. "I went to take care of her and stayed up all night with her. I rested her head against a chair, covered her with animal skins, and kept the fire going. She was so sick she could hardly talk. But she started making motions with her hands, as though she was beating a drum. We call that *machitucando,* and it means that the person wants to become a *machi.* 'What do you want?' I asked Juana. She kept showing me the motions of beating a drum. 'Do you want to be a *machi*?' Then she nodded her head, meaning that she wanted to learn to be a *machi.*

"We called Segundo Wenchunpán, and he reached an understanding with her. Through him, Machi Isabela Queopán came and taught Juana Namuncura how to beat the drum and be a *machi.* And she's kept it up ever since—it must be about thirty years now. Some of her patients get better, others get worse—just like at the hospital. She likes to treat her patients by killing a pig and putting its entrails on top of them. But what she did best was delivering babies. As a midwife she was good, very good."

When I asked about Machi Juana's dream after the earthquake of 1960, the Opazos just started laughing. "The earthquake and the tidal waves came so fast there was no time for anyone to dream anything," they said. "The people got together very quickly and decided to do a sacrifice, and within three hours the whole thing was finished."

"*Machis* are great liars," Rosario said. "That's part of their mystique—they don't want anyone to know how they learned their practices. And this Machi Juana is particularly clever. She has some real histories behind her! Her whole family are known for being animal thieves, and she had a special shack where she used to cook and cut up the stolen animals. Well, one time when there was a feast-day celebration and all the neighbors went to Puerto Saavedra, she stayed behind to cook all the animals. But her shack caught on fire and burned down! Everyone laughed at that. It served her right.

"People don't like Juana Namuncura. They often beat her up at the *guillatúns*. But that may be because she's a good fighter and starts trouble herself. That whole family is bad. Her husband's uncle was killed by the police, and another relative was beaten so badly he later died in his home. It doesn't pay to get involved with that lot. You have to be careful. I heard the *machi*'s family once saying, 'What is that *huinca* doing around here? Maybe it would be better if we killed him.' They were talking about some other *gringo*, not about you. But they don't like strangers."

The most amusing thing about this revelation was that there'd been no time for Machi Juana to receive a divine message from God before the sacrifice of José Luis Painecur. In the tribal lore about the sacrifice of 1960, the responsibility for killing José Luis Painecur belonged directly to Machi Juana. But God was indirectly responsible, because God supposedly commanded her by way of a dream-vision. By now I knew that the whole dream sequence was phony. But, in a strange way, it had become even more revealing of the Mapuche attitude toward human sacrifice and guilt.

"The Mapuches always say they've had a dream about some event after the event has occurred," anthropologist Lydia Nakashima told me. Nakashima was completing a Ph.D. at UCLA on Mapuche dreams. She'd found that dreams are used to justify illnesses, calamities, and other difficult-to-explain events. "Whether it's an illness or an earthquake, they'll always claim to have dreamed about it first. It's a way of fitting the occurrence into their belief system. In fact, the dream always comes later."

Not *always*, as we've seen in the case of Machi Juana's forthright predictions about earthquakes. But the supposed dream about the sacrifice of 1960 fits this category.

As I crossed Lago Budi on the old wooden raft, the mists covering everything around me, I reflected that I still didn't know anything about Lago Budi. There was a persistent duality and contradiction. I knew two chiefs, Toro and Felipe; two dreamers, Machi Juana and Manquián; two Manquiáns, the oracular old man and the sea god. And, as a *gringo* intruder, I had so many personalities I'd lost count of them.

Underlying these rivalries and contradictions was a depressing pattern of violence. Almost everyone I knew had a homicide in his family—Lorenzo's father had been murdered on the beach and buried God knows where; the same had happened to one of Machi Juana's brothers. These killings were frequently by members of the same family. "A man's enemies are his own household" (Micah 7:6) was sadly appropriate at Lago Budi.

When you consider the history of Lago Budi, the bloodshed makes tragic sense. If the stubborn Spaniards were forged between the hammer and the anvil of the Moorish wars, the Mapuches were forged by the unbelievable brutality of Spanish chivalry. There were at least half a million Mapuches when the Spaniards arrived in Chile in the 1540s; by the end of the nineteenth century, only one hundred thousand were left.[3] The Mapuches occupied rolling pasture lands in a parklike setting which appealed to the Spanish conquistadors. They were blessed with a moderate climate, plenty of pasture for animals, and good agricultural land for crops, along with rich alluvial deposits of gold. And, best of all, there were tens of thousands of slaves to pan the gold, tend the animals, and raise the crops.

Of the ten settlements built by the Spaniards in sixteenth-century Chile, seven were in Mapuche country. None of them survived without being burned down. Most Spanish settlements were burned down several times. One of them was burned down eight times.

But the Spaniards also burned down the Mapuche villages. Actually, the Spanish chroniclers mention three Mapuche cities, with some five thousand *rucas* apiece, in the heartland of Mapuche country. One of those three cities was built along the shores of Lago Budi, not far from Machi Juana's home. The Spaniards attacked that settlement in 1555, swimming across Lago Budi with their horses by night to catch the Mapuches unaware. But the Mapuches anticipated the Spanish assault, and counterattacked while the Spanish cavalry was still in the water. A long battle ensued, which the Spaniards finally won. Rather than surrendering, many Mapuche warriors deliberately drowned themselves in Lago Budi.

Sometimes I could have sworn the ghosts of those dead warriors were still hovering around, trying to drive me off as another invader. And since this old warrior-instinct reasserted itself with particular force at organized games and *guillatúns*, I wasn't overjoyed at attending the coming *guillatún* at Tragua Tragua. Especially after I'd been told that Lago Budi's *guillatún* at the Tragua Tragua hilltop in 1983 had degenerated into a huge battle between two groups, who fought all the way to Machi Juana's house, about two miles away. I feared this year could bring a repeat performance. And I didn't want to be near angry Mapuches, now that Toro Aillapán had fueled the crazy rumor about my stealing the *ngenpín's* job. I would make an ideal scapegoat. So I told Felipe Painén I didn't plan to attend.

"Don't worry about Toro," Felipe Painén told me. "You're my guest, and I'll guarantee your safety."

The day of the *guillatún* was December 6, 1986. By 9:00 A.M. hundreds of ox carts jammed the roads, and prayer flags fluttered in a grand procession to the Tragua Tragua meeting place. I eventually reached the hill with my jeep, which I parked in the circle around the *guillatún* field. I purposely put it as close to the gate as possible, in case a rapid exit was required.

I'd come with Lorenzo's wife and two of his children. But Lorenzo had excused himself, saying he preferred to come alone. I thought that was extremely unusual: Lorenzo accompanied me everywhere.

I was relieved to see Toro Aillapán in the assembly of leaders addressed by Felipe Painén at the start of the ceremony. At least Toro hadn't carried out his boycott threat. Felipe told the chiefs that I had permission to take pictures of the *guillatún*. No one objected. I walked over to Toro Aillapán when Felipe was finished.

"How are you?" I asked respectfully.

"Not too well," Toro answered gruffly, and went off without shaking hands.

I wore a poncho over my camera, to take pictures with a little more decorum. A couple of hundred devotees formed straight lines in front of the *rehue*, where Felipe began invoking God in a singsong fashion, while the *machis* around him took turns drinking home-brewed wine from small jars around the *rehue*. After everyone had drunk a good bit, the horns, drums, and *trutrucas* began blowing to accompany the rhythmic repetition of OM and the up-and-down movement of the sacred maqui-tree branches, which all the dancers held. The entire body of worshippers marched in unison back and forth along the east-west axis of the field, with the *rehue* as the starting and stopping point of each movement. Machi Juana looked very spaced out—whether from alcohol or chanting, I don't know.

I was beginning to enjoy myself, relaxing with the chanting and dancing. Everyone was in a good mood, and all the fears and spectral dreams of *huitranalwes* and other demons seemed banished in the bright-blue December sky. Soon the number of participants doubled as a solemn procession arrived from the coast. These coastal people normally worshipped at a sacred mountain closer to the ocean. But, like a majority of the fifteen-hundred-odd participants, they'd come to help out at this ceremony.

After two hours of nonstop dancing, the pace suddenly quickened and the rigid, linear formation changed into a circle. At this point the men on horseback, who still didn't seem uncontrollably drunk, began galloping in good grace around the dancers. There were now two concentric circles, people dancing up and down around the *rehue* while horseback riders galloped around us.

Next the center of devotion shifted from the *rehue* to a makeshift altar on the northern side of the field, where two white sheep were tied. The *machis* began screaming and quickening their drumbeats as the circle closed in, bit by bit, on the two victims. The circle grew tighter and tighter, until we were all pressed against each other, yelling loudly now, and waving our leafy sticks with great vehemence, creating a bristling thicket of green branches that rose and fell with our wild movements. I had the fleeting impression that I was in a jungle where our tribe was hunting a quarry driven out of its lair. As the knife plunged into the sheep, Felipe Painén and Machi Juana came together, ahead of all the other *machis* and leaders, to lead in the frenetic spraying of sacrificial blood in the four cardinal directions.

Machi Juana and Felipe worked as a team. Machi Juana held the sacrificed blood in an orange bowl while Felipe set the pace for the chanting, as we all headed to a hill, Piedra Alta (the High Rock), overlooking the coast.

At Piedra Alta there was a marvelous view of the South Pacific, foaming breakers smashing the isolated beaches for miles on end while horses galloped and the splendidly dressed women danced in another set of concentric circles. Eventually, Machi Juana and Felipe came to the cliff overlooking the ocean and began praying and shaking the sheep's blood toward the waves. Felipe cried, "Oh, God, grant us good harvests and good health; Rich Man of the Sea, share your wealth in animals, fish, and food with us."

Then Felipe broke away from the main body and began the sharp descent down to the beach, followed by about twenty people, including me. Felipe waded into the waves, holding a big container of sheep's blood and a maqui branch. He lifted up his branch, now dripping with blood, and cried to the ocean for blessings. Then he emptied the whole container into the waves, smearing the white foam with a dark-red patch that churned for an instant before disappearing into Manquián's domain.

On the way back to Tragua Tragua, I asked Machi Juana why they'd poured blood into the ocean. "Because the ocean is very rich," she said. "So you ask Lafquén Ullmén [The Rich Man of the Sea] to give you everything."

A woman next to Machi Juana remarked pointedly that the *guillatún* used to be better when there weren't as many *huincas* allowed near. "That's why we have more droughts these days," she said.

Back at Tragua Tragua, a man objected to my tape recording of the final prayers.

"He has permission," another man said.

"Who gave him permission?" the first man asked.

"Felipe Painén."

"Well, he's the maximum chief," the first one admitted. "But you're going to have to excuse me. A lot of people here believe these prayers don't have power, and aren't listened to by God, if the *huincas* are allowed to participate. Before, not a single *huinca* could come to the *guillatún* field. Later they let some come, but they couldn't interfere with the ceremony. Now, look at this, here you are with a tape recorder right next to the *rehue*."

A *gringo* next to the *rehue*! Toro Aillapán's great fear was a common fear, and one that started surfacing now that everyone was intoxicated. An extremely boisterous inebriated man came up shortly after this exchange, and started hollering in my face. Although he was practically incoherent, I understood that he didn't want me near the *rehue*, either.

I left in a hurry.

The drunken man followed behind, still complaining.

"Why are the *gringos* so interested in us? What do they want?"

At this point I just wanted to get out of the *guillatún*, but the man was determined to make this as difficult as possible. He began menacing me, shoving himself against the jeep.

"Leave him alone," one of my neighbors shouted, a man who was equally drunk. Eventually, the first drunk left.

"Things are really ugly now, because everyone is drunk with wine," Lorenzo's wife said nervously. "I've been to other *guillatúns* which are nicer because they don't permit wine. But this is bad."

"I think it's time to go," I said.

"I think so, too," she agreed.

I headed back to the *rehue* to tell Lorenzo that I was leaving with his family. But I hadn't quite reached Lorenzo when two of the *guillatún* leaders rode up on horseback, right into the inner circle of *machis,* where Felipe held sway, and violently interrupted the solemn conclusion of the *guillatún.* The drums, horns, *trutrucas* all went silent. The dancing came to a halt.

"Quiet, quiet," a man shouted. "Listen to what the chiefs are saying."

I couldn't hear all that the chiefs were saying from my vantage point, but what I did hear, coupled with the riders' furious gestures, told me all I needed to know.

"The *huincas* . . ." one of the riders kept saying. "You're the *guillatún* chief, and you've allowed the *huincas* . . ."

I turned around, badly scared, and rushed back to my jeep.

"Go and get the children," I said to Lorenzo's wife. "And tell Lorenzo to come, too, if he wants."

In a minute Lorenzo's wife came back with the children. She was in tears. "Lorenzo says you have to leave immediately, immediately, *immediately!* He says that the shit has hit the fan [*quedó la escoba*]. He doesn't dare come over to your jeep, because if he does it will be worse for you and he will also be in danger." Then she broke down and said, "Please, let's go quickly. I don't want anything to happen to my children."

I put the jeep in four-wheel drive and ran over the front of an ox cart that blocked my way. We drove very quickly down the dirt road from Tragua Tragua, faster than I had ever driven on any of those roads before. I was still shaking and scared when we reached the raft at Lago Budi, and I was immensely relieved when I saw that the raft was on our side, ready to go. As we crossed the waters, I had time to reflect on what had happened and to curse Toro Aillapán silently.

"I'll bet that old fox put those two chiefs up to their trouble-making," I said.

"I think so, too," Lorenzo's wife agreed.

When we reached the far shore of the lake, I gave the raftsman a big tip and told him, "If any of those horsemen from the *guillatún* come galloping up, don't go and fetch them in a hurry, O.K.?"

He laughed. "So they've chased another *gringo* from the *guillatún,* have they?"

I didn't laugh. I smiled, very faintly, and got going, very quickly, down the roads that led far from Lago Budi, fleeing, as the Spaniards and Incas had before me, from a race of people too tough for *huincas.*

▣ 10 ▣

ONE MORE VICTIM

After escaping from the *guillatún*, I waited anxiously for news from Lorenzo. When I finally spoke to him, I was pleased to hear that nothing serious had occurred at the close of the *guillatún*.

"Several of the chiefs were trying to start a fight because of all the pictures you took," he said. "They'd been drinking a lot and they wanted a conflict. But Felipe defended his actions very well, and Toro Aillapán supported him."

"Toro supported Felipe?" I asked incredulously.

"Yes, Toro said you had permission to take pictures," Lorenzo added. "After the ceremony was over, he asked about you. 'Why did the Holy Father leave so soon? I wanted him to eat with us,' Toro said. Machi Juana also asked about you, but she agreed that you did the right thing in leaving early."

Still, I'd had enough of Lago Budi. I packed my bags and loaded my jeep, then drove to a little hostel by the ocean, to have a meal before leaving.

"Are you the one who's a friend of that Machi Juana Namuncura?" a young Mapuche girl named Adela asked me outside the hostel.

"Yes," I answered.

"I know about her," Adela said. "I'm a Namuncura, too. And my father is a friend of Bombero, Machi Juana's son."

"What do you know about Machi Juana?"

"Do you remember that her granddaughter was pregnant last year?" she asked.

I remembered.

"People say Machi Juana killed the baby that was born to her granddaughter a year ago."

"Are you sure about that?"

"What happened to that baby?" Adela demanded. "If it had been stillborn, people would have been told—the *machi* would at least have let the people at the medical post down the road know. But no one heard a word. Then, about the time the baby was expected, my father and Bombero were out late at night because they'd been near Piedra Alta doing some leather work for a saddle. As they went past Machi Juana's house in the darkness, they saw a light, and Machi Juana was dancing, holding the heart of her granddaughter's baby, praying with it. Machi Juana prayed that no one would find the place where she'd buried the baby. So that's how we know that Machi Juana cut out the baby's heart and buried its little body by her house."

When I spoke with Adela's father, Pedro Namuncura, he denied having seen Machi Juana praying with the heart of her grandson. But he admitted that Bombero had told this story.

"Machi Juana is my legitimate aunt, the sister of my dead father," Pedro said. "But I believe she killed that baby. The girl was pregnant. That's not a lie. So what happened? There was no burial or public notice. The head of the medical post, a man from Toltén, wanted Machi Juana put in jail."

I felt Bombero was almost certainly lying about seeing his mother dancing with the heart of her dead great-grandchild. After all, he'd claimed falsely that his mother was dead in an effort to steal her land. But his description of the ceremony probably reflected real customs once practiced—maybe still practiced on rare occasions—at Lago Budi.

"We don't go near Machi Juana," Pedro said. "People believe she is a witch, a bad *machi*. That's why people treat her so badly and make her life unbearable. They don't treat her with the respect due to an old lady. Twelve or thirteen years ago Ricardo Culminao, the nephew of the *machi*'s husband, accused Machi Juana of being a witch. He broke into her house and broke her bones, and her head, too. Machi Juana spent two or three months in the hospital after that. That's when Bombero protected her. He took Ricardo Culminao to justice, and they put him in prison. Later Culminao got sick and died. He was a young man. So the people say that the *machi* used witchcraft to kill him."

My conversation with Adela and her father reminded me that I still didn't know enough about Lago Budi.

It wasn't time to pull out yet.

So I returned to my best informants at Lago Budi, Senovio and Rosario Opazo, who lived barely two hundred yards from Machi Juana's *ruca*. Senovio was not Mapuche, and Rosario was only a half-blood. But Rosario, despite her golden hair, spoke Mapuche eloquently and, like half-bloods who feel they have something to prove, had become an expert on Mapuche lore. Machi Juana spoke highly of them both, mentioning that they always helped out at the *guillatún*.

I interviewed each of them separately, found their accounts almost exactly the same, and, on checking details through Lorenzo, Felipe, and others, was satisfied that their information was the most accurate I'd received on both the history of Machi Juana and the sacrifice of 1960. In the end, I learned far more from the Opazos about the ritual at Cerro Mesa than from any full-blooded Mapuches.

The Opazos said that Domingo Manquián's father had been the real *ngenpín* at the time of the earthquake. Domingo had considerable authority because he acted as his father's representative—a typical Mapuche custom, since the son of a *ngenpín* often succeeds his father. But they said Domingo Manquián was not present at the sacrifice of the little boy in 1960.

"Domingo Manquián was with us on the hill over here," Senovio said. "The word went out that they were looking for an orphan to sacrifice on Cerro Mesa. The *machi* wanted an orphan, they said. That message came almost immediately after the first tidal wave, around three in the afternoon. Then they tried to get a girl about eighteen years old from Pu Budi, but her family hid her. So they settled on Vargas's little grandson because there was no one to stand up for him.

"At six in the afternoon the third tidal wave came. By that time the whole community of people around Cerro Mesa was on top of the hill. From our mountaintop we could see hundreds of people dancing there. But that third wave almost washed them all away—we saw the water smash against the hill and burst on top of them, soaking all the dancers on Cerro Mesa. That wave must have been twenty meters [sixty-five feet] high. Cerro Mesa was completely isolated by the ocean. There was nothing but water here, water there, and waves everywhere. We thought that the world was going to end. We didn't care about our house, our furniture, or the animals, because we thought everything was at an end. We never want to see that again."

I asked who the tribal leaders of the community, the *loncos*, had been at that time.

"The chief of that community was old Trafinado," Rosario said, using the nickname for the dead chief, Juan Nahuelcoy. "As they cut the boy's arms and legs off with a knife, the *machi* received them and passed them on to old Trafinado. And old Trafinado danced with both of the boy's arms, waving them about as he went. They cut out the boy's heart, too, while the *machi* played her drum. After he was dead, they took the boy and placed him in the ground, like a stake, in front of the ocean. They didn't throw the rest of him in, like some people say.

"Then the *machi* announced, 'Here are my two black sheep.' And out from behind a bush jumped two naked men, who danced with spears, shaking them as though they were defending themselves. But when the people saw the naked men waving their spears, they became terrified and ran away. They arrived here crying and told us all about it."

Lorenzo and I found ample confirmation for this report when we spoke with Segundo Aillapán, father of the *ngenpín* who'd given me valuable information on mountain spirits, and his mother, Machi María Huechacona, perhaps the oldest *machi* at Lago Budi, and one who occupied the most prestigious position at the *guillatún* ceremony after Machi Juana.

"Three years before the earthquake of 1960 I dreamed that the waves had risen," Machi María Huechacona said. "I spoke to the waves, holding a maqui branch, telling them to dissolve. Then a couple appeared on Cerro Mesa, Une Fuche and Une Kuche [the Mapuche Father-Mother God; literally, the First Man and the First Woman]. They asked, 'Where is the *guillatún?*' "

From this dream, Machi María claimed, she learned that God proposed to destroy everyone. When I asked her why God appeared on Cerro Mesa, she answered that Cerro Mesa is a *conlil*, a sacred place. She said that *conlil* also meant "a place of fighting," which is why Machi Juana had the naked men simulate a battle with their spears, defending themselves from the rising ocean.

Segundo Aillapán added that Cerro Mesa had a "fighting spirit" from ancient times, when three hundred dead warriors were cremated on top of the hill. "In the last war between the chiefs here and the chiefs in Temuco, we were allied with the Chileans, and many people from Temuco and Imperial died on the beaches. They were burned with firewood on Cerro Mesa, but their spirit remained. Their bones were collected in ox carts."

This war must have occurred sometime between 1818, the date of Chilean independence, and 1880, when the final conquest of the Mapuche heartland by the Chilean army began. Now, Cerro Mesa, in addition to being a hill with Machi Juana's spirit and direct access to Volcán Llaima, was also a place of ancient fighting and ceremonial cremations, a logical stronghold on which to wage a spiritual battle against the serpent monster Cai Cai Filu, whom Machi Juana's naked dancers had threatened with their spears. The use of the archaic spears, the nakedness of the dancers, and their identification with the most common animal victim—black sheep—indicated the primitive origin of the ritual.

I wanted to know more about this ritual with the spear dance by the so-called black sheep. Unfortunately, the old chief Trafinado was dead, and so were the two men who had acted as the naked dancers. But one of Trafinado's daughters had married Lorenzo's grandfather, the last great *lonco* at Lago Budi. She was his fourth wife and, as Mapuche kinship systems go, was one of Lorenzo's grandmothers. We took the opportunity to pay the grand old dame a visit.

María Nahuelcoy gave Lorenzo a big hug. I was struck by her effusiveness, not customary in the reserved Mapuche protocol for greetings. But her mood changed quickly, and she began crying as she told us that a nephew of hers had just been taken to jail. She insisted on a drink before she'd talk to us. We poured her a glass of wine.

"This tastes like horse piss," she said appreciatively.

"Can you tell us something about Mapuche customs during earthquakes?" I asked.

"No, no, no," she answered. "I want to sing. Can't you understand that they've just taken my nephew to prison in Santiago? I don't know what he did."

"These things frighten her, because her own children and her nephews have been involved in so many crimes and murders," Lorenzo explained. In fact, María Nahuelcoy said that all her sons were dead, two of them murdered. And it turned out that Machi Mariano was her adopted son, so she was also planning to visit his boy, now sentenced to three years in prison at Imperial. "These things astonish her and she's afraid to speak. But if you let her sing, everything will come out."

After taking another swig of wine, María Nahuelcoy, the last wife of the Lago Budi's last chief, announced, "I'm great for singing." Then she started into a wailing, tearful dirge in Mapuche:

> I'm very sad,
> I didn't know what was going to happen;
> My heart is in pain
> Now that I've learned that my nephew is imprisoned.
> My heart is in pain,
> How badly I've been wounded. . . .
> When I learned this, all my thoughts concentrated on it alone.
> I left my house happily,
> And reached town safely.
> But how sad I am now that I know.
> I am the same María Isabel Nahuelcoy,
> But now I walk with affliction,
> Like a different person,
> And stumble over everything I encounter.

She paused and cried a bit, then announced, "One more song." She started up again, singing in cadences that reminded me of Indian chants from the American Southwest:

> My heart was orphaned
> When I was just a little girl.
> My dead father made me cry very much.
> He was four times a widower,
> Four times a widower.
> My father gave me away to be married
> Because he was very poor,
> Because he was very poor.
> I suppose he gave me away because he was poor.
> That's why my father sold me like an animal.
> He ruined all my luck.

"I was twelve years old when they betrothed me to Juan Aillapán," she said. "He paid for me with animals, and I was his fourth wife. I had four children with him. But I was just like his maid—he never married me legally. So I ran away one night. My father was angry, but it was his fault. I never wanted to marry Juan Aillapán. That old man was blind. What could I get from him?"

When I asked her about Cerro Mesa, María Nahuelcoy immediately said that her father, Trafinado, and her brothers were present at the sacrifice of little José Luis Painecur. She also said they'd told her all about it, down to the last details. Maybe her resentment against her family made her open to talking. Maybe it was the wine.

"My father was the chief over there in Collilelfu, near Cerro Mesa," she said. "I grew up near Machi Juana. We knew each other when we were little girls, though she was a couple of years older than me. [María Nahuelcoy's ID card shows her to be seventy-nine years old.] She's the one they took to jail because of what happened after the earthquake.

"The people over there went to the *conlil*, Cerro Mesa. A *conlil* is like a Tren Tren, a defense against the sea. They have a big snake inside them which makes the noise TAANG TAANG as it rises above the ocean. That *machi* ordered the sacrifice there. Who knows why she wanted it. There were people dancing with drums and whistles and *trutrucas* as they quartered the boy. 'I'll fetch firewood and water,' the little boy promised his grandfather. 'Just let me live, Grandfather.' He cried a great deal to live. He was pretty well grown, about this tall [she motions with her hand]. But they cut out his heart and intestines and threw them into the sea."

María Nahuelcoy said Machi Juana had collected the boy's blood in a bowl, then dipped a maqui branch in the boy's blood and started waving it toward the ocean, splattering warm blood on the waters swirling all around them. "And the *machi* sang like this," María Nahuelcoy said.

Here María Isabel Nahuelcoy stood up and began waving an imaginary stick in the air, singing in Mapuche:

Feytata yetuafymy
Kelluayyn taty kullyuguayn
Ynchyn mayta kunyfall
Chumelu kam castigaynmu
Tachy Ngnechen
Kullyuguayn tachy pgnen
Eluayn regalautuayn feymu
Calmape tachy marremoto
Feymufey ngneuekynope

Take this boy now,
We are helping you,
We are paying you with this boy.
We are all orphans.
Why do you punish us, God?
We sacrifice this boy to you,
We give him to you as a gift,
So that the tidal waves are calmed,
So that there are no more disasters.

"That's what the *machi* sang," María Nahuelcoy said. "That dirty shit of a *machi*. I don't even want to look at her. I can't stand the presence of those people who made a little child suffer so much. And it was the child's own blood, his own relatives, who did it. Why did they make him suffer so? The father of the boy was also to blame, and he was my nephew. So that little boy they killed was a relative of mine. They went and got that poor child." Here she began sobbing. "Please don't ask me any more questions about it."

I was stupefied when María Nahuelcoy spontaneously sang the *machi*'s invocation to the sea—I'd always wondered what the prayer formula was like, but never expected to find out. On the surface it was quite straightforward—a simple payment to the sea—similar to the invocations made to the ocean waves at the last *guillatún*. But there was a subtle identification of the sacrificed boy—an orphan—with all of the participants—"We are all orphans." The message seems to be: This catastrophe has made orphans of us all, and we will all die like this orphan if you don't stop punishing us. There is also an underlying threat to the ocean here: If all the "orphans" die, no one will feed you any more.

And there was another revelation: the identity of little José Luis Painecur's father. The father never came forward, and I'd wanted to know what his family's reaction to the sacrifice was. Now I knew: the father was María Nahuelcoy's nephew, which meant that Trafinado, the old chief who had danced with the victim's two arms in the ceremony, was dancing with his great-grandson's body. This incensed María Nahuelcoy as she thought about it, and she continued to denounce José Vargas, the little boy's maternal grandfather, for turning the boy over to the *machi*.

"Is it true that José has become an Evangelical?" she wanted to know.

"Yes, when I visited him he had a special chapel with an altar set up on his property," I answered.

"What the hell is he doing being an Evangelical?" she asked angrily. "That little boy they killed didn't do anything—he's the only one who has the right to be an Evangelical."

María Nahuelcoy didn't have a good impression of Evangelicals. "They once tried to convert me," she recalled. "They gave me old clothes and invited me to their Sunday service. I sat there a while, listening to the minister. 'God! God! God!' he shouted. 'He's in bad shape,' I thought to myself. So I asked to go to the bathroom. 'Just knock on the door when you want to come back in,' the guard told me. But I went outside and got the shit out of there. I don't need old clothes that badly."

She also had a bad opinion of *machis*. "All that *machis* do is make the Mapuches fight among each other," she said. "When my son died, my daughter-in-law called in a *machi*, who said that another *machi* had made him sick with evil spirits. So then they hired still another *machi* to do witchcraft against the one who killed my son. What stupidity! But my son died from a brain tumor—they diagnosed it at the hospital. So why spend all this money on witchcraft? *Machis* are pure shit."

Machis certainly were responsible for plenty of fights, just as they were frequently victims of such fights. Before the Chileans conquered Lago Budi in the 1880s, it was customary to take a *machi* accused of witchcraft, tie the *machi* to two horses, and pull the unfortunate individual apart.

Many people sounded as though they would like to resort to these old methods in dealing with Machi Juana. Her neighbors shared María Nahuelcoy's lack of appreciation for her: people didn't even want to look at her. But it wasn't until my last few days at Lago Budi that I realized what this really meant.

"We kept having bad crops here," Rosario Opazo told me. "And Senovio was constantly sick. Finally, we asked another *machi* to come in and tell us what sort of person Machi Juana was— whether she was causing all these misfortunes with her witchcraft. And, sure enough, Machi Juana was behind it all. We learned she was taking dirt from the cemetery and sowing it on our lands, to kill all the crops. And we found a rotten egg buried near our house, which always brings sickness."

This is how *machi* warfare is waged. "I've seen many groups hire a *machi* from outside the community to come and investigate a suspected witch," said anthropologist Lydia Nakashima. "I've even observed one. He was actually very clever at learning a lot about all the local people in a very short time. So they can be very skilled at investigating."

The spiritual private eye who investigated Machi Juana was a male *machi*, Antonio Paineo. We had a hard time locating him, and we wouldn't have tracked him down at all except that several young girls knew him well. Perhaps too well.

"Where is Antonio Paineo?" Lorenzo asked them.

"You mean the *machi?*" one asked. "He's the one we call Big Penis." Although they did not reveal how they'd come upon this information, they all giggled hysterically. Then they directed us to an isolated valley, with sharp rises and woods all around, some twenty miles inland from Lago Budi. We crossed a stream with a small waterfall cascading near us on our way to his solitary *ruca*. From the steep hillside we spotted a tall *rehue* planted in an open clearing, with prayer flags and flowers adorning it.

"Are you detectives?" Paineo asked at once. On hearing that we wanted to know about Mapuche customs, he invited us to sit in front of the *rehue*. "I dreamed that two detectives would come and visit me in a car," he said. "So I suppose that must have meant you."

He wasn't too far from being right.

"That Machi Juana Namuncura is very famous," he said in response to our questions, "very famous indeed. I was called in to prepare medicine for Rosario Opazo. I entered into the center of a real fire there—I learned all the evil things they were doing to each other. That *machi* went to the cemetery, where she got dirt from the dead. Then she took that dirt and sowed it on the lands where her neighbors were going to plant wheat and peas, in order to sow death there."

"Why would anyone waste her time doing a useless thing like that?" I asked.

"You think it's useless," he answered. "But how much money was she paid to do that? A lot, that's for sure. Many people pay *machis* to do spells that bring people poverty, so that their pigs will die. And that *machi* was involved in the death of more than pigs. I learned that she killed the son of Juan Pañán. He also asked me to investigate her."

"How did you find these things out?" I asked.

"I came before my *rehue* and God revealed it to me in a dream," he said. "I also learned it from the urine of those attacked by the evil." This meant he'd performed the urine divination ceremony for the Opazos and Pañán.

"God has revealed everything to me through visions," he said. "I've seen all the types of *machis*. There are *machis* who learn from big snakes, others who learn from spirits of water sources, others from *huitranalwes*, and others from the spirits of the volcano."

When I asked what spirit Machi Juana had, he immediately answered: "The spirit of Machi Juana Namuncura is the spirit of Cerro Mesa. And from that hill she takes hold of the spirit of the whole ocean with one hand, and with the other hand she takes hold of the volcano. That's why she's so powerful. Because, having the ocean and the volcano, she also takes hold of all the mountains in between. For example, this mountain here is my Tren Tren, the place where I pray for water. It gets its power because it's connected to another mountain, about five kilometers [three miles] from here, and that mountain is connected to both the volcano and the ocean, and to other mountains as well."

"It sounds like the connections between the mountains are all computerized," Lorenzo whispered.

"So that Machi Juana Namuncura is very powerful with her Cerro Mesa," Paineo concluded. "And when she dies, her spirit will go to a niece or a daughter of hers—that's how it always works. That power will go to them. But God is not going to let Machi Juana Namuncura die for a long time. He's going to keep her poor as a flea until she's very old, maybe ninety years old, as punishment for that boy she killed. And so that everyone will see her punishment."

Of course I'd known that Machi Juana was taboo from the beginning. But Paineo spelled out the strange way in which she was taboo—everyone had to see her and hate her as a scapegoat. "I don't want to look at her," María Nahuelcoy said, calling Machi Juana a "dirty shit of a *machi*." But it was precisely Machi Juana's function to be a very visible "dirty shit of a *machi*" so that everyone *could* look at her. This explained why, at the big *guillatún* ceremony, she presided along with Felipe Painén. Her role was to be a victim: old, poor as a flea, and punished by everyone's disgust.

And this seemed to make Paineo very happy, in a perverse way.

Everything I now knew about the sacrifice at Cerro Mesa showed that hundreds of people had participated. Perhaps the people who claimed to have learned about it from relatives, or seen it from a distant mountaintop (and there were a lot of these), were also participants. However many participated, a human sacrifice couldn't have occurred without the permission of both male chiefs— Trafinado and possibly Manquián. But in spite of all this, the only person blamed for the sacrifice was Machi Juana.

And this made all the people who participated in the sacrifice, along with all those others who still believe they were saved by it, just as happy as Paineo.

The hate game against Machi Juana is complex and contradictory, like everything else at Lago Budi. Her son Bombero is spreading the terribly damning claim that he witnessed his mother praying with the heart of a sacrificed infant in 1985. Machi Juana's neighbors blame her for crop failures, illnesses, and death. One of her nephews tried to kill her a dozen years ago; another nephew robbed her last year. She's one of the most frequent victims of beatings at *guillatún* celebrations. And yet Machi Juana remains the most prominent female at the same ceremonial occasions at which she is beaten.

Machi Juana is a surrogate victim—and a perpetual orphan— in much the same way that the five-year-old orphan José Luis Painecur served as victim. The difference is that José Luis Painecur expiated the communal sins that had caused the calamitous earthquake and tidal waves, whereas Machi Juana soothed the communal feelings of guilt about an action most people felt was as horrible as it was necessary.

Another key item in Paineo's discourse was his confirmation of Felipe Painén's claim that Machi Juana's spirit was identical with that of Cerro Mesa, and that Cerro Mesa was connected with Volcán Llaima. Furthermore, he revealed the intricate relations between *his* mountain and both Volcán Llaima and Cerro Mesa. Lorenzo's description of a computer network seemed as apt as it was anachronistic. Thomas Zuidema's statement about Inca religion seems accurate for the Mapuches around Lago Budi as well: "The mountains on the horizon were organized into an ever-expanding geographic hierarchy of more potent sources of water." The ocean, source of all waters, and the snowcapped volcanoes, origins of the major rivers, headed the Mapuche hierarchy in a polarity that compares to the Inca worship of both coastal mountains and snowcapped peaks. Moreover, for Mapuche shamans, intermediate peaks are connected with both snowcapped peaks and hills by the ocean—a circumstance that exactly reflects Reinhard's research on Cerro Blanco in Nazca.

Curiously, the more I learned about Cerro Mesa's secret identity—as a Tren Tren, a magical hill that rises as a serpent above the sea; as a *conlil*, a place of fighting, where dead warriors were cremated; as a hill connected to the sea and to the spirit of the monster Cai Cai Filu; as a point of contact, via a line of blue light, to Volcán Llaima; as a shrine where the soul of the sainted José Luis Painecur presided—the more I learned about Machi Juana's shamanic identity. Her neighbors said Machi Juana was a good fighter; from her dreams about the serpent spirits, it was obvious Machi Juana was on intimate terms with these beings; and, according to Paineo, Machi Juana's spirit had a hold on the entire ocean, the volcano, and all mountains in between, through Cerro Mesa. Paineo's metaphor of Machi Juana, standing on Cerro Mesa, holding the ocean with one hand and Volcán Llaima with the other, completed the mutual metamorphosis: Cerro Mesa had become Machi Juana's body, and Machi Juana was planted on the coast like a hill.

My investigation at Lago Budi began with an attempt to understand Machi Juana, human sacrifice, and mountain worship. In the end there was only one subject. Machi Juana and the mountain were inseparable, and they were both united with José Luis Painecur. In fact, Machi Juana had become a communal scapegoat, a kind of eternal twin to José Luis Painecur, so that her life and status were bound up with his sacrifice. There was the circular connection: Machi Juana–Cerro Mesa–José Luis Painecur; mountain-shaman-victim.

I felt I was getting solid, repeated testimonies from unconnected sources over a broad area. But the source I most wanted to hear from was Machi Juana. And, as usual, Machi Juana's family was making my contacts with her difficult. They were getting nastier and nastier about my hanging around. The solution seemed to be to get Machi Juana out of the house, but a new tactic was needed. Fortunately, an interesting case arose that required the skills of a powerful *machi*.

María Alcavil was a talented ceremonial drummer, and would have become a *machi* except that she had some French blood in her. (The Mapuches also have their racial prejudices.) She lived thirty-seven miles from Lago Budi, in a place called Boroa, located between two fast-flowing rivers.

María Alcavil was in her late fifties, energetic, unusually tall for a Mapuche woman, with gray-white hair, light skin, and a direct, no-nonsense style of talking. Alcavil's husband, José Huintrilaf, was in his seventies, a short white-haired man with a gentle demeanor. He limped badly, however, and complained about his left leg. When he showed it to us, we couldn't detect any wound, but it looked completely withered.

"I've had a pain in my leg since I was eleven years old," he said. "I've always been treated by *machis*, in the natural way. But the majority of *machis* don't know anything these days. The first *machi* who treated my leg boiled herbs in a kettle until the kettle was red-hot. Then she put the scalding-hot herbs on my leg and tied them there. I went crazy. The sickness exploded out in other parts of my body—my thumb and my face. Pieces of bone came out. The bone in my leg is still very thin as a result."

I asked him if he'd been treated by normal medical doctors.

"The doctors don't know what it is, either," he said. "This is a sickness that is peculiar to Mapuches—it's a *perimontún*."

Perimontún means "vision" or "apparition." According to José Huintrilaf, the cause of his withered leg is "a water creature," a type of snake called Chunufilu. Just as the Eskimos have hundreds of names for snow, the Mapuches have numerous names for snakes, many of which—like Cai Cai Filu, Tren Tren, and Chunufilu— are what we would consider imaginary. Chunufilu means "Basket," and the vision of this creature reveals a multitude of snake heads all woven together like strands in a wicker basket. It's a multiheaded snake monster horrible to look at, a sort of Mapuche Medusa.

"My mother saw that snake come right into this house in a dream," he said. "And in the place by the river where I used to play, she saw an old man with a beard come out from behind a bush. 'Where is my son?' my mother asked in the dream. 'If you have enough money, you may be able to save him,' the old man replied. Then the old man showed that I was chained up there by the river—my leg was chained in the place where it hurt."

Since that time Huintrilaf and his family have spared no expense in paying various *machis* to perform complex ceremonies, all aimed at freeing him from the chains of the many-headed monster. He also went to regular doctors, but found them less effective than the *machis*. For years now he'd been commissioning a full *machitún* ceremony once a year, a procedure that requires an all-night prayer vigil at the full moon, conducted by a *machi*, several assistants, and many participants, all of whom pray, chant, perform an animal sacrifice, and finally shout at the prostrate patient to get up and walk. Many do get up and walk, proof of the power of positive suggestion. Unfortunately, the benefits are sometimes short-lived. Huintrilaf claimed the *machitún* made his leg feel better for a year or two, after which he paid for another ceremony.

"My father was feeling fine," one of his daughters said, "but then he saw a red snake, and immediately the wound got worse."

"The problem is that one *machi* betrayed my husband," María Alcavil said. "We paid for a *machitún* with a couple of sheep, one of which was sacrificed at the ritual. My husband thought everything went well, but that night I dreamed that a small woman covered with jewels came to speak with me. 'That *machi* has cooked the meat from the sacrificed animal and given it to her dogs,' the woman with jewels told me. 'For that reason I'm going to punish her.' "

According to the tradition of the *machitún*, the bones and meat of the sacrificed animal have to be thrown by the *machi* as an offering to the water source where the Chunufilu dwells—in this case the river by which José Huintrilaf believes the water spirit chained his leg. By feeding the bones and meat to her dogs, the *machi* committed a grave sacrilege. As a result, the serpent's hunger wasn't satisfied, so it kept gnawing away at Huintrilaf's leg and appearing in his dreams.

Lorenzo called me aside and said, "This is an incredible medical history—a man who's been suffering from a snake nightmare for over sixty years."

"Do you think Machi Juana could help this man?" I asked.

We told José Huintrilaf about Machi Juana, whom we described as a great healer—one who would never stoop to feeding the animal sacrifices to her dogs. He immediately brightened up and asked if he could go see her.

"We'll have to consult with the *machi*," Lorenzo said. "And with the *machi*'s partner, Felipe Painén."

Felipe was doubtful. "That Chinufilu is a very bad snake," he said. "And this man has been sick a long time. To treat that illness, you have to get a *machi* who knows the snake. There are some *machis* who have studied with that snake, and some who haven't. To really heal him, it must be a *machi* who knows the snake's trail from the beginning and can follow it all the way to the end."

Machi Juana said she knew this snake, Chinufilu. This in itself was important, because it suggested that Machi Juana's "spirit" was a snake entity, something I'd suspected anyway because of Cerro Mesa's connection with the great serpents Tren Tren and Cai Cai Filu. Trying to find out the exact name of a *machi*'s familiar spirit is a source of huge interest to the Mapuches. *Machis* never reveal that information.

Machi Juana now asked to see a urine sample from José Huintrilaf, to determine how serious the case was. When I brought the urine sample, she held the yellow bottle against the sun. "There's pus in his leg," she said immediately. "He has a bad wound which is full of pus. He still has life force, but there is putrefaction, too.

This will require a lot of effort. And I'll have to see him personally before deciding if we can do it."

When we were alone, Lorenzo commented admiringly, "How well the *machi* knows her profession. She didn't hesitate or give some vague answer. She said he has a wound which is infected with pus. We didn't see any wound or any pus, so if that turns out to be true it will be good proof that there is a science in her urine analysis."

We returned to Boroa and set a date for the visit with Machi Juana. I said I would pay the expenses of the visit and whatever additional costs a *machitún* would entail—provided everyone agreed to proceed. I naturally assumed we would perform a *machitún* because Huintrilaf was hopeful and his family enthusiastic at the prospect.

But when I went with Felipe Painén and Lorenzo Aillapán to pick up Machi Juana at 7:00 A.M. on the appointed day, she was in a very curt mood.

"How did you sleep?" Felipe asked her.

"Bad," she said. "But we have to keep our word. Let's go."

When Lorenzo asked Machi Juana what was bothering her, she said, "The Evangelicals are mixed up in this."

"No," Lorenzo said. "This woman has been a legitimate Mapuche ritual expert since she was a child. She's a *thungulmachín* [a shaman's assistant]. And her husband, the sick man, only goes to *machis*, not medical doctors."

"The Evangelicals are trying to stop me from treating him," Machi Juana said firmly. She set her face resolutely, looking almost majestic with her earrings, her pectoral decorations, and her black-and-green blanket, which she wore as a cape.

In spite of Machi Juana's imposing pronouncement, I almost laughed at her paranoid fear of the Evangelicals. This was one case, at least, of projecting an Evangelical under every sickbed.

We arrived in Boroa about 9:30 A.M., and found everyone there in a bad mood, too. "We don't have enough strength to do a *ma-*

chitún right now," María Alcavil said shortly. It was really an amazingly direct, rude way to handle a meeting with a *machi*. But at least we knew where she stood.

Nevertheless, Machi Juana had brought an herbal remedy for external application to José Huintrilaf's leg. He sat in the sun, took off his shoe and sock, and showed Machi Juana a very nasty pus-filled open wound on his right leg. I hadn't seen this before, but it coincided with Machi Juana's diagnosis. The man's whole leg was disfigured—emaciated in some places, swollen in others. It was a real mess. I hadn't told Machi Juana anything about the man's physical condition, as a way of testing her diagnostic ability. I had just recounted his episode with the snake, and his suffering from a pain in his leg, in a general way.

First Machi Juana held the man's leg with her left hand and gently massaged it with her right. Then she applied the herbal remedy she'd brought. When I asked her what herbs were in the preparation, she answered with a smile, "Oh, any old plants. You know me, I'm just a poor, ignorant woman. I pluck any old weeds growing on the mountain and use them in my medicines."

Her diagnosing the man's infection from his urine also convinced me that she was no charlatan. A number of doctors who've gotten acquainted with *machis* share this respect for their techniques, although no one has found a way to codify them in a way intelligible to Westerners.

Of course, Machi Juana's fear of the Evangelicals was pretty silly. But she'd been right about the presence of discord in the air, and her prognosis that things weren't going to work out proved accurate, much to my surprise and in spite of my careful planning.

As we left the *ruca*, José Huintrilaf thanked Machi Juana, and told her that the herbal massage had already made him feel better. Perhaps this was only a formality, or a fleeting benefit born of simple suggestion. Then María Alcavil asked to be taken to the house of a close friend of hers who was very sick.

"She's my *comadre*," Alcavil said, referring to the artificial kinship created between the mother and godmother of a child, a common way of extending the family in Latin countries. In this case, the *comadre* in question was the godmother of one of Alcavil's children, meaning that at least one of her children had been baptized, which was a bit unexpected.

When we reached the *comadre*'s house—a house of cut and painted wood, which indicated a superior economic status—Lorenzo and I accompanied Maria Alcavil inside. She also invited Machi Juana, but Machi Juana refused.

"Evangelicals," Machi Juana said.

I couldn't see any sign of these people's being Evangelicals, and I thought Machi Juana was fixated on her favorite enemies. But when we entered the crowded sickroom, the Bible, crucifix, and prayers made it clear we were in a *very* Christian home. The *comadre* was, in fact, an Evangelical. And one of the first things she asked María Alcavil, in a disapproving tone, was whether "that *machi*" had come to treat her husband after all.

"No, no, we're not going to do the *machitún* after all," María Alcavil quickly responded in a defensive way. "She just gave him some herbal remedies."

Lorenzo learned that the *comadre* was a kind of patroness of María Alcavil, and that her opinion, perhaps because of her superior economic and social status, carried quite a bit of weight.

"I think that the Evangelicals were opposing Machi Juana after all," Lorenzo said. "She was right again."

At Felipe's request, we went to the city of Temuco, where he and Lorenzo had business. I dropped off Felipe and Lorenzo, which left me alone with Machi Juana. I parked my jeep at the Triple AAA garage, and asked Machi Juana if she'd like to go see a movie.

"No, movies are pure nonsense," she answered. "That kind of stuff makes you sick."

She agreed to eat lunch with me.

We started walking toward a restaurant about a block away,

but I quickly saw that we weren't going to make it that far. Machi Juana stumbled on in a daze. She bumped into telephone poles twice.

Fortunately, the Triple AAA is right next door to the Frontera Hotel, the nicest place to eat and sleep in Temuco. I helped Machi Juana through the hotel's glass doors, into the red-carpeted lobby, and down a flight of stairs to the dining room. At the landing halfway down the stairs was a big mirror that completely covered the wall. I barely paid any attention to it, but Machi Juana walked straight into it before I could stop her.

I watched her pull up, stand back, and look closely at her own reflection, which stared right back at her. She pawed her reflected face, grunted in disbelief, and tried to step down a reflected stair. Her foot slipped off the glass again and again, to her increasing confusion. She also saw my reflection in the mirror, and tried talking to it. She kept struggling with her illusory self in the mirror, while I stood there too amazed to say anything.

I redirected Machi Juana down the stairs and to a table. Three waiters immediately came up to take our order—soup for Machi Juana, an omelette for me. But long after our orders had arrived, the waiters kept hovering around, whispering to themselves. Finally, the headwaiter came over to our table.

"You know, this is the first time in all our years at this hotel that we've seen a Mapuche Indian come in here as a customer," he said. "I just want to tell you that we're so happy you're taking this dear grandmother out to lunch. It's the most beautiful thing we've seen."

One of the waiters had gotten his camera, and wanted to take a picture of Machi Juana. She looked as out of place as E.T. in the comfortable hotel setting, where soft yellow lights and piano music cascaded around us. Machi Juana appeared as innocent and inoffensive as a "dear grandmother."

"Would you dance with me, Grandmother?" one of the waiters asked, thinking perhaps that this was a gallant gesture on his part.

Machi Juana looked up quickly.

"No," she said, "you're much too ugly. And, besides, you're not the one who's taking me out to lunch."

The other waiters burst into hysterics. The "dear grand-mother" had let herself be cooed and oohed over without objection. But when the young waiter moved in for what he thought was the grand gesture, she delivered a deadpan sucker punch to the male ego.

I asked the headwaiter if Machi Juana and I could go to a conference room for a private talk. The management quickly let us have a room on the second floor, where I laboriously conducted Machi Juana. After we sat down in a couple of armchairs, I started asking a few questions about mountain worship and the sea god Manquián. Then I asked her how old she was.

"I have no idea how old I am," she said. "Today, when a baby is born, they tell it immediately how old it is. But when I was a baby, they didn't tell us. I must be more than eighty years old. I'm very old, so old I can remember the steamships that used to come along the coast."

"I understand that you really became a *machi* when you were already grown up and had children," I said.

"I had to do it like that, because my father wouldn't let me be a *machi* when I was little," she answered. "Later my husband wouldn't, either. The old people were like that."

"Wasn't Isabela Queopán the *machi* who taught you to be a *machi?*" I asked, basing the question on Rosario Opazo's account.

"Isabela Queopán cured me when I was sick," Machi Juana said. "I was already married and with children when they told me that my poor brother was murdered on the beach. When they told me that my brother was murdered, I got sick, and every day I got thinner. So I paid Isabela Queopán a cow to cure me. But she never taught me anything. I taught myself.

"The Mapuches are a very envious, slanderous people," she continued. "They're always lying about other people. They say that the house you built me is for yourself, not for me. They make up all kinds of stories. They say that you needed a house, so you built one on my property. In the same way, they are always telling stories about me."

"There's one story that I'm very interested in," I said, seizing the opening. "I've heard that at the sacrifice of the boy at Cerro Mesa there were two naked men who danced with spears, who were called 'black sheep.' Where did that custom come from?"

"That's a big lie," she said. "There wasn't any time after the earthquake to go and get naked dancers. And there wasn't any sacrifice of any little boy, either. That boy disappeared collecting firewood."

"Lots of people have told me about the men who came out and danced with spears on Cerro Mesa," I countered.

"People lied about me the same way they lie about you," she said. "The people say you're a communist, or a spider merchant. They say I sacrificed that boy at Cerro Mesa. The Mapuches are a dirty, lying people, always full of envy."

Here Machi Juana bewailed her bad luck among the Mapuches, reciting a litany of complaints that included all the attacks and accusations against her as though they'd happened yesterday. "And because of those accusations of sacrificing that boy, I was taken by the police to jail."

Machi Juana started crying as she recalled her experiences in jail. "They hung me upside down for days," she said. "They tied me up from my ankles and hung me upside down like a pig, to make me confess."

She burst into tears again and spoke in a plaintive, pleading voice. "The people all hate me. 'She's the killer of grandchildren,' they say to me. The Mapuches are such an envious, hard, and lying group of people."

When I remember what happened next, I am still ashamed of the way I acted. But I must confess that I wasn't moved by Machi Juana's words or tears. I just thought to myself, "Well, she's giving me the old tape-recorded announcement about Cerro Mesa, so we're back to square one. I guess this must be a signal for a bribe before she'll say anything more."

But then I reached into my wallet and found that I only had $150 in cash, part of which I needed to pay for the return trip to Santiago. "Maybe I can afford to offer her a hundred dollars," I thought. "If she was once willing to talk for twenty-five, when her family stopped her, she might give me the remaining details for a hundred now."

The only problem was that I couldn't change a hundred dollars into Chilean pesos for a very good exchange rate at the Hotel Frontera, so I had to figure out a way to run to a jeweler's about two blocks away, while keeping Machi Juana busy.

"All right," I finally said out loud. "Look. Why don't you just have some tea? I'll send up a waiter with tea and some snacks, and I'll go see what's keeping Lorenzo and Felipe. Don't go anywhere, all right?"

So I ran out, leaving instructions for Machi Juana's tea, and asking the waiters to keep an eye on her. "Make sure she doesn't wander off," I told them. Then I dashed to the jeweler's, changed a hundred dollars at the more favorable rate I wanted, and dashed back to the Hotel Frontera conference room, where I rushed in breathless.

"Machi Juana . . ." I started to say. . . . But Machi Juana was sound asleep, curled up on her side, her black-and-green blanket covering her huddled body. She looked so peaceful there, and her peace contrasted so much with my breathlessly frantic entry, that I was shocked into something like a realization. It suddenly hit me how horribly I was acting, mercilessly isolating, pressuring, and bribing this poor old woman. In her song at the *rucán* ceremony she'd said I was "like a son of God," so good and kind in building her a house. But I didn't care about her, only about the human-sacrifice story.

I put away my wallet, filled with the proceeds from the most favorable exchange rate in town, and watched her for a few minutes in silence. I feel that if my spirit ever spoke to me about Machi Juana, it spoke to me then. Because, as I looked at her, huddled in the fetal position, wrapped in her Andean blanket, wearing her pectoral decorations and jewelry, with that utterly peaceful expression on her face . . . I thought I was looking at the Inca child of Mount Plomo.

◪ 11 ◫

LAKE TITICACA

Colonel Sabino Rodríguez, the chief authority for the Investigating Police of Peru (PIP) in the large department of Puno, Peru, wouldn't have been pleased to see me even if he'd been completely sober, which he was not. But he might have been friendlier if I'd been investigating a more routine murder.

"Human sacrifice?" the colonel said angrily. "We aren't savages around here, you know. We're living in the twentieth century, too."

I read the colonel the March 3, 1986, report from the newspaper *La República:*

PEASANT SACRIFICED IN PUNO

As a final recourse to calm nature's wrath, which has caused the extraordinary rise of the waters of Lake Titicaca, the loss of tens of thousands of acres of cultivated lands, and close to 200,000 homeless, members of an ancient peasant community in the province of Azangaro cut the father of a family into four pieces, as a sign of "sacrifice." His remains were buried in the four cardinal directions.

For this effect, the members of the community revived old magico-religious rites of their ancestors and chose as a gift offering, not an animal, but community member Clemente Limachi Sihuayro, whose remains were spread in the four cardinal directions.

Close to a hundred peasants, all of them Aymara Indians, participated in this "human sacrifice." All of them, once they'd completed their labor of killing and cutting up the body of the victim, offered the blood of Limachi Sihuayro to the Sun God.

The charge concerning this macabre act was presented by one of the nine sons of community member Clemente Limachi Sihuayro (37 years old), to the PIP (Investigating Police of Peru) of Azangaro. . . .[1]

"No one named Clemente Limachi Sihuayro was killed," the colonel replied. "And no one was sacrificed in Azangaro. You think I just sit around here letting people do human sacrifices? Where are the authorities while all of these massacres are going on? Ask the people if they've done a human sacrifice. Try to find this Clemente Limachi Sihuayro."

The colonel laughed in a way that seemed to say, "No one in his right mind would be stupid enough to go and ask the peasants if they've done a human sacrifice."

Lake Titicaca was the cradle of Andean civilization. The Inca child frozen atop Mount Plomo possibly came from the vicinity of Titicaca as well. What made the newspaper report even more tantalizing was the description of the victim's being chopped into four pieces in an effort to stem the rising floodwaters—the same motive and the same method as for José Luis Painecur's sacrifice on Cerro Mesa. Other details sounded odd. If the Aymara Indians really offered Limachi's blood to the Sun God, it might illuminate the issue of solar worship in Andean religion. Recent scholarship has discounted the role of sun worship as a superficial Inca imposition that died out after the Spanish conquest. But the survival of a solar-dominated human-sacrifice ritual at Lake Titicaca would challenge that view. For all these reasons, I had to find out what happened to Clemente Limachi Sihuayro.

Joao Ecsodi, the U.S. Embassy's press attaché in Lima, was not encouraging when he heard my plan. "Frankly, I don't recommend it at all," he said. "The Shining Path guerrillas have been infiltrating Puno, and their next offensive may be in the Puno area. You see murders and explosions everywhere now. I would say going to remote villages there to do research on human sacrifice is one of the worst ideas you could have. The law of the mountain prevails out there. You don't know how people will react to you."

The Shining Path (Sendero Luminoso) terrorists have several thousand members in the highlands, and they follow a political program that mixes Maoism with Andean mysticism. Although Sendero calls their hybrid ideology Inca socialism, their program sounds more like that of Pol Pot's Khmer Rouge: they want to destroy all advanced technology, return to subsistence agriculture, expel all foreigners . . . and live happily ever after. Peasants who disagree with Sendero get shot in their "take-no-prisoners" approach to warfare. Since 1980 ten thousand people have been killed in an escalating spiral of atrocities, committed by both government forces and leftists. This is South America's bloodiest guerrilla conflict.

The police and army have fared poorly against Sendero Luminoso, a situation that has spawned peasant paramilitary groups to protect villages from Sendero attacks. These paramilitary groups add to the general confusion. "Eight journalists were apparently killed by peasant paramilitary," U.S. Vice-Consul Jeff Levine told me, pointing to a story in the newspapers about the ongoing trial of the accused peasants. By some accounts, the Indian peasants mistook the journalists for Sendero guerrillas, and shot them on sight.

"The highlands are not a safe place for journalists," Levine warned me. "The Indians have little idea of what a journalist is or what he does. They may just think you're some kind of spy. Or a revolutionary. Or a drug dealer. And none of those are particularly welcome."

At the Civil Guard Station, I met with the sergeant in charge of public information. (In Peru's complex military estalishment, the PIP is supposed to function like the American FBI, while the Civil Guard is closer to the local police force.)

"Yeah, I remember that sacrifice of Clemente Limachi," the sergeant said. However, as he pulled out archive after archive, he just couldn't locate it. "Seems to be lost," he concluded. "But if I remember correctly, this guy wasn't sacrificed in Azangaro, as the newspaper says. He was killed over by Yunguyo, near the Bolivian border.

"You know, we have quite a few human sacrifices around here," the sergeant said, matter-of-factly. "We hear about them all the time from the mines. North of here, in Madre de Dios, they just tried to sacrifice a fifteen-year-old girl. She escaped from the mine and, fortunately, we had an alert out for her in the area, because we figured she was going to be sacrificed. The mine owners like fifteen- and sixteen-year-old virgin girls for their ceremonies. Plenty of *muchachas* disappear in the mines."[2]

Later that day I met Roberto Zegarra, a university professor and a mine owner, who told me that the custom of offering virgins in the mines goes back to the Incas, who made similar sacrifices at their own mines at Tambillo, Patambuco, and other gold-producing sites. The connection between blood sacrifice and mineral wealth intrigued me, especially since some high-altitude sanctuaries, like Mount Veladero, are near Inca mines. It seemed remarkable that the Andean sacrificial ideology has been adapted to high-tech mining operations.

On September 7, Francisco Paca, a respected journalist for *La República*, and I left for Yunguyo in a white Toyota van with a dented front, which I rented from the Hotel Don Miguel. Paca is well informed about local folklore, and speaks Aymara, the language of the people in southern Puno Province, where we were traveling.

As we pulled out from the hotel, I noticed an odd thing: the building's metal girders were exposed, and loose plaster lay all around. Our driver, who worked for the hotel, explained that the building had been rocked by a terrorist attack on July 5, 1986. "A couple came in to ask for a room," he said. "While the attendant was distracted, three masked men ran in, tied up the night man, and placed two bombs about two meters away from him. The attendant managed to loosen his bonds, and he crawled behind the desk, where he set off an alarm with his chest. That brought the owner and his daughter, who threw the bombs out into the street, where they exploded, blowing out all the windows of the hotel, breaking up the walls, furniture, doors, everything."

"There are probably no more than two hundred Senderistas in this region," Francisco Paca said. "They function Robin Hood–style to get popular support. Recently, they stopped a bus and forced everyone out. Then they killed all members of the government Aprista Party, whom they recognized by their ID cards, and forced everyone else to participate in an attack on a rich cooperative farm, La Cooperativa San José. They murdered four leaders of the San José Cooperative and gave away all the tools, animals, butter, and everything else. Naturally, many people were happy for a little while.

"But the Senderistas disappeared, of course. And then the army retaliated both against those who'd been forced to attack the cooperative and against those who received the stolen goods. Supposedly, the armed forces just came into the village and drove all two thousand residents out like a herd of animals, with machine-gun fire. No one knows what happened for sure, because the press still hasn't been allowed in there. So you can see why, although the people hate Sendero, they sometimes hate the police and army even more." For this reason, Paca says his brother, the mayor of Puno, opposed the use of army combat units in the province, even though Sendero now has "liberated zones" which are outside government control.

Sendero Luminoso is not the only armed force in Puno outside government control. We were passing through a prime smuggling area, where huge international deals are cut for the cocaine trade. Paca pointed out the peninsula of Cachipucara, an isolated and heavily armed center of coca production along Lake Titicaca, where President García Mesa of Bolivia supposedly came by helicopter in 1978–79 to meet with Peruvian narcotraffickers. "García Mesa was so involved in the cocaine trade that he used to receive the head of Peru's cocaine mafia, a man nicknamed 'The Joker,' at the Presidential Palace in La Paz, Bolivia, with the full honors accorded to a head of state," Paca claimed. The coca crop has become the best business of the highlands, the logical choice of farmers in a decade of falling agricultural prices. The pervasive coca trade represents a perverse triumph of the free market against government regulation. Coca is particularly important because the flood of February 1986 destroyed the best farmlands for potatoes, peas, and grains.

"Getting worse every day in every way" seemed to be the motto up here, between guerrilla and government atrocities, peasant paramilitary counterattacks, and drug mafias. But this pessimism is not shared by the peasantry, many of whom feel that life is getting better. Today they have bicycles and radios. Tomorrow they hope to buy cars and televisions. Those who smuggle already have cars and televisions. After centuries of stagnation and serfdom, the black market has spawned a revolution of hope in the highlands.

We reached the Ilave River, Lake Titicaca's main tributary, a creek two to three feet deep and fifty feet wide during the dry season. During the winter flood, however, the river rose torrentially, and badly damaged a new steel bridge across it. Nearby was an old stone bridge that went unscathed.

"Everyone knows that a child was sacrificed and buried in each one of the pillars of the old bridge," commented Pablo Paredes, an engineer we'd picked up along the way. "The people think that sacrificing and burying a child inside makes the bridge strong, so the river won't carry it away. When the new bridge was built, the people said they needed those sacrifices of children to sustain it, and when the sacrifices weren't made and the bridge later collapsed, they blamed the absence of child sacrifices for the problem."

I knew of an incident in the 1960s at the Peruvian town of Moya in which police prevented the sacrifice of a child to the local mountain deity, who was angered at the construction of a new road through his territory.[3] Sacrifices of children to promote construction projects, such as the one attempted at Moya or the one rumored for the Ilave River bridge, recalled Tanta Carhua's sacrifice during the building of an irrigation canal in Ocros, over five hundred years ago, as recorded by inquisitor Hernández Príncipe. Of course, Father Hernández Príncipe actually dug up the body of Tanta Carhua, with great effort; there was no chance I could tear down the stone bridge to look for the eleven saints among the stones.

Paca also pointed out a modern white-walled building by the Ilave River, with the sign ISRAEL CONGREGACIÓN DE JEHOVAH (Israel Congregation of Jehovah). This was a sect that literally followed the Old Testament's Mosaic Law—including the sacrifice of sheep on the High Holy Days. They believe that the Promised Land has moved to Peru, an idea expressed in their slogan: *"Israel en el Perú."*

Our ninety-mile ride from Puno ended just a mile short of the Bolivian border, in the town of Yunguyo. We walked into the barracks of the Civil Guard, and waited to meet the commanding officer beneath a giant mural, painted in screaming colors, depicting a heroic Civil Guardsman carrying a beautiful, bloody woman in his arms, past an iron gate into a protected enclosure, while other guards with machine guns stave off the black-and-red chaos of a burning, bomb-ridden city.

"I don't remember anything about Clemente Limachi Sihuayro," Captain Díaz said in response to our questions. "But that was during the flood, wasn't it? Around that time we did find a dead baby in a field about two kilometers [one and a quarter miles] from here, which we thought might be some kind of a sacrifice. But the investigation of any homicides is immediately turned over to PIP."

Although Captain Díaz did his best to help us, we were unable, during the first day, to locate the Civil Guard's initial report on Limachi's murder. Feeling frustrated after a couple hours of searching through notebooks kept in a cardboard box, we looked up Víctor Avendaño, a friend of Paca's and an agricultural engineer who was in charge of a technical station in Yunguyo.

We found him at his Ministry of Agriculture office. "Human sacrifice is the most normal thing in the world for these people," he told us. "Why, Mr. Uriarti, the biggest beer distributor in town, took his wife to Mount Santa Bárbara and gave her to the devil there. And they left her body there on the hill, because they say that her blood has to pay the earth." In this way, Uriarti expected to increase his profits from beer sales.

"People here are accustomed to sacrificing someone when the weather gets bad," Avendaño explained. "It could be during a drought, or a flood, or after hailstorms. I remember in 1983, during the Feast of Santiago of Pocona, they hanged a man. I saw his dead body myself when I went there—the body was inside a circle where they'd offered sweets and incense."

"Yes, but that man was executed because he was a thief," one of Avendaño's assistants interjected.

"But it was still done with a ceremony, and at the conclusion of the solemn festival," Avendaño answered. "In case of a drought or flood, it's assumed that a sin has destroyed the balance of nature. So they look for a person who is responsible. I've heard of instances where all the single women in a village are lined up naked and a village elder comes and feels their breasts to see if they have any milk in them. If milk comes out, he knows there has been sin and that's the reason the weather is bad. So they kill that girl right away."

Avendaño and his assistant started talking excitedly about all the human sacrifices they could remember. It was quite a list, and I had trouble keeping up. What interested me most, however, was Avendaño's personal witnessing of the bodies in two cases—the one of a thief at the Feast of Santiago in 1983, and the other of a woman found on the slopes of Mount Santa Bárbara the year before.

"Mount Santa Bárbara is the preferred place for human sacrifices around here," Avendaño told me. When I asked him if he'd accompany me up to the peak to look around, he shook his head vigorously. "I've never gone up there, because the devil is there," he said. "Right now the Indians are celebrating the Feast of Kasani. And the witches are doing their rituals up on Mount Santa Bárbara. They say the *yatiris* (Aymara word for shamans) kill people who go near on nights when there are rituals."

With the help of Víctor Avendaño, I located Clemente Limachi's uncle, a stocky, sturdy-looking farmer aged about sixty, named Clemente Fargín. Clemente Fargín was surprisingly outgoing. He impressed me with his desire to see justice done to his nephew's murderers, as well as his disinterested offer of help to the deceased's family, which included nine orphans. Fargín kindly agreed to arrange an interview for me with the victim's widow, Leucaria Limachi.

When Clemente Fargín brought a tiny wisp of a woman dressed in black into my Toyota van, I was struck by how pretty she was. But I realized there was something wrong with her. She acted dazed and zombielike.

"She's not well since her husband died," Clemente Fargín said in good Spanish. "Leucaria has to take care of nine orphans by herself, and they don't have food."

Fargín proceeded to explain what they knew about Clemente Limachi's death. "It was Sunday, the last day of the Carnival, and lots of people were dancing," he recalled. Leucaria was selling caramels when two of Clemente's cousins, Fausto Quispi Limachi and Alejandro López, came along to buy sweets and a quart of liquor. They asked Clemente to go dancing with them. So the three of them went off together alone. No one knows where they went, but it was toward Mount Chuchape, on the road to Chinumani.

"Around five A.M. Leucaria came to tell me that Clemente was dead. 'Do you want to come and investigate?' she asked me. We found Clemente's head cut off and placed at the narrow mountain pass up on the hill, at the place called the Apacheta. The body was a few feet away. "This is my husband,' Leucaria told me. 'Here are his clothes.' "

According to Fargín, Clemente Limachi's face had been scalped off, then pushed up above his head, where it hung like a mask. He and Leucaria went to the PIP, which sent two officers to photograph the body and question the suspects. "They beat up Alejandro and Fausto pretty bad," Fargín said of their interrogation technique. "But the murder happened at night. No one knew anything. The police didn't find any weapon around there. And there wasn't any blood, either."

Fargín admitted the whole thing was very mysterious. No, he couldn't imagine why this had happened or who would want to kill his thirty-seven-year-old nephew. "Clemente was a very responsible person," he said. He couldn't account for anyone scalping his nephew's face off, either.

Leucaria Limachi was not playing so dumb, however. When I asked her who had killed her husband and why they did it, she answered quickly in Aymara, "Pagans killed him to pay the earth. The narcotraffickers did it so they could make more money."

"Paying the earth" is the standard expression for blood sacrifices to Pacha Mama (the Earth Mother) and the mountain gods. I'd already learned that human-sacrifice ideology could adapt itself to modern mining technology, bridge building, and beer distribution. Now it seemed that the international cocaine trade was also claiming its quota of martyrs to ensure production.

I was struck by several details of Clemente Fargín's account.

First, he and Leucaria both said that the victim had been decapitated—not quartered, as the newspaper fancifully reported. Nor did the ritual appear related to the Sun God.

Fargín also said that the body of Clemente Limachi turned up at a mountain pass—a place he called the Apacheta. I knew that Apacheta means both "Mountain Pass" and "Mound of Stones." Andean believers often build stone mounds at mountain passes, and the two have become closely linked. At Mount Pilar, by the Laguna Brava, Antonio Beorchia, Mario Muñoz, and I found a stone mound at a pass just below the peak—a peak that had firewood and a simple Inca altar. Other *apachetas* have yielded more impressive finds. In fact, several of the largest Inca statues yet discovered were buried at mountain passes near Cuzco. Anthropologist Thomas Zuidema at the Smithsonian Gallery in Washington once told me that, in Andean religion, "The entire horizon was critically important, not just mountain peaks. *Apachetas,* mountain passes where you see your home village for the last time on a journey, were particularly revered. People still make offerings at these *apachetas* today, to ensure safe travel from the gods."

When I examined the *apacheta* where Clemente Limachi's body and decapitated head were deposited, I found that it was the highest point on the road between the town of Yunguyo and the community of Chinumani.

"We found the body inside this narrow stone canal," Fargín told me, as he pointed to the exact spot. The "stone canal" was a natural formation, but it was curiously smooth and stood out, with its white color, among the dark rocks at the pass. I noticed that we were on a narrow isthmus, with Lake Titicaca's waters on both sides of us. The small hilltop to our right was called Mount Chuchape; to our left was Mount Santa Bárbara, the most prominent hill within an area of a few miles.

"I hear there was a woman sacrificed at this same mountain pass in 1982," I remarked to Fargín.

"I don't know much about that, but some people say that's true," he answered. "I'm a Christian myself."

"Isn't this Mount Chuchape, where you said Clemente Limachi's cousins invited him to dance?"

"People were dancing all over the place," he said defensively. "It wasn't just one place."

"Well, do you think we might find an altar with offerings to the mountain gods on top of that hill?"

"No," Fargín said. "There's nothing up there but rocks."

I'd been clued in that old Fargín was really a shaman himself, and knew all about the mountain gods. His statement that there was nothing but rocks on the mountain was about as believable as his protestations of being a Christian.

High-altitude archaeology also gave me an advantage. I could see that the ceremonial importance of the *apacheta,* where at least two bodies had popped up in the last three years, was related to the lake and hilltops on either side of it. In Andean worship, a mountain can be tremendously important if it's located next to a large body of water—like Cerro Mesa, between the ocean and Lago Budi, or the hills where we'd found ceremonial remains by the Laguna Brava.

I also noticed that a well-worn path coming down from Mount Santa Bárbara ended just a few feet from where Limachi's head and torso were tossed. Since Mount Santa Bárbara was much higher than Chuchape, and since locals had already identified it as the preferred place for human sacrifices, I naturally wanted to follow that path.

"Do you think we might find an altar up on Mount Santa Bárbara?" I asked Fargín.

"I don't think so," he answered. "I've never been up there myself."

"I know we'll find something up here," I said. "What worries me is that we might also run into some *yatiris* and their assistants, since it's the last day of the festival. And they might be angry to see us intruding on their rituals."

Fargín considered this silently for a moment. "No," he said finally. "They were busy last night, and they'll be coming up again at sunset. But now, at one in the afternoon, we shouldn't have any problems. I'll go with you."

Andean peoples love Saint Barbara because she was a virgin who was tortured and beheaded by her pagan father—a death that made her the appropriate patroness for this mountain. According to tradition, Saint Barbara's father was killed by a lightning bolt as a divine punishment, thus making Saint Barbara the patroness of thunderstorms—a principal attribute of Andean mountain gods. In Yunguyo alone there are two mountains named for Saint Barbara.

The peak proved to be the best high-altitude sanctuary I'd ever seen. There were hundreds of little stone circles and mounds all over the peak, which was maybe a half-acre in area. Incense wafted upward from dozens of little containers, proof that the shamans had indeed been busy the night before. Ubiquitous crucifixes, champagne bottles and piles of half-burnt offerings testified to a major ceremonial center. We could see Lake Titicaca on both sides, and Fargín said that on a clear day you could see Mount Illimani (21,201 feet) in the distance. According to Johan Reinhard, Illimani was the chief weather god of the Tiahuanaco civilization. Thus, Mount Santa Bárbara was connected to Lake Titicaca on two sides and the great Illimani in the distance, just as Cerro Mesa at Lago Budi was connected to Volcán Llaima and the ocean.

Ironically, the biggest crucifix of all was planted in concrete in the middle of the peak by a Catholic priest. "That was put here by the priest when he said Mass up here to drive away the devil," Fargín commented. But the "pagans," as Fargín called them, simply incorporated the crucifix into their mountain rituals—as the dozens of incense burners in front of the cross proved.

"You know an awful lot about what's happened on this mountain, and what you can see on clear days, for someone who's never been here before," I said.

"I only came for the Mass," Fargín answered. Then he quickly changed the subject. "This is what the police should have done when we showed them Clemente's body. If they had come up here, they would have found evidence—blood, and other things, to prove that the pagans had done it."

"What's the name the pagans have for this mountain?"

"They call it Incahuási," Fargín said. *Incahuási* means "the house of the Incas."

If Clemente Limachi had been killed on the mountaintop and dragged down the well-worn path to the *apacheta*, this would explain why there was no blood and no weapon near the *apacheta*, what the body was doing so far outside the town, and how the body got there. After all, it was much more sensible to take a body downhill than to drag it uphill from the nearest houses in either Chinumani or Yunguyo.

But Limachi's death still concealed a surprise.

Víctor Avendaño had located a man in Yunguyo whose grandson had disappeared. From what I could gather in talking to him, this man suspected his grandson might have been sacrificed, and in the course of searching for him had learned about a pattern behind such disappearances.

"What happens is that, two or three times a year, at the main festivals, there has to be a human sacrifice," he said. "At that time the chief *yatiri* talks to the devil, and the devil tells him, 'I want you to sacrifice your son.' So he has to sacrifice his son, no matter what age his son is, or some other relative. The devil tells him [the *yatiri*], 'Get this one over here [the son or relative].' And so he does it. That's what happened to Clemente Limachi. You see, his father is the biggest *yatiri* around Chinumani. He's always talking to the devil."

It seemed that Mr. Limachi, Sr., like Abraham, had also taken his son to the mountain.

But how did this accusation mesh with Leucaria Limachi's equally enigmatic testimony that her husband had been sacrificed by cocaine dealers in a blood ritual to increase the narcotraffickers' wealth? The two versions were obviously contradictory.

Unless Clemente's father was a cocaine dealer as well as a shaman.

Or unless "the devil" Mr. Limachi communed with was a cocaine dealer.

▣ 12 ▣

THE SNAKE MOUNTAIN

News reports of more bombings in Puno discouraged me from continuing my investigation in 1986. But then a lull set in; the Shining Path guerrillas apparently moved north, having failed to recruit peasants in the well-organized Aymara communities of southern Peru. By early 1988 I felt secure enough to go back.

I decided to live across the border from Yunguyo, Peru, in the peaceful resort of Copacabana, Bolivia. The Copacabana Peninsula begins in the swampy lowlands near Yunguyo, then rises into the rocky mountains that break into Titicaca's waters in a series of sharp descents. The drama is reminiscent of the Spanish Costa Brava, except that these Andean cliffs are carefully terraced, a seemingly miraculous feat that epitomizes the Incas' most distinctive agricultural achievement.

When the Spaniards conquered Copacabana, they found that one of the local idols was a blue rock, carved with the face of a man and the body of a fish, worshipped on a height overlooking the lake. *Copacabana* (or *copacauana*) apparently means "the place where you see the blue rock."[1] Blue is definitely the color of choice here, with the lake and sky both painfully bright in the clear air of the high mountains. A blue rock is an apt artistic embodiment for the meeting of mountains, water, and heaven in Copacabana.

Today Copacabana is what it has been for thousands of years— a place of pan-Andean pilgrimage. Five thousand visitors a week come here from Bolivia, Peru, and other countries, ostensibly to pray at the Basilica of Our Lady of Copacabana. Yet the real climax of these pilgrim visits, and the object of countless vows, is reaching the peak of Mount Calvary, a red-rocked hill at Lake Titicaca's edge. Converging streams of penitents reach the bottom of the hill, where the First Station of the Cross on the Via Dolorosa begins the three-hundred-foot ascent. For most people, the Via Dolorosa takes on literal meaning here. I climbed Mount Calvary, huffing and puffing along with hundreds of other pilgrims, all of us struggling with the thin air of the altiplano. At 12,500 feet even a short climb like this is a painful experience. Each station of the cross, where huge cement statues mark the stages of Jesus' agony, serves as another resting point. Those who climb on bloodied knees, to fulfill particularly demanding vows, arouse general admiration and consternation.

The peak of Mount Calvary offers both a sweeping view of Lake Titicaca and a summary of Andean sacred history. The Copacabana Peninsula divides Lake Titicaca in two—the northwestern part being called "the big lake" and the southeastern part "the small lake." Andean peoples consider Lake Titicaca the birthplace of the sun and the source of all highland waters through a supposed underground connection to the ocean. Even before the Incas expanded to this area in the fifteenth century, the Colla culture of Titicaca identified their chief deity with a feline-shaped rock located on an island just off the coast of Copacabana. They called this rock Titicaca (*titi* is "cat," *caca* is "large stone"), the same name given to the island and the lake as a whole. Franciscan scholar Julio María Elías says that, long before the Incas arrived in Copacabana, the sacred rock of Titicaca "was frequently sprinkled with the blood of llamas and persons, especially children." For the Collas "the sacrifices of animals and persons . . . constituted the most important manifestation of their religiosity."[2]

The Incas adapted Copacabana and its islands to their own solar cult, making the area one of the three most important places of pilgrimage in the entire empire. Inca conqueror Tupac Yupanqui went to great expense to inculcate the worship of the sun and moon in Copacabana, especially at the ancient sanctuary at the Island of Titicaca. Here Tupac Yupanqui pursued a clever policy—he kept in place the worship to the feline god, while at the same time laminating the concave, cat-shaped rock with gold sheets, making it a refulgent mirror of the Sun God, from whom the Incas claimed descent. Thus the Island of Titicaca became the Island of the Sun. The Incas extravagantly imported earth to terrace the island's rugged, barren hills into gardens, whose produce was then sent to monasteries around the empire as a sacred food. This is one of the clearest examples we have of Inca solarization, the co-opting of ancient traditions in the name of the new state cult.

The Incas also rebuilt their own creation myth around the renamed Island of the Sun. Whereas their original creation story described the Incas emerging from the creator god Viracocha at Tiahuanaco, the new variation said that Manco Capac and Mama Ocllo, the Incas' Adam and Eve, were born on the Island of the Sun. At the birth of a royal prince, the Inca sent a messenger who climbed a stone staircase up to the terraced gardens of the Island of the Sun, where, in a fountain of pure water, the messenger filled a golden goblet that he then took to the Inca ruler in Cuzco.

The Incas built a shrine to the moon on another nearby island. Vestal virgins lived on this Island of the Moon, where they wove, fasted, and prayed under a strict monastic discipline. Some of them were honored by being sacrificed on the Island of the Sun, in a ritual that combined both the old Colla customs and the new imperial cult:

> The immolation of the virgins followed a special ritual. A number of months before the feast in which they would be sacrificed, they were moved from the retreat of Titicaca to an enclosure called Tahuacouyo, located in Copacabana

at the foot of [Mount] Calvary. . . . Here they were celebrated with banquets that lasted until three months prior to
the sacrifice. From that moment onward they had to abstain
from salt, pepper, and meat, and eat modestly. When the
feast arrived, they were carried on richly adorned rafts to the
sacred rock. Before their throats were cut, the virgins were
intoxicated until they lost consciousness. As the blood flowed
from these virginal offerings, the sacred ministers collected
it in order to spread it upon the Rock of the Cat and to smear
it on their own faces. The victimized body of the chosen of
the sun, forever the bride of Inti, was buried with signs of
reverence and veneration between curious blankets. . . .[3]

Although no memorial stands for the virgins who were killed
here, the feminine presence predominates at Copacabana. The Virgin of Copacabana is the Andean goddess of abundance, not easily
recognizable to a Western Roman Catholic, but almost indistin-
guishable from the ancient Andean Pacha Mama.

At the peak of Mount Calvary, around a golden statue of the
Virgin Mary, there's a virtual supermarket of plastic objects—cars,
trucks, motorcycles, all-terrain vehicles, three- and four-story
houses, TV sets, stereos, passports, university diplomas, large
stacks of phony money—all waiting to be blessed by La Mamita,
the Little Mother, as the Virgin of Copacabana is affectionately
called. I asked a woman what all this non-religious-looking paraphernalia was supposed to accomplish.

"We believe that whatever you want in the coming year you
have to first obtain in miniature form," she said, holding up a three-
story plastic house and a Ford truck. "If you choose a house or car
here, you'll acquire the real thing in the upcoming year, provided
you get it blessed by the Virgin."

Copacabana is a strange tribute to both the triumph of native
beliefs over foreign impositions, and the triumph of twentieth-
century mass production over everyone. In his book *El enigma de
los santuarios indigénas de alta montaña*, Antonio Beorchia describes
the Incas' mountain altars as "external signs of the Indian's mystical

search."[4] But here on Mount Calvary, amid the hundreds of pilgrims searching for TVs, household appliances, and other goodies, there was no sign of anything but externals. Almost all the elements of Inca worship could be seen—stone circles and rectangles dotted the landscape like miniature sanctuaries, where shamans burned offerings with the help of firewood and alcohol—but the name of the game was getting a house or a car. There was not a mystical sign on the vast horizon, nor was there any "enigma" to these high-altitude rituals. Janis Joplin's chorus, "Oh, Lord, Won't You Buy Me a Mercedes Benz" was no joke on Mount Calvary.

But Mount Calvary does hold a pivotal position between the Andean present and the remote past. The great pre-Inca religious center of Tiahuanaco is forty miles across the lake from Mount Calvary. This Tiahuanaco civilization dominated a thousand-year epoch of Andean culture (A.D. 100–1100), when much of southern Peru, Bolivia, and northern Chile came under its sway.

There is a simplicity and austerity about Tiahuanaco's monumental temples, temples masterfully built with stones of staggering size, some weighing several tons, quarried and carried from distant mountains, then assembled on this barren plateau 13,000 feet above sea level. There's a shock intended, like the one you feel at Stonehenge. The rectangular stone precincts at Tiahuanaco are masterpieces of geometric purity embedded with mystery. One remarkable feature of Tiahuanaco's Semisubterranean Temple is the presence of several hundred stone heads, without bodies, jutting out of the red-and-white stone walls. In the center of the Semisubterranean Temple there's a monolith of a god whose most prominent feature is a snake slithering up his side. The stones are perfectly cut. The walls around the precinct are perfectly regular, all rectangular. The place is a Cubist dream. Yet the embedded heads, some delicately sculptured, awkwardly intrude on the abstract elegance of the design, silently asking questions that no one has been able to answer.

One challenge for research on human sacrifice in this key area of the Andes was the hope of breaking the silence. Could there be a connection between the stone heads of Tiahuanaco and Clemente Limachi's gruesome beheading?

Mount Incahuási (also called Mount Santa Bárbara), where Clemente Limachi Sihuayro was decapitated on February 17, 1986, rises between the mountains Calvary and Kapia. Mount Kapia is by far the highest mountain of the Copacabana Peninsula; in fact, at 15,778 feet it is the highest mountain by the shores of Lake Titicaca. Clemente Limachi's sacrifice was so close to the quarries that gave Tiahuanaco some of its sacred stones, and to the temples where the Incas redefined their creation myth, that I felt I was also getting close to the Andes' inner mysteries.

Leucaria Limachi's house, or hovel, sits just beyond the southern slope of Mount Incahuási. I made my way to her house across potato fields that were covered with white blossoms, like thousands of flags waving in the wind. When she saw me she came out, crying. Her brood of half a dozen children also came out, crying. They were all weeping because one of their rabbits had just died, a serious food loss. But they had other causes for distress as well.

"I wasn't able to get that money that you sent me," Leucaria said, referring to a hundred-dollar deposit I'd made for her at a local bank.

"Clemente Fargín took half the money," chimed in a man who identified himself as Agustín Leiva, the president of the community of Chinumani.

Worse, one of Leucaria's daughters, who worked for a local beer distributor named Mengoa, had been accused of stealing from her employer. The beer distributor accused both Leucaria and her daughter of the theft.

"Leucaria was captured by the Civil Guard and spent four days in jail," Leiva explained. "Then she was captured by the PIP. I had to go and get her out of jail both times. The beer distributor threatened Leucaria: 'We're going to kill you.' "

Here Leucaria broke down crying. "With the money you left me when you came I bought some clothes for the children," she said. "But the beer distributor's wife came with a court order and took all the clothes away, claiming that I'd bought them with her stolen money." This explained why the children looked like the Rag Army, clothes so tattered and faded they conformed more to the wind than to the little bodies they covered; no shoes, no sweaters. Their best protection against the cold was a formidable layer of dirt and sweat each of them seemed to have developed.

Leucaria was sobbing hysterically as she showed me another court order, one that required the beer distributor to give back the children's clothes. She'd obtained this court order, at great cost and with great difficulty, through the help of the community president. But the beer distributor had simply ignored the order, and the children's clothes never reappeared. Leucaria knelt down and begged me to help her.

My meeting with Leucaria Limachi was emotionally draining. The money I'd sent her had been stolen . . . she'd been put in jail for a crime her daughter had supposedly committed . . . death threats . . . lawsuits. . . . She spilled sixteen months of calamities on me in twenty minutes. Leucaria herself appeared on the verge of a nervous collapse, dazed and bleary-eyed, barely able to talk for a minute without compulsive crying.

Leucaria Limachi needed a lot of things, starting with a monthly stipend to put food in the mouths of her children. She also needed a much larger house. But I knew I couldn't help Leucaria Limachi alone. I went to the Ministry of Agriculture, where Engineer Víctor Avendaño was still in charge. Fortunately, Víctor agreed to help. "You can count on me to do whatever we can for that poor widow. And it will be good for your study of human sacrifice, too, because the widow will be so grateful to you she'll tell you what she really knows. And you can be sure she knows everything."

That thought *had* occurred to me.

When we reached Leucaria Limachi's house, she came out and

quickly poured out her litany of troubles to Engineer Avendaño, sobbing as she did.

"All right, that's enough!" Avendaño said, with surprising brusqueness. "Nothing's to be gained by crying. Who's to blame for all these troubles, anyway? No one forced you to have nine children. We're going to try and help you, but you have to learn to help yourself."

If Avendaño sounds harsh, he has a license to be. He is a native Quechua speaker from the northern part of Puno Department, raised on a farm. He's also fluent in Aymara, having worked for years in Yunguyo. Like virtually everyone in the highlands, he is a mestizo, coming from mixed European and Indian ancestry, as his short, broad frame and darker skin suggest. He always wears a baseball cap, often with a sports outfit, which gives him an impish look. But he has a no-nonsense approach that gets things done. The people respect him because he works brutally hard, far longer than his job officially requires, and he doesn't demand bribes. We were quickly surrounded by a crowd of perhaps twenty people, who'd come to hear what we planned to do for the widow and the orphans.

"We're going to try and help this woman start a business," Avendaño informed them. "There are no stores around here, are there?"

"No, we need a store," Agustín Leiva responded.

"Well, I suggest that, with the help of our friend from the United States, we build Mrs. Limachi a new house big enough to serve as a store. It will face the road here, so it's well positioned. But I expect you all to help build the house. Our friend here from the United States is a writer, and he's interested in how Clemente Limachi was sacrificed and what your customs are."

This drew a lot of blank stares. I assumed it was because people were shocked at the mention of a human sacrifice, but that wasn't the case at all. The problem was that they'd never heard of a writer before.

"You know what a writer is, don't you?" Avendaño continued. "A writer writes books. And this man is going to write a book about you." There was still a blank look on Leucaria Limachi's face. Avendaño got a little impatient. "You know what a book is, don't you?" he asked her, while creating a book in the air and pretending to hold it. "The books that we have in our schools didn't just appear out of nothing. Someone had to write them. This man here is one of those people who write books."

I liked the way my job was explained to the whole community at the outset. We were being very up-front about my mission: to write a book about Clemente Limachi's death and the religious customs surrounding it. I was amazed that most people accepted this, which they would not have done, under any circumstances, at Lago Budi.

By now there were over thirty people milling about, all promising to help build Leucaria's new house. There was a lot of enthusiasm and there was, it seemed, a well-established institution of communal labor, which made projects like this possible. At Lago Budi communal labor was practically extinct. And I'd never seen this kind of spontaneous combustion of neighborly interest.

While Avendaño discussed with the leaders the details of building a house, I looked around, curious to see if I could locate any of the local shamans. Sometimes these ritual experts wear pointed woolen caps, pulled down over their ears, which make them look more wizardly. Although I didn't notice anyone with such a cap, I saw an older man join the group and I immediately thought, "That's got to be Clemente's father."

"Who is that old man there?" I asked.

"That's the dead man's father."

"Is he a *yatiri?*"

"Yes, he knows."

I don't know how I was so sure from the start—what exactly betrayed the old man's religious vocation or his relation with Clemente. I'd never seen a picture of Clemente, and the old man didn't approach Leucaria or the children in any way, which was odd in itself. There were half a dozen men around his age in the large group, and he dressed, like most of them, in Western pants and a dark coat. He acted like an outsider, yet he had a very erect bearing and an almost exaggerated way of staring straight ahead. He had stage presence.

When Avendaño had finished his discussion, I addressed the president of Chinumani, Agustín Leiva.

"Mr. President," I began, taking care to address him by his title because these signs of rank are particularly important in the native communities, "Engineer Avendaño will direct the construction of the widow's new house and I will supply the materials. We're both very grateful to the community for your strong support. But building the physical house isn't enough. We want to follow the traditions and perform the necessary ceremonies to inaugurate construction. Is there any *yatiri* here who can invoke the help of the *achachilas* [ancestral mountain spirits] before we lay the first stone?"

Some people smiled and nodded their heads, but others looked uncomfortable. The president spoke to a couple of men in Aymara before answering.

"There's a man named Fortunato who knows."

I was taken to a nearby house, where I met a small, barefoot man who agreed to perform a ritual to bless our house-building activities.

"But it has to be secret," Fortunato said. "You can't talk about these things in front of everyone."

"Why not?" I asked. "Everyone believes in worshipping the mountains, don't they?"

"Not everyone," he answered. "Most of the people around here are Evangelicals now. They're opposed. Agustín Leiva, the president of the community, and all those leaders are Evangelicals. They'll get angry."

"What about Clemente Limachi's father? Doesn't he do these rituals, too?"

"Oh, yes, Angelino Limachi is my teacher," Fortunato said. "He'll come. But we have to do it all in secret, on the mountaintop, where the Evangelicals won't see us."

"Is there any particular mountain where we should go?"

Fortunato pointed to Mount Incahuási, just behind us. "That's a powerful mountain, superior to all the other mountains. Did you bring everything we need to offer a Misa?"

"Offering a Misa" means burning an assortment of sugar objects as a sacrifice to the mountain gods, Catholic saints, and other deities. Misa also means the Roman Catholic Mass. Fortunately, I'd bought a standard Misa for the occasion—a bag full of sugar houses, cars, llamas, people—so we could proceed.

"You go on up to the Apacheta," Fortunato said. "I'll send word to Angelino, then I'll follow."

I couldn't understand how everyone could take my interest in human sacrifice as natural, yet insist on performing rituals with such privacy. Fortunato obviously didn't want to be seen climbing the mountain with me, but that gave me time to enjoy the surroundings. It was a lovely day, and from the Apacheta I had an excellent view of Mount Kapia, the Island of the Sun, and the whole surrounding area. Chinumani, where Leucaria Limachi lived, had good farmland, as the highlands go. Leucaria's own plot of land was tiny, but the lakeside soil was rich and deep. Even so, she'd suffered two consecutive bad harvests, one because of the flood in 1986, which covered much of the community's land, and the other because of a drought in 1987. This year, the potato crop looked robust. But there was always the danger of hail or frost, which could wipe out crops as well. It was a precarious existence.

I could see how precarious by looking at the abrupt change of terrain just a few yards above the marshlands. Once you left Lake Titicaca's immediate rim, things turned barren. At the Apacheta of Mount Incahuási I was entering another ecosystem, with rocky soil and sparse growth, a high-altitude wasteland of stunted shrubs and needlelike grasses.

Fortunato arrived alone, saying that Angelino Limachi would join us in a few minutes. We sat in the sun together, looking out over the lake.

"Apacheta is the name of this place where they left Clemente Limachi's head and body," he said.

"Why do they call it Apacheta?" I asked.

"They call it Apacheta because the Incas did things here. The Incas used to live here. Now all the dead Incas are buried inside this mountain."

That was an interesting development, given that Incahuási means "House of the Incas." Apparently it was the house of the dead as well, much as Cerro Mesa had the spirits of dead warriors attached to it.

We started climbing Mount Incahuási in a leisurely way, following a well-worn path that cut across the rock face. Thousands of feet must have made that path over hundreds of years.

Angelino caught up with us, even though he was shouldering a supply of firewood. Whenever we rested, Fortunato and Angelino shared coca leaves, which they offered me. I joined in, although I found the taste of the leaves bitterly disagreeable. Angelino poured alcohol from a small flask onto the ground, and in the direction of Mount Kapia, muttering an invocation in Aymara.

"Now that mountain is just called Kapia," he said. "But in the old days it was called Mallku Kapia [the Great Kapia]. It was much bigger then."

According to Angelino, Mount Kapia had once been the highest mountain in the world. He described a time of primeval darkness when waters covered the whole earth except for Mount Kapia, which, as a huge snake, reigned alone. "But then the Incas came, and they cut Kapia into pieces. Because of that, Kapia is no longer the highest mountain." Angelino pointed to the ridge of Kapia as it descended, in broken stages, to the edge of Lake Titicaca. "You can still see the body of the snake if you look closely."

I could see the snake's head by the water's edge, and its body coiling toward the peak three thousand feet above the lake.

"That's why we call Kapia 'Aserropatahata'—'The Cut Snake.' There are great snakes in that mountain."

This story was similar to the Mapuche myth of Cai Cai Filu and Tren Tren, the great serpents who became mountains. I had been told by several anthropologists not to expect much common ground between the Mapuches and the Aymaras, but this belief in the original Serpent Mountain was suggestive of at least some shared beliefs. Serpent deities have always been worshipped around Copacabana. In 1619 a Spanish priest destroyed a snake idol on a mountaintop near Yunguyo. This idol, called Copacati, belonged to "the sorcerers of Yunguyo." It was "made of stone, with an extremely ugly figure and all wound up with serpents." There were live serpents around the idol, which the priest killed and threw into the lake. According to this account, the natives prayed to this serpent god during droughts, specifically to get rain.[5]

Although I'd expected Angelino and other *yatiris* near Yunguyo to have some beliefs about the famous feline god of Titicaca, instead I kept hearing about snake deities that reside on mountaintops, in gullies, in mountain lakes, and in Lake Titicaca itself. "These *yatiris* think there are snakes everywhere," Víctor Avendaño told me. "What I want to know is, why do they have more faith in the snake than in God?"

Curiously, archaeologists have discovered that snakes are the most frequently carved animals on a type of ancient stelae found all around Lake Titicaca, going back not only to pre-Inca times but possibly to pre-Tiahuanaco times. So Angelino and the "sorcerers of Yunguyo" have preserved an ancient legacy that has outlived the state cults of both the pre-Inca kingdom, with its feline god, and the Incas, with their Sun God, as well as the Roman Catholic inquisitors.

Angelino sees rocks and mountains as personalities with differing degrees of power, often with blood relations. Mount Kapia is the most powerful entity in the broad region of Yunguyo, Incahuási the most imposing local deity. Thus Kapia belongs to a category of supergods called *tius*, or *tiós* (uncles), while Incahuási pertains to the smaller mountain spirits. Still, Angelino sees Kapia and Incahuási as complementary. "Kapia is the man, and Incahuási is the woman," he said. "Kapia doesn't have any fertile valleys or fruit trees. But Incahuási has all these crops nearby."

When we reached the top of Incahuási, we could make out some of the snowcapped peaks of the Cordillera Real to the east across Lake Titicaca. Clouds quickly covered them again.

"Illimani is over there," Angelino said. Then, turning in the opposite direction, westward, he said, "On this side there is Mount Azoguini, near the city of Puno. Illimani, Kapia, and Azoguini are the three *tius*, the greatest mountains. We always pray to the three *tius*." At this Angelino once again pulled out his liquor flask and sprinkled the spirits, first toward Illimani, then toward Kapia, and finally in the direction of Azoguini. He then handed me the bottle and ordered me to do the same thing, calling each of the three mountains by name, and taking a swig of the liquor myself. I nearly choked on the white liquid, which was real fire water.

We sat down in the middle of a stone circle off to one side. He pulled out an old Latin Bible and began to pray, "In the name of the Father, the Son, and the Holy Spirit," in a highly eccentric, singsong way. Then we started to pray the Rosary. That is, we prayed the first sentence of the Hail Mary fifty times, with the first sentence of the Our Father at various interludes in between. Angelino didn't seem to know the whole prayers, but he certainly put a lot of enthusiasm into it.

After completing the Rosary, Angelino began invoking Illimani, Kapia, and Azoguini, along with Mount Calvary, Illampu, Incahuási, and many other mountains. Then I heard him invoke Clemente Limachi. He invoked Clemente again and again, as a kind of deity, as often, if not more often, than the greatest mountain gods.

Angelino then wanted to sing the litany of the saints in Latin, and when he found that I could read, he told me to stand up and start the responsorial prayer. As I invoked the Virgin Mary, John the Baptist, the apostles Peter and Paul, and the long list of saints and angels included in the beautifully phrased litany, Angelino would sing back, *"Ora pro nobis"*—"Pray for us."

Once again my sacrificial suspect was a complex character. Instead of being an Andean heretic, he was a Tridentine Latin–rite fanatic, worthy of the Archbishop Lefebvre. This was an altogether different holier-than-thou hazard from the one I'd met with Machi Juana, the Mapuche fundamentalist.

When the time came for us to take our place at the main altar, before a terribly ugly iron crucifix, I took out my candy Misa.

"This is no good," Angelino said. "You don't have all the *tius* or the saints." Angelino had very exact requirements for his Misa— there had to be one collection of items dedicated to the three *tius*, another for Pacha Mama, and another called *glorias*. My Misa just didn't measure up. It was a cheap version that I'd bought at a local fair.

"You don't have any cigarettes, either," Fortunato complained. "You've got to come better prepared."

Angelino and Fortunato ended up by giving me a long list of essential spiritual items: pure alcohol (one bottle); beer (several bottles); wine (at least one bottle); *pisco* (a native liquor, one bottle); cigarettes (several packs); a bag of coca leaves for divination; and three Misas, one for the *tius*, one for Pacha Mama, and one for the Christian saints.

"We'll make a very good Misa on top of Mount Kapia," Angelino said.

"But to reach Kapia we have to start at five in the morning," Fortunato said. "It's best to burn the offerings before it gets too late in the afternoon. It takes about four hours of hard climbing to reach the peak."

I agreed to meet them at 5:30 A.M. to climb Kapia. On our descent, I asked Angelino about how he had become a shaman.

"I was struck by lightning," Angelino said. "Right over there by Chuchape [the hill next to the Apacheta where Clemente was deposited]. That hill is very superior, much better than this one. It has lots of minerals."

I thought he'd just established this beautiful hierarchy where Incahuási was the main local mountain. Now Chuchape was competing, and it turned out to be Angelino's personal mountain, much as Cerro Mesa was Machi Juana's "spirit."

"After that the mountains spoke to me," Angelino said. "All the mountains—Illimani, Kapia. Even the rocks talk to me. You see this rock here? This rock is in charge of automobiles. If you make an offering here, you'll get a new car for sure."

"He was an orphan, and the mountains called him to be a *yatiri*," Fortunato explained. "The mountains have given Angelino faith. First he started off as a fortuneteller, divining people's luck with coca leaves. Then he became a maestro, a *yatiri*. I was an orphan myself, and I started off in the same way. It's like going to school—first you go out and do prayers to Pacha Mama so she'll help people's crops. Then you become a fortuneteller, throwing the coca leaves. Once people know you're a good fortuneteller, then you can become a *yatiri*. But I'm not like Angelino. He knows. He can talk to the mountain."

How devout and deeply religious Angelino Limachi seemed, and how gentle at the same time. His prayers to his son, Clemente Limachi, seemed—no, were—heartfelt. And yet the last, fatal invitation Clemente had received in his life was to dance in Chuchape, right underneath the hill that was the personal tutelary spirit of his father.

"Why did you mention your dead son, Clemente, so often?" I asked Angelino.

"He's a saint," Angelino said.

"He's here with us now," Fortunato added. "Clemente is united with this mountain."

⊡ 13 ⊡

BLACK MAGIC

"**W**e have to hurry," Fortunato scolded me the next morning, when I reached Angelino's home. "The old man has already started up the mountain. We told him the weather was too bad, but he said, 'If we've told the mountain we're coming, we have to keep our word.'"

By now it was light enough to see Kapia's peak, covered with a light dusting of snow, more than three thousand feet above us. That was a good sign—the storm was clearing. We could also see Angelino high on a ridge. He turned and spotted us, then pointed to the peak of Kapia. He held this pointing posture for several seconds, standing straight, rigid as a road sign. We got the message.

Fortunato relieved me of my heavy cargo of holy goods—the three Misas Angelino had ordered, numerous bottles of beer, wine, *pisco*, and pure alcohol, along with some sardine cans. He shouldered about half of the things and gave the rest to a little boy who accompanied us. I felt a bit embarrassed about having the little boy carry so much stuff, but as he walked easily on ahead of us I was sorry I hadn't given him my camera and tape recorder, too.

"Who's going to bring the firewood?" I asked Fortunato, in between deep breaths, when we stopped to rest for a minute.

"The widow [Leucaria] has to bring the firewood," he answered. "This ceremony we're doing is mostly for her, so that her house will be built. She agreed to bring the firewood."

After an hour we caught up with Angelino Limachi, who was wearing dark pants, a suit coat, and an Andean wool cap that is commonly worn by *yatiris*. He walked with the help of a long stick, making frequent offerings of alcohol to certain rocks we came across. Artificial stone mounds marked these spots. Whenever you reach one of these stone heaps, you're supposed to add a rock to the growing pile, while uttering prayers to the mountain gods, Pacha Mama, and ancestral spirits. Fortunato told me it was a good idea to invoke Clemente Limachi as well.

"What do these piles of stones represent?" I asked Angelino.

"These are the mountains," Angelino replied.

These stone mounds modeled the great mountains, like miniature pyramids.

Whenever Angelino made an offering of alcohol, he also took a good swig himself, then passed the bottle to Fortunato. When my turn came I spilled the alcohol, first toward Mount Kapia, then toward Mount Illimani, then toward Mount Azoguini, following Angelino's routine as closely as I could. I barely touched the burning liquid to my lips.

"You have to drink it," Fortunato said. "The white alcohol is what the *tius* like."

We'd just begun hiking to a rocky pre-peak above the lake when Leucaria, her eldest daughter, Primitiva, and several others caught up with us. Leucaria nimbly worked her way barefoot over the sharp volcanic rocks. "She must have spectacular calluses," I thought.

There were eight of us, scrambling up and down the serrated ridge that was our only route to the peak. The rocks were deep red, the color of the great stone slabs of Tiahuanaco. But wherever we went there were more stone cairns, signs that our route was heavily traveled. Once we came to a clearing with hundreds of little square stone structures, some with three or four stories carefully built up. With the mists floating around, it looked like a city for sprites.

But it was actually the world's most impractical home-improvement project.

"You have to build yourself a house here," I was told. The theory was: the bigger and better you make your miniature stone house here on the mountain, the bigger and better your real house will become. Everyone set about constructing a stone model of the home he wanted to acquire. The more ambitious members of our group built several-story houses. They were simple enough—just four stones and a roof, then four more stone walls and a roof—but moving those big stones was not a great joy. "Do they really think this is going to get them all new houses?" I wondered. Judging from the proliferation of multistoried minihouses, hundreds of people had participated in this ritual over the years. But I hadn't seen anyone in Chinumani with a three- or four-story house. I wanted to blow the whistle on this inefficient Andean dream construction. But maybe I was just jealous that the others were having such a good time while my heart was beating out of control because of the altitude.

The mist lifted off Lake Titicaca, revealing its sky-blue waters on both sides of the peninsula. But even as the weather below seemed to clear, clouds rolled in around us.

"This is just to protect us from the sun," one man said. "If we didn't have some clouds, it would be too hot to continue."

We edged up the mountain and crossed a stream only a few hundred feet below the peak. Now we were in another world, as different from the dry tundra of Kapia's lower reaches as the barren tundra was from marshy lake lands by Titicaca's shore. There were half a dozen lakes all around the peak, and the ground was sopping wet. Although we were over fifteen thousand feet high, water abounded. And we soon learned why.

A storm closed in, and hail mixed with snow began falling heavily.

We all huddled under an overhanging rock, which provided

partial protection against the hail and wind. Angelino won the pre-
paredness award, because he pulled out a black umbrella that kept
him completely dry. He was quite elegant with his dark suit and
umbrella, standing as stiff as a British aristocrat, a strange symbol
of order who appeared to have magically emerged from the envel-
oping clouds. The rest of us were soon soaking and freezing beneath
the hail, which blanketed the rocks and our entire world under an
inch of ice.

"Kapia has two brothers," Angelino said, pointing to two of
Kapia's pre-peaks which appeared to be about the same altitude as
we were. "The brothers are getting angry that we're about to climb
higher than they are, so they sent this hailstorm to stop us. But it
won't last long." Since we were taking offerings to Kapia, we were
bound to triumph, with his help, over the other mountains.

The hail let up after twenty minutes. So we proceeded, often
sliding on the now-icy rocks, to the final ascent. We chose the
eastern slope, which is steep under normal conditions but became
treacherously slippery with all the sleet and hail. Leucaria kept
going with her bare feet, and seemed to be enjoying herself. Angelino's daughter gave several high-pitched screams, when we had
to make leaps from one rock to another. For someone with climbing
boots and gear, this was a place to be careful. But for someone in
bare feet or sandals, it was a good place to break a leg.

I was relieved when we made the 15,778-foot summit. All of
us threw ourselves on the ground and rested near a four-foot-high
altar.

Angelino spoke to Fortunato in Aymara, and Fortunato translated for me. "This mountain has a lot of money. The maestro says
that the real purpose of this ceremony is to get the mountain to
reveal where its gold and silver are hidden. Then the American
mining companies will come and we will all get good jobs."

"Are there powerful mountains where you live in the United
States?" Angelino asked me.

"Mount McKinley is the highest mountain in the United
States," I said. "It's in Alaska. But I spend more time in Chile,

near Mount Aconcagua, which is the highest mountain in North
or South America."

Angelino muttered "McKinley" and "Aconcagua" while sprin-
kling more alcohol all around to the mountains on the horizon. He
said he wanted to include the mountains from my homeland in the
ceremony.

"I've climbed a number of high peaks in Chile and Argentina
where the Incas built altars on the summits," I said. "In fact, they
sometimes buried children at those altars. Have you ever heard of
them doing such things?"

"The Incas also did that around here," Angelino said. "In the
old days the people would take any child who was an orphan and
kill him on the mountain. So it's very possible that there's a child
buried right here on top of Kapia."

Now Angelino started organizing the ritual. First he requested
a single bill from me, which he placed inside a bag of coca leaves,
wrapping the coca leaves and the money inside a rainbow-colored
blanket. He mixed the leaves up, then asked each one of us to come
forward and choose a leaf. If the leaf was large and whole, it meant
good luck; if not, Angelino asked us to choose again, until our luck
improved. "The coca leaves say that we are all doing very well up
here," Fortunato said. "And no matter how much money you spend
on this Misa, you're going to get much more in return."

Everyone seemed happy to hear this pep talk, although I was
more cautious, since I had to pay the *yatiris* at the end of the Misas
and it looked as if Fortunato were trying to up the ante.

Angelino then started sorting out our three Misas—one dedicated to Pacha Mama, the Earth Mother; one for the three *tius;*
and one for *glorias*, a more confused category originally connected
with the thunder god, Illapa, a generalized mountain deity, but
now including many Christian saints, particularly Saint James, the
patron saint of thunder and lightning. The two *yatiris* had long
discussions over which items belonged in which Misa—whether
Leucaria's house, represented by a candy model, should go under
the patronage of of *tius* or of Pacha Mama. It was as though this

were a scientific formula requiring utmost precision. In the end, they decided to subdivide the Pacha Mama Misa into two—one for Pacha Mama and one for "the Virgins," a category presided over by Mother Mary.

After dividing the objects up, Angelino spread old newspapers on the ground to receive them. But even the newspapers had to meet certain requirements. Angelino searched until he found a picture of a bare-breasted woman—a popular porno queen who appeared in a cheap Peruvian publication. He nodded his head approvingly. "This will be for the Virgins," Angelino said, placing various Madonna figurines on top of the scantily dressed dancer. I thought that it was one of the few times this professional stripper had been associated with the Virgin Mary. What also caught my eye was the plurality of the "Virgins." For Angelino the Virgin of Copacabana was one Virgin, the Virgin of Puno another. Like the mountain gods, they were related—cousins or sisters—but they had to be invoked separately.

At this point Angelino called Leucaria forward and asked her some questions about her projected house. Then he took a candy house and, making the sign of the cross, placed it on the improvised altar for the Pacha Mama. He next offered a piece of candy to the Virgins for each member of Leucaria's family, and everyone else's family. The list of family members was very long, since it encompassed brothers, sisters, parents, grandparents, and even deceased relatives. In the Aymara scheme of things, you can't ask for good luck for yourself alone. Your sense of self is so closely tied to a wide kinship group that the whole network has to be invoked and protected before you can begin to consider your private concerns.

Angelino spent more time praying for his dead son, Clemente, than for any other individual. He had me read a whole Latin litany for the dead in Clemente's honor. This confused me, because I wasn't sure whether Angelino was praying *to* or *for* Clemente. If Clemente was a saint, as Angelino said, united with the mountain spirits, he didn't need any prayers. If he was a suffering soul in purgatory, Clemente certainly didn't merit all the praise and petitions they were showering on him. But this contradiction, though it bothered me, was unintelligible to them.

Angelino placed three candy mountains at the top of the *tius'* Misa. These represented Illimani, Kapia, and Azoguini. He played his role magnificently, seated erect, closing his eyes and meditating from time to time, then making his pronouncements with eyes raised to heaven and arms outstretched, as though he had just spoken to God. The surroundings lent power to the proceedings. Clouds suddenly enveloped us, blocking out the world, and creating a feeling of floating above the earth. Then, just as suddenly, the clouds would vanish, and Lake Titicaca would reappear, serene and blue, along with the many-colored lakes of the high mountains surrounding us, which reflected the changing skies. When the brilliant sun came out, the ice all around glinted like a field of diamonds.

If the setting was mystical, the prayers were terribly practical. Family and business. Money, money, money. Angelino had to take everyone through his private wish list, putting houses, cars, llamas, pigs, and every goody under the sun on the altars. Everyone placed a stack of money while requesting a specific amount from the gods. A large amount.

"Five million Intis," one man asked.

"Fifty million," Angelino corrected, who was always generous with the mountain gods' money. When he placed the money on the altar he said, "Five million times fifty million." Why not? Although the Third Mystery in the Rosary we recited was "the imitation of Jesus's poverty," the whole purpose of our ceremony was the imitation of wealth.

Even when we buried a little llama fetus, all covered with colored paper, we were performing a commercial exchange with Pacha Mama.

"We bury this fetus so the earth will give us more produce," Fortunato said. "It goes under the earth and brings more things up."

By now we'd been going for three hours on top of the mountain, taking a beating from the constant winds and the occasional rains mixed with hail.

"You're pretty cold, aren't you?" Fortunato asked me. "But we still have a lot of work to do."

I was freezing, my shoes and socks still soaked from all the hail and rain. But I warmed up after we built a big bonfire in front of the stone altar. Now I started to enjoy the Misas, as we danced around the bonfire, shaking our beer bottles and spraying the foam in all directions, calling on the mountains and the Earth Mother to bless our offerings. Finally, we placed the Misas on top of the fire, watching the candy universes we'd created blacken, wilt, and melt into running masses that seeped into the earth. We all prayed and embraced.

Fortunato made me turn my jacket inside out and wear it that way, like all the other men. Perhaps this showed we'd changed ourselves through the ceremony. Fortunato certainly seemed transformed. He whirled around the bonfire, shaking his outstretched palms, possessed by the liquor and good feeling, as though he were a mountain god himself.

Angelino picked up a stone and threw it down the mountainside, toward a boulder a hundred feet below. "Follow the stone," he shouted. I followed the stone to the boulder, which had a hollowed-out center where there was a pool of water. Angelino drank from the rock and prayed. He wanted everyone to do the same, but by this time discipline had broken down—and so had Angelino. He fell down, too drunk to retain command of himself, let alone anyone else. His daughter just laughed at him and told him to get lost.

"The old man's had too much to drink," Fortunato said with a slur that indicated he, too, had imbibed a little too much. "He wants us to do what he says. But he has his ideas and I have mine."

So the harmony on the mountaintop didn't survive our first steps toward Yunguyo. I walked ahead, alone, while the others took another route back to Chinumani. I passed cows, sheep, and llama herds guided by little shepherds. As I got closer to town, and as night fell, I also passed quite a few intoxicated men. I hadn't seen this much alcoholism since Lago Budi. I could understand that drinking was about the only entertainment available. But why did every ceremonial occasion degenerate into drunken disputes? When I later asked Fortunato and Angelino why they drank such appalling amounts at each Misa, they said, "We don't drink for ourselves. The *tius* drink through us. If we don't drink all of the liquor, the *tius* will be angry. You can't leave any for the next time—whatever you bring to the mountain you have to drink that same day." And when Fortunato wheeled around the burning offerings, hands outstretched and prancing like a madman, he seemed to say, "I *am* the god dancing," just as he *was* the god drinking.

Clemente Limachi's fusion with the mountain was more drastic and more permanent. When his head was cut off on Mount Incahuási, he changed from an impoverished peasant into a rich demigod—who was now in charge of protecting poor travelers like me.

The next day I returned to Chinumani, where I paid Angelino for the ceremony. But he was strangely reserved and unenthusiastic— a markedly changed attitude from the previous day. In fact, no one in his household wanted to talk to me. The same thing happened at Leucaria's house.

The agronomist Víctor Avendaño didn't look too happy, either, when I finally caught up with him that night. He put his head out his window and said, "Come and see me tomorrow morning, about five-thirty."

When I came the next morning, Víctor was still asleep, but farmers were already waiting to see him. At six o'clock Víctor emerged and was swarmed over by people wanting animal vaccinations, agricultural loans, technical advice. . . .

"It goes on like this all day," Víctor said. "Last night I didn't get back until eight. My official work hours are supposed to be from 7:00 A.M to 2:00 P.M, but I can't turn all these people away."

Some of those waiting to see Avendaño had made great sacrifices. "I've been walking since 3:00 A.M. to get here," said a young man with a businessman's briefcase who was the president of a community called Tacapisi.

Avendaño came over and said to the community president, "Let me introduce you to . . . " He had forgotten my name, so I introduced myself. He'd also forgotten the name of the president of Tacapisi, Gerónimo Bonifacio.

"Patrick is studying people's customs and climbing the mountains with the *yatiris*. A few days ago he climbed Mount Incahuási to do a Misa."

"Oh, Incahuási, some people call it Mount Santa Bárbara," Gerónimo said. "That's where they have to kill people." He made a motion of slitting his own throat. "They cut off the head."

"You see?" Avendaño said. "Everyone around here knows that. In order to get money, the people turn over a family member to the devil. And they do it on Mount Santa Bárbara or on Kapia. In the community of Chimbu, near here, the people climb Mount Kapia, where they have a deep well, and they throw a person down it—often a bad person who's committed a crime. It especially happens during a dry year. They have faith in the devil. In a way, you have to admire that incredible faith they have. And it's not only a belief in riches. They're convinced that if they do these sacrifices they'll become immortal—they'll never die."

"Yes, it's very common still, especially in the more backward communities, where they sacrifice someone during difficult times," Gerónimo said. "We ourselves just had a case like this a couple of months ago, in November of last year, when three young boys involved with black magic killed someone."

"Who was the victim?" I asked.

"He was the son of a sorcerer [*brujo*]," the president claimed. "This man is known to be a *liquichiri*, a vampire who transforms himself into an animal—a dog, a cat, a snake, or a donkey. Then he goes out at night and sucks people's fat. And he sets a date for that person to die."

According to Gerónimo, the *liquichiri*, in his animal shape, simply looks at his victim from a distance. The *liquichiri*'s gaze alone is sufficient to inflict an invisible puncture wound, through which the vampire magically extracts the person's "fat" or flesh—without the victim's even realizing it. He uses this stolen fat for the manufacture of powerful charms that can either bring wealth or work mischief. Lots of people are suspected of being *liquichiris*, particularly shamans, Catholic priests, and white-skinned foreigners. I didn't believe the death of this shaman's son had anything to do with black magic, or vampires. But I decided to visit Tacapisi to see if I could extricate the facts from this fantastic mythology.

I quickly confirmed that a teenage boy had been murdered in Tacapisi in late November 1987. Furthermore, the murder took place at a ritual site on a prominent white mountain, called Janq'u Qhawa. Janq'u means "white," and Qhawa means "armor." This name belongs to a mountain deity—Janq'u Qhawani Achachila—who controls hailstorms.[1]

I climbed Mount Janq'u Qhawa with two leaders of the community. "This is a very bad place," one said as we passed a series of ravines, some of them twenty feet deep and so narrow they invited accidents. "Crazy people come here at night." He pointed to one of the deepest chasms and said, "That's where we found the body."

But the boy was actually killed a few yards away, in the shallow bed of a dry stream. It reminded me of the dry watercourse where Clemente Limachi's body had appeared. "One of the boys has admitted that they did the killing here, with a stone. Then they threw their dead friend down in the ravine.

"The dead boy was fourteen years old, an intimate friend of the other three. They all came here to make a payment to the devil to get gold. They paid to find a treasure. They weren't drunk. But they followed some three books they'd obtained—the books of *Black Magic*, *Red Magic*, and *White Magic*."

"Where'd they get these books?" I asked.

"They got them from the dead boy's father, who is a *yatiri*. All of the boys were studying magic with the dead boy's father. People say that the father was involved, that he is responsible because the books were his. The son started to do experiments."

According to these men, the streambed where the boy was killed is a special ritual spot. *Yatiris* make offerings where this gully meets the main road below. "At night there are strange spirits here, and sometimes a red cock flies around," one man explained.

There have been other sacrifices in this gully as well. "About three weeks ago we found a black dog dead in the same spot where the boy was killed." Together we examined bits of black hair that still remained. It certainly looked like an animal sacrifice, and one that was particularly relevant to the dead boy's fate. On top of Mount Tortolas (20,770 feet), in northern Chile, the Incas sacrificed a dog. Although the large altar-platform on top of Tortolas has never been fully excavated, the presence of the dog there suggests to some archaeologists the possibility of a human-sacrifice victim. That's because dogs—black dogs, in fact—are still believed to accompany the dead souls of Peruvian Indians when, in the afterlife, they pass a sacred mountain where the dog spirits dwell. The sacrifice of this black dog on Mount Janq'u Qhawa suggested that someone else was involved who knew a great deal about Andean rituals. The teenage boys reportedly responsible for the initial sacrifice were all under detention when the dog appeared.

"Someone must have directed the ritual," Gerónimo Bonifacio told me. "Boys wouldn't do this alone."

"Who do you think directed it, then?"

Gerónimo paused. "It can't be proved. But it might just be that the boy's father himself was behind it all."

Marciano Víctor Copa, the boy's father, admitted to being a *yatiri*. "Kapia is the strongest mountain around here. I sometimes go up to do a Misa, whenever the weather is bad and hail falls."

He seemed to have forgotten about his dead son, whom he did not include when he named the rest of his children.

"What about the son who died?" I asked.

"Oh, his name was Rolando Adolfo Copa," answered Marciano. He didn't show any sign of grief. "He wasn't a very good student. He left home November 20 and they found his body in

Tacapisi eight days later. I don't know how he died. The *yatiris* know."

"Which *yatiri?*"

He didn't know any of the other *yatiris.*

"But aren't you a *yatiri?*"

"No, I'm not a *yatiri.*"

"But you just said you go up to Mount Kapia to perform Misas. . . . "

"No, only the *yatiris* do that."

He also denied teaching any rituals or magic to his son.

"The one who killed my son was Mario Gregorio Cotipu. The police put him in jail. But the police said there were footprints of more than one person around my son's body."

My next step was to find Mario Gregorio Cotipu's family and from them—I hoped—learn where the police were keeping the boy. Although it was 3:00 P.M., everyone was celebrating a feast to the Virgin of Copacabana. Many men were playing soccer, so I started asking for the Cotipu family at the field.

I was lucky to meet an uncle of Mario's, named Gregorio Churro, immediately.

"I'd like to find out about why your nephew was arrested," I said.

"Are you some kind of a police detective?"

"No, I'm doing a cultural study of sacrifices. That's why I'm interested in what happened at Tacapisi."

"If you really want to know about that sacrifice, why don't you ask my nephew about it?" Churro suggested. "He's been released from jail and he's staying at home. I'll show you where he is."

On the way Churro talked about his nephew's involvement with the reticent shaman, father of the dead boy. "All of these boys were studying magic. My nephew says they went to that hill in Tacapisi to study the books of *Black Magic, White Magic,* and *Red Magic,* along with the *Book of San Cipriano* and another book about discovering treasures."

Churro steered us to an adobe hut where his nephew's family lived. "We have to be careful not to scare them," he said. "I know what you're doing, because I have a brother-in-law who's studying anthropology at the university. But they might not want to talk with you."

While Churro went inside to negotiate, I sat, cold but as stoic as possible, looking out across Lake Titicaca at a few visible peaks in the Cordillera Real of Bolivia. Kapia was behind me, obscured by dark rainclouds, which were already beginning to thunder in the distance. I waited twenty minutes, but the negotiation continued without any good result. Then it started raining, and I decided to take advantage of Andean hospitality and force myself inside the hut whether they wanted me or not.

They were not delighted. But they did not throw me out, either, a sign of triumph for door-to-door salesmen and investigative reporters. Mario, just back from jail, was sitting in a dark corner of the room, wearing a white baseball cap with FANTA emblazoned in orange letters. He still had the baby fat of early adolescence, and a round face to go with it. Mario told me he was fifteen years old.

After some preliminaries, Mario admitted that he and his friend Rolando had gone to Mount Janq'u Qhawa in Tacapisi to perform a ritual for obtaining treasure. "We were studying two books. One was the *Book of Black Magic*. The other was the *Book of San Cipriano*. While we were reading"—one read in Spanish, the other read the same text in Latin— "I had a vision of armed men riding on horseback through the air. I was afraid. Then my friend turned into a snake, a big green snake. I threw a stone at the snake's head and left the place. People told me later that I had killed a person."

At this point everyone in the room, including the boy and his uncle, started giggling nervously. Then the giggles gave way to outright laughter. I wasn't sure how to react, so I just kept asking questions.

"Was he a good friend of yours?" I asked, when things had calmed down a little.

"Yeah, he was a good friend."

"Are you sorry you killed him?"

"No, I'm not sorry."

Now everyone burst out laughing even more uproariously than before. "What are they laughing about?" I wondered. Surrounded by this sea of mirth, I felt pretty awkward, so I smiled a little and tried to manage a laugh or two. The Aymaras are famous for their absolute reserve, which borders on melancholy. This was so strange it felt like a ritual catharsis.

"Maybe you could give my nephew some advice on how to live his life," Churro said to me, as I was preparing to leave.

I asked Mario what he planned to do in the upcoming year.

"I'm going to high school," he said.

"What do you like to study?"

"Mathematics."

"Well, maybe you should put your mind on math and stay away from these . . . um . . . esoteric subjects, like black magic and treasure hunting. Keep your attention on concrete problems."

Everyone thanked me for my words of wisdom. It occurred to me, as I left, that I ought to start following my own advice.

"They didn't want to let you in," Churro said. "So I had to tell them that you were a professor of anthropology at the university, and a friend of my brother-in-law's."

"Do you believe all this stuff about the *Book of Black Magic* and so forth?" I asked.

"I saw the books myself," he answered. "When the cadaver of that boy was found in Tacapisi, the whole community went over there. Afterward they assigned a commission to search for these books the boys spoke about. The commission went to Copa's house, and they found the *Book of Black Magic*, the *Book of Red Magic*, the *Book of Oracles*, the *Book of Discovering Treasures*, the *Book of San Cipriano*. Then they took all these books and they burned them on the white mountain, a hundred meters from where the body was found."

"I don't believe they found a real *Book of Black Magic*," I said.

"I was present when they burned them," Churro insisted. "The vigilantes shouted, 'Here is the *Book of Black Magic*.' And everyone screamed back, '*Yes! Burn it!*' Then the vigilantes brought out another book: 'Here is the *Book of Red Magic*.' The people answered, '*Yes! Burn it!*' I told them that we should save the books as evidence for the judge, but the people, half crazy, shouted, '*Burn them!*' They didn't want to wait. They were afraid of the power of those books."

I didn't know what to make of all this. I didn't believe the largely illiterate people of Tacapisi would know what books they were burning on Janq'u Qhawa, the white mountain. After all, Leucaria Limachi didn't seem to know what a book *was* when Víctor Avendaño told her that I was a writer. It seemed like a case of collective hysteria. The murder of Rolando Copa was also eccentric. Maybe young Mario, his friend, really did commit accidental homicide in a hallucinogenic fit—Mario had possibly imbibed enough booze and chewed enough coca leaves to have visions of monstrous green snakes and a cavalry of ghostly warriors. Or perhaps Mario was not altogether sane to start with.

On the other hand, maybe he was making the whole thing up under the influence of skillful coaching. The story had certainly proved useful to him: Mario was released from jail on the grounds of temporary insanity, according to his family. Several elements in the death followed the pattern of Clemente Limachi's sacrifice— the victim was the son of a local shaman, his body was dumped in a white-water channel at a well-known ritual site—but the reliance on the *Book of Black Magic*, with parallel recitations in Spanish and Latin, sounded strangely skewed.

In any case, I had to make a decision about Leucaria Limachi's family. The rainy season was now in full swing, and the house-building project had to wait until the weather cleared, which wouldn't happen until April. I offered Leucaria a choice: I would give her fifty dollars a month for twelve months, or come back and build her a large adobe house with a tin roof.

She said she wanted the money *and* the house.

On February 4 Víctor Avendaño and I had a meeting with Leucaria, her daughter Primitiva, and Agustín Leiva, president of the Chinumani Community, at the Ministry of Agriculture. I explained to Leucaria that I was giving six hundred dollars to Víctor Avendaño, who would apportion it to her in monthly installments. As for the house, I promised to give all materials for the roof, provided the community made the adobe bricks and built the house free of charge. President Leiva (that's how we always had to address him) agreed to have the adobe walls ready for roofing by early April.

We then asked to speak with Leucaria alone. Avendaño called in a native Aymara speaker to translate.

"We want to know how they sacrificed your husband," Avendaño said, in an extremely direct and demanding style. "You know very well everything that happened there, and we want to know the truth."

Leucaria told how, on February 16, 1986, the last day of the weeklong Pre-Lenten Carnival, her husband had gone to sell a donkey at Yunguyo's main plaza. After giving her the money, Clemente went off to drink and celebrate with Fausto Quispi and Alejandro López. The next thing she knew, she was awakened in the early hours of the morning and told her husband was dead. She and her daughter Primitiva went to the Apacheta, where they saw his severed head, with tongue and ears cut off, and all his facial skin scalped.

"Why did they do it?" I asked.

"They were all drunk, and that's why they paid the earth," Leucaria answered. "Every four years they have to perform that sacrifice there. Four years before, in 1982, they killed a young woman in the same place, too."

"I am interested in knowing why the *yatiris* cut off the facial skin and the head," I said.

"They have to pay the mountain," Leucaria answered, as

though she didn't quite understand the question. "As to why they have to cut off the face and head, I don't know. It's always been that way."

"But who was responsible for killing Clemente?"

"Fausto Quispi and Alejandro López were the assassins," she said. "But Simón Montoya, a rich man who owns many cars and donkeys, must have contracted them to do it, and others as well, in order to pay the earth. Simón Montoya is the one who went to take care of Quispi and López when they were in jail; he visited the judge and got them free. I saw him when I was there myself."

"But I thought you said that the people who killed your husband were cocaine dealers?"

"We don't know, but we suspect Montoya of being a cocaine trafficker. How else did he get all that money for his big house and cars?"

"But who actually performed the Misa to pay the earth?"

"We hear that Montoya hired a *yatiri* from Bolivia."

"But I've heard that it's customary for the *yatiris* to sacrifice their own children on these occasions."

"Sometimes that does happen."

"And I heard that Angelino, being an important *yatiri*, was involved in the death of Clemente."

Leucaria admitted that she suspected as much, too. "We had a falling out with Angelino on the day we found Clemente assassinated," she said. "The first thing I did was go to Angelino's house, which is near the Apacheta. But when I told him that his son was murdered, he refused to come and see. 'That's nonsense,' he answered. When I insisted, he got angry and told me to stop making such a fuss, to keep quiet."

"I think it's extremely clear that the father was mixed up in this," Víctor Avendaño interjected. "The *yatiris* always try to calm the people down after a sacrifice, so they won't investigate it."

Avendaño seemed uncharacteristically excited as he continued. "You know, this is the second time I've seen a case like this one, almost exactly the same situation. I heard from very truthful sources that the beer distributor Uriarti sent his woman to be sacrificed on that same hill. These were very reliable sources, you know what I mean? I mean that the two men who did it told me so themselves, after they'd been drinking with me. They said they'd taken her to that hill [Mount Incahuási], they lifted up her dress, and they cut her. . . . [Here he pantomimed the act of stabbing a woman in the vagina.] Do you know how terrible that is? And Uriarti did this, just like Montoya sacrificed Limachi, to get more money. That's why these guys are millionaires. They have faith in the devil, they perform the sacrifice, and the devil gives them what they want."

It appeared, then, that the two apparently conflicting stories I'd heard about Clemente Limachi's death might both be true: his father was involved and so was a suspected narcotrafficker. Their exact relationship wasn't clear; nor could I be sure that Montoya was a cocaine smuggler. But Leucaria and her daughter were both certain that Montoya was the patron of Clemente Limachi's sacrificial death. And that he was threatening them, too.

"We're very frightened," Leucaria said, as she started to cry. "Alejandro López has threatened to get revenge if we talk about this. Simón Montoya has also been asking all over about you. He's traveled to Puno and Juli asking, 'What's that *gringo* doing around here? What is he doing with that widow?' "

We tried to reassure Leucaria as best we could. Then we went to the local judge, who dictated an act legalizing the gift of six hundred dollars to Leucaria. It was a nice occasion. We all hugged each other under the national emblem of Peru, an insignia that includes a llama and a condor, representatives of the mountain gods. After we came out of the judge's office, Avendaño turned to me and said, "Now you'd better get out of here and let things settle down for a while."

⊿ 14 ⊾

REVIVING
THE INQUISITION

I didn't want to return to Lake Titicaca. I now knew of three sacrifices around Yunguyo—one of a young girl on Mount Incahuási in 1982; Clemente Limachi's death in 1986, also on Incahuási; and Rolando Copa's strange murder on Mount Janq'u Qhawa of Tacapisi, around November 20, 1987. Was there anything that tied these deaths together? Apparently, rich people, allied with shamans, were paying for the sacrifice of human beings in order to get richer. The worst elements of the Andean past were being employed by powerful entrepreneurs to advance their business.

I hadn't believed what Leucaria Limachi had told me from the beginning—that narcotraffickers sacrificed her husband to "pay the earth." My experiences at Lago Budi steered me away from accepting the weird syncretism at work in Yunguyo. I expected to find a communal sacrifice, with widespread participation, whose purpose was to stem the floodwaters during the 1986 disaster. When people told me this was a common, seasonal occurrence, which merely happened coincidentally during a flood, I couldn't digest it. Even stranger was the fact that these acts were performed *against* the community, not in its behalf, by a murky underworld elite.

The forces behind the sacrifices had more money, and more control of the local police, than the recently conquered and relatively unacculturated Mapuches. The wealthy merchant Montoya was furious that I was helping Leucaria Limachi. His hirelings threatened reprisals. I realized that going alone, and at night, to ceremonies on top of fifteen-thousand-foot mountains was not necessarily wise. Nor was it a good idea to wander on foot, far from Yunguyo, in isolated fields and farms, asking about human sacrifices, as I'd done in Tacapisi.

Since my friend Francisco (Pancho) Paca lived in Puno, I decided to move there. Together we struck a deal with a local taxi driver, who agreed to drive us to Yunguyo daily, a round trip of about 160 miles.

When we visited Leucaria Limachi in late April 1988, I was disappointed to find that her house was not ready for roofing, as we'd agreed in February. In fact, the community hadn't even begun drying adobe bricks for building the walls.

"The rainy season has lasted far too long," Agustín Leiva said, "so we haven't dared make the adobes yet."

This was partly true. The rains were still falling, and it was now April 27—well into the normal dry season. But the community had shown little interest in helping Leucaria. Nor had they expected me to return.

Pancho and Víctor Avendaño suggested setting a date for laying the first stone. "That's the most difficult part, the beginning," Víctor said. "They have a ceremony to perform, with offerings and animal sacrifices, so it'll be interesting for you. After that, the community will pitch in. You'll see."

"The Feast of the Holy Cross is coming up next week," Leiva said, "and the people will be celebrating for several days. Then comes the Feast of the Ascension, and then comes Pentecost. People will be celebrating for about a month."

We finally convinced Leiva to set the laying of the first stone for Saturday, April 30. Then we consulted separately with Angelino Limachi and his assistant, Fortunato, to see if they would perform the traditional house-building Misa and llama sacrifice on that day. But they vehemently refused.

"It has to be secret," Fortunato said, over and over again. "We would like to go to the public ceremony, but the Evangelists are against it."

In the end, Angelino and Fortunato agreed to meet Pancho and me the next day on top of Mount Incahuási, to perform a ceremony for good luck in raising the house.

"But be careful that no one sees you," Fortunato warned. "The last time, people laughed and said we were doing things with the *gringo*."

"These country people have great fear of *gringos*," Pancho said. "They think that if a *gringo* visits a community, they'll suffer a bad harvest, or some other calamity."

"I didn't know that."

"Now you know."

The next day we rendezvoused with Fortunato at 10:30 A.M. near the Apacheta of Mount Incahuási. We were late and Fortunato was annoyed. "We wanted to burn the offerings at noon," he said. "And now we'll have to postpone it until two in the afternoon." The offerings could only be burned at certain hours, and we'd interfered with the schedule. Fortunately, I'd brought two beautifully made alpaca-wool ponchos as gifts to the *yatiris*. They were delighted with them, and quickly forgot about the delay.

We followed the usual routine of Latin liturgy, the Rosary, prayers for Clemente Limachi, more prayers *to* Clemente Limachi, invocations to the mountain gods with candy offerings. . . . Fortunato was terribly deferential toward Angelino, calling him *"mi máximo jefe"* ("my highest chief"). Pancho and I each had to light a candle and place it in a niche at the main altar. Mine lit without incident, but Pancho's broke in half.

"That's very bad; something is going to happen to you," Fortunato said. "Someone is envious of you and wants to harm you. You know that someone is envious of you, don't you?"

Pancho, who'd been taking things with a grain of salt, now looked scared.

"Yes, someone is envious of me at my office," he admitted. "My boss is trying to get me fired."

Fortunato started upbraiding Pancho for holding back. "You have to tell us these things, so we can take care of them. We're masters. You can't fool us. When the candle breaks, there's an envy."

Angelino received the news of the broken candle with muttered prayers and imprecations. It was a bad omen that upset the proceedings. Now we had to change our approach and perform a special exorcism on Pancho, as a partial solution to the negative forces intruding upon us all. So Pancho was assigned a prayer—"the prayer of the glorious San Cipriano"—against evil spirits. (This was the same San Cipriano who figured prominently in the treasure-hunting ritual that resulted in the death of Rolando Copa at Tacapisi. For the first time it occurred to me that the *Book of San Cipriano* might be real, after all.)

Pancho stood off to one side, calling on San Cipriano to intercede "against all witchcraft." Pancho looked like a child sent to the corner for being bad; the rest of us continued talking and praying over the Misas, without having anything to do with him for a long while. Once again Angelino and Fortunato kept invoking Clemente Limachi for all kinds of projects.

"Clemente brings good luck," Angelino explained. "You should always ask Clemente for help—when you go on a trip, when you need support in your work, when you build the foundations for your house."

"Now that we're friends, we can tell you this," Fortunato said. "Anywhere you go and pray to him, Clemente will be there with you."

"How do you pray to Clemente?" I asked them.

Angelino immediately responded:

> Padre Clemente, que estás en los cielos,
> Sanctificado sea tu nombre.

> Father Clemente, who are in Heaven,
> Hallowed be thy name.

It was strange to hear Angelino and Fortunato asking that Clemente's "will be done on earth as it is in heaven," that Clemente supply their daily bread, forgive their sins, and deliver them from evil. Later I learned that shamans from other communities were praying to "Father Clemente" in the same fashion.

"Can you talk to Clemente for me, and ask him some questions?"

"No, you have to talk to him yourself," Fortunato said. "If you have faith, he'll present himself to you just like I'm in front of you now."

"Does either of you speak with Clemente?" I asked.

"He speaks to me just like you're speaking to me," Angelino claimed.

After Pancho finished his prayer to San Cipriano, Angelino sent him back to read it twice more. Then, at two o'clock on the dot, we burned the candy offerings in front of the altar, dancing and spraying beer toward the mountains on the horizon.

"You two must stand back now," Angelino ordered Pancho and me. At the end of the ceremony there is supposed to be a backlash of *contra*—negative reaction from evil spirits—who oppose the blessings of the Misa. The *yatiris* take this *contra* upon themselves. They believe it's dangerous for untrained people to battle these forces.

As Pancho and I waited off to one side, I asked him how he felt.

"Now I feel a lot better," he said. "But I was worried there for a while."

"Do you really have a problem with your boss, or did you make that up to keep Fortunato happy?"

"No, I have a problem with my boss. Just a few days ago I received a reprimand and a fifteen-day suspension for supposedly revealing government secrets to the press. It concerned an interview I did with an engineer who accused the Fishing Ministry of a disgracefully inefficient trout-raising project. *I* didn't say it was a disgrace—the man I interviewed did. But my boss is afraid I'm after his job, so he wants to fire me."

Angelino and Fortunato said that Pancho needed to complete his exorcism the next day, with a complete Contra Misa, also called Misa Negra (literally, a Black Mass), to crush the forces lingering against him. We agreed to buy the Black Mass and finish the job.

Both Angelino and Fortunato were now reasonably content, as well as reasonably drunk. Angelino told us how happy he was that I had returned to Chinumani. My return had confirmed his faith in the power of Clemente Limachi's soul.

"Clemente made you come back," he said. "This is proof to everyone of his greatness."

I agreed. But I said I wanted to know how Clemente had died in the first place.

"Simón Montoya did it to get rich," Fortunato said. "He has three cars because of the sacrifice. The rich people do it for cars."

I asked Angelino if this was true.

"I don't know anything about it," he answered.

"What do you mean, you don't know anything about it?" Fortunato said derisively, pushing Angelino. "You're the dead man's father; you know very well who killed him." Surprisingly, Angelino didn't defend himself. He just shrugged and looked fatalistic.

In fact, Angelino looked as though he might reveal something under all this pressure. But when he opened his mouth to speak, Fortunato reversed field and told him to shut up.

"I'll tell you," Fortunato said. "I found Clemente's body in the Apacheta with his head cut off. Clemente was my *compadre* [Fortunato was the godfather of one of Clemente's children]. I'll never forget how I found my beautiful *compadre* dead, with his head and face cut off, even his tongue and ears." Fortunato cried.

"Why did they cut off his face?"

"They cut off his face so the dead man won't have power," Fortunato said. "They cut out his tongue so he won't be able to talk.

"Clemente wasn't the only sacrifice," Fortunato added. "We found another woman here a few years back; she had her breasts cut off and her vagina slashed. Her face was all painted black."

"We heard that Uriarti, the beer distributor, sacrificed his wife on this mountain several years ago, and the men who did it slashed her vagina," I said. "Was that woman you found Uriarti's wife?"

"No, they took Uriarti's wife up to Mount Kapia, not here, to sacrifice her," Fortunato said. "But she refused to be sacrificed. She's still alive."

Neither Angelino nor Fortunato knew who the young woman they'd found on Mount Incahuási was. Angelino pointed to a dry canyon, perhaps two hundred yards from the Apacheta, where the female victim was left. "It's near Clemente Fargín's house," he said, referring to Clemente Limachi's uncle, the one who'd originally accompanied me to Mount Incahuási. "Fargín knows a lot about that sacrifice."

I thought—I wasn't sure, but I thought—I saw the shadow of a smile on Angelino's face.

"Fargín knows a lot about that," Angelino repeated. "He's a *yatiri*."

And this time Angelino definitely smiled.

Then Fortunato said that, although he suspected Angelino was paid off by Montoya to keep quiet, the presiding *yatiri* at Clemente's sacrifice had been brought from Bolivia. Leucaria Limachi had also referred to a Bolivian *yatiri*. Who was he? Angelino looked like an accomplice, but a minor one. Perhaps Angelino was present at his son's sacrifice. Perhaps he merely consented to it.

But there was no doubt Angelino considered it an honor to have his son chosen for sacrifice. In fact, promoting Clemente's cult had become his father's major passion.

Angelino explained that he hoped to build a new tomb for his son Clemente, where people could come and place flowers. Then he could recommend that people pray to Clemente, to obtain his help. And they would keep coming "for centuries of centuries." Angelino promised that if I helped build this tomb they would place my name on it, along with Clemente's, and Clemente would become my special protector.

For a human-sacrifice detective like me, this was a dream come true. Seeing Clemente's cult rise out of nothing was like being a geologist watching a volcanic eruption grow into a mountain before his eyes.

The next day we took our Misa Negra to the mountain for Pancho's exorcism. Fortunato didn't come. He was afraid of being seen in our company again, and his absence upset Angelino. "You have to have an assistant to help fight the *contra*," he said.

Angelino pulled out a large book and started to thumb through it in preparation for our ceremony. I asked him if he knew how to read. He replied that as an orphan he'd grown up alone, without knowing either parent, so he'd never gone to school. That's why he hadn't learned to read very well, even though he understood what was "inside the books."

"How can you understand them if you can't read them?" I asked.

The books "explained themselves to me without teaching, from one moment to the next," he said. "My head got hot, I went crazy, and I started sweating. This happened to me on Mount Chuchape. I thought I was going to die. But I didn't die, because my wife came and helped me."

Angelino claims this fit came over him after lightning struck the house where he lived as a young man on Mount Chuchape. "The lightning burned down everything in the house, but nothing happened to me," he says. Afterward he prayed to the Virgin Mary and to the *tius*, or high-mountain gods. "Other *yatiris* told me that I had to serve the mountains, the lightning." From then on he understood the books, such as the Bible, that *yatiris* rely on.

Like Machi Juana, Angelino claims he is blessed with a prophetic dream before each ceremony he performs. "Last night I saw a large stone that wanted to fall down on Pancho and crush him," he said. "But then I pushed the stone away." He stood up very straight and did a pantomime of driving the stone off. This meant that our Misa Negra was going to reverse the attack on Pancho and bring him good luck.

Angelino began by sorting his coca leaves to see which of us should assist him in the ceremony. I got the call—which I knew was fated, since Pancho, as the patient, couldn't serve as assistant. The old man kept sorting the green, aromatic coca leaves to find out who was "envious" of Pancho.

"It's possibly your boss," Angelino said. "He doesn't want you to be on top."

Maybe Angelino had heard us talking together, although Pancho thought not. Anway, it was both a shrewd and an obvious guess. If he had guessed wrong, Angelino would have sifted again and guessed again.

"Ah!" Angelino exclaimed, looking dismayed, as he held up a broken coca leaf. "Your boss has done witchcraft against you," he declared solemnly. "He has hired a special *yatiri* who performed spells against you in the lake."

It was another clever suggestion. Pancho was a fishing engineer, so hiring a *yatiri* to work black magic through the water spirits of Lake Titicaca sounded appropriate. Angelino explained that candy objects shaped like fish were used in Misas for the lake gods—who could hurt Pancho's hatchery projects or even kill him through a storm. Angelino's further divinations revealed that Pancho would have become ill because of the hexes against him. Fortunately, the final three coca leaves came up whole, meaning that Angelino's ceremony would save him from serious harm.

Angelino resumed his stern warrior pose. He took a knife in his hand and announced: "We're going to kill these enemies." Then he hunted a little black caterpillar wandering by our altar. He took a tremendous swipe at the tiny creature, cutting it in two, releasing a dark, viscous mess onto the ground.

"That's how we're going to kill them," he said.

I whispered to Pancho, "Just tell him that we want you to have good luck, without killing anyone else." Pancho suggested this to Angelino, who merely shook his head and repeated, "No. There are *contras*. We're going to kill them."

Angelino asked me to begin reading the San Cipriano prayer from an archaic Roman Catholic missal. The word *contra* ("against") came up over and over again. I invoked the venerable San Cipriano, along with Jesus, Mary, and Joseph, Archangel Michael, and all the angels, to battle *"contra enemigos"* ("against enemies"); *"contra Satanás"* ("against Satan"); *"contra hechicería"* ("against witchcraft"); *"contra diablos"* ("against devils"); *"contra hechiceros"* ("against sorcerers"). Pancho had to name his enemies specifically at the office—San Cipriano was ordered to especially swoop down *contra* them. Now I knew the origin of *contra* as a generic term for witchcraft in the highlands. It came right out of the Roman Catholic manual once used by the "extirpators of idolatries" like Hernández Príncipe, and was now the exclusive property of the very idolaters they'd come to extirpate.

Angelino took his knife and drew three crosses on the ground in front of the black candy objects on the altar. Then he slammed the knife into the ground. It stood erect, like a sentinel, for the rest of the ceremony, except when Angelino pulled it out to kill bugs wandering nearby. He killed the unsuspecting insects with a vengeance apparently intended for Pancho's envious boss.

After placing the power objects—representing saints, Pacha Mama, and the mountain gods—on the altar with appropriate prayers for protection, Angelino started dancing around Pancho. It was intense—as if Angelino were stalking him. He circled with exaggerrated slowness, like a Tai Chi master, bending his torso back and forth, taking a drink of pure alcohol as he bent backward, then explosively spitting it out. He amplified the spitting sound into a loud "Shshuuh!" to scare away all demons. Angelino repeated this in the four cardinal directions, calling on the mountain gods Illimani, Kapia, Calvary, and others. Finally, he took his knife and, with increasing frenzy, began making cuts in the air all around both Pancho and me, getting close enough to make us hope he wasn't too drunk yet. Angelino was setting us free from the demons of envy and witchcraft.

We knelt before Angelino to receive his final blessing—a thunderous blow on the head with the heavy Roman Catholic missal. Now the exorcism was complete. As Angelino burned the offerings, Pancho said that he felt much better. I had a slight headache.

Angelino seemed happy, too, as he sat down with us. The sun was out, and Lake Titicaca surrounded us, its white-sailed reed boats floating like toys far below. Angelino pointed in the direction of Mount Illimani, under clouds, saying that he'd gone there twenty years before to perform a ceremony. Traveling to a distant community is a sign of prestige for a *yatiri;* making a pilgrimage to Illimani at the behest of a community there is a special mark of status.

Angelino thanked me again for the gift of the new poncho the day before—he said he would never forget it. I asked him if he would like to have lunch in town with us, but he said, with genuine graciousness, "No, I am satisfied with what you have already given me."

I asked him what kind of son Clemente had been.

"He worked hard, but he was always poor," Angelino replied. "He was very affectionate to his parents."

"Why haven't you demanded a police investigation of Clemente's death?" I asked.

"The day the body was found I was very sick," he said. "And

talking to the police is the widow's responsibility. But when she went to the police, they just yelled at her. They said, 'Why don't you keep a better watch on your husband instead of letting him go around alone at night?' Anyway, since then Leucaria and her children don't visit me any more. They don't miss me."

Since when?

"Since Clemente died, Leucaria hasn't spoken to me. Neither do my grandchildren, and that hurts me. I would like my daughter-in-law to approach me as she used to. Now that Clemente has died, she's my full daughter. I'd like her to come and say, 'Father, will you help me?,' to see what I can offer. Good manners require her to approach her father-in-law. I would like to be there when the stone is laid for the new house, so that we could be reconciled. She needs help, because there's a lot of envy in the community against her. People ask why you are helping one widow and not all the others. But I'm willing to help, even if all I'm able to do is lift one stone."

I could understand why Leucaria refused to speak with him any more, blaming Angelino, as she obviously did, for Clemente's death. Watching old Angelino, knife in hand, decreeing, "We're going to kill those enemies," I knew his intent was nothing if not literal. After all, Angelino was performing magic that, according to his belief system, was as lethal to its intended recipients as the knife was to the squirming bugs. Whether Angelino, directly or indirectly, killed his own son when the occasion demanded it, his attitude toward deadly rituals was terribly impersonal. His philosophy reminded me of the official interrogator in the movie *Brazil,* who told his best friend as he began to torture him, "This is a strictly professional relationship."

Although Angelino hoped that laying the first stone for Leucaria's house would be an occasion for reconciliation, the project began with a series of conflicts. First Angelino and Fortunato objected to its inauguration without proper offerings to the Pacha Mama and mountain spirits. But President Leiva and the Evangelicals wanted only Christian prayers. The two groups, of about ten men each, stood apart, arms folded, without speaking to each other.

The women sat away from the men, cooking for everyone, without the obvious divisions that marked the male world. But when Angelino tried to approach Leucaria, the widow yelled at him in Aymara, motioning for him to go away. This is almost inconceivable rudeness from a woman toward an elder man, much less toward her father-in-law.

My driver, Víctor Aquispe, shook his head. "This is all very strange," he said. "When the foundation for the house is placed, the *yatiris* have to do their work, praying to the hills and Pacha Mama. It's like getting permission from the earth to build the house. Without it, the house may not stand. But the *hermanos* [Evangelicals] are opposed."

President Leiva took me aside. "There's a lot of envy going around, you know," he said.

Yes, I knew. I was also beginning to appreciate the need for cathartic ceremonies, like the Misa Negra, to deal a psychological swat to the stinging furies buzzing around everywhere.

"I'd expected many more workers to come today. But some people say that you're a communist organizer. Others want to know why you're helping only this woman. Even Angelino, the widow's father-in-law, doesn't want the house to be built. He says we should build a house for his other daughter, who's also a widow, before helping Leucaria."

"They tell me that Simón Montoya doesn't want me helping the widow, either," I said.

"Simón Montoya is the father-in-law of Fausto Quispi, one of the two men who was taken to jail for killing Clemente," Leiva said. "Montoya helped him get out of jail, just as we were on the verge of finding out what really happened. I almost had a fight with Montoya about this—he knows very well what happened to Clemente. So do Fausto Quispi and Alejandro López. That's why they're afraid. Fausto Quispi is going around asking, 'What's that *gringo* doing here?' "

Just as in Lago Budi, everyone wanted to know what the *gringo* was doing. In fact, when I went past Fortunata Limachi, Leucaria's eldest daughter, she asked disdainfully, in Aymara, "What's this *gringo* doing here?"

On that particular Saturday, I felt it was a good question. I was suffering from a case of dysentery, which made me feel weak and miserable. Eating compounded my discomfort, but eating was the main social grace of the day. And as the official sponsor, or *padrino* (godfather), of the house, I was obliged to eat enthusiastically. I explained that I was sick, that I was a vegetarian, but to no avail. I was soon feeling sicker. All I wanted to do was escape. When people kept squabbling over the ceremony, I was tempted to tell them all to forget about it.

Fortunately, Víctor Avendaño arrived, and he was able to convince the warring factions that some traditional ceremony could accompany the Evangelists' prayers. So we proceeded to hear the Our Father recited in Spanish and Aymara, followed by Angelino's offerings of alcohol and coca leaves to the earth and mountains. Each of us—including the Evangelicals—then filed by Angelino, selecting a bit of *kopala* (a resinous substance from a tropical tree, used as a fragrant offering in most Misas) and a coca leaf, depositing them in one cup, then pouring a few drops of wine into an adjacent vessel. After everyone had made his offering, a man and a woman were chosen to compete in burying the offerings in the northeastern and southeastern corners of the building. The male and female groups both laughed and clapped, urging their representatives on. Leucaria moved back and forth quick as a cat, and easily won. I'd never seen her so happy.

Now it was my turn to lay the first stone—a big rock which I barely lifted into the prescribed hole of the southeastern corner. Pancho came over with a champagne bottle and said, "You have to break the bottle on the first stone. But before you do, give a little speech."

I took a deep breath and made my first speech to the Aymara Indians.

"I know that some of you are wondering, 'What's the *gringo* doing here?' " Everyone laughed, which was a good sign. "I've been wondering myself. Angelino told me that I had returned here because the soul of Clemente Limachi called me. According to Angelino, Clemente's soul is very powerful. I myself don't know, but I'm beginning to believe it. When I came here originally, all that interested me was finding out how Clemente had died, so that I could write about it. We all know that he had been sacrificed. Traditionally, anyone sacrificed to the mountain gods here in the Andes became sacred, and it was a sacred responsibility to take care of his family with honor. Some of you, the *hermanos*, say Clemente died in a pagan ceremony, which you consider a sacrilege. But we also know that Jesus continually told his followers to help widows and orphans, and Clemente Limachi left nine orphans and a widow. So whether you are Christians or you believe in the old religion, whether you think Clemente is a saint or not, there's an obligation to assist innocent victims like these children. On behalf of Clemente, I'd like to thank you for being here, for helping build this house for his family, which has also become *my* family."

I shattered the champagne bottle on the rock, and applause burst out with the foam. Immediately men lined up and began carrying rocks to lay the foundations, one rock at a time. Angelino asked Leucaria for an empty kerosene can to gather dirt fill, which he wanted to pour between the rocks. Leucaria spoke sharply to him—but she got him the kerosene can. At least they were talking.

I'd brought beer and Coke for everyone to drink, but no one made a move to open the bottles; Pancho explained that I had to go around and serve everyone, or they would never drink anything. So I went from person to person, filling the same dirty glass over and over again, realizing, as I got big smiles from formerly reticent faces, that this was probably the best way in the world to make friends. I enjoyed serving the children, and when Leucaria's little boys came up, I took the opportunity to wipe their very dirty noses.

I couldn't shed my desire to civilize the natives. Wiping their noses was only the first step—in my ideal world they would all have become teetotaling vegetarians who practiced yoga. I never really thought such a fantasy was possible, but nothing else was quite good enough for me.

People noticed this. I got my first inkling that I was not meeting native standards from Víctor Avendaño. Víctor was a key contact— he knew more about native customs than did I, or many anthropologists. For instance, when I mentioned that Clemente Limachi's face had been cut off, he said that this custom was similar to that of the local undertaker, who covered dead people's faces with mud to prevent the souls of the dead from doing evil.

More important, Avendaño actually knew two men who'd sacrificed a girl on Mount Incahuási. The victim was supposedly "Uriarti's woman," a rather vague designation that could refer to Uriarti's wife or lover. I'd confirmed that such a sacrifice had indeed taken place in 1982, and that the young girl had had her vagina slashed, a key fact which corroborated Avendaño's story, as told to him by the sacrificers themselves over drinks. But I wanted Avendaño to tell me more about the sacrifice. Why had they slashed the woman's vagina? Why had they cut her breasts off and painted her face black? Yet, whenever I raised the subject with Víctor, he looked embarrassed, muttering that I would have to ask the men myself. If I asked who the men were, he was equally evasive.

During the celebration of the house inauguration, Pancho pulled me aside and said, "Avendaño complains that you enter in too directly when you ask about sacrifices. He's ashamed just to come out and talk about these things. He's afraid you'll think he's some kind of savage. He has to have a drink or two in order to talk. But since you don't drink, he's also ashamed to tell you this."

"I don't care if he drinks."

"But you keep yourself aloof, as though you were better

than everyone else. Here society revolves around communal drinking. The success of every project—from doing a Misa to building a house to harvesting the crops—depends on everyone's joining in and drinking together, so the *achachilas* [mountain spirits] can be fed."

"Look, I'm not telling them whether they should drink or not. I accept their traditions. But my tradition is not drinking, O.K.?"

This was not O.K.

President Agustín Leiva insisted that Pancho and I accompany him to yet another house-building ceremony—this one the roofing of a large cement-block home for his son. I desperately wanted to get out of it. "It's impossible to avoid going without insulting the president," Pancho said. "The president," I thought disgustedly. "The president of *what?*"

You have to remember that I was feeling sick—weak, dehydrated, and feverish. My patience was wearing thin. So, when we arrived at the second, unexpected house ceremony, it proved a trial. The level of intoxication was surrealistic. I felt drunk almost by infection—the ground seemed to wobble from all the swaying that people were doing. Everyone arriving was supposed to bring a crate or two of beers with him (Pancho bought one for us to present). I tried not to forget that this staggering quantity of liquor was for the gods.

Various inebriated individuals came up and saluted me as though I were a member of their family. They kept trying to offer me beer bottles.

"No, thank you," I said.

"I want you to drink with me," one man insisted.

"No, thank you."

At this point the man, whose eyes were so bloodshot they looked almost fake, became offended. He loudly insisted that I had to drink with him. Pancho intervened and sent him on his way.

"The ritual here is that one person fills his glass, then gives the bottle to the next person," Pancho explained, gesturing toward me. "He then drinks from the glass, toasting you, the mountains, and the good fortune of the house. Then you have to take the glass and follow suit. Even if you don't drink, you must pour some beer onto the ground and invoke the mountains, asking for blessings on the house."

I got pretty good at invoking the mountains—I knew the names of more snowcapped peaks than most of the people at the party. That, along with the technique of putting the glass to my lips and pretending to drink, seemed to satisfy everyone.

"Let's go, Pancho," I said, after we'd been at the celebration for two hours. "It's eight o'clock now, and we've got to drive all the way back to Puno."

"We have to wait until the *padrinos* break the bottles of champagne on the roof," Pancho said.

"How long is that going to take?"

"Well, they have to go out and buy some more champagne bottles, because they've added another *padrino* at the last moment. They want you to be *padrino* of this house, too."

I made a very ugly face, so ugly, in fact, that Pancho came over and grabbed my arm, saying, "The object of this whole thing is to have everyone here in your hip pocket by the time the ceremony is over. Just go along with everything, and I'll explain it later."

Someone handed me a bouquet of flowers. I smiled and handed it to Pancho, thinking that we were passing it around. People stiffened.

"He doesn't understand," Pancho said. "He's not trying to insult you; he just doesn't know what this means." Then, turning to me, Pancho said, "As the *padrino*, you have to keep the flowers and put them on the roof of the house when you break your champagne bottle."

After the longest time my champagne bottle arrived, we climbed onto the wet cement of the roof, broke the bottles, laid the flowers, invoked the mountain gods, saints, and Pacha Mama, and came down again.

"Now can we go?" I asked Pancho.

No. We could not. The hosts wouldn't hear of it. Besides, it was very bad luck for the *padrino* to leave the inauguration. And it was impossible even to consider doing so before being worshipped by your new godchildren.

"Worshipped" is the right word. Leiva's son and daughter-in-law, the owners of the house, came up and knelt down in front of me, prayerfully stretching out their arms and saying to me, "Godfather, dear Godfather, give us your blessings." Others also joined the line to greet me in the most effusive fashion. I was so tired and bewildered I just thought, over and over again, "Who the hell are all these people kneeling down to me?"

It wasn't until an hour later, when Pancho and I managed, with great difficulty, to have a few words in private, that I began to understand who the elite of Yunguyo, the people at my feet, really were.

"Look, the people here in Yunguyo are all very nervous about outsiders," Pancho said. "They're defensive, because the people in this town who aren't involved with smuggling goods are involved with smuggling drugs. So any new person around here scares them. This afternoon Avendaño told me that the people here suspect you're a top-flight CIA agent. With your strict style of life, you seem like a secret agent to them. Avendaño told me these people are angry, and that's why he warned you to stay away from Yunguyo for a while, until things settled down. In fact, Avendaño has been told to stay away from you—his friends are accusing him of betraying them, of receiving money from you. That's why he'd prefer you not approach him directly anymore."

Here Pancho gave me a big grin. "And that's why I decided tonight that you should be the godfather of Leiva's new house," he said. "I suggested to Leiva that you would be honored by being the godfather. Being a godfather is an extremely important thing to them—from now on you're related to Leiva and his son in a special way. You can go and stay at their home any time you want; you can stop and eat lunch without any notice. And they expect you to be like a family member to them. I arranged this, even though you didn't want it, so you would be less threatening to them. So that you would be incorporated into their system of *compadrazgo* [fictional kinship]. Everything revolves around *compadrazgo* here—the smuggling, the drug running, and probably the sacrificing, too. So getting you to be the godfather is a spectacular coup.

"Avendaño also told me that he has definitely spoken with the two people who sacrificed Uriarti's woman," Pancho said. "But he's a good friend of Uriarti's, a very good friend of Uriarti, whom he drinks with all the time. That's why he also feels bad about giving any more information that might compromise his friend."

"That's some friend he has, then," I answered. "Whose side is Avendaño on, anyway? The poor people who are being sadistically sacrificed, or the sadists who are making the sacrifices?"

"That's why the people don't have confidence in you," Pancho said. "You seem outraged at everything—all their customs disgust you. I'm often disgusted myself at the filthy food they offer us, at their alcoholism, and at these terrible sacrifice practices. But you have to swallow those feelings if you want to get beyond their defenses. And here in Yunguyo you at least have to go along with them by taking a drink. They can't understand someone who won't drink. Avendaño told me, 'I don't trust someone like the *gringo*, who doesn't drink.' He also warned me that you would betray me."

"Yes, Pancho, I'm going to betray you," I said.

"Oh, it's not just you," Pancho said, laughing. "He thinks that *I'm* going to betray him, too—in spite of the fact that I've known him for years. And when I told Avendaño that I was going to Leiva's roof-raising party, he said I should be careful, because the people there might harm me when they get drunk. He says they're all very dangerous."

On that score, at least, I agreed with Víctor Avendaño. I thought the elite of Yunguyo were very dangerous, especially to me, and especially when they were drunk. For that reason, I had no intention of hanging around and getting drunk with them far into the night. Getting drunk with friends like this was the last thing Clemente Limachi had done in his life. And it was the last thing I planned to do.

The drive back to Puno was long and cold, punctuated by a couple of cloudbursts of hail. As we drove, I mused over the different answers people around Yunguyo were giving to the question: "What is the *gringo* doing here?" Avendaño suspected that I was a CIA agent; others feared I was a detective investigating drug smuggling; many more thought I was a Catholic priest. It occurred to me that, as far as the people of Yunguyo were concerned, I was the local incarnation of Father Hernández Príncipe—part priest, part policeman. As in Lago Budi, I'd become the embodiment of an ancestral nightmare—in this case, I was the the Inquisitor.

I was startled several times on the road to Puno, when we swerved to avoid big rocks—boulders, actually—treacherously placed at curves near cliffs. These sabotage stones were a regular part of our travels. At first they'd confused me. Then a resident of Pomata explained: "The people deliberately put the stones on the highway to cause accidents. They say that the highway must drink blood. When someone dies in an accident and his blood spills on the road, then the highway is satisfied, and everyone is safe from accidents for a while."

We were lucky that a full moon, a giant spotlight, illumined the dangerous road. From the white stubble on the hills I could see that the highlands were frosting over, glittering in the freezing light. The only warm spot in our journey came as we passed the Israelite Temple near the Ilave River. Here devotees were celebrating the Sabbath of an animal sacrifice, judging from the big crowd, waving banners, and the blazing bonfire lit outside the temple. They were singing and swaying around that huge, burning circle, led by a woman dressed in white—almost a banshee in the moonlight. She knelt next to the fire with her arms outstretched, her head thrown back, and her mouth agape, probably in rapt song. But to me she looked like a lunatic raving at the sky, another citizen of this promised land, "Israel in Peru."

◫ 15 ◫

TRACKING THE
SACRED EXECUTIONER

For several days following my godfather duties, I was so ill I couldn't get out of bed. When I returned to Chinumani I saw that no progress had been made on the house during these days. Monday had been the Feast of Saint Philip; Tuesday, the Feast of the Holy Cross. Today, Wednesday, I could still hear the drums and horns from nearby bands celebrating the Holy Cross. Nobody was working on the house, and nobody seemed to think that such a thing was conceivable. "People are afraid to work because of the feasts," I was told. Being a Peruvian peasant doesn't pay well, but there are lots of fringe benefits.

Fortunately, Leucaria Limachi's brother, Luis Flores, was hanging around, and he agreed to introduce Pancho and me to a knowledgeable *yatiri*. "Angelino Limachi is a good *yatiri* but he's old," Luis said. "Now more people go to Ramón Jiménez, because he's younger and he remembers the names of the mountains better than Angelino does."

We met Ramón Jiménez as he was leading a bull to his brightly painted two-story house. A profusion of flowers marked the outside patio, where we sat down to talk. Jiménez told us he'd been a *yatiri* for over twenty-five years. Now, at the age of fifty-six, he had plenty of people requiring his ritual services—something he recounted as a sign of his prestige. When asked how he became a *yatiri*, Jiménez sounded a little embarrassed to admit he hadn't been struck by lightning—the traditional way of being commissioned by the mountain gods. Yet Jiménez claims superiority to older *yatiris* like Angelino because, unlike them, he knows how to read.

"When I do a ceremony, I take all my books to show them to the *achachilas* so that the books will be successful," Jiménez said proudly. "I've cured people of vampire attacks using the San Cipriano prayers and a black sheepskin."

Jiménez agreed to perform a ceremony for us the following day, on top of Mount Incahuási. In addition to the three Misas for the *tius*, *glorias*, and Pacha Mama, he ordered us to bring a Ñanqha Misa, a group of offerings for the *ñanqhas*, or "devils." He said this was necessary to drive off the *contra*.

The next day we met Ramón Jiménez and Luis Flores at the Apacheta and climbed the well-worn path to the peak of Mount Incahuási, where Jiménez set up four pieces of white paper to receive the many-colored candy offerings of our Misas. I was struck by Jiménez's calm, controlled style, a great contrast to Angelino's drunken, Dionysian approach. Jiménez, wearing sandals, a gray business suit, and a blue-tasseled cap, marshaled his offerings with reserve and precision. There was none of the ecstatic improvisation—sometimes highly inspired, sometimes incoherently rambling —that marked Angelino's Misas. Jiménez invoked an impressive list of mountains, including the distant Volcán Misti (18,360 feet, site of an Inca high-altitude sanctuary),[1] a few hundred miles from Yunguyo. "If you don't name all the mountains, sickness and bad luck will catch you," Luis Flores explained.

Jiménez departed from his beloved books, however, in one peculiar respect: he summoned the spirit of Clemente Limachi even more earnestly than Angelino had. Which is to say that Jiménez spent more time praying to Clemente than to any mountain god or saint—and possibly more than to all the mountain gods and saints put together. He and Luis kept asking Clemente to help Leucaria build her new house; to help Pancho and me with our investigation; to help everyone with good health, jobs, rich crops, cars . . . the whole shopping list.

"Clemente has a lot of power," Ramón said. "When you perform a Misa to Clemente, you'll never lack work, or water, or good health. We get everything from him."

"Why does Clemente have so much power?" I asked.

"He has so much power because the people killed him," Ramón answered, explaining that all people sacrificed like Clemente are good intercessors. "There's another man the people killed who is named a lot in Misas—Sexto Aratia. A few years ago, at the Feast of Saint James, on the 25th of July, they tied him to a pole and flogged him to death. Then they placed a sign on his body which read I AM A THIEF. But he wasn't a thief. The people were all drunk and crazy from the celebration. He begged them not to kill him, saying, 'I have seven children.' But the people answered, 'That's all the more reason to kill you.' "

Although Sexto Aratia was Ramón's brother-in-law, Ramón hadn't bothered to mention his name at our Misa. Ramón justified this by explaining that praying to Clemente produced better results. In the course of his Misa, however, Jiménez made a general invocation to cover all human sacrifice victims—"all those who died in *wak'ani.*"

According to Juana Vásquez, an Aymara folklore expert at the Museo Etnográfico in La Paz, Bolivia, "*wak'ani* is a place of power which belongs to the serpent. It's usually a gully, a canyon, or a cave. People go to the *wak'ani* to perform rituals at night, even though the *wak'ani* is malevolent and dangerous—a place where you have visions of snakes, tigers, and red roosters."

Jiménez pointed to the dry stone channel where Clemente's body was deposited and said, "That's a *wak'ani*. The place where the girl was killed on this mountain [another dry channel] is also a *wak'ani*." The boy who was sacrificed in Tacapisi in November 1987 met his end in a dry streambed similar to these two spots Ramón Jiménez indicated on Mount Incahuási.

"But was Clemente Limachi killed at the *wak'ani*, or did they decapitate him on top of this mountain and then leave the body below?" I wanted to know.

"They did it right there in the *wak'ani*, in the canal of the Apacheta," Jiménez said. "The sacrificers pay the *tiu* of the canal because those are places of power, where the devil keeps his treasures. So they kill the victim right there, at night, bringing offerings of a cow horn, a green shirt, a golden slipper, the ear of a donkey, and the tongue of a dog. Then they make a circle out of chicken's blood and from within the circle they call on Lucifer three times. When Lucifer arrives, he asks, 'Why have you called me?'

"You have to answer, 'I want money, lots of it.' The devil receives your request, but he tells you first to bring him a person—man, woman, or child. Once you've made this pact, you have to fulfill it with a human sacrifice right then and there. If you don't have a human victim on hand for the devil, you'll go crazy."

"You have to comply with that responsibility," Luis added solemnly.

"I've read the exorcism of San Cipriano from a Roman Catholic missal, but there was nothing about golden slippers, cow horns, or human sacrifices in it," I objected.

"The Catholic exorcism of San Cipriano has nothing to do with the *Great Book of San Cipriano*," Jiménez said.

This story has marked coincidences with the bizarre murder at Tacapisi, where the confessed killer said he was using the *Book of San Cipriano* for a nocturnal ritual, at a dry channel or canal, whose purpose was to secure treasure from the mighty, and malevolent, spirits of the place. Juana Vásquez says that the *wak'ani* is virtually a serpent's lair, and that's precisely what Mario Cotipu saw his friend, Rolando Copa, turn into—a giant green snake. Furthermore, Mario claimed he had committed his crime during a fit of insanity. The murder at Tacapisi was still bizarre, but it no longer looked like a local eccentricity. It fit the sacrificial pattern.

According to Luis Flores, human sacrifices near Mount Incahuási were a fairly frequent occurrence. "A human sacrifice gives a person money for only a half-year, or a year at most. Then they have to sacrifice someone else."

"Why is this place near Mount Incahuási so popular for human sacrifices?" I asked.

"They used to do the sacrifices somewhere else," Jiménez said. "Did you know that Mount Kapia is a snake cut up in pieces? Well, the head of the snake rests right on the shore of Lake Titicaca, over there." He pointed to a small hill, the last extension of Kapia toward Titicaca; from our angle, the mountain did look like a partitioned serpent, with its head lapping the water of the lake. The hill Jiménez pointed to was obviously a choice spot, right next to the lake but directly connected to Kapia, a symbolically perfect union of the mountain and water through the snake deity. Unfortunately for the sacrificers, the government built the Pan-American Highway right across the "snake's" neck, effectively decapitating the serpent, and bringing a permanent flow of traffic within a couple of hundred yards of the ritual site. So the sacrifices were moved to the relative privacy of Mount Incahuási.

"Why did the sacrificers cut off Clemente's face and tongue?" I asked.

"They cut his tongue off so Clemente wouldn't be able to talk and tell who his assassins were," Luis said. "At midnight the devil can speak through the corpse of the victim. But when they cut his tongue off, he keeps quiet. As for the face, they use it as an offering, as a *kucho*, which they bury at the Apacheta for the *tius*. There's a lot of fat and blood in the face, which makes it a good offering to the *tius*. That's the same reason they cut the vagina of the girl who was killed here—to get a lot of blood. Only blood satisfies the *tius*. The *tius* always want blood."

Another reason for cutting off the face and tongue, Luis explained, was to deprive Clemente's soul of power. "If they don't scalp his skin and tongue, Clemente could avenge himself against his killers. But even though they've done these things, Clemente still has a lot of power." Proof of Clemente's power, in Luis's eyes, was that one of his suspected assassins, Fausto Quispi, lost a cow the previous year. "The soul of Clemente is not helping him as he is helping us," Luis concluded.

"How can you be sure Clemente is the one who's giving you jobs, health, and rainfall?" I asked. "And how can you be sure it's the same Clemente who seized Fausto Quispi's cow?"

Ramón Jiménez and Luis Flores exchanged quizzical glances, as though I was a little daft. They finally answered, matter-of-factly, that Clemente was always assisting them and everyone else in the area. There was no doubt about it. That's why they all performed Misas to him.

"Well, how do you know it's Clemente? Can you see him?"

"Of course, Clemente is here with us now," Luis said.

"Can't *you* see him?" Ramón asked me, incredulously, gesturing to something that seemed to be in front of his face. "He's right here, like the wind."

I'd thought of the Aymara religion as excessively materialistic, with its candy houses, cars, animals, and people revolving in a supermarket constellation of goodies and gods. But the spiritual presence of Clemente Limachi seemed as tangible to them as a toy house or any other object. They could see him. Why couldn't I? It occurred to me that my view of their world hadn't been materialistic enough. I was blind to the object of my inquiry.

As we huffed our way down the mountain, Pancho took time to sound Jiménez further, in Aymara, about the sacrifice of Clemente Limachi. Pancho pulled me aside, showed me his notebook, and said, "I know the name of the *yatiri* who sacrificed Clemente Limachi."

"What's the *yatiri*'s name?"

"The sacrificer's name is Máximo Coa.* That's a pretty good scoop, isn't it?"

It sounded like a great scoop. And one that we pursued the

---

*Máximo Coa is an alias, the only alias used in this book.

next day by paying another visit to Ramón Jiménez. We found him at home, sitting at ease by his flowers. After some small talk, we raised the subject of Máximo Coa.

The mention of Máximo made the relaxed Ramón uneasy. He said Máximo was a great magician, but one who was too deadly to deal with. Coa was a shaman who specialized in human sacrifices.

"He's a fugitive," Ramón said. "And you only meet him in the mountains. The last time I saw him was by chance, at the Feast of Saint Anthony last year, on top of Mount Incahuási. He'd been there since midnight the night before, with nothing to eat but a piece of bread and oranges. He was fasting, like Jesus Christ. I was so scared when I saw him that I started to tremble. 'Maybe he'll sacrifice me up here,' I thought, since we were all alone. But we started drinking together, and we drank a lot, enough so that I wasn't so afraid of him after a while. Then I got up the nerve to ask him about those human sacrifices. I said to him, 'Well, uh, what about all these human sacrifices the people say you've done?' But Máximo just took off his hat and put it over his heart, saying, 'Only God knows the truth.' "

"He's a real cynic," Francisco Paca said, "making God his partner in the human-sacrifice business."

Jiménez told us that Máximo Coa had once lived in a community called Queñuani, but that the people had thrown him out because of his reputation for human sacrifices. "Now Máximo just goes around at night on his donkey—you have to catch him in the mountains."

According to Jiménez, Máximo's power derived from several mysterious books that he carried around with him. "I saw him with three books," he said. "When I asked him what books they were, he said they were the Bible. But you could tell those books couldn't be the Bible."

Pancho and I decided to go to Queñuani. Again Pancho proved invaluable, because, as a fishing engineer, he already had contacts in the community. He quickly gained the confidence of the president of Queñuani, and in the course of an introductory conversation

The Inca boy of Mount Plomo
(Museo Nacional de Historia Natural, Chile)

Detail of Inca boy
(Museo Nacional de Historia Natural, Chile)

Female idol buried at Mount Plomo
(Museo Nacional de Historia Natural, Chile)

OPPOSITE: Mount Veladero and the Laguna Brava (Patrick Tierney)

Tierney excavating ceremonial quadrangle atop Veladero (Johan Reinhard)

Angelino Limachi and his assistant, Fortunato, atop
Mount Incahuási, where Clemente Limachi
was sacrificed (Patrick Tierney)

Angelino in ecstasy with a Bible in
one hand and a bottle in the other (Patrick Tierney)

Author inaugurates Clemente Limachi's grave, as Leucaria, her children, and her brother, Luis Flores, look on. (Preben Kristensen)

The figurine of the Tiu that was used in a ceremony on Mount Azoguini (James L McGuire)

asked the president if there was any shaman who really knew what
he was doing in the area.

"Yes, the best *yatiri* for sacrificing llamas is a man named
Máximo Coa," the president said. "Every December he used to
perform that ceremony for the crops. But the man got carried away
several times, and sacrificed some people—women especially. He
was even in the Puno jail because of sacrificing people. The police
let him loose, but he went back to his old ways. In fact, he even
wanted to sacrifice his own wife. Finally, the community got angry,
sacked his house, and kicked Coa out. Coa's son took his wife away
to Arequipa. Máximo doesn't come around here anymore."

Queñuani was far more prosperous than the neighborhood of
Chinumani, some six miles distant. Here, right next to the Pan-
American Highway—and not far from where Mount Kapia's snake
head slithers into Lake Titicaca, the former site of human sacrifice—
people had diversified their economy. They raised beef as well as
potatoes and traded heavily with the coastal city of Tacna. Pancho
thought they were also heavily involved in smuggling across the
Bolivian border, like most enterprising people around Yunguyo.

If Evangelical Protestantism had made large inroads in Chinumani, it appeared to have definitively conquered Queñuani. The
Baptists were stong here, but the Seventh-Day Adventists were even
stronger; they'd grown so numerous that they'd divided into two
groups, the Vegetarian Seventh-Day Adventists and the Meat-eating
Seventh-Day Adventists. All of them emphasized sobriety, hard
work, and family responsibility. The strength of the Protestant
congregations explained, in part, why the community was clean and
prosperous—and why they had not suffered a witch like Máximo
Coa to live among them. Yet people still believed in the efficacy of
his black magic.

"Máximo is the only *yatiri* who knows how to perform the Misa
to get riches," one man said. "Máximo is the only one who works
with Ñanqha, the devil."

It took us several days of discreet questioning to locate Máximo
Coa's old neighborhood. Since the slightest mention of Máximo's

name made people bristle, we asked instead for directions to another old shaman's house, someone we hoped would know our sacred executioner. After getting the wrong directions several times, I happened almost to collide with an elderly man on a bicycle.

"Where are you going?" he asked, in a friendly fashion.

"I'm looking for an old *yatiri* named Toribio Mamani," I said.

"Why do you want to see him?"

"I want him to perform a good-luck divination for me."

"I'll take you to his house," the man said. "He's my brother. It looks as if people were pointing you in the wrong direction on purpose. They probably thought you were a police detective."

We went to a dilapidated shack, one of the poorest dwellings in the whole locality, and found an emaciated man, perhaps sixty years old, who turned out to be Toribio. I told him that I was going on a trip and wanted to know whether it would prove safe. Toribio immediately produced a paperback, *El libro del oráculo, The Book of the Oracle,* which, according to the title page, "was the exclusive property of the Emperor Napoleon, translated from the 22nd English Edition of the 1864 German Edition of an Egyptian Manuscript found in the royal tombs of Upper Egypt." The title struck a chord—the people of Tacapisi told me they'd found and burned *The Book of Oracles* in the *yatiri* Copa's house.

Toribio's method of consultation was to throw a coca seed onto a checkered page, get numerical coordinates, and read from them, in uncertain style. The oracle prophesied that I would have a safe trip.

"I want to ask the oracle one question," Pancho said. "We're looking for someone, someone who is a powerful *yatiri*. So far we haven't been able to find him. And we need to find him so that he can perform a ceremony for us."

"Who's this *yatiri*?" Toribio asked.

"What's his name?" Pancho said to me. "Something strange like Máximo . . ."

". . . Coa," Toribio finished. Yes, he knew Máximo, who'd lived just a few hundred yards away. But he hadn't seen Máximo for years, and he didn't advise us to try and see him, either. "He sacrifices people. He's butchered three people already."

"Four," his brother corrected. "He killed a woman over at Chimbu a few years ago—a boy saw him there, so the police put Coa in jail. Before that he killed a mother and her daughter in his own home. He cooked their flesh, made cebo [fat extracted from the victims and used in Misas] out of them."

"Why did he do that?" I asked.

"He probably did it for the owners of automobiles," Toribio said. The fat from a human sacrifice is supposed to have multiple uses in acquiring automobiles, running machines, and even driving spaceships. In Aymara mythology, the whole economy is fueled by human flesh. "Only he knows for sure why he did it. He has three books he uses to study these things—the books of *Black Magic, White Magic,* and *Red Magic.*"

"He must know a lot," I ventured.

"People say he's a good *yatiri,*" Toribio's brother agreed. "But I don't know about that. You can't go alone to the mountain with him. He might end up sacrificing you."

"It sounds like he only sacrifices women."

But both brothers said that Máximo had also sacrificed a man that they knew. I asked Toribio's brother what the man's name was, but he refused to tell me. "What would happen if Máximo found out that I was talking about him?"

"Why are you so afraid of Máximo?" I asked him. "Isn't your brother a *yatiri,* too? Can't he protect you from Máximo's spells?"

"*Him?*" he said, pointing to his brother in disgust. "All my brother handles is this book and some Misas. I can do that myself. I used to be a *yatiri,* too. I'd get drunk every day at the ceremonies and chew so much coca I was always hungry for more. But neither of us knows anything compared with Máximo. Máximo is much more powerful. And he gets his power from those books that he carries."

Those books that Máximo carried. I kept hearing about the three books of *Black, White,* and *Red Magic,* along with the *Great*

Book of San Cipriano, although no one had been able to show me the texts. I still suspected this was a kind of illusion or exaggeration until I went to the local market and found that the *Great Book of San Cipriano* and the books of *White* and *Black Magic* were on sale at several different booths. "The *Book of Red Magic* is out of stock right now," an apologetic vendor said. "But we expect it from Bolivia some time soon."

The Sorcerers' Guide, or The Great Book of San Cipriano dedicates chapter XIII, "El santum regnum," to "The True Method of Making Pacts with Infernal Spirits Without Suffering Harm." The method is similar to that outlined by Ramón Jiménez and others: the supplicant should go to a mountaintop (or a crossroads near a river or a ruin) and, carrying various talismans, make a cabalistic circle on the ground, from which Lucifer is invoked three times. The first invocation goes as follows:

> Emperor Lucifer, owner and lord of all the rebellious spirits, I beg you to favor my request. . . . Appear to me tonight in human form, without any awful smell, and grant me, by means of the pact which I am going to present to you, all the riches and gifts that I need.

An infernal representative of Lucifer then appears, demanding to know why his rest has been disturbed. On hearing the request for riches, the devil refuses, saying, "I can't accede to your demand, except on the condition that you give yourself to me for twenty years, to do with your body and soul what I want." Negotiations follow, a pact is signed in blood, and the devil leads the individuals who have sold their souls to the nearest treasure.[2]

The protocol of the *Great Book of San Cipriano* has suffered a distinct transmutation in the oral tradition around Lake Titicaca. Here the very masochistic, and Christian, notion of selling your own soul to the devil in exchange for a treasure never caught on— or made much sense. The Aymara *yatiris'* more practical approach was to sell someone else to the devil, "body and soul." In the

Aymara adaptation of the rite, the way to avoid harm in making a pact with the devil was simply to give the devil a human victim.

The sense of selling the victim "body and soul" is crucial to the magical efficacy of human sacrifice. Obviously, someone is physically killed in this diabolical exchange, conducted at night and in a place of power. Not so obvious, however, is the sinister underlying deal whereby the soul of that person is permanently enslaved. This is the most terrifying aspect of human sacrifice to the poor people around Yunguyo—not just the fear of violent death, but the fate of lingering forever in a demonic hell, carrying out the wishes of the sacrificers.

All the facts about the death and subsequent cult of Clemente Limachi point in this direction. But perhaps the shaman who expressed the problem most clearly was a healer named Eduardo Calderón, who lives on the Peruvian North Coast, six hundred miles from Lake Titicaca, near the city of Trujillo. I went to visit this shaman because I couldn't locate Máximo Coa anywhere around Yunguyo, and I needed another perspective on my growing body of research. Eduardo Calderón has become the principal celebrity of Peruvian shamanism—subject of UCLA anthropologist Douglas Sharon's Ph.D. thesis and book, *The Wizard of the Four Winds*, and numerous other scholarly and popular works. British archaeologist Evan Hadingham, author of *Lines to the Mountain Gods: Nazca and the Mysteries of Peru*, may have summed up Eduardo's role when he told me, "Eduardo is a bit of a charlatan, but there's no doubt he has tremendously improved our understanding of Andean shamanism."

What makes Don Eduardo, as he's called, so useful, is his ability to verbalize the inchoate concepts latent within Andean religion—putting into Western terminology ideas that are implied but unexpressed in the world of the *yatiri*. Don Eduardo has Chinese blood and looks like a more powerfully built version of the martial-arts master in *The Karate Kid*. When I asked him about current human-sacrifice practices, he grunted and didn't say much about it for a few hours, launching himself instead on a series of fantastic stories about his encounters with thieves, several of whom he claims to have murdered in cold blood; mountain gods, who opened up a sacred peak and showed him rooms stocked full of gold and jewels; and black-magicians.

I was particularly engrossed in one story about a black-magician, whom Eduardo called a *brujazo*, or "big witch." Don Eduardo claimed to have been participating in an all-night ceremony with the big witch when the *brujazo* ordered him to leave the room and spit outside (spitting being a way of driving off certain evil spirits). "But when I went outside, I saw this kind of gorilla, which was half drunk," Eduardo said, emitting a series of guttural sounds as he got up from his chair, stooped over, his arms extended almost to the floor, and staggered around in imitation of a drunken gorilla. "It scared the hell out of me, and I bolted back into the house. But when I got back to the Mesa [North Coast equivalent for Misa], the gorilla was seated right next to the big witch. The *brujazo* looked at me and laughed. 'You see him, don't you? This is my guardian spirit, Chicanga. He does anything I want him to.' That's when I realized he was a black-magician. You'd never catch me working with a creature like that big black thing. It was really ugly."

"Do the *yatiris* who perform human sacrifice try to use the souls of their victims like that?" I asked.

"Of course," Don Eduardo said. "Obviously. That's what the guys who perform human sacrifice are trying to do with the souls of the victims. They want to control the disembodied soul and make it into a guardian spirit who will serve them."

Don Eduardo maintains that such entities are "thought-forms" trapped by the minds of magicians, for good or evil. As an example of "positive thought-forms" Don Eduardo mentioned Jesus and Buddha. "A thought-form like Jesus or Buddha can go on for eternity. As long as people think of Jesus, it's like continually charging a battery. But if people forget him, then, like others before and since, he'll be dissolved. Now Clemente Limachi is a thought-form that people are charging up where you work. By praying to him, they are giving him greater potential. They believe he's a saint, which means they've made him a necessity. He's been crystallized into a deity, a high power."

According to Eduardo, shamanism is the art of dominating and using these thought-forms. "When an animal is sacrificed, and the smoke from the offering rises skyward, everyone prays, 'Let us have bigger flocks.' But it's not the smoke from the animal—it's the united thoughts that rise upward and produce results. These are thought-forms, too. The black-magician concentrates his mind to cause an automobile accident and—THWAACK!—it happens. A white-magician also uses these forces. But the forces themselves are neutral."

"What about these pacts with the devil that precede human sacrifices?" I asked. "Are they neutral?"

"The devil here is different from the devil in Europe or China," Eduardo said, laughing. "San Cipriano is an adaptation from Europe, but it has found local roots. All these pacts are just a way of making concrete plans. People want something. They think they're going to get it through a certain ritual. But it has nothing to do with the devil. Europe and America have their own distinct devils. Here in the Andes the feline god of Chavín, the Lanzón, is an example of a devil."

I wanted to know if Don Eduardo could see any esoteric justification for human sacrifice. Did it serve any useful purpose from a magical standpoint?

"These guys who do human sacrifices are regressing to something that is so ancient, a real throwback," he said, shaking his head disdainfully. "It's almost commonplace. Here at the Huaca of the Dragon, a Mochica site (the Moche culture flourished in northern Peru in A.D. 250–750), we found the skeletons of children and llamas. In other places we've found heads of adults. The decapitation of this victim, Clemente Limachi, sounds like the cult of the trophy head, which was common here, at Nazca and Tiahuanaco. The Jivaro Indians of the Amazon still do it. It's almost normal."

Don Eduardo continued, "Now, what's the purpose of a sacrifice? In an ultimate sense, it's the sacrifice of man, the microcosm, to the universe, the macrocosm. A sacrifice is a channel between the microcosm and the macrocosm. The channel is always the same, yet between the past and the present there are many accidents, many uncertainties. So the disembodied soul of the sacrifice is a channel between the living present and the dead past. I believe that the soul of the sacrificial victim, if he is fully aware of this great honor, can become such a cosmic channel. In the case of the Moches, there is a beautiful painting of a warrior whose heart is being torn out. You can see from the look of peace on the warrior's face that his mind has transcended the pain. But to sacrifice a person without preparation, as this guy Máximo Coa does, is a terrible thing."

Killing someone without preparation is a terrible thing, in Eduardo's view, because it allows the black-magician to convert his victim into a monster. Eduardo contrasts this with the idealized purpose of traditional sacrifice, wherein the victim, accepting his fate, transcended material life and entered a higher realm of consciousness.

One may wonder to what extent human sacrifice was ever performed with the wholehearted acceptance of the victim; and one may wonder even more about Don Eduardo's optimistic projections of life-after-death. But there's no doubt that some of Eduardo's observations are insightful. His suggestion that Clemente Limachi's decapitation was a "normal" continuation of an ancient cult of the head—known at Nazca and Tiahuanaco in the remote past, while still continuing among the Jivaro Indians of the Amazon today—seems on the mark.

But how valid a comparison can be made between actual human sacrifices involving pacts with the devil and classic Andean beliefs? Here Don Eduardo's observation that the Andean "devil" of Yunguyo has more in common with the Lanzón (Great Image) of Chavín than with a European demon is extremely apt. Chavín, in northern Peru, was the first great pan-Andean religious center, whose artistic style spread over a wide area starting around 800 B.C. Chavín's

THE EVOLUTION
OF THE ANDEAN GODS

LEFT: Lanzón (Great Image), Chavín (800 B.C.)

The Lanzón has snake hair and feline fangs.
Recent excavations have suggested that
this deity was the recipient of
human and animal sacrifices.

RIGHT: Gateway God, principal figure
on the "Gate of the Sun" at Tiahuanaco
(A.D. 100–1100)

The Gateway God has trophy heads
dangling from his arms and waist.

LEFT: Aiapaec, Moche divinity (A.D. 250–750)

Shamans around Yunguyo identified Aiapaec
with their Tiu, who, like the Lanzón and
the Gateway God, has animal fangs for
teeth and serpents sprouting
from his head.

Lanzón is a gruesome-looking humanoid stone statue with the fangs of a feline and snakes for hair, which dates from Chavín's earliest period. Feline, serpent, and bird characteristics can be seen in later developments of Chavín religious art, particularly in a figure called the Staff God, considered to be a precursor of the central deity of Tiahuanaco's Gate of the Sun. All of these—Lanzón, Staff God, and the Gate of the Sun figure—have serpent and other animal traits. But so does the "devil" now worshipped around Lake Titicaca.

I found this out at a market in La Paz, Bolivia, where hundreds of "devils" were on sale for less than a dollar each. These devils are tourist trinkets, miniatures of masked figures who annually reenact a battle between Archangel Michael and Lucifer at the Carnival of Oruro. Because of the Christian overlays, anthropologists haven't considered these masked dancers, or effigies of them, as embodiments of the mountain gods. Aymara natives, however, say that the many "devils" at the Carnival celebrations are mountain spirits—*achachilas*. Lucifer, their leader, is really the Tiu, also known as "Supaya" or "Tiu Supaya."

Tiu Supaya lives in the mountains, and has great power to bestow wealth—particularly mineral wealth—or to harm people. In the early days of the Oruro Carnival, one of the names for Tiu Supaya was Huaricoto—the representative of Huari, the mountain god. In fact, the Pre-Lenten Christian battle between Archangel Michael and Lucifer, written by a Spanish priest in 1818, is really a continuation of a much older battle between the god Huari and the Inca state cults of Inti, the Sun, and Pachacámac, a coastal deity whom the Incas also brought into their solar pantheon:

> Near where Oruro stands, there lived the Urus, who were chiefly fishermen and pastoralists. Huari, a giant, lived inside the Uru-uru mountains. He fell in love with Inti Huara, the Dawn, who awakened him every morning. When he attempted to take her in his arms of fire and smoke, Inti buried him in the hills. To revenge himself, Huari took human form

and preached to the Urus against the rule of Inti and Pachacámac. He told them they would grow rich by seeking the metals concealed in the hills. He prompted them to steal the crops of the valley and made them drink chicha [a beer-like beverage made of corn in the Andean highlands] until they became drunkards. . . . Huari would not give up . . . and sent, one after another, a snake, a toad and a lizard, all of monstrous size, to wipe out the [Inca] people and their crops.[3]

The Urus were among the oldest and most primitive inhabitants of the Lake Titicaca region. Their deity, Huari, dwells in the hills and bestows wealth. He's also pleased by drunkenness. In all of these respects, Huari is just like the *tius* who are worshiped with alcohol around Mount Kapia today.

According to the above legend, Huari finally sent three monsters—a snake, a toad, and a lizard, all of gigantic size—to wipe out the Incas. Today, Yunguyo shamans connect snakes and toads with rainfall—toads are sacrificed atop Mount Kapia during droughts. Snakes, toads, and lizards also adorn Tiu Supaya at both Oruro Carnival and the Diablada in Puno. The little statue of the devil I bought shows him with a serpent coming out of his head and animal fangs, along with the bulging eyes of a frog or lizard. This mixture of animal traits is typical of shamanic visions of mountain spirits. When I asked Angelino Limachi what spirit Mount Chuchape had, he answered, "Snakes, lizards, frogs—devils." The crude but complex "devil" sold at the handicrafts market is a mountain god directly descended from ancient Andean beliefs, as Don Eduardo pointed out.

Don Eduardo isn't the only shaman with such ideas. When *yatiri* Andrés Jiménez, who lives on Mount Kapia, saw pictures of several classical Andean gods—ranging from the Lanzón of Chavín to the Gateway God of Tiahuanaco—he identified each of them as "the Tiu." I pointed to the miniature heads hanging from the belt of Tiahuanaco's Gateway God, the principal figure of the Gate of the Sun and asked what they were. "They used to chop people's heads off in the old days," he said. "They were like that." When I asked why people in "the old days" carried human heads around on their belts, Jiménez replied, "Because two heads are better than one [*Dos cabezas piensan mejor que uno*]."

The meaning of these frightening animal features is very clear in the natives' minds: "The *tius* always want blood." In exchange for blood, they bestow all the gifts of this world, from rain to Mercedes-Benzes. The *tius* are responsible for giving wealth to miners and merchants, many of whom buy the same diabolical images of him I got in La Paz. The Spanish friars told the Indians their mountain gods were devils, and the label stuck. But the power of the "devil" didn't diminish as a result. Nor did he lose his taste for blood.

Johan Reinhard has concluded that the central figure of Tiahuanaco's Sun Gate, the Gateway God who has a row of trophy heads around his waist, is a mountain god who was in charge of weather and fertility. He also thinks that Tiahuanaco's ranking mountain god was probably Mount Illimani, since Reinhard's research in the area shows that today's residents worship Illimani as the preeminent mountain deity. This view challenges assumptions that Tiahuanaco was primarily an "astronomical observing station," as my own guide to the ruins proudly stated, and as many academics have maintained over the years.

Like Reinhard, I've found that Mount Illimani is central to the Misas offered all around Yunguyo. Illimani is one of the three *tius*, along with Kapia and a high peak near Puno, Azoguini, described by Angelino Limachi as the paramount deities of the Yunguyo region. Illimani is thought to have decapitated its nearest neighbor—a snowcapped peak named Mururata (The Decapitated). Thus the Gateway God on Tiahuanaco's mammoth stone lintel—with serpents for his hair, feline fangs for his mouth, and human heads suspended from his waist—shares characteristics with the Lanzón from Chavín and my marketplace devil, but also his mythical beheading of Mururata perfectly matches the ritual activities associated with both of them.

In 1988, University of Illinois archaeologist Alan Kolata and an internation team uncovered ancient evidence of human sacrifice at Tiahuanaco. While excavating a ceremonial pyramid, called the Akapana, they discovered "a series of presumed human sacrifices— 16 burials of human parts, from the pelvis to the knee, where the question remains what happened to their corresponding torsos and skulls. These burials, found together with the burial of llamas, and puma bones, have an obviously ceremonial character, and they are found at only one level, at the foot of the first step of the pyramid."[4]

The three most striking aspects of Clemente Limachi's sacrifice were that he was decapitated, his facial skin and tongue were cut off, and all his blood had been drained out of his body for use somewhere else. Are there parallels for any of these practices? Archaeologist Evan Hadingham, who was influenced by Johan Reinhard's theory, connects the gigantic desert drawings of the Nazca plains to fertility rites involving mountain worship and an obsessive cult of the head. Deities sporting trophy heads from their belts, similar to the feline-serpent god of Tiahuanaco, or holding trophy heads by the hair, abound in Nazca pottery. Even more telling has been the discovery of physical trophy heads, complete with cords for carrying them around.

Excavations at the Chaviña Cemetery, in Nazca territory, uncovered eleven trophy heads, inside what archaeologists Máximo Neira and Vera Coelho identified as a ceremonial building. These trophy heads were buried along with offerings of food such as peanuts and maize. All of the skulls were pierced for carrying cords. At least one of the victims had been violently beheaded. This is consistent with Nazca iconography. "Many of the trophy heads that appear in Nazca pottery are dripping with blood, apparently from recent decapitation," Hadingham told me. Once the sacrifice was completed, the skin was stripped off the skull and the skull was boiled; then the skin was painted red and pulled over the skull again.[5]

The shamans around Mount Incahuási believe that blood from a human sacrifice "pays the earth," thus ensuring wealth, rain, and good crops—beliefs that would perfectly explain all the ceremonial trappings around the burial of the Nazca trophy heads. The only major difference is that the Nazca peoples, who didn't have to worry about the police, could afford to prepare their trophy heads leisurely and carry them around. Yet there is even a hint of these ancient practices at Mount Incahuási, in the ceremonial scalping of Clemente Limachi's face, reminiscent of the Nazca skinning procedures.

An even closer parallel emerges from a sixteenth-century text, *Ritos y Tradiciones de Huarochiri* (*Rites and Traditions of Huarochiri*), assiduously compiled by the Spanish priest Francisco de Ávila from the statements of native informants. In this book there's a fascinating account of how warriors were sacrificed, following which their facial skin was cut off and turned into masks worn in sacred dances. The whole ceremony, which included food offerings to the masks, served to reenact the natives' creation myth, wherein their founding deity, Namsapa, was similarly sacrificed:

> Of him [Namsapa] they said: "He is our origin; he was the first to come to these lands and he took possession of them." For that reason they cut his face (and, transforming it into a mask, they placed it on top of their own faces) and danced thus disguised. Afterward, whenever they captured [someone] in war, they cut off his face [and, transforming it into a mask] danced wearing it. They said that they derived their courage from this. And the men themselves who were captured in war used to say: "Brother, now you will kill me. I've been a man animated with great powers. You'll make a *huayo* [mask] out of me and, when you're going to go out on the plains [where the dancing is held], you'll offer me great quantities of food and drink.[6]

The warriors, in death, became identified with the mythological Namsapa and, like him, received offerings of maize, potatoes, and other gifts. All the masks (or the men wearing them) were carried around on litters for two days, as a sign of reverence. This is certainly a more elegant end than the one that met Clemente Limachi. Yet it is recognizably part of the same Andean continuum. Clemente, too, is transformed into a god, one who receives all kinds of offerings. Clemente, like the warriors, has his face scalped as part of his transformation into a spiritual entity capable of bestowing riches on the living.

The *yatiris* around Yunguyo may have only a vague notion of why face scalping still takes place when they say it is to take away Clemente's power. Yet this notion of seizing the victim's "power" was precisely what Francisco de Ávila's sixteenth-century informants told him about the goal of human sacrifice. The victim is someone "animated by great powers," which, after his death, pass to his sacrificers, who become braver warriors.

Don Eduardo completes this picture when he says there is a struggle for dominion over the soul of the sacrificial victim—the black-magicians want to turn Clemente's soul into a ghoulish protector who will carry out their evil commands. But to do so they have to neutralize Clemente's personal power by cutting off his tongue and face and using his blood as an offering to the *tius* of the mountains. According to Luis Flores, Clemente's face made a specially potent offering to the mountain gods. Others believe that the wealth achieved through human sacrifices stems from the supernatural properties of the *cebo*, or fat. This *cebo* is the choicest portion of the sacrifice and is reserved for secret Misas.

In Andean shamanism, power is never lost; it is transferred from one being to another, often through talismans fashioned from the body of sacrificial victims. The Indians of Huarochiri told Francisco de Ávila that their ancestors derived "courage" from the skin masks of the sacrificed warriors. Among the Jivaro Indians of Ecuador, similar ideas centered on trophy heads, the most valued booty from any Jivaro raid. Jivaro men had to kill in order to acquire guardian spirits, known as *arutam* souls. The heads of victims were shrunken both to neutralize backlash from the dead soul, and to harness its power. Unfortunately, the protection of the *arutam* ghost-soul was only temporary, and had to be extended by repeated sorties to kill more victims. In this most dangerous game of serial murder, warriors with the most killings to their credit did achieve some safety, because others feared their magical powers and considered them invincible. This closely parallels the shamanistic philosophy around Yunguyo, where those who pay for human sacrifices supposedly become immortal through the protection of spirits similar to the *arutam*. Yet their immortality is also tenuous, since the sacrifices have to be repeated annually, thus locking the sacrificer into a cycle of killing not unlike that which once possessed the Jivaro warriors.[7]

The close similarities between twentieth-century head-hunting by Jivaros in eastern Ecuador, the sixteenth-century warrior sacrifices in Peru's central Andes of Huarochiri, and the continuing immolations around Yunguyo can't be a mere coincidence. The vast span of nearly identical beliefs over the hurdles of geography, time, and differing social organizations is impressive enough to suggest a core of data for interpreting the often misunderstood past. For example, I think the Inca's *capacocha* child sacrifices—though they served multiple purposes, including the initiation of fertility cults like Clemente Limachi's in Yunguyo—can also be seen as a method of manufacturing guardian spirits for the Inca. These guardian spirits, the souls of the victims, were guarantors of the Inca ruler's longevity; their yearly sacrifice, like the yearly sacrifice of people by the rich merchants in Yunguyo, was an installment payment to prolong the royal patron's lease on life. If the Inca child of Mount Plomo was anything like Clemente Limachi, he was simultaneously a god and a slave.

That's only one of the paradoxes of human sacrifice. The image of a snake devouring its own tail sums up one of the relations of the god and the victim. The god was created in a primeval sacrifice; the victim becomes a god through sacrifice in time.

▣ 16 ▣

THE GOOD SEED

"When I climbed Mount Kapia a few years ago," Johan Reinhard told me when I visited him in La Paz, Bolivia, "I heard about a rich man in the town of Pomata who had sacrificed a couple of his young servant girls to Kapia. They said his business wasn't doing well at that time, and ever since then he's done extremely well. I dismissed this as a typical projection of jealousy, which often happens toward wealthy people in traditional cultures. But with the data you're getting, I'm beginning to wonder."

I contacted Johan's informants and learned that the man rumored to perform human sacrifices in Pomata, some twenty miles from Yunguyo, was none other than Mr. Juan de Dios Uriarti, the beer distributor in Yunguyo who, according to Avendaño, paid two men to sacrifice a young girl on Incahuási in 1982. Actually, Uriarti moved to Yunguyo from Pomata about the same time as the sacrifice.

"It's a family tradition with the Uriartis to do human sacrifices," one of my informants said. "They've always kept too many young servant girls around, and then one or two disappear from time to time. These girls are brought in from out of town, so no

289

one really knows them or misses them. All their wealth comes from those human sacrifices. But they say that he has to keep doing them, or else he'll have bad luck, or an automobile accident."

According to my sources, Uriarti was definitely mixed up in smuggling. One of them actually saw Uriarti cutting a deal with a captain of the Immigration Department, which is one of the agencies that control border traffic, so that his trucks wouldn't be molested as they crossed to and from Bolivia. Another one had seen Mrs. Uriarti—his wife—carrying speakers under her dress (they're much cheaper in Bolivia, where she was coming from). Of course, this was small-time smuggling, but Uriarti's trucks which plied the border trade were not small-time. And it was thought that coca-leaf paste, the first elaboration of the coca leaf on its way to cocaine, had also been a family business. One of Uriarti's brothers, they said, had been in jail for cocaine smuggling. He'd run a kerosene business, a vital ingredient in cocaine production, since coca leaves are mixed with kerosene and mashed together until they form a whitish paste that's sent to Bolivia and Columbia for further refining. After paying a bribe, Uriarti's brother supposedly went free.

Everything is a family operation in the Aymara world. "Uriarti's father used to sacrifice people to Kapia before he died a few years ago. He and his wife would climb up to the peak with the *yatiris* for the ritual. They say that the old woman, Uriarti's mother, would then let her long hair out of all its braids and go flying around the mountains. Her hair stood out straight as she went flying around the peaks."

Mrs. Uriarti, with her hair extended straight, flying around Mount Kapia, sounded like a female supernatural being from ancient Peru. In fact, I found Mrs. Uriarti by chance—on a postcard displaying a brilliantly embroidered Paracas blanket from around 300 B.C. There she was, Mrs. Uriarti in Technicolor, red body, blue-green face, with her yellow hair perfectly straight and extended behind her, flying through the air, a sacrificial knife in one hand, a serpent with a trophy head in the other. This, then, was the other, less painful way to become a divinity in Peru—to perform a human sacrifice and join the flying immortals on the mountain of the gods.

Yunguyo was starting to look like a museum in which the exhibits walked and talked, sacrificed and séanced, after the lights went out at night. I felt as if the gods and goddesses emblazoned on ceramic vessels and woven in tapestries thousands of years old had abandoned their stiff poses and were now wandering here by Lake Titicaca's shores.

The great Andean gods, with their animal fangs, trailing serpents, and trophy heads, are a day-to-day threat in Yunguyo. The *liquichiri* myth—about evil men who convert themselves to animal forms in order to hunt human flesh by night—is no myth. As Johan Reinhard explained it: "The basic idea behind the vampire stories, which you hear from Bolivia all the way to Ecuador, is that certain people, who are usually rich and dress in Western clothing, turn themselves into animals at night to kill local people and take their body fat, which they then sell for many uses—including rocket fuel. The basic premise is right—there are rich people who are part of a clandestine economy waiting to catch unaware individuals and sacrifice them for the sake of gaining wealth." People *are* vanishing at night, and their blood is offered to demon-gods whose mixture of animal ferocity and human form recalls both the ancient Lanzón and the contemporary *liquichiri* stories.

"It's very dangerous to pass by the Apacheta at night," Susana Sihuayro, Leucaria's sister-in-law, said. "There's a chance they can sacrifice anyone there."

I asked who "they" were, while Pancho translated.

"Simón Montoya has done various sacrifices," she said. "There's a white stone by Montoya's house where it is suspected that a number of sacrificed people are buried. They do these sacrifices to get money. Now, Montoya has three houses—one in Puno, one in Lima, and one in Tacna—in addition to the big house he has here. But they always find poor people to sacrifice. They look for people who don't have money, get them drunk, and lead them off staggering to where they do the sacrifice. I'm afraid they'll sacrifice my husband, Luis, because he's helping his sister Leucaria."

How often do they sacrifice people?

"Every year. When they sacrificed Clemente, it was because they couldn't find someone older: he was pretty young to be sacrificed. And it's too bad, because he was the only support for that whole family until you came along."

According to Susana, Simón Montoya worked in league with Alejandro López and Fausto Quispi, the assassins. But Montoya's man behind the scenes, coordinating the affair, was Clemente Fargín, who, in addition to being Clemente Limachi's uncle, was also Montoya's brother-in-law. This was a surprise to both Pancho and me, since Fargín had originally been the widow's great protector. Hadn't he gone to the police with Leucaria? I asked. Didn't Fargín later arrange for Leucaria's daughter to work for Mengoa, a beer distributor?

But Susana said that Fargín was actually Montoya's spy. When he got a job for Leucaria's daughter with Mengoa, it had been a ploy to frame her on a charge of theft, so that Leucaria would be further intimidated and silenced. I remembered that Leucaria's daughter had been accused of stealing by Mengoa's wife, a charge that was never proved, and that Leucaria was beaten up and put in jail as a result. As Pancho and I asked around, we found that others shared Susana's opinion: the whole thing had been a setup to imprison Leucaria and her daughter Primitiva, thus "liquidating" Clemente's family, and eliminating any possible demands for justice against Montoya and his assassins.

I kept getting bits and pieces of the puzzle as work progressed on Leucaria's house. Adobe bricks were made and baked in the sun, the walls started to rise, and, as they did, Montoya and Co. started to raise their heads as well. Clemente Fargín appeared regularly, asking what I was doing. Montoya demanded to know why the president of the community, Agustín Leiva, was helping Leucaria. Alejandro López came to laugh at Leucaria when the rains, which continued until the middle of May, ruined a large number of adobe bricks. "I'm glad it rained and your adobe bricks are destroyed," he jeered. "I hope you can't build your house." Susana Sihuayro said she overheard López say, "We're going to sacrifice Leucaria just like Clemente."

Many people were intimidated by these threats. Others refused to join the communal building, which made work on the house fitfully inefficient. Finally, laborers had to be contracted. Leucaria didn't have much support. But now that Leucaria had seen the adobe walls of her new house, she seemed like a new person. She dropped her depression and started fighting back. "You're trying to kill me just like you did to my husband!" Leucaria shouted at Alejandro López when she saw him in Yunguyo. "You murderers!"

López just laughed at Leucaria, but he and his friends were getting scared. The wives of the two suspected assassins also got in on this bullying act. One of them told Leucaria, "Just wait and see what we're going to do to you." Clemente Fargín publicly threatened Leucaria and Primitiva. "We're going to put you back in jail," he warned Primitiva. Neighbors said that once, when Fargín got drunk, he tried to hit Primitiva.

Others said that Clemente Limachi was last seen alive, not at the home of Fausto Quispi—as López claimed—but at Clemente Fargín's house, in the company of Quispi, López, and López's wife. Leucaria claimed that when she went to tell Fargín of her husband's death in the early hours of February 17, 1986, Fargín answered, "That's a lie. Clemente went off with Alejandro Lopéz and a thousand Intis worth of liquor."

How could Fargín have known about that unless Clemente Limachi and López had visited him on their way?

"Clemente Fargín is my big buddy," one man told me. "He's dedicated to business along the Bolivian border, where he goes on his bicycle. But I think that his other job is looking for poor people who can be sacrificed. As he travels, he keeps an eye open." We had overlooked several clues to Fargín's involvement. The first time Víctor Avendaño saw Fargín he laughed and said, "That guy knows the whole story." Angelino likewise smiled and said that Fargín "knows a lot" about the sacrifice of the girl in 1982. Fargín was, after all, a *yatiri*, and the two sacrifices on Mount Incahuási had taken place within scant yards of his home. We still didn't know who had presided over the sacrifice—whether Angelino or Fargín or a high-level specialist like Máximo Coa. But many people believed that both Fargín and Angelino were conspirators in Clemente's death.

Leucaria claimed that she had first learned of Montoya's involvement in her husband's murder on the night of his wake, when a neighbor overheard Simón Montoya, López, and Quispi arguing about the way that Clemente's body had been dumped in the Apacheta.

It was hard to know how much of all this was gossip and how much was fact. An elaborate mythology had sprung up about Simón Montoya that was revealing in its own right. People said that he was enormously rich—he led donkey trains loaded with saddlebags full of gold coins. Anyone who so much as touched one of his treasure-filled saddle bags was instantly changed into a snake.

In Tacapisi, the teenage boy Mario Churro claimed that he mistakenly killed his friend Rolando when Rolando suddenly turned into a giant green serpent during a nighttime ritual to get hidden treasure. In Chinumani, Simón Montoya supposedly converts his enemies, who want his treasure, into serpents. Since the concrete threat hovering over Leucaria and her family is that Simón Montoya will pay to have them sacrificed, this farfetched story has a real message behind it: If you cross Simón Montoya, you'll be sacrificed and changed into a serpent spirit.

This Montoya myth hints at how practitioners of human sacrifice build up their storehouse of magical powers, assimilating their victims as guardian spirits. There's a triple identity between the sacrificer, the victim, and the mountain gods. Mount Kapia is a gigantic snake; victims are turned into serpents; the sacrificer,

Simón Montoya, is now lord of these serpents. The story of Simón Montoya with his train of mules carrying saddlebags full of gold is nearly identical to myths about the deity Supaya, who, in addition to commanding huge snakes, "goes abroad at night, leading his trains of beasts bearing ores to be spread among the hills."[1] People who reportedly pay for human sacrifices, like Uriarti and Montoya, imbibe the divine powers of these deities, becoming demigods themselves, with attributes of immortality and near omnipotence. This is a crosscultural theme.

Jivaro Indians believe that it's perilous to kill any warrior who has the protection of an *arutam* guardian spirit. That's because his *arutam* spirit is likely to change into a serpent and avenge itself upon the man's murderers, much as Simón Montoya's serpent spirits supposedly ward off his enemies.[2]

On the Melanesian island of Malekula, a man who sacrifices a young boy along with a special boar becomes the Lord of the Underworld, with power over the whole tribe. "He is a very picture of that immortal person for whom death has no sting," writes Joseph Campbell, one of the foremost twentieth-century experts on mythology. Campbell suggests this Melanesian example underscores a universal principle at the core of all primitive religions: "A magical power is gained according to the measure of one's sacrifice." Each offering is "a captured quantum of divine power, which, through its sacrifice, is integrated with the giver. The giver climbs, so to say, on the rungs of his sacrifice."[3] In Melanesian rites, the greatest sacrificers become mythological hawks and, spreading their arms like wings, go flying through the heavens, not unlike Mrs. Uriarti of Pomata.

Within this framework, there's a constant contradiction between the victim of human sacrifice and his sacrificers. Around Yunguyo, the sacrificers and their shamans write a pact to give their unwilling victims' souls to the *tius*, who then make the sacrificed souls slaves of both the devils and the killers. But that's not the end of the matter. The sacrificers continually dread that the dead man will break free and avenge himself—a terrible threat, since the dead man has now become a dangerous spirit himself, wielding powers like the *tius* of the high mountains. To avoid this backlash, the dead spirit is propitiated by Misas and prayers, as in the standard practice of invoking "all the spirits who died at *wak'ani*" (all the spirits sacrificed in the dry canals on the sacred mountains) during mountaintop offerings.

This is the same promise offered to the first victim of human sacrifice in the Mayan *Popol Vuh*. An ancestral hero is decapitated and his head is left in the sacrificial Ball Court, where it sprouts fruit and engenders offspring (much as Andean trophy heads sprout plants). When the victim's magically engendered children find him, however, they refuse to remove him from his place in the Ball Court. He's needed there:

> And so it remained that they were respectful of their father's heart, even though they left him at the Place of Ball Game Sacrifice:
> "You will be prayed to here," his sons told him, and his heart was comforted. "You will be the first resort, and you will the first to have your day kept by those who will be born in the light, begotten in the light. Your name will not be lost. So be it."[4]

And so it was with Angelino Limachi's relationship to his son, Clemente. He wanted a special tomb for his son, where people would come and pay homage to him "for the centuries of centuries." Clemente would be the first resort. His day would be kept. His name would not be forgotten. Thus Clemente would be comforted while continuing to fulfill his necessary fertility function.

Although the local *yatiris* insisted that Clemente bestowed nothing but good on the people of Chinumani, there was actually a strong ambivalence concerning him. "He's a martyr," Angelino said, "but since he died before his time, we don't know if he is with God or whether he is still floating around us."

To settle this matter, Angelino kept asking me to supply cement for Clemente's tomb. After I bought the cement and some paint, Angelino commissioned a worker to make Clemente a memorial, which he inaugurated with a two-day double ceremony. The first day Angelino performed his shamanic Misa de los Muertos (Mass for the Dead); the next day the local Maryknoll missionary performed Roman Catholic rites.

For weeks it had been raining on and off, far beyond the normal season; many layers of clouds had sat like permanent, unwanted guests on the Cordillera across the lake. But today the whole Cordillera Real stood out. We could see nearly ninety miles of uninterrupted snowclad summits, ending in the three towering peaks of Illimani, the highest mountain of the range. On a day like this you could see why the peninsula of Yunguyo, and Mount Incahúasi, were so revered. We had a commanding view of the lake, Mount Kapia, and a whole stretch of sacred mountains. For the Incas, who valued sightlines to eternally snow-covered peaks, this was a resource as valuable as the water and weather these mountains controlled.

Clemente's tomb was a simple two-tiered cement square, but painted in bright blue and etched with white trim. At the top, painted in white, stood a cross flanked by two branches. The inscription read as follows:

REST IN PEACE
THE SOUL OF CLEMENTE LIMACHI SIGUAIRO
BORN: JANUARY 23, 1949
DIED: FEBRUARY 17, 1986

HE WAS SACRIFICED IN AGONY ON THIS HILL.
MAY OUR LORD JESUS CHRIST, WHO WAS ALSO
SACRIFICED,
RECEIVE HIM IN HIS KINGDOM

REMEMBERED BY HIS PARENTS, WIFE,
CHILDREN, AND BROTHERS

CHUCHAPI, MAY 12, 1988

WITH THE COLLABORATION OF FRIEND
PATRICK TIERNEY

Angelino began the ceremony by giving a short sermon. "Today is Ascension Thursday," he said. "This is a very great day, the day of the Ascension of our Lord. This is a good sign that means that our Lord is going to receive Clemente's soul." Today, Angelino said, Clemente would also ascend to heaven—if he wasn't there already.

Although it was just a coincidence that Clemente's tomb was dedicated on Ascension Thursday, it was a very auspicious one. It was also good luck that the mountains all showed themselves: Angelino took this as a sign of approval.

The following day Father Edmundo came to Clemente's grave, accompanied by his parochial assistant. Father Edmundo Cookson is a Maryknoll priest from New York who's spent twenty years in the altiplano—long enough to earn his "Edmundo" instead of "Edmund." He speaks Spanish fluently and climbs rapidly. And he has a very busy schedule. The U.S. Catholic Church considers its current ratio of one priest for every nine hundred parishioners to be a crisis. Father Edmundo ministers to the wide area around Yunguyo, with over sixty-five thousand people. Although he'd come to bless Clemente's grave, someone immediately grabbed him to perform the last rites for a dying relative, which Father Edmundo did on the spot. A short, robust man, he was wearing the white clothes of a Maryknoller, and showing the businesslike speed that characterizes overworked priests these days.

"Why is Clemente buried here instead of in the local cemetery?" Edmundo asked his assistant.

"Well, since the man was sacrificed, they were probably afraid someone would try to steal his body," the assistant replied.

As people gathered for Father Edmundo's blessing, he told us that the next day, Saturday, he was leading a large group of worshippers to the peak of Mount Kapia (15,778 feet), where they planned to celebrate Mass. "I've done it once before," he said.

"Excuse me, Father," Pancho interjected, "but why are you going with the people to a place of pagan worship, where they perform offerings to the earth and the mountains? Wouldn't this have been considered heretical by the inquisitors who once controlled this place?"

"The mountain is a place of meeting between the earth and sky, between man and God—a very natural place to pray," Father Edmundo said. "We respect that. On top of the mountain one sees everything. One prays for everyone. We see something valuable in the traditions that revere the earth. It's not a blind syncretism, but there is a mutual respect. Of course, you have to clarify certain things. Our people know that this kind of human sacrifice just shouldn't be done."

Pancho and I stood along with Leucaria and her children by Clemente's grave—still adorned with flowers, somewhat wilted, and ribbons, somewhat sagging, from the previous day's festivities. Father Edmundo chose a passage from Saint John's Gospel to read:

> In truth, in very truth I tell you, a grain of wheat remains a solitary grain unless it falls into the ground and dies; but if it dies, it bears a rich harvest. The man who loves himself is lost, but he who hates himself in this world will be kept safe for eternal life.
>
> —John 12:24–25

"This is a beautiful tomb that you've built here," Father Edmundo began in a voice with just the hint of a foreign accent. "But we are not here to celebrate Clemente Limachi's death and burial in the ground. We are here to celebrate the fact that he is risen. Clemente Limachi was a good man. The life he lived was a life of giving, of voluntary sacrifice. How many times did he rise early in the morning to climb high on these mountains, in the midst of cold and hail, in order to get ice, with which he made the ice cream he sold in the town? It was a hard life he lived. For this community Clemente was the good seed which gives much fruit. Today his body is buried in the ground like a seed. We pray to God that he flowers, that he rises to be received in paradise by the angels and saints."

And we all said, "Amen."

■ ■ ■

The next day, Saturday, May 14, Father Edmundo led two hundred fellow worshippers to the peak of Mount Kapia—the place of encounter between earth and sky, God and man. But around noon, when they were just a few feet from the summit, a bunch of young boys went browsing among sharp rocks and encountered something that wasn't on the agenda.

It was the body of a young man. His clothes were still on, but his flesh had been eaten away by birds and his features were unrecognizable. Someone had the presence of mind to take a shoe from the body and carry it back to Yunguyo. As word raced around town, a family definitely identified the shoe: it belonged to their son, Camilo Loza, a twenty-year-old boy who'd been missing since mid-March.

When the PIP in Yunguyo heard about the cadaver's discovery they responded with admirable tranquillity. "We have to eat lunch first," they said, in declining to go up the mountain in search of the body. After lunch something else must have interrupted them. And the next day. And the day after, too. The Loza family finally had to organize their own expedition on Tuesday, three days after the initial find, without any help from the officers of the PIP.

"How could you possibly let your son stay lost for two months?" the PIP demanded of the Loza family when they brought the body back. It was the same complaint they'd made to Leucaria when she'd reported the murder of her husband: how could she let her husband wander about at night alone?

"The medical analysis of the corpse is inconclusive," said Horacio Benavides, mayor of Yunguyo. "There are several theories about what happened. One theory is that this could be a *kucho,* what they call a 'payment to the earth,' done by the narcotraffickers. Another theory is that the boy was killed by other youths with bad reputations. Still others say that this was the work of the *liquichiri,* people who go around and extract human fat with a syringe."

According to Mayor Benavides, several unknown men followed the Loza family from a distance when they climbed Kapia to retrieve the boy's body. He believes these men were sent to destroy the evidence, but found they'd been beaten to the peak by the Lozas. "If the Lozas hadn't gone to get the body on that day, it's certain that the corpse would have disappeared," said the mayor.

Camilo Loza's father, Dionisio, didn't have much doubt about why his son was killed. According to him, Camilo was a good student with a quiet life-style. He used to read the Bible avidly, but things changed after a friend of his started showing up, calling Camilo at night, inviting him to drink at the local bars. "I'm sick and his mother is busy," Dionisio said, "so the boy took advantage of the situation. From last December on, he would go out with his friend to get drunk. Then he disappeared on long trips—one to Tacna, the other to Bolivia. He sneaked out his window at night and left a note behind both times. Now, I'm a photographer with barely enough money to get by since I've been ill. So where did Camilo get the money to go out drinking and traveling? 'Don't worry, Dad,' Camilo said. 'My friend pays for everything.' Finally, Camilo disappeared a third time, on March 15. He'd sneaked out the window again, but this time taking his ID card and pictures of himself. He didn't leave any note."

When Camilo vanished the night of March 15, the Lozas figured he'd gone off again with his friend, who'd become so intimate with Camilo that he could summon the boy with a special whistle from outside the house. Now they believe this "friend" tricked Camilo into climbing Mount Kapia. It would have been extremely difficult to carry a twenty-year-old to the 15,778-foot peak of the mountain. When the Lozas saw their son's body, the face was completely missing and the intestines were torn out.

Dionisio Loza would not tell us the name of his son's friend. Nor would he venture a guess as to who the killer or killers behind the sacrifice were. He was afraid of reprisals. It was clear, however, that the people who had paid for this murder were rich enough to spend lavish amounts for Camilo's trips and entertainment, and had carefully managed the circumstances around the boy's disappearance to make him seem like just another adolescent runaway. Only the accidental curiosity of some small boys accompanied by Roman Catholic missionaries brought the case to light. And even so the police didn't want to investigate. "If there is no money involved, the police won't do anything," said Dionisio Loza, meaning that you had to pay the police before they would act.

We learned much more from the Dominican nuns who had accompanied Father Edmundo to Mount Kapia. The sisters told us that Camilo Loza's friend was named Rufo Lerma, and that he had once been caught stealing books from a local school and trying to sell them in Bolivia. After hearing that Camilo's body was found, he tried unsuccessfully to commit suicide on Mount Santa Bárbara. No one knew where he was now. These nuns also knew that a razor had been found next to Camilo's body on top of Mount Kapia, along with a plastic hood that covered his whole head. "They always cover the head of a human-sacrifice victim before they kill him," one of the nuns explained. The only really odd thing about this sacrifice was that the body had been so carelessly disposed of, they said. Normally the bodies were hidden in nearly inaccessible caves. "How strange that the body wasn't thrown in a cave!" the people had commented to the nuns on Mount Kapia. The sisters were very well informed. In fact, the four nuns we spoke to had been conducting their own investigation into human sacrifice for some time.

"When I first came here, in 1984, I thought these cases were just crimes," said Sister Liticia, a middle-aged woman from Colombia, dressed in the Dominican's flowing white habit. "But now, with this case of Camilo, we are convinced that it is something more than just another crime. Mayor Benavides himself says that there are two cases a year like this. That's about how many we've had since I've come here."

"We know of four or five cases like this one," said Sister Gabriela, a slighter, younger woman, who seems precise and intense. "Everyone is talking about this. Everyone is frightened. And everyone—simply everyone—in the countryside says, 'This is a payment to the earth,' or 'This is a human sacrifice.' None of us has heard of any other explanation. And when we ask who does these sacrifices, the answer is always the same: 'The rich people who own cars.' "

The sisters agreed with the peasants that rich smugglers and drug dealers were behind the ritual deaths. "There's a lot of money from contraband here in Yunguyo," Sister Liticia said.

According to the sisters, there were four big smuggling mafias in Yunguyo. The richest smugglers were involved in "everything," especially drug running. "There is no one with money here in Yunguyo who isn't involved in narcotrafficking. We started investigating the matter and learned about the interconnections between these groups. There's no question that the rich people made their money in that way."

Some people, however, suspected the Loza family of complicity in their son's sacrifice. "The Loza family has a long reputation for being *liquichiris*," said Gabriela.

"Well, some people think Pancho and I are *liquichiris*," I said. "When we went to buy the items for a Misa the other day, we heard the local *yatiris* grumbling that we were working black magic against them."

"Oh, yes!" Gabriela laughed. "The people are always claiming that we sisters are *liquichiris*, too. They think that we're after human flesh to make communion hosts."

It's commonly supposed among Aymara Indians that the communion wafers—which, after consecration, become "the body of Christ"—are fabricated from stolen bits of human bodies, and that changing themselves into flesh-sucking vampires is the real, professional occupation of Catholic priests and nuns. "A woman came to the church here in town and demanded to see Father Edmundo," recalled Sister Liticia. "She wanted to buy human flesh from him."

The nuns had drafted a petition calling for the provinical prosecutor to open an investigation of the serial sacrifices around Yunguyo. They showed me a copy:

WE SOLICIT: THE INVESTIGATION AND PUNISHMENT OF
THOSE RESPONSIBLE FOR MYSTERIOUS CRIMES.

TO THE PROVINCIAL PROSECUTOR OF CHUCUITO JULI:

> We the undersigned, the Provincial Mayor of
> Yunguyo and staff, the Parish Council, the
> Dominican Sisters, Civil, Political, and
> Military authorities, and the general public
> of the Border Province of Yunguyo-Puno,
> respectfully introduce ourselves to you and
> urge:

First—that since 1986 a series of mysterious crimes has been occurring, like that of Clemente Limachi, which happened in 1986; on the 20th of November 1986 the corpse of a young boy was also found in a place called Tacapisi; and recently, on May 14 of '88, the body of the young boy, Camilo Loza, in the place called Kapia, whose medical certificate indicates death from undetermined causes; it being presumed that around these places there are abnormal elements or people who are also practicing paganism or perhaps the narco-trafficker Pistacos [vampires] according to Vox Populi.

Second—Mr. Prosecutor, the Authorities of the Defense Front, and others worried about this type of crime cannot permit these acts to continue, and for this reason we ask you to carry out a severe investigation to punish those responsible.

THEREFORE:

> We ask you, Mr. Prosecutor, to carry out
> the pertinent investigations.

Yunguyo, May 26, 1988

Although the date of Rolando Copa's death in Tacapisi was wrong (it took place in November 1987, not 1986), the charges of "mysterious deaths" related to "paganism" and "narcotrafficker vampires" would have been spectacular enough to grab headlines almost anywhere on earth—especially if it was signed, as this petition was, by a mayor and other local leaders. In spite of the explosive accusations, the sisters were pessimistic about its accomplishing anything at all. The leading human-sacrifice patrons would be the first to sign the petition—and the first to make sure nothing was done about it.

The police wanted to end the investigation of Camilo Loza's death before it began. They said they didn't know anything about the murder of Camilo Loza—the medical diagnosis turned up inconclusive—what murder? Nor could they speak of human sacrifice without better evidence. At first, they said the body of Camilo had been discovered without any accompanying objects. Then, when we pressured them with the knowledge we had gained from the Dominican nuns, they admitted that a razor and a plastic hood had been found next to the body. The hood, of a light-green color, had a rope threaded through holes at its open end, so that it would have fit snugly over a person's head.

"We think that some shepherds must have found the body and covered the head to keep it from being eaten by birds," one of the policemen said.

This hypothesis made little sense. The cord around the hood would have kept it in place if it had been tied, especially with the body cradled among the protecting rocks. But since the hood was found next to the body, whose face was exposed and obliterated, the hood must have been loosened long before. It had probably been removed by the same people who had tied it around the boy's head in the first place, after they had cut his throat.

We asked the police if they knew who might perform a human sacrifice. They said they knew of no human sacrifices.

"We've heard of a *yatiri* named Máximo Coa who's rumored to be mixed up in these things," Pancho said. "He's been arrested twice before for sacrificing people, so you must have heard of him."

The three policemen exchanged glances. The two younger men denied knowing anything, but it didn't ring true. The older man, a sergeant, tried to open up a little bit.

"We've been trying to question that Coa guy ourselves," he

said. "It's commented that he sacrifices fifteen-year-old girls. But the people are hermetic. They won't say where he is. If you hear anything about him, let us know." Then, more confidentially, he added, "Look, we know these things happen. I've been around a long time. I knew of one case around here where the whole community got together and hanged a man as a collective justice. That was in Isani, fifteen or twenty years ago. And after the people hanged this man, everyone had to cut a piece of his flesh and eat it." Since Pancho knew of a nearly identical instance, they discussed group executions with cannibalistic participation—a common story around the altiplano—before we excused ourselves and left.

So—our secret quest to find Máximo Coa had become a police priority. We'd learned that Máximo often stayed with a *compadre* in a community across the Bolivian border, although the *compadre* denied it. Again I saw how social relations revolved around *compadrazgo*—the acquired "godfather" and "godmother" roles as they related to baptism, marriage, house-building, and other rituals. By knowing someone's *compadres*, you knew a lot about him. Máximo had many *compadres* on both sides of the border. This made him very mobile, since *compadres* are obliged to give each other food and lodging on a moment's notice. Significantly, Máximo's most intimate *compadres*, and most frequent hosts, included several of the richest people in Yunguyo, people who were widely believed to head the drug mafias. Further inquiries revealed that Máximo did indeed frequently stay with one of these patrons. Then Pancho heard that Máximo was living with a young girl near the Yunguyo cemetery, close to the Bolivian border.

With Máximo's reputation for sacrificing fifteen-year-old virgins, living with a young girl next to the cemetery sounded like an all-too-perfect place for him, but the arrangement held few long-term prospects for the girl.

◩ 17 ◩

THE SOULS CRY OUT

The Civil Register in Yunguyo's municipal offices had drawn up a curt document on Camilo Loza's death:

Certified May 26, '88
CAMILO LOZA UCEDA
AGE: 20 years old, single, male, Peruvian, born in Yunguyo, student
PLACE OF DEATH: supposedly Mount Kapia
CAUSE OF DEATH: Undetermined (not determined)
DATE OF DEATH: Hour____Day____Month____Year 1988

The official report states that Camilo Loza was "supposedly" found on Mount Kapia. But Seferino Loza, Camilo's paternal uncle, has no doubts on that score. "I went up the mountain to get my nephew's body," he said. "We were followed by several men. They kept far enough away so that we couldn't identify them. If we hadn't gotten the body that day, there wouldn't have been any evidence left.

"Even so, when we brought the boy's body down, farmers from the community of Choquechaca tried to stop us," Loza continued. The natives didn't want Camilo moved from the mountain, since the victim's body is supposed to stay at the place of sacrifice, where it ensures good luck for nearby communities like Choque-chaca. "I had to pull out my gun and threaten them. Then one asked me, 'Which of the cadavers did you bring—one of the fresh ones or the one eaten by condors?' When I showed them Camilo's skeleton, he said, 'Oh, this is an old sacrifice. Farther up there are two girls freshly killed, one of them more or less twenty years old, the other sixteen years old. Both of them are well adorned with flowers around their necks, and *mistura* [religious confette used in most Misas]. Didn't you see them?' "

Loza, a small, skeleton-skinny man with unusually fair skin for an Aymara native, is both a journalist and a radio announcer. He also worked as a police investigator for many years. As an Aymara speaker, a journalist, and an ex-policeman, Loza knows what's going on in Yunguyo as well as anyone. When I'd first met him, months before, he'd been reluctant to tell me anything about human sacrifice. He simply shut up when the subject was raised. But now, with his nephew as victim, he started telling us what he knew. At least, part of what he knew.

Loza found Camilo's body less than three hundred feet below the 15,778-foot summit of Mount Kapia. At the spot, he noticed a huge, flat rock "like an altar." He thinks the rock played a role in the rituals that accompanied Camilo's sacrifice. He also thinks his nephew was killed on the day of Christ's Passion.

"I spoke to shepherds who said they found my nephew's body, freshly killed, on Good Friday, at six in the evening. They say he was decapitated—his throat was cut from ear to ear. He must have died on Good Friday, the shepherds say, because they found him surrounded by *mistura*, and at that altitude the wind would blow the *mistura* away very quickly. By the time we got there, no *mistura* could be seen. But we did find broken alcohol bottles, and that's a sign they did a Misa around there."

This presented a problem: Camilo Loza sneaked out of his house sometime between the night of March 14 and the morning of March 15. Good Friday, the day the shepherds found his body, was April 1. Why had the sacrificers waited so long?

Camilo's uncle says that Camilo was seen several days after he disappeared from home, in the company of several men, in a white van right in Yunguyo's public plaza. People think this white van belonged to a group of narcotraffickers, though Loza could not— or would not—tell us which group it was. He felt that Rufo Lerma, Camilo's friend, was an agent for this group. Lerma had been assigned the job of seducing Camilo up to Mount Kapia to sacrifice him. Some people said that Rufo had been initiating Camilo in magical practices. But, since going up to Mount Kapia on Good Friday is a traditional thing to do, Camilo might have been invited to a Misa there without arousing his suspicion.

"Rufo Lerma was Camilo's friend since childhood," Seferino explained. "They knew each other by name, they hugged each other whenever they met, from school days. But Camilo didn't know that Rufo's heart had changed. He still seemed to be his friend when he inivited Camilo out to parties, when he took him on trips to La Paz and Tacna. But then he invited him on the last trip—the one with no return."

It was no accident that Camilo was sacrificed on Good Friday, one of the most important ceremonial occasions of the year, when hundreds of people climb the high mountains to make offerings. Loza said the narcotraffickers have to make regular human sacrifices, and these accompany the major festivals. The narcotraffickers have their own *yatiris*, who specialize in this work, he claimed. He thought Máximo Coa was behind the sacrifice of Camilo.

Loza claimed to know quite a bit about Máximo Coa's history. "Máximo conducts a special Misa for people who pay for human sacrifice," he said. "Both the husband and wife of the family who want the sacrifice have to participate, with the husband on the right side of the *yatiri* and the wife on the left. Coa uses a white llama-wool cloth for his Misa. Everything is very expensive. The husband and wife toast the mountains with champagne glasses filled with a mixture of blood and champagne. Blood is never found around the victims' bodies, because it must be used in the Misa, when the mountains are invoked. I didn't find any blood near Camilo's body, so that part of the performance was probably done somewhere else— perhaps on the peak."

The husband-wife team sponsoring the human sacrifice request a specific amount of money from the mountain gods. Then they must place a percentage of it on the altar, to be burned along with the rest of the offerings.

"But Máximo is very astute," Loza claims. "There comes a time in the ritual when the husband and wife must come forward and toast the mountains with their champagne glasses. Máximo makes them step in front of the Misa to do this, and while they're occupied with the toast, he secretly steals the money that is to be burned. Later he quickly burns the Misa as though the money were still present."

Máximo has become a legendary trickster. Apart from stealing the offerings, Loza says, Máximo also receives a huge fee for each human sacrifice. Unlike Catholic priests, who suggest specific donations for baptisms or Masses, Máximo leaves the contribution entirely up to the individual. "You can pay me whatever you want," he supposedly tells his clients, "but God sees everything. If you have a lot of money and you only give me a little, you might die."

Máximo's human-sacrifice ritual is strikingly similar to one performed seventeen hundred years ago by Moche warrior-priests. In 1987, at a Moche site in northern Peru, archaeologist Walter Alva excavated the richest tomb ever found in the New World. A fantastic collection of gold ornaments accompanied this Moche lord, along with six human-sacrifice victims—four adult males and two teenage girls. The elaborate dress and grave goods enabled Moche expert Christopher Donnan to identify the dead ruler as the same figure who presides over human sacrifices in Moche iconography. "The killing of captured warriors occurred at a special ceremony in which their throats were cut and their blood presented in tall goblets to elegantly dressed individuals," Donnan writes. "The warrior-priest, with rays emanating from his head and shoulders, is the primary figure of the sacrifice ceremony."[1]

"If you're going to perform a complex ceremony for, say, an hour and a half after cutting your victim's throat, then you must have some way of preventing the blood from coagulating," Donnan said when I spoke to him in northern Peru in December 1988. "Normally, human blood turns into a viscous, yogurt-like substance when left alone. So preserving the liquidity of the sacrificial blood was an extremely important concern for the Moches. Interestingly, there's a seed which always appears in the drawings of Moche sacrifices. Henry Wasen, of the University of Göteborg, Sweden, identified this seed as *ullucu,* and he's proven that it acts as an anticoagulant. A month ago, we found an *ullucu* seed at Sipan, underneath a floor of the burial platform, in an offering placed between two spondylus shells."

The warrior-priest receives his victim's blood in a tall cup, which is presented to him by a man dressed in a bird costume— possibly a shaman, judging from the drum the bird-man carries. Donnan told me that the warrior-priest is always accompanied at these sacrifices by a woman with long hair. This completes the analogy to Máximo's immolation ritual: a shaman cuts the victim's throat, and a rich couple receives the blood in an elegant cup, which they then offer to the gods. In Yunguyo, however, they have no technique to prevent coagulation, so the offering of blood has to be done quickly, right after the sacrifice.

Seferino told us the name of a young girl Máximo had sacrificed in Chimbu around 1980: Nieves Chipana Ucharico, from the community of Unicachi. It took us several hours to reach Unicachi, located on an isolated inlet on Lake Titicaca. Since the lake had risen abnormally high with the long rains, parts of the marshy pasturelands were flooded. But the peasants were prepared for that. As our car inched over narrow causeways, with water on both sides of us, we saw dozens of children expertly maneuvering little boats through the wetlands. Each wielded a long stick with a knife at one end to cut the underwater grasses and load them onto the precariously balanced boats. The boats filled to the brim, sinking almost to water level, as the children steered them home again to unload their cattle fodder.

Much of this territory belonged to Bolivia until a recent treaty changed the frontier. The women we saw on the dirt roads dressed in Bolivian style, their dresses a bit longer in back than in the front. Loyalty to Peru wasn't strong, and smuggling with the help of relatives across the border was a way of life.

The ex-mayor of Unicachi remembered the sacrifice of Nieves Chipana, though he seemed a bit surprised that we were interested in a sacrifice that had taken place such a long time before. The story was that Nieves Chipana had been living with a man named Kalisto Ramos, who'd spent time in jail for cocaine smuggling. Ramos had once driven his car through a police roadblock, which had caused the irate guards to shoot up his vehicle, though he escaped unharmed. In general, the whole Ramos family was believed to be behind the sacrifice of Nieves Chipana. "They all took her, because of their illicit business," the ex-mayor said. "It's a belief they have. They cut her throat with a complete ritual ceremony. They were accused of killing her, but they fixed it up and now they're free." Máximo Coa had been Ramos's friend. The man who had accused Coa of murder was Nieves Chipana's uncle, who'd raised her.

We found Nieves Chipana's uncle in a clean, white Evangelical church, La Iglesia de Dios de la Profecía (The Church of God of the Prophecy). A Bible and various study books were open on a table in front of us as we sat down on plain wooden benches to talk.

"They decapitated Nieves about five years ago," said Paulino Chipana, an energetic man who appeared to be in his fifties. "A *brujo* did it. They pay the devil and call it *kucho*."

Kucho is the generic term for a sacrifice in Aymara. The word itself literally means "fetus," since llama fetuses are one of the most common types of offering.

"Nieves met the old guy, the witch named Máximo Coa, in

Ramos's home. We never met him ourselves. Nieves liked him. She used to say, 'He's a good person. He speaks so well.' He's an old guy, with a bad limp. It looks as though he has a knot in his knee, so he has to lean on a big cane to walk."

The Chipanas aren't certain why Nieves developed a close relationship with Máximo Coa. But they suspect he was performing love magic for her in order to win back her man, Kalisto Ramos, who'd left her with two children to go off with another woman. Since Nieves made her living by knitting skirts and blankets, she paid Coa with these items. She also gave him some clothes and blankets as an advance for the magical "cure" he was working on her.

"Nieves went alone to be cured by the *brujo* at his house in Queñuani [over twelve miles away]," Paulino explained. "She told my wife, 'I'm going to go and ask him for some of the things I've given him.' But she never came back. Later the police found her body in Chimbu, where she'd had her throat slit like a lamb. The rest of her body was intact, except her hair, which had been cut off. We found one of her long braids, along with the clothes she'd knitted, when we went with the police to search Coa's house in Queñuani. That's when we finally believed Coa did it."

Paulino Chipana said that a rich man named Víctor Ceballos paid for Nieves's sacrifice. Ceballos was an Aymara native, too, but he'd changed his name to sound more like the Spanish upper class. On the day Nieves Chipana was murdered in Chimbu, people noticed a strange car come into the area, a Dodge pickup belonging to Ceballos. Ceballos and his wife, along with two other couples (his brother-in-law and his wife, along with his father- and mother-in-law) were all observed in the car.

"An arrest warrant was put out for Máximo Coa," Chipana said. "After a year they caught him. But then Coa accused me of paying for the sacrifice of Nieves, and I was put in jail. I suffered a lot. But I pursued a three-year case against them. Finally, the old witch confessed that the seven of them [he and the three couples of the Ceballos family] had done it together. Ceballos had paid him to do it. Coa had promised Ceballos, 'If you pay the devil, you'll get a new car.' Ceballos wanted that new car."

Chipana maintains that Coa worked for "a band of drug traffickers." Kalisto Ramos and Ceballos were both drug smugglers, he says. Another man, Conejo Rocha, thought by many to be the biggest drug dealer in Yunguyo, was also involved. "Conejo Rocha threatened us, too," Paulino said. "He yelled at me, 'Coa is my *compadre!*' All the big guys are with him. Paredes [another man frequently mentioned as a major drug smuggler] is also his *compadre.* He's their *brujo.*"

Paulino says he's now given up his hatred of Máximo Coa and Víctor Ceballos. Both Ceballos and Coa spent years in jail as a result of his accusations, he says. "I was ruined by the death of my niece, but so were they. Víctor Ceballos lost his truck." To Paulino this is the ultimate irony: Ceballos paid for a human sacrifice to get a new car, and ended up losing his old one instead. He sees this as proof that pagan rituals don't work. So, he figures, there's no reason to oppose them anymore. "I've given up the fight," he says. "That belongs to the world." But then, a few minutes later, Paulino bursts out vehemently, "He [Máximo Coa] has killed a lot of people. Someone should kill him."

Quite a few people shared this sentiment, particularly in Máximo Coa's own community of Queñuani. On returning there, we met Anastasio Rivera, a retired army officer and a sworn enemy of the great *brujo.*

"Máximo Coa is very famous, very famous indeed," said Rivera, an unusually tall man for the highlands, with an upright military posture and bearing. "People have gotten to hear of him in other countries by this time. He once tried to kill my wife. But she escaped."

Rivera called his wife, Pascuala, into the room to speak to us. Pascuala explains that she is a first cousin of Máximo Coa. "About twenty-five years ago he invited me to visit his house to peel peas," she says. "He fed me and then gave me a bed to sleep in. I was lying there in bed when Coa's brother-in-law, Gringo Máximo Choque, came by and saw me through the window. 'What are you doing in that house?' he asked. 'Don't you know that's a bad place? Get out of there!' Then I looked under the bed and found a pan smeared with blood, and next to it were two knives, one long and one short. After that I ran out the house, leaving my clothes and everything else behind."

Not long after this episode, it became public knowledge that Máximo Coa was a sacrificer. "Twenty-three years ago Herminia Alave and her baby daughter were killed," said Mrs. Rivera. "Máximo was convicted of that and spent six years in prison."

Sergeant Rivera pointed to a place along the shore of Lake Titicaca where he says Coa deposited the remains of Herminia Alave and her daughter. "He had a special room in his house for sacrificing people. That's where he quartered their bodies, chopped them up into pieces," the sergeant said. "He carried the pieces of Herminia Alave and her young child down to the shore in two bags on top of two burros, and buried them in a little mound by the water. No one knew what had happened to them for a long time, until a dog dug up the head of one of the victims. That's when the outcry came and the whole community went down to investigate."

At first no one suspected Máximo. He came to the funeral bringing flowers, and wept louder than anyone else. "He took off his hat and cried," Sergeant Rivera recalled. " 'Who has done this?' he asked."

But eventually Coa was linked to the murder. The two victims had been seen in his house. The young mother had been separated from her husband, and she'd probably gone to ask Coa to perform love magic—his specialty.

"Coa confessed to the whole thing very cynically, without any remorse," Rivera said. "He said he had done these things to pay the devil and get rich. But he never revealed the names of his clients. You should have seen how they rewarded him—he lived like a king in jail. The rich people of Yunguyo made sure he had everything he wanted.

"In the case of Nieves Chipana, who was sacrificed by Coa in

Chimbu eight years ago, we found out because the rich people who paid for this ritual went to Chimbu in a car. The local people keep an eye on strange cars. One of them asked the chauffeur of the rich people's car what these outsiders were doing in the community, and he answered, 'They've gone to pay the earth with Coa.' The patrons who pay for the sacrifice always have to be present for the killing."

"Why do you think Máximo does these sacrificial murders?" I asked.

"Maybe he's mentally ill, some kind of a sadist," Rivera answered. "In the case of Nieves Chipana, the police found that he'd cut off the hair on her head and her vagina. Why would you do something like that? They say that he always rapes the women before he sacrifices them. To me that's a sign of cynicism. I mean, he's supposed to be sacrificing virgins, right? If I pay for the sacrifice of a young virgin, I'm not going to like it if an old guy violates her before the sacrifice."

Coa's preference for pubic hair rang a bell—shamans in Nigeria use human blood, female breasts, and female pubic hair in special charms.[2] The anonymous girl found in a canyon by Mount Incahuási in 1982 had her breasts cut off; Nieves Chipana was missing her pubic and head hair; all the victims we knew of so far had been drained of blood.

"Do you think Coa might have some use for the victims' hair or other parts of their bodies?" I asked.

"Well, Coa's family has a *liquichiri* tradition," the sergeant said. "They supposedly have lots of uses for human fat. People say that the priests need that for the little wafers they bake for the hosts. That's why the priests in Copacabana pay a good price for human fat. At least, that's what a *liquichiri* named Jacinto told me. Coa got the *liquichiri* inheritance from his father. They killed the old man and buried him in the same house where he had lived."

"Máximo Coa's killed five women and two men," Mrs. Rivera said. "I'm still afraid myself. And I'm not the only one. That's why no one does anything."

"I'm not afraid, because I don't believe in anything," her

husband stated. "I wanted to kill him—I once went to find a gun to kill Coa. He's a *liquichiri*—he steals fat from people after changing himself into a dog or donkey—but he doesn't really do this except through hypnosis." Rivera brooded for a moment in silence, and seemed to lose a bit of his bravado. "Maybe it's because of Coa that I'm so impoverished now. Eight years ago I told him I was going to kill him, and he probably performed some witchcraft against me after that run-in. Coa must have some influence with the devil, or I wouldn't be so badly off now. But if he had as much power as people believe, then he would have eliminated me right off, wouldn't he? He would have murdered me just like a mafia chief.

"He works with the mafia. They ritually kill people in order to make pacts with the devil, so that they'll get money. It's like this: I give you a gift, and you give me something in return. That's what they believe. This is written in the *Book of San Cipriano* and other books that I've seen. I've read some of these witchcraft books. But I think it's impossible for the devil to bestow such great benefits on us. Of course, in some way, yes, the devil may help you progress. But I don't believe in these sacrifices. If I sacrifice a person and then I go home and sit down without doing any work, the devil isn't going to come and hand me money."

Behind Rivera there was a Christian poster, showing a blue-and-white-robed Jesus kindly hovering over the right shoulder of a young man; over the man's left shoulder stooped a black devil with menacing horns. The poor man seemed torn by doubt, as the caption indicated: "Will you serve God or the devil?"

Rivera also seemed to doubt whether or not the devil could serve man's "progress" more effectively than God, just as he wondered about the extent of Máximo's powers. Yet, although Rivera claimed to believe in nothing, he was in fact convinced Máximo's black magic had caused him, Rivera, eight years of poverty. I asked Rivera what had prompted him to threaten to kill Máximo so many years—seventeen by their count—after his wife had escaped being sacrificed. By this time his wife had left the room.

"Well, my wife told you that she'd gone to Coa's house in order to shell peas. That's impossible. She'd left me, because we weren't getting along well. And she went to Coa to bewitch me. She went to pay the earth because she was having problems in her marriage, to get Coa's help in some rite. It's to people like that, poor and needy, that he always promises things, solutions. That night when she found the knife under Coa's bed, my wife was the chosen one. And after he'd killed her, no doubt he would have accused me of doing it.

"You don't forget something like that. I always held it against Coa. But eight years ago, when I threatened him, it was right after my wife had finally confessed she'd once gone to him for help. I was afraid he might still be doing witchcraft against me. We got drunk. We exchanged words. People have told me we should just kill him. But they'll put us in jail for ten or fifteen years if we kill a *brujo*, even if he gets off much easier for killing innocent people."

After meeting Rivera, I discussed Máximo Coa's bloody career with Víctor Avendaño, who said: "All of these sacrifices, whether of humans or animals, stem from the same, sadistic idea—one creature has to suffer and die so that other creatures can be rich and live."

There is, however, another perspective. Why are Simón Montoya and Juan de Dios Uriarti, men who are accumulating capital, collecting trucking fleets, and building factories, devoting their time to the performance of ritual crimes? For an ancient culture like the Aymara, in which people worship mountains and streams, and define themselves by their defense against the outside world, the cost of building factories and roads and turning all relationships into money-making ventures is immeasurable. People who participate are committing a crime—digging up the sacred mountains and causing untold disturbances in the magical web of life. They believe that only human sacrifices can atone for these sacrileges. Capitalism, which writes off pollution and social disruption as "external costs," has no answer for their anxieties. For the Aymaras, the costs of technological change are not "external." They are central and paramount.

But it would also be a mistake to think that human sacrifice only eases anxiety. Communities that perform collective sacrifices achieve tangible results. These communal offerings are also frequent, though they contrast with the surreptitious, secret-society types of killings I've investigated. Sexto Aratia was killed by an angry mob at the Feast of Saint James of Pocona in 1983. Another communal murder took place in 1988, not long after Camilo Loza's death, when the people of Queñuani collectively stoned and beat Juan Condori Quispe to death for supposedly stealing.[3] I say "supposedly," because Sexto Aratia, after being flogged to death and his body hung on a pole, where candy and *mistura* were offered, had a sign placed on him describing him as a thief. But most people say he wasn't a thief at all. In fact, Sexto Aratia was an unusually honest person, which is why he's now worshiped along with Clemente Limachi. The same thing was apparently true in the recent stoning of the "delinquent" at Queñuani. According to *yatiri* Andrés Jiménez, the unfortunate victim had an "impeccable background." As far as Jiménez was concerned, the stoning at Queñuani was just another human sacrifice. "Generally, the accusation of crime is a pretext to absolve people of responsibility," Pancho told me.

Oscar Wilde captured the dilemma behind communal scapegoating when he said, "It's always a mistake to be innocent."[4] If you're chosen to be the victim, and you refuse to accept your "guilt," you commit the greatest possible offense.

Queñuani is a prosperous community, almost the direct opposite of impoverished, disorganized Chinumani. In both places, however, ritual killings take place. Chinumani has become a favorite sacrificial spot, in part because no one initiates any reprisals against the perpetrators. Queñuani, by contrast, is famous for its harsh collective justice. In Queñuani, human sacrificial rites *are* reprisals—or at least they pretend to be. But this pretense effectively keeps thieves out and also pressures community members into behaving themselves. Anyone in Queñuani who doesn't work on communal building projects, for example, is likely to be flogged and have his house ransacked. Máximo Coa was also a target of this mob action in Queñuani; his house was torn apart and he was expelled. But when we spoke to the president of Queñuani, he sounded almost regretful about Máximo's expulsion. He regarded Máximo as a valuable *yatiri*, one who, unfortunately, got carried away by his private lust for human sacrifice. The people don't categorically object to human sacrifice. They simply want these violent rites to be exercised by and for the community, not on behalf of a gangster elite.

Human sacrifice remains a powerful social force in Andean society, with real and rippling consequences in rank, status, and wealth. Just as mountains are the great manufacturers of all material riches, so they are the undoubted generators of new gods in every generation.

Human sacrifice creates three types of deities or demigods. The first, and most obvious, is the victim—like Clemente Limachi or Tanta Carhua. The similarity in these fertility cults, in spite of the passage of 360 years, points to a fundamental Andean institution. Obviously, the control of any such dispenser of good weather, good health, good jobs is a political boon. "Father Clemente," as his devotees address him, is now the Creator, and his grave, like Tanta Carhua's, is a focus of magical power.

The second deity created by a human sacrifice is the patron, or controller, of the offering. In the case of Ocros, the person who most immediately benefited from Tanta Carhua's sacrifice was her father, Caque Poma, who went on to become chief as a result of his daughter's death, and then became a god in his own right and a lineage founder. In Yunguyo today, the patrons of human sacrifices also acquire immense prestige. People are intensely afraid of men like Simón Montoya, Uriarti, and others. They consider these men invincible, partly because of the powers they get from their human-sacrifice pacts.

The third supernatural produced by human sacrifice "fission" is the sacrificer himself—the shaman who presides over the offering. In Ocros, shamans were the third type of mummified ancestor—together with Tanta Carhua and Caque Poma's lineage—to get special prayers and offerings. Today a sacrificier like Máximo Coa is feared more than anyone else around Yunguyo. He holds the keys to wealth and success through pacts with the all-powerful *tius*. If he curses you, you'll suffer poverty, like Sergeant Rivera; if he blesses you, you'll get rich, like Uriarti. In 1988 people were also blaming Máximo for bad weather, as though he were a regional storm god.

The main difference between Ocros under the Incas and Yunguyo in democratic Peru is that human sacrifice is now clandestine. The victims used to be sons and daughters of nobility, who were carefully prepared for their role, whereas today they're all poor people betrayed by unscrupulous shamans. The number of human sacrifices may actually be greater in Yunguyo today than it would have been in a similar population under the Inca system. Admittedly, general population estimates for the Inca Empire and human-sacrifice calculations are so uncertain that I'm only making a semieducated guess. Ocros sent four boys every four years to Cuzco, meaning that the formal *capacocha* system claimed one victim per year in Ocros. Figures for the number of human sacrifices around Yunguyo vary, but Mayor Benavides's off-the-cuff estimate of two a year is conservative. In the communities near Yunguyo, there is talk of three or four victims per year *per community*. This is no doubt exaggerated. Nevertheless, many communities mention several people who have disappeared, often crippled or mentally retarded children or old people. I don't think ten victims per year for the whole Yunguyo area is an outlandish estimate.

Nor is this situation unique to either the cocaine trade or Yunguyo. A colonel in the Civil Guard told me that the highest frequency of human sacrifices occurs in the mining towns. "When you first started telling me about human sacrifices, I didn't believe it," said Romeo Paca, the ex-mayor of Yunguyo, a professor who has a master's degree in statistics from the University of New Mexico. "But I've been asking around, and it's true. In fact, in the mining town of Madre de Dios, it's very common for them to sacrifice fifteen-year-old virgins. The female population is very small. And there's even a time of the year when the Catholic Church collects the adolescent girls and keeps them interned doing handicrafts, just to protect them."

The spectacular wealth that has accrued to native leaders has given them new means of kidnapping and coercion, and new incentive to do it. There is a big difference between two human-sacrifice cases in Lampa, a town north of Puno. In the 1940s the parents of child victims demanded that the children's sacrificers be released because the community was in agreement with the act. In 1974, miner Guagua Condori sacrificed a fifteen-year-old girl in Lampa. Condori kidnapped the girl without her parents' consent. That's why he ended up in jail. Condori performed the sacrifice because the local shaman told him it would increase the returns from his already profitable silver mine; the sacrifices in the 1940s aimed to overcome a drought. Condori's was a private sacrifice; the earlier ones were communal. The traditional concern was survival; today's sacrificers are already fantastically rich by Andean standards—they just want to get richer. Human sacrifice has entered a capitalist growth cycle, where the laws of supply and demand rule. Since the demand for sacrifices is as limitless as the desire for new wealth, the number of human sacrifices is theoretically limited only by the supply of victims.

The Incas had good reason to place limits on human sacrifice: they didn't want local leaders to become immortal and invincible (in people's eyes), and thus threatening to Inca domination. To this end, the Incas centralized human sacrifice, and tried to make it a state monopoly. Thus Caque Poma had to apply to the Inca to make his daughter a *capacocha* victim. She was dedicated to the Sun God, so that she would be a satellite to the solar cult, not a new, rival power. As a "royal offering" she increased the Inca ruler's prestige, becoming one of his tutelary spirits; at the same time she enhanced her father's political position within the imperial hierarchy. Finally,

Inca priests supervised the whole *capacocha* process, starting with the inspection by the High Priest (who was often a brother of the Inca ruler), and probably continuing to the final immolation itself. Thus the tremendous social energy released by human sacrifice was channeled in directions that all reinforced the Inca's incipient imperial order.

Under the Incas, leaders were expected to sacrifice more than common people; someone who aspired to rule an imperial domain was obligated to perform a sacrifice of commensurate proportions. If the Inca succeeded in meeting expectations, people would be afraid to attack him, just as the natives of Chinumani are afraid to attack Simón Montoya. If you touch Montoya's saddlebags, you'll be converted into a snake. Likewise, the Inca became an untouchable figure. Each sacrificial victim was added to the Inca royal person like another protective amulet. He was literally accumulating spiritual wealth, filling his storehouse of guardian spirits with each new Tanta Carhua. Like the present sacrificers around Yunguyo, however, he was obliged to keep sacrificing. If the Inca stopped, the whole system would backfire. His guardian spirits might rebel. The mountain gods would escape his precarious control and destroy him.

What both the Inca *capacocha* system and the present, seemingly haphazard sacrifices around Yunguyo have in common is social control. The Incas utilized ritual death to assert the superiority of the Inca's person over local chiefs, the supremacy of the sun cult over local mountain deities, and the ascendancy of an institutionalized priesthood over charismatic local shamans. In Yunguyo today, wealthy individuals can terrorize poor people like Leucaria Limachi. They threaten to sacrifice her if she doesn't accept their conditions. Their conditions at one point included keeping Leucaria in jail and committing one of her daughters to thirty years of indentured service without pay—slavery. The esoteric purpose of human sacrifice is to make the victim a spiritual slave, a sort of demon-in-the-bottle who answers every command of the sacrificer. The social consequence of random, unpunished, predatory killing

is the intimidation of the poor. Víctor Avendaño summed up the
situation when he told me, *"Todo el juego es dominación"*—"The
whole game is domination."

Thus the wealthy can take poor servant girls into their care
and make them disappear—like the adolescent girl found hideously
murdered in a gully by Mount Incahuási in 1982. Everyone is afraid
and suspicious. Who is a spy for Montoya? Who is working for the
narcotraffickers? Why hasn't my son come home tonight? These
are the incessant questions of the underclass in Yunguyo. Unfortunately, it is a paranoia based on reality—a reality related in myths
of the *liquichiri* and the mountain gods. Although the perpetrators
of these sacrifices are sincere in their faith that human sacrifice is
the ultimate magic, the resulting violence is conducive to their illegal
and immoral purposes. It continues because it works.

Human sacrifice around Yunguyo today resembles the unpredictable violence of the Jivaro Indians—where stealthy nighttime
attacks to accumulate new trophy heads were the rule rather than
the exception—more than the comparatively elegant Inca *capacocha*
system. No efficient state would tolerate the lawlessness that cur-
rently reigns in Yunguyo, and the Incas had especially strong motives to exercise careful control over human sacrifice. It's ironic
that, as drug money and technology come to Yunguyo, the culture
finds in the practice of human sacrifice a mark of status and success.
In Yunguyo today, aspiring smugglers seize genuine advantages by
sacrificing human beings, just as aspiring warriors among the Jivaros
established genuine security by hauling around the greatest number
of trophy heads.

The problem I faced in Yunguyo was like the one homicide detectives in the United States encounter with satanic cults. Although a
number of detectives, police officers, doctors, and psychologists
believe that satanic cabals are performing human and animal sacrifices around the United States, hard proof is hard to come by.

Bodies of dead children found with pentagrams and other satanic paraphernalia constitute only circumstantial evidence. The one way to break a satanic ring would be for an undercover agent to infiltrate it. But police have been unwilling even to attempt this so far.

If I wanted incontrovertible proof of human sacrifice around Titicaca, I would have to go underground myself.

I began toying with the idea of pretending I was a wealthy mine owner who wanted a human sacrifice to increase his gold production. Although I was well known around Yunguyo, no one believed I was a journalist. I felt that if I told local shamans that I was really interested in human sacrifice because I wanted to *perform* one, they might accept it more readily than anything else they'd heard about me.

I didn't like the idea of tricking shamans. But, as one anthropologist said when I asked him about this plan, "An anthropologist has to adapt to the local culture and blend in with it. The local culture you're studying is based on lies. People pretend to be honest businessmen when they're really smugglers and drug dealers; shamans pretend to be harmless Christians when they're really killing people. You won't penetrate their disguises unless you wear one yourself, pretending you're part of their illegal subculture."

By great good luck, Pancho met a young man named Silberio Cori, who lived in an ample two-story house with a lovely young Aymara woman and several children. "Máximo Coa is my uncle," Cori told Pancho cheerfully. "I was his cellmate in the Puno jail."

Cori confessed that he'd been put in jail for cocaine smuggling. But he considered himself lucky to have been picked up by the Peruvian authorities. "In Bolivia they confiscate all your possessions if you're convicted of drug trafficking," he said. "In Peru you at least keep what you've earned after you get out of jail."

Silberio was in his twenties. He lived a few hundred yards from the Bolivian border, on a road parallel to the Pan-American Highway—but without the inconvenience of customs and border police.

Not everyone living in this neighborhood was doing so strictly out of reverence for their ancestors in the nearby cemetery. Cori promised to find his uncle for us, after I explained that I needed Máximo to perform a ritual for me. I said I was willing to pay Máximo a lot of money. I gave Cori a few dollars, too.

"Right now he's being discreet about where he goes, because of the death on Kapia," Cori explained.

Pancho and I came back once, with no results. But on our second return, Silberio reported success. "I was walking around the plaza last night about ten o'clock and I saw my uncle go in to have a drink at one of the bars," he said. "I told him a *gringo* wanted to see him about paying the earth. My uncle told me he already knew a *gringo* was looking for him. 'Is he a policeman or something?' he wanted to know. 'No, Uncle,' I explained. 'He just wants you to pay the earth for him, because he's heard that you're the real master.' He said, 'That's something which must be done with great seriousness and tranquillity. It's not something that can be done rapidly or lightly.' He finally agreed to meet you here on Sunday. On Saturday night, without fail, he'll come here to sleep."

But Máximo failed to show Saturday night. And on Sunday both Pancho and I were nervous. Actually, I'd never seen Pancho in such a state of anxiety as when we approached Cori's house. Pancho refused to go directly to Cori's door. Instead he walked around the house from a distance, inspecting the whole area, silently watching for . . . "What are you so worried about, Pancho?" I asked him.

"I want to make sure we haven't been set up for an ambush," he said.

"Do you really think these little thieves are going to dare to shoot a journalist like you or a *gringo* like me?"

For the first time Pancho got mad. "These narcotraffickers have their own hit squads. Why do you think the police are so scared of them? Because they can kill the police and anyone else who gets in their way. It's just possible that they're the ones acting behind the façade of Cori's cooperation with us. They might be intervening today in order to protect Coa, their witch. They will protect their witch if they think we're a threat to him. They've got their own intelligence services, too. Why didn't Coa come yesterday as planned? He should have come. And I noticed something funny about the way Cori was behaving. There was some fear there. I don't know what's going on. It could be that Coa was really there last night, that he was hiding inside the house to find out if we were setting *him* up, if we'd truly come alone. We have to be very careful."

Eventually, we saw Cori coming on his bicycle. He was crestfallen. "My uncle hasn't come. I've been searching for him all morning. He was taken in a van to Puno yesterday. This morning another van took him to Paredes's house, where he must be doing some work."

This was how Máximo lived, going from one rich person's house to another. He was a permanent outcast, always on the run. There were occupational hazards to being a professional human sacrificer.

There was nothing to do but wait. Pancho and I took a walk on the road that passed in front of Cori's house. It took us to the Bolivian border in five minutes. Not that you could see any official border. But the road reached a crest on a hill whose ridge defined the national boundary. This was a busy little road, judging from the big truck we saw people loading on our little stroll. We didn't ask them what they were loading. We were told, however, that these trucks reached the top of the ridge, where waiting workers unloaded their cargo onto carts and hauled them to nearby trucks.

Most of the volume in smuggling consists of foodstuffs, dairy products—all going to Bolivia—and electronics equipment coming into Peru. It was no accident that Peru had shortages of most foodstuffs. Government price restrictions seemed perfectly designed to force this result. Peasants had to smuggle for a living. This was a very old business, going back to the artificial division of Peru and

Bolivia by Simón Bolívar. Unfortunately, this established culture of illegality lent itself efficiently to the new cocaine trade, "the best business in Yunguyo," as one ex–police officer told me.

I headed down to the cemetery while Pancho had a long talk with Silberio in Aymara. When Pancho came back, he was smiling and relaxed, waving his little notebook at me.

"Silberio doesn't understand why you're so keen on seeing Máximo. He says lots of *yatiris* do what his uncle does. Then he asked me if you'd ever seen Máximo. When I said no, he suggested we get another lame *yatiri* to pose as Máximo. 'The *gringo* will never know the difference,' he said.

"Silberio also claims human sacrifice is super-common around here. He says a man paid eight million soles in 1980 to sacrifice someone on a hill near the Bolivian border. The hill is called Janq'u Janq'u, which means 'White White.' It's a white mountain."

The mountain where Rolando Copa was sacrificed in Tacapisi was also a white mountain (Janq'u Qhawa). The name of the chief mountain of Nazca, which plays such a key role in understanding Nazca water rites, is Cerro Blanco (White Mountain).

"The cocaine trade revolves around these *yatiris*, according to Cori," Pancho continued. "Whenever they have to cross the border with a shipment, the *yatiri* has to consult an oracle with coca leaves. If the leaves come up whole, then the shipment crosses. If not, no matter how favorable other conditions look, the shipment stays put. A good *yatiri* is considered responsible for a person's success in this business. Cori says that Máximo is especially intimate with Uriarti, the beer distributor. 'Uriarti is my son,' Máximo supposedly brags. Máximo claims he's responsible for all of Uriarti's wealth."

We kept waiting. But Máximo didn't show. "He's too suspicious now, with all the clamor about the boy killed on Mount Kapia," Silberio said. "He's afraid you might be with the police."

⧉ 18 ⧉

THE HIDDEN GOLD MINE

Six months later, I still hadn't met Máximo. Although I'd left my Puno hotel phone number with Máximo's nephew Silberio, I'd given up hope of ever meeting the fugitive shaman, when the hotel's receptionist called me one night and said, "We have a message for you from Yunguyo: Señor Máximo will be coming to see you tomorrow morning at 9:00 A.M."

That night I nervously prepared my hotel room desk as a makeshift altar. First, I covered it with blue and red wrapping paper. In the center, I placed a book of divination, and on top of that a six-inch-high statue of the *tiu*. I put the *Book of Black Magic* to the *tiu*'s left, and the *Book of Red Magic* to his right, so that they flanked him, propped up against the wall. Since the *Book of Red Magic* displayed a white-bearded wizard with a pointed hat, while the *Book of Black Magic* showed a black-robed sorcerer invoking a demon, they made appropriate company for the *tiu*. I hoped all this paraphernalia would convince Máximo that I was a genuine devotee of his *tiu*. And that I was very rich.

When Máximo came through the glass doors of the Hotel Sillustani the next morning, there was no mistaking who he was. I'd seen a photo of him taken at the time of his last arrest, around

1981. He now looked much older and more fragile. He wore sandals, a woolen cap, and a faded blue coat, and he stooped over a thick wooden cane with a big handle. When one of the bellboys directed him toward me, he came over slowly, as though he was very tired and every step was an effort. In one arm he was carrying a bundle, which he placed on the sofa next to me. Then he looked at me for a moment without speaking. He sighed audibly and started to speak softly.

"My son, why have you troubled yourself searching everywhere for a poor old invalid like me?" he asked, almost reproachfully. "You've wasted so much of your time looking here and there for an old cripple. But now that you've found me, with God's help, I am going to assist you *with all my power*."

I felt kindness and concern flowing from him so palpably it was as though he'd just opened a spigot. If he was reproachful, it wasn't of me, but of himself—for being so much trouble to me. When he said "I am going to assist you *with all my power*," he raised his hands and eyes to heaven, and took off his cap, revealing streaks of gray hair.

"I don't receive any new clients," he added. "I have so many clients that when someone new asks me I just say"—here his voice changed to a whining, pleading tone—" 'I can't read at night anymore' or 'Forgive me, sir, but I'm just a cripple.' That's why I didn't want to meet with you. But several days ago I had a dream in which a woman appeared to me, a rich woman, neither very old nor very young, very *simpática,* who told me to come and see you. 'You'll make a lot of money out of it,' she told me. 'And he'll make a lot of money, too.' That's why I came.

"I'm not like these other *brujitos* [little sorcerers] who run around here with their cheap tricks. They don't know what they're doing. There are *heaps* of these guys, who just do it as a business. They go somewhere and say"—here his voice becomes artificially loud and boastful—" 'I'm the healer.' 'I'm the fortune-teller.' 'I'm the one who knows how to present the Misa,' they say. 'I'm like God,' another one says. 'We'll kill your enemy. Lightning will fall on him, everyone in his house will die—they'll all go to ruin. I'm very powerful.' But it's all deception.

"But not me," he said, pulling two old books, wrapped in brown paper, out of his bundle. One of them was The *Great Book of San Cipriano;* the other I'd never seen before. It was entitled *La última palabra de la magia y del ocultismo (The Last Word on Magic and the Occult).* "Whatever I see in the book, I do. Nothing else has any value. I know how to act correctly because God has punished me in both legs."

To illustrate his point, Máximo quickly rolled up his right pants leg, revealing a horrible-looking knot, swollen to the size of a baseball, at his knee joint, which he pointed to with apparent pride. "I got this in a car accident nine years ago." He was now declaiming in a loud voice, oblivious of the bellboys and tourists who were looking at us with trepidation. "Since this is the punishment of the Lord, my God, I obey [what the books say] without tricking anyone. That's how I go, fulfilling my profession. I serve only God, and Jesus Christ, who has created the whole universe. I don't drink alcohol—nothing! Nor do I have anything to do with women. I just go alone to the mountains, with my little donkey, asking God's help for all."

Máximo explained that being a cripple gave him special powers. He claimed that any *yatiri* who endured great suffering acquired the ability to foretell events and heal the sick. "When he cures people, when he prays to God, God forgives them, because he [the suffering *yatiri*] already carries His [Jesus Christ's] cross. This is why the Lord says in a book, 'I have been poor. In this world I've had neither a house nor property—not even a little piece of property—nor a car, nor money, nor cattle. I have been *poor.* I was abhorred in all places. People who are in this world as invalids, or without eyes—poor, ragged people—I am right there in the midst of them because these wounded ones are my family. All the big millionaires work with the devil.' "

I then asked Máximo if he would perform a Misa for me.

"I'm sorry, this afternoon the smugglers are taking me to offer a Misa at the peak of Mount Azoguini, behind the city of Puno here," he answered. "I work for all the multimillionaires, the big guys. Some of them have ten cars."

He agreed, however, to accompany me to my room, to discuss things in private. As we chatted, Máximo told me that he'd been born near Yunguyo to a landless family. "My father was illegitimate, a natural son. He was ignorant. Since I was poor, I suffered. I went across the Bolivian border to work in the mines, for the companies. Then I made a lot of money, but I got sick."

Searching for a cure, Máximo traveled to Charasani, Bolivia, home of the Callawaya healers, famous throughout five Andean countries as traveling ritual experts. Máximo said he had to wait in a long line until an old shaman could see him. According to Máximo, this old man was "a true *espiritista*," a *yatiri* who entered trance states in which he conversed with and became possessed by spirits. This type of shaman "summons the spirit," as Máximo put it, and "makes it talk." Máximo performed an impressive imitation of one of these "spiritist" sessions, filling my hotel room with choking sounds—*Bauuuuuuuuuuuugh*—followed by moaning—*Ooooooooooo*—which changed into whistling and blowing, and ended with an explosive *Puuumm!*, signaling the arrival of the spirit. Máximo laughed quietly after this performance, indicating that he himself does not practice spiritism; he uses his books, not mediumistic trances, to work magic. Certainly, such "spiritist" shamans are rare these days, though they were still common in the seventeenth century, when Hernández Príncipe reported that "sorcerers" at Ocros helped sick people by "assimilating themselves to Tanta Carhua," then "answered them as a woman: 'This you must do, etc.' "[1]

Máximo's Callawaya spiritist also told him what to do. "You're sick," Máximo recalled his saying, "but now you can be at peace about your life and your future because from now on you can prepare Misas, you can do payments to the earth, you can do everything [that a *yatiri* does]. You can pray to God. With that, you'll earn your living. You'll make progress."

Máximo received this "task" in 1956, when he was forty-one years old. "In 1962 I started [working as a *yatiri*] little by little—always afraid. By 1970 I was confidently going straight ahead. Then the great millionaires took me to cure a sick person in Lima. Since that time, none of my patients have died. All of them have been cured. I just pray—I don't make them take medicine or anything. I trust in the Lord, that's all. With my tears, on my knees, I beg the Lord. Then, little by little, that sick person starts to get better. That's when people first start to believe in me." He imitates the amazed voices of his converts: " '*And this old guy doesn't need to cure people with anything? He doesn't want to present Misas or anything? We thought he was an Evangelical or a madman. We wanted to kick him out of here!*' "

I was beginning to understand why so many people had told me—warned me—that "Máximo speaks very well." His command of Spanish vocabulary was, for an Aymara native, exceptional, even extraordinary. But far more arresting was his acting ability. Like his Callawaya master, Máximo is possessed by so many voices that he is a one-man theatrical production. He continually creates dialogues, with radical voice and posture changes. When he speaks for Jesus, he is close to tears, and the eloquence is moving. At other times he rages in a stormy cacophony of strident accusations and counteraccusations, as he acts out the roles of his admirers and detractors, who are equally vehement in attacking or praising him. And then there are the more subtle, internal talks—Máximo conversing with Máximo. Or Máximo's "spirit" speaking to Máximo's mind.

"Now my luck speaks to me in my dreams," he said. Máximo claims that his "spirit" appeared to him in a dream and told him to work as a traveling *yatiri*, wandering from the city of Juliaca, about twenty-five miles north of Puno, to Copacabana, just beyond Yunguyo. "If you follow your path, we're going to protect you. We're going to give you presents," his spirit told him. "If you go to some other place, we're going to treat you capriciously."

Máximo showed me written contracts he had to perform Misas

throughout his territory—one in Ilave, one in the distant mine of Toquepala. He also had several people a day waiting to see him in Puno. Judging from his crowded itinerary, Máximo was the busiest shaman I'd ever met.

The mention of a mine gave me an opening. I started telling Máximo a suitably magical version of my life story: how I'd encountered a giant serpent who smiled at me when I was a teenager; how I'd been transported to snowcapped peaks during dreams and spoken to the mountains, whose rocks assumed the forms of faces; how the mountain spirits had guided me to a valley in northern Chile where I discovered a rich gold mine, called La Escondida (The Hidden One), through the help of the friendly serpent who had appeared to me.

Máximo nodded approvingly.

"You have a lot of faith," he said. "And that's why the *tiu* himself appeared to you in that form. Good."

"This is the *tiu*, isn't it?" I asked, pointing to my little statue. The room was dark, or perhaps Máximo's eyesight wasn't good, because until this moment he hadn't noticed my altar.

"That's him!" he exclaimed happily, kissing the feet of the figure with real affection. "That's the Great Millionaire. And that's the *Book of Red Magic*—"

"And this is the *Book of Black Magic*," I added. "They're my favorite books."

"I have them, too," Máximo said. "Sometimes I use the *Book of Red Magic*. The *Book of Black Magic* . . ." His voice trailed off and he looked a little uncomfortable. "I almost don't use it. I have a superior book called *The Last Word on Magic and the Occult*. This is the divine science of the great magician King Solomon. Everything in this book has been decreed by God Himself—so it has to be valid. Everything that God has promised here, He has to fulfill." Máximo also showed me his worn-out copy of the *Great Book of San Cipriano*, which he opened to a picture of Lucifer, who had a trident in his right hand and a serpent coiled around his left. Lucifer was flanked by two other demons, Belzebuth and Astaroth, all enveloped in flames.[2] According to the book, Lucifer is the "Emperor" of hell, Belzebuth is the "Prince," and Astaroth is the "Grand Duke." But Máximo's views didn't entirely coincide with the book's, since he maintained that the greatest spirit of all was Lucífugo Rofocal, a being whom the text described as only the "Prime Minister" of "the infernal kingdom," subordinate to Lucifer in "The Complete Hierarchy of Infernal Spirits," as Chapter 7 of the book is entitled.[3] Nevertheless, Máximo has reason to prefer Lucífugo, since Lucífugo is Máximo's personal spirit guide. "Ever since 1962 I've surrendered myself to Tiu Lucífugo, body, soul, and blood," he explained.

"I need all the help that you and your books can give me," I interjected. "Because recently there was an accident in my Chilean mine: a forklift backed up and killed a worker named Tito Caniguantes. Ever since Tito was run over by that forklift my Aymara workers won't enter the mine. They say the mine has bad luck. And every day that mine is paralyzed costs me lots of money."

Máximo kept punctuating my terribly sad and entirely phony story with sighs and tears. He let out such a gasp of pain when Tito Caniguantes was run over by the forklift that I was afraid it would be the death of Máximo, too. Fortunately, he recovered enough to let me continue.

"Now the Aymara miners say that they'll only go back to work in my mine if I bring a great *yatiri* from Lake Titicaca to perform a special sacrifice to the *tiu*. They say that traditionally the only way to appease the *tiu*'s anger after an accident like this is by sacrificing a fifteen-year-old virgin girl. And since several of them have heard of how famous you are for these sacrifices, they specifically asked me to bring you back to Chile to do the sacrifice yourself."

"Yes," Máximo said. "Now I understand what you want. But first you have to give me an advance, so that I can go alone to the mountain. There, in accord with the universal magical science, only there will I know after one or two days of prayer what can be done. Prostrate on my knees I'll pray to the Lord: 'Lord, You are the one who has given this [money] to me, with Your help and mercy, You have given me this prize. And this money which You have given me is not for me to spend on myself; on the contrary, half of it is for me and half of it is for these other things [candles and incense]. That's why I don't take any people with me. I go alone."

"Couldn't I go with you?" I asked.

"No, if you have sufficient faith in me, I'll have more trust in you, and then you'll be even more in my prayers," he said. Máximo noticed, however, that I wasn't happy about paying him without knowing what he was really doing, and so, without missing a beat, he completely changed his approach. "Tomorrow we'll go to the mountain. There you'll hear how I sing to the Lord, how I can pray, asking for you and your companions, also for your mine, that your miners are safe, that there will be no danger, nothing of that sort, that God may bless you. First we'll ask the recognition of the Eternal Father, and His son Jesus, and the Holy Spirit—everything in the Catholic way. Once we finish with those Catholic books, the candles will be lit. Then we'll leave them and retire to another spot, where we'll celebrate a Misa. There, with my other book of magic, we'll talk and read, read and talk, and you'll give me your complete name. And only then, with alcohol, we'll adore the Friend: 'Tiu Lucífugo Rofocal, Belzebuth, Astaroth, I offer you this soft whiskey for this foreigner. Don't forget him. Keep your word, give him good luck and wealth. Do this because I have been your servant for years, since 1962 until the present. Faithful, I'm your cook, your servant boy who obeys you. Please, I don't want curses, but Tiiuuuuu! *Help him!* For his mine, for his wealth, winning or losing, may he always have luck and fortune, and his partners, too.'

"Then [the *tiu* answers], 'You've believed in me! You've offered me alcohol! That's what I wanted! Now I'm going to keep giving you wealth.' "

Máximo concluded by saying, "Tomorrow is Tuesday, sir, and with great pleasure I can walk with you to the mountain. I'll bring candles, incense, and fresh flowers. I can also bring alcohol to offer for your wealth, and a Misa, too. Some people think that Tuesday is bad, that Friday is bad. No. All days belong to the Lord. And the night, in certain places, belongs to the *tiu*."

"Thus, when we sacrifice a girl, is it always necessary to do it at night?" I asked.

"Yes. Since we're going to go alone, you and I, we need a woman we can offer. She can be married, single, or widowed. The important thing is that she be able to sign the contract, because the *tiu* says in his prayer: 'If you sign over to me your body, your soul, and your blood, then I'll give you riches.' That's why we have to dissimulate when we bring a woman. [We have to tell her,] 'You'll make offerings for your job, for your business.' So she answers, 'Oh, yes.' And at the moment she's offering alcohol I retire with the book and say, 'Tiu Lucífugo Rofocal, since this person, this woman named so-and-so, has prayed and offered to you, she has given herself to you on behalf of so-and-so, so that he may obtain good luck and wealth. Therefore, from today onward, for twenty years, she is *yours*.' Then we have to make her drink [indicates drunkenness from his slurred speech and limp body]. This is the business of paying—it's called a *human holocaust*. And since she has signed her hand with alcohol [there's a play on words which suggests she also "gives her hand" in marriage to the *tiu*], therefore the *tiu* recognizes that the chalice [cup used to make offerings] belongs to her. She gets sick or she dies. She belongs to him, that's all. We don't have to do anything. I'm already free. Yes. It's written in that book. It's also good to offer a little lamb."

Máximo made it clear that this was a form of symbolic sacrifice—the girl was "given" to the *tiu* without her knowing it, then allowed to return home. If she later became sick, or died of natural causes, so much the better, because it was considered a sign that the *tiu* accepted her. Although this sort of substitute sacrifice was an intriguing development in its own right, I wanted to hear about the real thing.

"The miners where I work are of a very fixed opinion," I said. "They claim that it's necessary to sacrifice a young girl exactly as if she were a little lamb, right? Do you know how to do this?"

"Of course. It's in the book. It's in the Sacred History [the Bible]."

"What's in the Bible?" I asked.

"That it's better to pay with a male lamb, a fat one. A two-year-old lamb and a fat bullock, it says. But nothing else."

"And what does it say with respect to the sacrifice of a girl, a little virgin?"

"Ah," Máximo said. "That also has its prayer. It has its prayer."

"The miners say it has to be a fifteen-year-old girl. Is that right?"

"It doesn't make any difference if she's fifteen, twenty, or forty years old. [The *tiu*] isn't demanding about that, he doesn't ask about that. She can be thirty or forty years old. The thing is to make her sign with her own hand—'For my business, for my wealth'—[once she says that] she's already signed."

"Well, what do you do with the blood of the girl that you sacrifice?" I asked.

"No," Máximo answered. "Alive, that's all. Some of the women get drunk, and, getting drunk, they get lost."

"They get *lost?*" I repeated, incredulous.

"They get lost," he said slowly and with emphasis. "You also have to dig a grave. Then the woman herself, singing, dancing—she's already inebriated, and she just puts herself into the grave."

"Into the grave?"

"Yes, into the grave. Then we just bury her alive."

"It's better to bury her alive?"

"It's much better."

"But the miners told me they have a custom of cutting the girl's throat with a knife and collecting her blood in a sacred cup, and that a *yatiri* would then offer her blood to the mountains."

"Of course," Máximo said. "Yes, that's also good. But since this is the first time I've met you, I'm afraid to tell you *everything* correctly."

"But which is better—to offer the blood or to bury her alive?"

"Both are good as long as the body is offered. Then the *tiu* is happy. 'Of course, that's what I wanted,' he says. 'There's no one in the world who pays me like that person.' Burying alive, or cutting the throat and doing a sacred aspersion (*santibañando*) with the blood, it's all the same."

"It seems like you have a lot of experience with this," I observed. "How many people have you sacrificed to the *tiu* over all these years—fifty?"

"No, not that many," Máximo answered. "Twelve or thirteen, that's all. With those who believe in the *tiu*, with those who've studied and have seen the book—those are the only ones I can count upon. And why should I talk to the rest? Nothing! Of course, with them I just show these little Catholic books and that's all." He begins a derisive, mealymouthed imitation of his Catholic persona: " 'I know how to sing hymns, make prayers, and burn incense, that's all.' What else can I offer them? *Nothing! Never!*"

He spoke these last words with shocking vehemence. Máximo's hatred for Catholicism burst out, but his anger quickly cooled down.

"Because it is *forbidden* to speak about these things, neither to the *gringos* nor to anyone else," he said in a whisper. "If the people hear it, they'll privately go to the PIP. The PIP don't understand—they'll put you in jail and at midnight they'll make you confess *everything*. But even if they kill me, I don't speak! I answer, 'I don't know' and 'I don't know.' It doesn't matter if they kill me. If I talk, the PIP says, 'All right! We condemn you to prison [under] article such-and-such.' The PIP don't understand anything. They're bad. They're donkeys."

"Have you ever been captured by the PIP?"

"No, no, because I walk around like a poor old man," he said, assuming his bent-over posture and whimpering tone. "So whenever they ask me anything, I just show them my little Catholic book and tell them, 'I know how to pray because I'm an invalid. I know how to pray for the dead souls, and how to sing hymns to the Lord, nothing else. People pay me for these things. This question about Red Magic, I have no idea what that's all about. I don't know what it is. Since I'm poor I just ask for alms.' Therefore, because of my age, they believe me. I'm seventy-three years old now, and people don't ask someone over sixty for a passport or documents. I just show them my lame leg." Again he lifted up his pants leg and displayed his deformity. "This is my passport."

Máximo was now in a hurry to meet the smugglers on Mount Azoguini. Before he left, however, Máximo gave me several reading assignments from the *Great Book of San Cipriano*—the first concerning "The Love of God," followed by a complex account of how planets, sacred metals, and hours of the day are all interrelated. Máximo regarded the planets as guides to all his ritual activities. "God first, then the planets," Máximo explained. "Little by little, you'll learn." He also looked over my altar, with its bright paper and multiple images of the *tiu*, and said, with just a hint of criticism, "You don't have to adorn so much. Keep it simple."

As we browsed through the book together, I asked him about the picture of Lucifer with a serpent. "Why does the *tiu* always carry a serpent?"

"Because if you make light of him, if you don't keep your word, or if you do evil to your neighbor, the demon has a snake [to punish people]. But I don't work with this demon in the book here," he said, pointing to Lucifer. "I only work with this Rich Friend here"—indicating my idol on the table.

"How does God feel about the *tiu?*" I asked. "Are they friends or enemies?"

"When our Lord God created all things," Máximo said, "he also created the *tiu*. So they should be friends, but . . ." Máximo looked doubtful for the first and only time in our conversations, as though this were a problem he hadn't worked out yet. "God doesn't really give wealth," he said after a moment. "God's all right for curing illness, or helping crops, but He doesn't have much money. When it comes to riches, you have to ask the *tiu*."

I accompanied Máximo out to the street, and walked with him a while to establish our rendezvous point for the following morning. I also gave him a good sum of money to buy a complete Misa.

"I don't really need these magic books anymore," he confided as we walked along the narrow streets. "It's all up here." He touched his head with assurance. "These other *yatiris* don't know what they're doing. They don't know if they're praying to a rock or to this car here." Máximo pointed disdainfully to an old beat-up Volkswagen beetle. "But I know who I'm praying to—I know the *tiu*. That's why he always helps me."

"Never go alone to the mountain with Máximo."

That was the advice I'd received from several shamans around Yunguyo, but Máximo insisted that I bring no one else with me when we climbed together to the peak of Mount Azoguini. He also objected to a taxi driver's taking us partway up the mountain. This sounded suspicious to me since I'd heard that Máximo gave exactly the same instructions to his female victims before sacrificing them in lonely spots.

My friend Pancho also feared foul play. "*You're* going to be alone on top of the mountain," Pancho predicted, "but Máximo is going to have his narcotrafficker friends waiting for you."

I decided to wait until 7:30 A.M., when there was full daylight, then take a taxi partway up the mountain in spite of Máximo's objections; if Máximo canceled our ritual as a result, that would be a sign that he was deceiving me.

But Máximo responded to the taxi's arrival with pleasant surprise. "You shouldn't have gone to such expense," he said. "I told you not to bring a taxi to save you money."

The road from Puno wound around Mount Azoguini, until we reached a new maximum-security prison, the cleanest, whitest building around, standing in fortresslike isolation, surrounded by barbed wire, high above the city.

The sight of the prison seemed to jog Máximo's memory.

"I was in jail twice for cocaine," Máximo told the taxi driver matter-of-factly. "The last time they gave me a twenty-year sentence. But money always rules. My sons paid a bribe, and the transcript of my sentence was destroyed before it reached Lima, so I went free. Who knows how many millions they must have paid?

My sons are professionals—military officials. They all have cars and money because they're paid big salaries to just sit around. They're lazy bums."

After the taxi driver dropped us off, we climbed the remaining distance to the peak of Azoguini, with Máximo leading the way at an almost frantic pace. In spite of his lame leg, he quickly wore me out, and I was glad when we stopped to rest.

"I may be a cripple, but I climb these mountains as though I were riding a bicycle," Máximo bragged.

It was a clear day, and by eight o'clock, as we neared the peak, we could see all the way from the colonial church towers of Puno, across Lake Titicaca, to Mount Kapia on the Yunguyo Peninsula. The tin roofs from Puno's congested residential districts flashed in the sun, like mirrors blinking out a fitful message.

Mount Azoguini is much lower than Mount Kapia or Mount Illimani. Despite its insignificant height, the *yatiris* from Yunguyo, eighty-seven miles distant, worship Azoguini as one of the three principal *tius*, along with Kapia and Illimani. "Why do so many *yatiris* invoke Azoguini?" I asked Máximo. "It's a very small mountain."

"This Mount Azoguini is pure metal," he answered. "You can see the minerals clearly in its roots—it has outcroppings."

We reached a large cross at the summit, with a set of cement stairs leading up to it. A young man was just finishing his prayers at the foot of the cross as we arrived. "We have to hurry," Máximo said. "Plenty of people will come before long."

As Máximo untied his bundle of books, I asked him, "How much do you charge to perform a human sacrifice?"

"It's not like taking a taxi, where you get in and the driver says, 'So much,' to go somewhere," he answered. "It depends on your goodwill."

I started to ask another question about human sacrifice, but he angrily cut me off.

"Not here! This is a purely Catholic place. Here we'll do nothing but Catholic prayers. Everything else, we'll discuss afterward, in a hidden place. Then we'll pull out the statue of the *tiu* and the books of magic. But here we're on sacred ground and we shouldn't speak of those things." He turned aside and whispered all of this, as though he were afraid the crucifix would hear us.

Then Máximo climbed the stairs and knelt before the cross, where he prayed a rushed Rosary. At the end of it, he exclaimed, "*Dios, todo es tiu* [God, everything is *tiu*]," but quickly caught his mistake and corrected it: "*Dios, todo es tuyo* [God, everything is Yours]. We all work with God. Without Your help, God, my foreign friend here will not be able to accomplish what he is planning. Because You are infinitely merciful, God, with Your help he can acquire many automobiles. It's not a lie!"

At this point, Máximo launched off into his own version of the Bible's Book of Genesis.

"We're all flesh, bone, and blood of God, because God took mud and breathed upon it, and that's how we were created, through Adam and Eve. Adam and Eve had three sons and four daughters. The first son was called Caiaphas—no, Cain. The second son was called Abel. Cain was strong, while Abel was weak. Cain, the strong one, killed Abel, the weak one, and that's why humanity is descended from Cain. Their third son was called Seth, and he was so good that God let him enter the Garden of Eden once again, where the guardian angel didn't forbid him entrance as he had to Adam and Eve."

Máximo's account of Jesus' life and death was equally creative, and even more revealing.

"When the multimillionaires in Jerusalem, along with King Herod, found out that Jesus was about to be born, they gave the order to kill all the little children under two years of age. They tricked the parents of these children by inviting them all to a big celebration, promising that they had presents for the children. But when the parents came with their children to the party, the children's heads were cut off and thrown into one pile, while their little bodies were thrown into another pile. After that, horses trampled on the children's corpses, squashing them like frogs. Mary and Joseph took Jesus to Egypt, however, where he escaped.

"At the age of twenty-eight Jesus was baptized in a big river, just like the Ilave River near here, and afterward he climbed a high mountain, just like that pointed peak over there"—he motioned to a high, pyramidlike summit on the western horizon—"where he fasted for forty days. John the Baptist also started preaching on top of a sacred mountain."

Máximo offered no further details from Jesus' life. Christ's death was far more important to him.

"I want to clarify this history," he began. "In the Garden of Gethsemane, the man who attacked Jesus was named Mallku Mallku Mallku [literally, Great Great Great, though *mallku* is a name for mountain gods]. Now, Peter got mad at Mallku Mallku Mallku and cut off his ear. But Jesus picked up the ear and, covering it with his own saliva, returned the ear to Mallku Mallku Mallku. Jesus said to Peter, 'Don't be rude to the *tiu*, Peter.' This was in spite of the fact that Mallku had mistreated Jesus more than all the others. 'Don't be bad, Peter,' Jesus said. 'With patience, with my suffering, with my precious blood alone, I am going to buy this world.' Then Mallku, very happy with his new ear, started to mistreat Jesus even more than before.

"Now, ignorant people think that the devil killed Jesus. That's a lie! The devil, the *tiu*, didn't have anything to do with the death of Jesus. It was his own cousins, the Jews, who abused and killed him. *All* the people in Jerusalem, the multimillionaires, the Pharisees, Caiaphas, the government ministers, the military, King Herod—who was like President Alan García in Peru today—they're the ones who killed Jesus. All the people in Jerusalem shouted, '*Crucify him! Crucify him!*' "

Máximo, grimacing and shoving his fist up into the air, became completely possessed by the hatred of this scene. He kept screaming "*Crucifíquelo!*" in such a shrill, high-pitched tone that his voice went momentarily hoarse, and he broke down with profuse weeping. When he recovered, he continued.

"The whole populace of Jerusalem shouted, 'Crucify him! Crucify him!' Even though you were blameless, Lord. They put you in jail and they killed you on top of Mount Calvary. They beat you, turned you into an old rag, they flogged you, and gave you six hundred and sixty-six wounds, by which you saved the world. They made the Lord carry the cross, saying, 'You stupid old *brujo!* You don't have any profession! Listen, old witch, aren't you the one who likes to climb the mountains to pray? Why do you pray on the mountains? Aren't you the one who knows how to heal people? Now we want to see you get down on your knees and pray to God!'

"So Jesus gave the cross to Simon the Cyrene for a moment, and he knelt down to obey them. Then, all Jesus' enemies started laughing. 'This old idiot, this filthy old guy, look at how he obeys us! The numbskull gets down on his knees! He's crazy.' Yes, they all asked Jesus to get down on his knees and pray. Therefore, the Lord, for the sake of the world, for our sake, knelt down. And because of his sufferings we, His creatures, must now repent."

When Máximo finished with this "Catholic" part of our ceremony, we went down the mountain until we were almost out of sight of the crucifix. I was struck by how, in Máximo's account, Jesus' detractors called him "old *brujo*" and mocked him for climbing mountains to pray—taunts Máximo could have received himself.

"Do people ever call you an old witch and laugh at you because you pray on top of mountains?" I asked Máximo.

"Yes, exactly," he answered. "They've accused me of being everything—that I speak with the devil, that I'm a *brujo*, everything. Like Jesus, they call me 'a stupid old man.' Jesus didn't have a house, or money, or a woman; I don't have a house, or money, or a woman. I also help sick people, just like the Lord. They put Jesus in jail and made him suffer; they've put me in jail and made me suffer. Wherever I wander I carry my cross, following the path of the Lord."

But now that we'd reached our new location, Máximo didn't want to speak about Jesus anymore. He took out a bottle of whiskey, which he sprinkled on the ground as he called on Mount Illimani, Mount Kapia, Mount Azoguini. He also offered whiskey to the statue of the *tiu*. Then we got down to the business of human sacrifice.

"If a person *comprehends,* if he's really convinced, and if he has enough faith to carry out this human holocaust to the *tiu* in order to obtain lots of good luck, and he carries it out, then we do it. Only then does good luck really come to you—loads of cars and houses, everything. But you can't tell anyone. Neither can I. We have to be ignorant about everything except those things we've just prayed about [in the Catholic ceremony]. Nor should all of your miners know about this. Only one person in your confidence should know about it, not the rest."

Then, after a pause, he asked, "And if it's possible, can you get her in Chile?"

"Get who?"

"The girl."

"Listen, I wanted to ask you about that, because, although I could buy the victim in Chile, I thought it might be easier to buy her around here in Peru."

"There aren't any for sale," Máximo said. "There aren't any Christians for sale."

"You used to be able to buy them, couldn't you?"

"Yes."

"How do you get a girl now?"

"For example, I wait until she asks me to present a Misa for her smuggling business. I agree, saying, 'Right. Let's take these books with us, and let's go because I'm going to present the Misa for you.' I trap them. I pretend. 'I'm afraid to offer a Misa alone. Come with me, and you can also make your offerings at the Misa,' someone tells her. That way, she comes along happily. The other people who also come with that person are all of one accord, without *anyone* saying anything. Then we make the preparations. We have to do it in a secret place. Only you and your wife should know. Just us three, that's all.''

"I don't have a wife, just a girlfriend," I answered. "Should I bring her?"

"Yes," he said, looking very interested. "By the way, how old is your girlfriend?"

"Twenty-three," I said.

"Does she have any disfigurations?"

"No."

"Is she pregnant?"

"No."

"Is she in good health?"

"Yes."

"Is she in your power?"

"Yes."

"Well, if we don't find any other girl, she would also be good," Máximo observed. His sacrificial criteria resembled those which the Incas used to select children for their *capacocha* ceremony. Like them, he preferred young, attractive, healthy victims. I must have reacted to his suggestion more than I intended, because Máximo quickly changed his tone of voice and said gently, "Personally, of course, I would prefer someone else. There are lots of poor girls we could get."

"Where do you find them?"

"We've found them in Juliaca [a city of 100,000 located twenty-five miles north of Puno] lots of times. Juliaca is nearby. We could go there with your girlfriend and converse with people, waiting for someone to ask for work. We'll sit down and three young girls will approach:

" 'Gentlemen, lady, we're looking for work.'

" 'What kind of work can you do?'

" 'I just want a job,' one says.

" 'Do you have a work certificate?'

" 'No, sir. I don't.'

" 'But how much do you want to earn?' we ask her.

" 'I'm not earning much, you can hire me cheaply, sir.'

" 'Yes, we can receive you as a cook, or to help around the house, to take care of the house. But all I can pay you is so much.'

" 'Oh, yes, lady, I'll come right now. I need the work anyway, because I'm poor, and I want the job no matter what.'

" 'Fine, we'll pay you so much. Let's go. We'll invite you to lunch,' we say. 'Do you want to buy something that appeals to you? Here, take this. I'll give you some money.'

"Then you give her money, and she comes *gladly*. The other two go away, and the young girl comes all *alone*. Then, when she arrives, you come and tell me: 'We've got her, Uncle. Her complete name is such-and-such. She has a social security booklet. So what can we do?'

" 'How old is she?'

" 'She's twenty years old, twenty or thirty years old. Or she's seventeen years old, or eighteen years old.'

" 'It doesn't matter. Everything's ready. With this sacrifice the *tiu* receives any woman, but not a man.' "

"The *tiu* doesn't receive any male victims?" I asked, interrupting his long, imaginary dialogue.

"No, no, no," Máximo answered emphatically.

"Why not?"

"Because he's a man, of course. The *tiu* is a man—so he wants a woman."

"But in Chinumani they're accustomed to sacrifice men. Two years ago, they tell me, they offered a man named Clemente Limachi at the Apacheta of Mount Incahuási."

"That's a lie," he said. "That wasn't the payment of a sacrifice. He was fighting with his neighbor over a little piece of property. They got drunk, provoked each other, and almost fought. That's why, when the deceased had been drinking in Yunguyo, and went walking home all by himself, singing, the other one went alone and waited for him at the Apacheta, and cut off his head. The people make unfounded accusations. One tells another, who tells someone else, and they all believe it, and say, 'Aha!' as though they'd seen it with their own eyes. That's false. The *tiu* doesn't receive a man as a sacrifice, only a woman.''

Máximo also denied that Camilo Loza had been sacrificed on Mount Kapia. He thought Camilo had been killed in a quarrel over a girl, though he didn't know the names of the people involved and admitted to having only a vague notion of what had happened. On principle, however, Máximo refused to acknowledge men as valid offerings to the *tiu*. He also considered himself the only *yatiri* capable of carrying out a successful human sacrifice, and he resented the notion that others might be competing with him. He mistakenly believed that no other *yatiri* possessed the *Great Book of San Cipriano* and the other magical texts required for these rituals. But when I told Máximo further details of the three male sacrifices I'd investigated—Clemente, Camilo, and Rolando Copa—he began to change his mind. I explained that all three of them were killed at ritual spots where they'd been led, unsuspecting, by their best friends—exactly as Máximo was planning to trick our own hypothetical victim. He seemed impressed by the fact that two of the victims were sons of *yatiris*, but he began railing against these rival shamans, accusing them of insulting the *tiu*'s masculinity by sacrificing men.

"They're confused!" he said. "They don't study. They don't have what it takes. They do them [human sacrifices] ignorantly. Because, with me, a man is never offered. He [the *tiu*] doesn't receive a man. That would be to make a mockery of the *tiu*. The *tiu* is a man, so he always accepts a woman—even if she's married, it doesn't matter. Even if she's only eight or nine years old."

"Some people have told me that a man can be a good sacrifice because the Pacha Mama, the earth, is a woman, and she receives him."

"The earth doesn't own anything," Máximo said disdainfully. "The *tiu* is the Great One who owns everything. He's the true one."

"But some *yatiris* invoke Mount Kapia as a *tiu*, while Mount Doña Juana is called the *tia*. They invoke many *tius* and *tias*."

"There aren't millions of *tius*," he answered. "There's only one *tiu*."

"Well, I'd better do what you say, then, and get a serving girl for the sacrifice."

"Then we'll bring that little girl [near the mine]," Máximo continued. "And your girlfriend will say to her, 'I've got a little grandfather whom I pay [to do Misas]. I'm feeling a bit sick now, so he's going to cure me. Would you accompany me?'

"[The maid answers,] 'Let's go, lady.'

"Then, man and wife, like this"—he indicates a man on one side and a woman on the other—"we'll prepare the Misas of sweets. It has to be a special Misa—a fine Misa. I'll bring three kinds of fat to offer—bull, sheep, and lamb fat. Llama fat doesn't have much value anymore. At eleven o'clock at night we burn the Misas. Finished. Then we turn on the cassette player and make her sing. [Máximo tells the victim,] 'We always have to offer alcohol.' So we all start offering alcohol, *challando*. She drinks liquor—*pisco* Vargas, champagne, and pure alcohol—these three liquors are called 'the three brothers.' We also make her smoke a red cigar."

"Why does it have to be red?"

"You get them over there in Bolivia. They're red."

"Is it some kind of a drug?"

"Yes. It's always cocaine. And we also make her drink beer. And since the little girl is ignorantly drinking, at that moment I go off to another place to praise the *tiu*: 'Tiu, she's right there signing with her own hand. Now you can take her. From now on, for twenty years, she's yours. Tiu Lucífugo Rofocal, this is what you desire.' Then he [the *tiu*] will become animated. The girl will get up to serve herself. I tell her, 'Little girl, don't drink too much, you can get dizzy. This is a bad place, just drink a little bit.'

" 'No! I want to marry the *tiu*,' she says. 'I don't want to be poor. More drinks! More drinks!'

"She herself has said it!" Máximo exulted. "No one else has said it. That's because the *tiu* has already entered into her mind. The *tiu* has enchanted her. So she says it herself. With that, we get her to smoke that red cigar, with its cocaine, along with some wine, and *pisco* Vargas, and white alcohol, and some black beer. With all that she can't even stand up. She sings, sings, sings, and . . . sings . . ." His voice trailed off. "Meanwhile, the rest of us are all preparing, retiring to another site. While she's still singing, we retire to another spot where we've got whiskey and pure alcohol. [We pray,] 'Tiu, we've given you this woman. Take her! Take her! But only on the condition that you give us *money*, riches! I've obtained this person for you.' The other person [paying for the sacrifice] also offers alcohol with me.

"A little while later, we go back. And then there's nothing left. Just her shoes, or a little bundle, the bag that she carried—that's all that's left. We pick those things up and carry them to another place where we've got kerosene hidden; with that, dowsing the things, we burn them. And then there's nothing left!"

"Doesn't the girl ever put up a fight?" I asked.

"No, she usually lets herself be killed," he said. "If the hour isn't right, if it's too early, we just bury her alive. But some people do the sacrifice at one in the morning, as the book says; if we can wait until one o'clock, then we grab her and cut off her head and with the blood we make holy aspersions around the place. The man [who pays for the sacrifice] makes holy aspersions. His wife does, too. And so do I."

"That's when we cut her throat and gather the blood," I said.

"Yes. You sprinkle it around. As soon as we receive the blood, we offer it."

"Toward whom do you sprinkle the blood—toward the mountains?"

"Yes. To the *tiu*, to the mountains, to the mine itself. Even if the mine is over there"—he pointed to the distance—"we can still invoke it by name."

"Do you also invoke the snowcapped mountains?"

"Yes, yes. And mountains that have minerals. For example, this Azoguini here. Kapia is also named—it has minerals. When it rains hard on Kapia, the mountain streams come roaring down, brilliant with gold. On the slopes of Kapia little boys are born with golden hair, too—they've been engendered by the *tiu*. Mount Illimani, which is near La Paz, Bolivia, is also named. It has eleven mines. Illimani is the big boss in Bolivia because of its mines. I've been there lots of times, to the Cholla mine, and also to the Mururata mine. I used to go to those places before I became crippled. I thought we were going to freeze to death on Illimani, with all the snow. We couldn't make it to the peak of Illimani because it was so cold."

"Have you done human sacrifices on Illimani?"

"Yes."

"My miners claim that I have to acquire a golden chalice in order to receive the victim's blood," I observed. "Is that true or not?"

"That's what everyone says," Máximo answered with a dismissive gesture. "But where are you going to find a golden chalice? You can't get them anymore. We have to use something else—a white glass which no one has drunk from. We buy that sort of glass, and we receive the blood in that."

Máximo explained that he was referring to a crystal glass, preferably a champagne glass, though almost any kind of unused glass cup would do. The main thing was to write the victim's name secretly on the glass and to invoke her name while making the blood offering.

"You use that cup while making the holy aspersions," Máximo said. "Then you bury it with her body. It has to stay with her."

"Do you do anything else with the blood?" I asked. "Do you drink it?"

"No. No. When she's dead you just cover her up, and you bury her. Down there"—he pointed down the slope of Azoguini—"that's where we have the tomb. That's where we leave her, covered up. The body can't be left out in the open."

At other times, however, Máximo indicated the girl's grave was very near to the place where the Misas were offered. Perhaps it depended on circumstances, and whether the girl was buried alive close by or beheaded and carried farther away. "It doesn't make any difference," he repeated, "whether we cut off her head and offer her blood or bury her alive."

"Why does the *tiu* like blood?" I asked.

"Because the *tiu* has received her body and soul. Don't you know that the book says, 'If you sign the pact with your body, with your soul, with your blood, I'll give you riches.'?"

"What happens to the soul of that victim?"

"The soul, of course, will be in the air," Máximo said. This was precisely what Angelino Limachi was worried about in the case of his son Clemente's soul—that it would be "in the air," hovering near the body and the place of its death, without going to heaven, thus posing a threat to the living.

"But will the soul of that person punish us or help us?"

"Well, that's part of the contract," he answered. "I pray to the soul: 'We've given you to the *tiu*. But it wasn't for any other purpose. We've given you and you'll be resting in this place until the day of the Final Judgment, when your spirit and body will be reunited. God also had to die and resurrect.' I do a Misa far away [from the place of sacrifice], so that the soul won't punish us."

He pulled out a Catholic prayer book, to the page entitled "Prayer for the Blessed Souls in Purgatory."

"Here are the prayers to free us from the sacrifice," he said. "To liberate myself, I go to that mountain which is off in the distance [a high, pointed peak northwest of Lake Titicaca, which Máximo had previously likened to the mountain where Jesus fasted for forty days], in order to do my penance. It's better to go to that high mountain which is close to the snowcapped mountains. That's where I go to do my penance, with my book [the *Great Book of San Cipriano*] and this book [the Catholic prayer book] also. I say, 'Lord, I have sinned. I made a contract against Your law, Lord. But it wasn't for her money, or for her clothes, or for her livestock. No, it was in compliance with what King Solomon had written in this book [the *Great Book of San Cipriano*]. It wasn't because I wanted to do it; it was because this *apu* [Quechua word for mountain deity], Your holy mountain, was so desirous of this sacrifice. Forgive me, Lord. And also forgive the person who has given you [the sacrifice]. Forgive him, too, Lord.' With that, we're free. He doesn't punish us at all."

"And does the dead soul which hovers at the place of sacrifice—in this case, at my mine—bring me riches? Do we keep calling on her to bring us money?"

"Yes, that's true," Máximo answered. "After we do that special Misa, everything gets better. For example, Tintaya, who lives in Yunguyo, has done this [human sacrifice] with me. That's why he has four trucks. And he's bought a house in Arequipa, another house in Lima, and one in Yunguyo, too."

"How many times has Tintaya sacrificed?" I asked.

"Just once."

"Once a year?"

"No. No. One time lasts for your entire life."

"And Uriarti?"

"The same. Just once, that's all."

"I was told Uriarti sacrificed a girl on Incahuási in 1982. Do you remember a little servant girl of his who was knifed in the vagina on Incahuási?"

"That's a lie," he said. "In the year '81 I was put in jail for cocaine. I was in jail here and in Yunguyo for cocaine. So that must be a lie. Why would I draw attention to myself like that? *Never!* When I do this thing I never let myself get caught. *Carefully thought out,* making plans, studying—only then do we do it. That way, they never catch us. Because the *tiu* receives [the body of the victim], he never lets that person['s body] appear."

"They say that Uriarti has sacrificed many times, and that's why he has so many trucks and cars," I insisted.

"Just once, that's all, sir," Máximo replied. "Why should we tell lies? After all, I'm the one who helped him do it. That was not here, but in Arequipa. There, too, since he's a millionaire, girls went to him looking for work. So he said, 'If you're looking for work for two months, then help me. I've sent my girl, my cook, on her vacation. She won't come back. Now I need a cook.' He gave her money to buy blankets, everything. From then on, the girl didn't know what was going to happen. From time to time I took her to the mountain. Then, one day, he [Uriarti] said to her, 'This afternoon I'm going to pay a Misa so that my cars don't have accidents. Since my car wants to roll over, I'll pay the Holy Earth so that nothing will happen; I'll pay the road. Will you accompany me?' he asked.

" 'Yes, sir. I'll go with you.'

" 'That way [Uriarti added], you can also make offerings for your health, for your work. And then someday you'll be in a permanent job and you'll have a good husband.'

"So she came along *peacefully*, singing," Máximo remembered. "She was a stupid little thing. We had already dug the grave, beforehand. Then, in the same way, we got her drunk."

I asked Máximo if he'd participated in the sacrifice of Nieves Chipana at the abyss of Nankhapi, in 1980.

"No. No. I do mine farther away. I never get mixed up in those ones nearby [Yunguyo]. *Far away!* Far away, here in Puno or in Arequipa, on this mountain, or on a black mountain whose name is Chiaraqui [*chiara* means black]. That mountain is very powerful because it's black—it has twenty kilometers [twelve miles] of pure minerals. We also take people to Cutimbu, where we sacrifice the person right at the peak, by the *chullpas* [twelfth-century pre-Inca funeral towers]. Another time, we offered a fourteen-year-old girl for Alberto Rocha Quispe [one of the richest men in Yunguyo]. That was fifteen years ago, on the slopes of Volcán Misti."

"But didn't you go to jail for the death of Nieves Chipana?"

"No. When the girl appeared [at Nankhapi], the people mentioned me: 'Máximo is a cocaine smuggler.' Then the police cars came. The investigator, searching in my house, really did find cocaine. The first bag had one hundred grams. The second bag had eighty grams. That's why they pursued me. But I turned myself in."

"But some *yatiris* around Yunguyo believe they know how to sacrifice people," I said. "One of them told me he knew how to perform a human sacrifice for my mine."

"That's a lie. Sure, they sacrifice, but they don't really know what they're doing. They do it because they feel like it. There's no benefit from it."

"They say that Montoya has done a lot of these human sacrifices," I ventured. "Has he ever done one with you?"

"No. I don't know him."

"He's a rich man who has lots of cars and houses. They say that every year he sacrifices."

Máximo confirmed that he'd performed ritual killings for three of the richest men in Yunguyo—Tintaya, Uriarti, and Rocha—the three men most often associated with him as *compadres*, and three of the biggest names in the smuggling business. The places Máximo chose for his sacrifices were farflung: Mount Illimani, Cutimbu, Chiaraqui, Volcán Misti, and Azoguini, among others. Volcán Misti (18,360 feet), near Arequipa, has the remains of two Inca ceremonial rectangles at its peak.[4] Misti's two nearest neighbors, Pichu Pichu and Chachani, also have Inca sanctuaries. At both Pichu Pichu (18,521 feet)[5] and Chachani (19,234 feet)[6] climbers found the skeletons of young girls sacrificed during Inca times. The adolescent at Pichu Pichu was sixteen to eighteen years old, about the same age as the fourteen-year-old Máximo offered on the nearby slopes of Volcán Misti in 1973. Perhaps Uriarti's young maid was also immolated on Misti, since Máximo said she was offered near Arequipa. When I told Johan Reinhard about Máximo's activities on Misti, Johan said, "That fits, because Misti has always had a reputation as 'the bad mountain.' The Incas could well have buried a victim on Misti, too, but we just haven't found it yet."

Máximo's choice of Mount Cutimbu for his blood rituals is even more interesting. Cutimbu is an imposing tabletop hill located in the center of a valley thirteen miles west of Puno, remarkable because of the high funeral towers on its altarlike summit. These towers, or *chullpas*, have a long history of human sacrifice. In fact, the seventeenth-century Spanish chronicler Ramos-Gavilán rescued a young girl who'd been buried alive in a *chullpa* near Lake Titicaca. In all of these cases, Máximo follows ancient antecedents for selecting sacrificial sites.

Máximo is careful, however, not to give too much information about his ritual killings, especially in the two cases near Queñuani, where he was reportedly convicted. Máximo's version of Herminia Alave's death, around 1965, had contradictions and omissions. Máximo insists that Herminia's husband waylaid her and killed her out of jealousy. Although Máximo admitted that he himself was jailed about the time of Herminia's death, he claimed it was for cocaine trafficking, not murder; later, he changed this story, confessing that he'd been sentenced to ten years in prison after being found guilty of Herminia's slaying. Máximo maintained, nonethless, that he'd been framed. Curiously, he said that ten people, all told, were convicted of conspiracy in this double homicide of Herminia and her daughter. He never explained why ten people were implicated if, as he says, Herminia's murder was a purely personal quarrel between herself and her husband.

Another large group—seven people, Máximo and three couples—reportedly went to prison for the sacrifice of Nieves Chipana in 1980. Máximo, however, blames her death upon thieves in Queñuani, leaving out any mention of his own role as Nieves Chipana's *yatiri*, or the inconvenient discovery of Chipana's clothes and body hair in his house. Máximo admits that he was jailed as an indirect result of Chipana's murder, but for the lesser charge of cocaine possession. He says the court gave him a twenty-year sentence in 1981 for the possession of 180 grams of cocaine. But a twenty-year sentence would have been a disproportionately heavy punishment for owning that amount of cocaine. Such a stiff sentence would, however, be about right for a second homicide conviction.

One part of Máximo's story which appears to be true is that his sons paid to have the records of the 1981 conviction expunged.

Although I hired a lawyer in Puno to find these records at all costs, they seem to have vanished, placing a question mark at the end of the whole affair.

I tried to resolve these questions, but Máximo became impatient, waving me off with "That's enough. I've told you enough already." He was starting the *challa*, alcohol offerings to the *tiu* and the mountains. After doing this for a while, he took a few sips of *pisco* and offered it to me.

Máximo was clearly enjoying the prospect of another human sacrifice. The strange thing about Máximo is not his penchant for human sacrifice, but his prosaic, almost scientific, approach to problems, one that's markedly different from that of all other shamans I've met. Other shamans have elaborate mythologies about snake spirits residing on mountaintops or in gullies on the slopes of sacred peaks, but Máximo says that the only reason to immolate a person in a gully is to get rid of the body more easily.

Máximo has strange new ideas, too. For instance, he regards the sacrifice of men and boys as a great heresy—he gets angry about it. Such intense intolerance is, in itself, uncharacteristic of most shamans. It's especially curious since there's abundant evidence that the sacrifice of males of all ages has gone on in the Andes for millennia. On this point Máximo is out of line with both the Andean past and other shamans in the present-day altiplano.

Yatiris such as Angelino Limachi have several, or many, *tius*, corresponding to major mountains that define a broad horizon. Máximo swears by only one *tiu*, a sort of supreme mountain deity in the making.

Máximo drinks very little liquor—only token amounts while invoking the *tiu*. This would be blasphemy to many *yatiris*, who consider that getting stone drunk is an indispensable ritual technique for feeding the spirits. Strangest of all, Máximo treats Misas as if they were of no account. He took money from me to buy a Misa, which he was to have performed that same morning on Mount Azoguini. I kept waiting for him to pull out the familiar collection of candy offerings, but he never did. For a normal *yatiri*, this would have been an inconceivable breach of faith. Yet Máximo wasn't even embarrassed when I finally asked him what he'd done with my money. "I didn't have time to buy your Misa. I'll buy a very good Misa tomorrow, or the next day, and I'll offer it when I'm alone on the mountain," he assured me. "That's how I always work. Wherever I go, I'll light a candle for you, just like I do for Juan de Dios Uriarti."

Máximo was discarding the traditional core of mountain worship—the candy offerings, the allegiance to particular mountain deities, along with concern about weather and water cycles. I never once heard Máximo mention the *tiu* in the context of crop or animal fertility. Máximo didn't have time for the peasant economy—he had become a prophet of "capital" and the acquisition of trucking fleets. Angelino Limachi might pray for automobiles and TV sets, too, but he never omitted his prayers for rain and his offerings to the earth. Máximo treated Pacha Mama with contempt. "The earth doesn't own anything." Of the dozen *yatiris* I've worked with, only Máximo would dare to say such a thing.

While traditional *yatiris* prayed for the protection of their own communities through the intercession of local mountains and ancestral spirits, Máximo had expanded his vision to a more impersonal, masculine, all-encompassing *tiu*, who still resided on mountains, but was not limited to any one of them, and was superior to all of them and the earth put together. In short, Máximo was creating a new religion.

Of course, this new religion still had human sacrifice at its center. But what interested me even more than the catalogue of these ritual slayings was Máximo's remarkable invention of a symbolic human sacrifice, one that offered a woman to the *tiu* without her even knowing it. Máximo described this procedure during our first talk at the Hotel Sillustani; from his account, I gathered that he performed such symbolic human sacrifices frequently. This was another practical innovation, since purely symbolic immolations involved none of the painstaking preparations, exact timing, and high risks of real killings. Oddly enough, I witnessed Máximo carry out such a symbolic sacrifice on Mount Azoguini.

While I was offering *pisco* to the *tiu*, a middle-aged woman, dressed in the Indian style except for a yellow sweater over her dress, appeared near the crucifix. She took her bowler hat off, letting her long braids down, and began crying, praying, and actually haranguing the crucifix all at once. From the sound of her wailing, I thought she must have just suffered a death in her family. When she spotted Máximo she pathetically called out to him, *"Abuelito!"*

Máximo got up, obviously annoyed, and said to me, "I'll have to see what it's about."

He limped over to her with that diffident, humble mien he'd adopted when he first approached me in the Hotel Sillustani. Once again, Máximo simply turned on his charm, overwhelming and calming the distressed woman with his kindness, quieting her crying, and captivating me in spite of myself as I observed. Máximo is a professional comforter.

But when he returned, Máximo looked over his shoulder to make sure the woman wasn't watching, then whispered to me in one of his exaggerated asides, "It's a good sign! She says that last night thieves stole all her sheep and her cow. It must be a lie! The *tiu* has brought her here to show that he'll also find us a victim when the time is right without our having to worry. Our victim will come of her own accord, just like this woman has come to the top of the mountain. We won't have to do anything." He started laughing and making intense invocations to the *tiu*'s statue, whose glittery cape caught the sun when Máximo held it up: "Take this woman in the yellow sweater, Tiu! Write her name down in your book! Take her for the sake of this foreigner, for the sake of his mine."

Máximo was beside himself with joy. As he cackled over our good luck, he exposed his missing teeth, which made him look primitive and ugly: the very picture of the "old *brujo*" his detractors called him. There was a harsh play of shadows on Máximo's face, caused by the angle of the sun and the way his gray-black hair protruded over his forehead. The contrast between his face and the luminous surroundings seemed to underscore his own dual identity—one, a kindly grandfather comforting the hysterical woman; the other, a fanatic gloating over her suffering as a promise of things to come. The contradiction was as dramatic as the conflicting images of the poor man on the cross and the rich, grinning *tiu* in Máximo's hand.

Now Máximo took out the *Great Book of San Cipriano* and told me it was time to "sign the pact with the *tiu*." This pact was both a promise to sacrifice a woman at my Chilean mine in the future and a petition to the *tiu* to bless our planned immolation by aiding us in finding a victim. To seal this pact, Máximo explained, we would verbally offer the weeping woman to the *tiu*, without doing her any physical harm. This would strengthen the covenant. It was also a token, a teaser to whet the *tiu*'s appetite for real blood.

"Tiu Lucífugo Rofocal, I promise to give you a human holocaust, on the condition that you give luck and fortune to—what's your name? Patrick Tierney. This will be a secret, *secret*, so that nobody, *nobody* may know. No one. He and I are the only ones who can know. This is a secret matter."

"Now we're going to pray to Lucífugo Rofocal," Máximo said, opening the *Great Book of San Cipriano*, and reading: "Great invocation for the spirits with whom you desire to make a pact, taken from the Great Key of Solomon."

As I followed the text at Máximo's side, I noted that he couldn't read very well. He knew most of it by memory, but he constantly interjected his own creations into the "pact." The book's ritual formula doesn't mention a single word about human sacrifice. What follows is the *Great Book of San Cipriano* according to Máximo, which is far more original than the pulp magic book itself. It is a dialogue between Máximo and Lucífugo, in which Máximo plays both parts.

"Emperor Lucífugo, owner and lord of all rebellious spirits. I pray to you, I, Máximo Coa Reyes, promising that I will offer you a human holocaust so that you will give fortune and luck, so that you will respond favorably to my petition."

[Lucífugo asks,] "Who desires to make a pact?"

"He and I both beg you," Máximo continued, indicating me. "We also ask you, Prince Belzebuth, spirit Belzebuth, that you protect me in my undertakings, O Count Astaroth, that you protect me tonight, Tuesday, when I am going to pray to you at this place, Mount Azoguini, right here in your own office. I am going to ask you to help us find a woman just like the one who appeared here now—a woman who is neither very old nor very young, who is crying. In the same way, O Lucífugo Rofocal, O great Lucífugo, I want you to appear to me in human form, without any noxious odors, and that you grant me all riches by means of this pact that I am going to give you. Because you're rich, of course, because of your powers, this foreigner is asking you. Nobody else knows. It's a secret thing. I need your powers.

"Great Lucífugo, I also ask you, I command you, to come from wherever you are and speak with me. If you don't, I'll oblige you by the power of mighty Alpha and Omega, the angels of light, Adonai, Eloim, and Jehovam. Obey me immediately or you will be eternally tortured by the powerful words of the Key of Solomon: Agión, Telegram, Voycehón, Stimulatón, Ezpares, Retragrammatón, Oryorám, Irión, Existión, Eryona, Onera, Brasimi, Moyn, Messiás, Soter, Emanuel, Sabaot, Adonay, I adore you, I invoke you."

After all these threats, Tiu Lucífugo made his appearance: "I am here. What do you want me for? Why do you disturb my peace?"

"Tiu, I promise you that this figure is yours," Máximo said, as he held up my little statue, with its green cape, orange vest, shiny metal trinkets, and multicolored crown of snakes. "Under this figure and with this magical science and philosophy, I, Máximo

Coa Reyes, ask for you to provide us with a woman just like the one who is appearing here alone. Tiu Lucífugo, I haven't asked her name, but mark it down in your book anyway. I have called you here to make a pact with you, so that, right now, Tiu Lucífugo Rofocal, Belzebuth, this little woman who has come here *all alone*— she's *yours!* She's yours, in whatever way you take her, from today onward for a period of twenty years, so long as you give him—"

Máximo turned to me again and asked, "What's your name?" When I repeated it, he went on. "—Patrick Tierney riches and luck in his mine, in his place, as soon as possible. If you don't, I'll torment you with the powerful words of the Key of Solomon. This is a secret thing."

Máximo now read Tiu Lucífugo's response. "I can't agree to your demand unless you give me, of course, this little woman whose name you haven't asked, for a period of twenty years, to do with her body, with her soul, whatever I want."

"Mark her down, Tiu!" Máximo exclaimed. "Mark her down! What good luck! She came all by herself for the purpose of crying. Lucífugo Rofocal, Belzebuth, Astaroth, I promise that she is marked down for you. I offer you, I *challo*, because she has come alone. What great luck! Take her away! And may another woman just like her appear somewhere else, Lucífugo Rofocal."

Taking the book again, Máximo read, "The pact should be written in your own hand, with the ink of the pacts, and on a small piece of virgin parchment, beneath which you'll sign your name, traced in your own blood."

Máximo ignored all this, however, and substituted the unsuspecting woman for ourselves: "This woman signs, with her own blood, her own body, her own soul, on behalf of Patrick Tierney, so that you'll grant him [what he wants] without her realizing that she is signing. We give her to you, and we promise her to you, Tiu Lucífugo Rofocal."

Lucífugo, however, contested with "I can't grant your request" and vanished. Máximo was supposed to read the Key of Solomon to make Lucífugo reappear, but he was now in a hurry, and just went on to Lucífugo's next apparition:

"Why do you keep tormenting me?" Lucífugo asked. "Leave me alone and I'll give you the treasure."

"Of course you have to give it to us," Máximo replied, "because she's come here alone and we're promising her to you. With these magical words, with her body, her soul, her blood, we sign. What good luck!"

Finally, Máximo read the surrender of Lucífugo.

"I'll give you what you want, on the condition that you give me a coin every first Monday of every month, and that you don't call me more than once a week, between the hours of ten at night and four in the morning. Pick up your pact. I've signed it. If you don't carry out your word, you'll be mine within twenty years."

"Yes, we're going to carry it out, Tiu Lucífugo Rofocal," Máximo promised. "What good luck that she's come alone. You brought her here, Tiu. And since she's truly crying, she is given to you, Tiu Lucífugo Rofocal. She is yours, here on this holy mountain. She's good—neither tall, nor short, nor old, nor young. We've promised you a little girl because this is a good sign for us."

Máximo looked pleased with the completion of the ceremony. He was also getting hungry, and had brought only enough food for himself, so I think he wanted to be rid of me.

"Did you have any breakfast?" he asked.

"No," I answered.

"My son, I'm worried about you, coming up to this mountain fasting like this. I think you should go back to the city and take some nourishment. I'll stay here praying. I'm very grateful to the *tiu* for the arrival of this woman. And she called to me. Did I ever call her? No. She called to me twice, weeping. I had to obey her. The *tiu* was attracting her by his power.

"Since you love the *tiu*, this woman has appeared here. Because your heart is good toward the *tiu*, how could the *tiu*'s heart fail to warm up toward you?" Here Máximo raised both of his hands over me as though he were conferring a special blessing. "And since

THE HIDDEN GOLD MINE

you've come fasting, the spirit of God is upon you. All of this means that God has accepted our plan. Go in peace back to the city. We can proceed with our human sacrifice."

That night, I saw Máximo for the last time. I told him that an American multinational mining corporation had purchased my little gold mine, giving me a fabulous profit. I told him the *tiu* also appeared to me during my *siesta*, telling me that he had accepted our symbolic sacrifice of the woman on Mount Azoguini, and had rewarded me with this unexpected takeover. The *tiu* also revealed to me, I said, that real human sacrifices were no longer necessary. I emphatically canceled the planned sacrifice in Chile.

Máximo took it kind of hard at first. He kept telling me that "lots of fat women kept coming up to the mountain today. *Really* fat ones." Apparently, the *tiu* preferred fat victims. But I firmly explained that I had no further need for a human sacrifice, while paying Máximo generously for his day's work.

He recovered instantly when I handed him the money. Máximo took off his cap and looked to heaven, saying, in that outstandingly sincere style of his: "My Lord, my God, with great faith and good-will I am receiving this money from your afflicted son, your creature, who has had a heart for a poor old man, for the invalid that I am. Just as you were on this earth, without anything, so, too, I am in your center, on your path, Lord. I don't own anything to speak of. I don't have a house, not the smallest piece of land. Yet, even though I haven't sweated or worked, you've given me this money, Lord. For this money, Lord, I give you thousands and thousands of thanks. You will also return this money to him, Lord, through your mercy, so that, whether he wins or loses, he will always have your mercy, just as was decreed today when we left that holy place of the Catholic Church. My Lord, Jesus Christ, Blessed Father, many thanks."

⊟ 19 ⊟

THAT OLD-TIME
RELIGION

Osvaldo Salamanca was afraid of dying as he lay in a creaky old bed in a crude wooden shack, whose rough, unvarnished walls were papered over with pictures of Jesus, the Bible, and promises of salvation. In the midst of the religious paraphernalia, Salamanca complained of stomachaches and disturbing visions. Once he found himself floating out of his bed up into a realm peopled by men and women dressed in white cloaks; at other times he saw the spirit of a bloodthirsty vampire approach him, anxious to drink his blood. But what most worried Salamanca was the hyperkinetic quality of his old bed, which, he claimed, started moving back and forth of its own free will, accompanied by weird supernatural sounds. Surely the devil was behind all this, Salamanca's family concluded. Osvaldo Salamanca was too tired and sick to reach many conclusions of his own, except that, promises of salvation notwithstanding, he had stumbled into a deathbed nightmare where demonic forces lurked all around, waiting to seize his soul.

Fortunately, the sixty-year-old Salamanca lived in a community that knew how to handle this kind of crisis. Almost all members of the tiny Vista Hermosa community, located among the foothills of Chile's southern Andes, had been visited by a group of "prophets" who converted the lonely inhabitants to the "Evangelical Army of Chile." These so-called prophets made quite an impression at Vista Hermosa—they spoke in tongues, held all-night vigils, performed exorcisms of evil spirits, healed people with the laying on of hands and anointing with oil. Sometimes, when the spirit possessed them after all-night vigils, they broke into ecstatic dancing. The prophets claimed all these practices were exactly in accord with mystical traditions of both the Old and the New Testaments. Pretty soon the people of Vista Hermosa received the baptism of the Holy Spirit and began displaying prophetic abilities themselves. One community member, Hernán Italo Cofre, offered his house as a temple for the sect. And it was inside this temple that the most unusual events in the otherwise monotonous history of Vista Hermosa began to take place.

It was also to this improvised temple that Osvaldo Salamanca was conducted for the Sabbath prayer meeting on Saturday night, August 16, 1986. The presiding officer at the meeting was Pastor Segundo Cares, who had traveled thirty miles from his home to officiate. First there were prayers and songs. Then, in a candlelit atmosphere, the pastor anointed Osvaldo Salamanca with holy oil, practiced the laying on of hands, and prayed for the exorcism of the demons possessing him. Unfortunately, the demons did not move out as requested. And since this was the third time Salamanca had received the ritual, with little to show for it, it seemed that some more effective method of dealing with the demons was called for. Without consulting their pastor, two particularly fanatical members of the sect decided to perform a more drastic ceremony.

When the other participants left the temple, two adult children of the sick man remained behind. They were María del Carmen and Edgardo Salamanca. Together they slipped into an adjoining room where María del Carmen's three children were sleeping. Then Edgardo pulled out a sharpened wooden stake and drove it through the heart of his nine-year-old nephew, Hernán Edgardo Cofre, while reciting invocations to drive out the vampire spirit disturbing the community. The child struggled, and his mother held him down, while the boy's two little sisters, aged five and seven, watched the spectacle in absolute terror.

Either shortly before or shortly after this sacrifice took place, the boy's father arrived and tried to enter the house. He was surprised to find the door locked.

"Let me in!" he shouted to his wife impatiently.

"Go away," his wife shouted back.

"What do you mean, 'Go away'?" the man answered angrily. "This is my house, and you'd better let me in."

"Go away, vampire spirit," his wife said over and over again, in what her husband thought was a weird, hollow voice. "In the name of Jesus Christ, I command you, vampire spirit, to go away from this house. Your boy is also possessed by a vampire spirit."

"Cut this shit out about the vampire spirit and let me in," her exasperated husband rejoined. "It's just your old man out here, not a vampire."

"In the name of Jesus Christ, we abjure you: begone, spirit of the vampire!"

After this final, vehement exorcism from his own home—in which he heard the voice of his brother-in-law Edgardo join in with his wife—Hernán Italo Cofre left in disgust, reflecting to himself that his wife and brother-in-law were out of their minds. He didn't return until thirty-six hours later, Monday morning, eight-thirty. Then he saw the gaping wound in his son's chest and called the police.

What seems peculiar, and un-Christian, about the sacrifice at Vista Hermosa was the belief that they could save the grandfather's life by murdering a child. But on closer inspection this isn't so peculiar or un-Christian. The core of human-sacrifice ideology is that a surrogate victim in one way or another saves others by his or her death. Christians believe they are saved by the blood of sacrificed Jesus. If God the Father sacrificed His own Son by allowing nails to be driven through him, to save humanity from the power of Satan, a simple person like María del Carmen Salamanca might not see any difference in driving a stake through her own son to save her father and vanquish the demonic powers threatening the community that constituted her whole world.

Although such beliefs seem bizarre from a modern Christian perspective, Andean peoples can be amazingly literal in interpreting, and reenacting, the Bible. Camilo Loza was sacrificed on Mount Kapia on Good Friday, in an imitation of Christ's Passion so concrete as to appear blasphemous. Máximo Coa apologizes to his human-sacrifice victims by telling them, after they're dead, "God also had to die and be resurrected." The two killers at Vista Hermosa were the strongest adherents of a "letter of the law" interpretation of scriptures. "They went around talking about nothing but the Bible," Esnelson Cofre, an uncle of the victim, told me. "They sounded fine. Everything was pure Bible."

Some Andean natives feel they have a more "pure" understanding of the Bible than the missionaries who gave them the book in the first place. "I want to clarify this history," Máximo Coa declared, almost defiantly, at the peak of Mount Azoguini, as he offered his own versions of Genesis and Christ's Passion. Would viewing the Bible through the optic of Andean mountain worship really "clarify" our own sacred histories? Could these South American shamans know something about the Bible we don't—or something that we've forgotten?

> The time came when God put Abraham to the test. "Abraham," he called, and Abraham replied, "Here I am." God said, "Take your son Isaac, your only son, whom you love, and go to the land of Moriah. There you shall offer him as a sacrifice on one of the hills which I will show you."
> —Genesis 22:1–2

Yahweh is often called "the rock of Israel" (Isaiah 30:29). This holy metaphor becomes a dark, hard, and heavy reality with a visit to Mount Moriah, where you can see the Rock—the immense stone where Abraham tried to sacrifice his only son, Isaac. Solomon built the Great Temple nearby. Today the Mosque of Omar, third-holiest shrine of Islam, stands in the Temple compound, with its magnificent golden dome surrounding the sacrificial rock. The circular dome, all dazzling blue mosaics and brilliant stained-glass windows, gives the odd impression of being a polished jewel revolving around the rough, uncut boulder that sits, like a trophy from the moon, as the centerpiece. This particular Rock, which is the foundation stone of Judaism, Christianity, and Islam, is literally "the Rock of Ages."

The Supreme Muslim Council expressly forbids anyone other than Muslims to pray on the Temple Mount. When right-wing Knesset members tested this restriction by praying outside the Dome of the Rock in January 1987, Muslim riots rocked East Jerusalem. Arab nations have voted to wage a jihad against Israel if the mosques are destroyed. This actually pleases the craziest of Christian fundamentalists and ultra-Orthodox, since they believe an all-out war, the Armageddon, must come along with the Messiah. If such a conflagration breaks out in the Middle East, it may explode over this big, unattractive, and intensely disputed rock on top of Mount Moriah.

The Hebrew name for this ordinary-looking rock, Even Hashettiya, means "Rock of the Foundation." Jewish tradition places this stone at the center of the earth, an idea borrowed by medieval Christian maps that put the world's hub at Jerusalem. Some Jewish sages go even further, claiming that, when God gave the original creative fiat, "Let there be light," the first light shone forth upon universal darkness from this exact spot on Mount Moriah.[1]

When Abraham bound Isaac and drew his knife to sacrifice his son on top of Mount Moriah, on the Rock of the Foundation, God promised to make Abraham the father of a great nation:

> This is the word of the Lord: By my own self I swear: inasmuch as you have done this and have not withheld your son, your only son, I will bless you abundantly and greatly multiply your descendants until they are as numerous as the stars in the sky and the grains of sand on the sea-shore. Your

descendants shall possess the cities of their enemies. All nations on earth shall pray to be blessed as your descendants are blessed, and this because you have obeyed me.

—Genesis 22:16–18

Jews reverently recall the Akedah, the "binding of Isaac," each year at Rosh Hashanah and Yom Kippur. According to the Bible, Abraham "bound" Isaac but did not kill him because an angel appeared saying, "Do not raise your hand against the boy; do not touch him"(Genesis 22:12). Yet Jews call on Isaac as the first of Israel's long line of martyrs and ask God to keep this great event in mind as an eternal blessing for themselves and their descendants. This is curious: Isaac supposedly escaped sacrifice, yet he is treated as a perfect sacrifice.

Saint Paul compares Jesus' sacrifice on the cross to Isaac's willingness to lay down his life. Even the language in the Gospel's description of Jesus' death on the cross echoes the language of Isaac's near sacrifice.[2]

Mohammed also seized on the Akedah, when he rewrote Abraham's sacrifice. The Koran's version of the Akedah is that Abraham tried to sacrifice another son, named Ishmael, near Mecca. Since Ishmael went on to become the father of the Arabic peoples in the Hebrew Bible as well as the Koran, Mohammed thus expropriated Judaism's foundation sacrifice for his desert tribes and their own ancestral place of pilgrimage at Mecca.

The almost desperate desire of Jews, Christians, and Muslims to claim the salvific power of a distant event on Mount Moriah shows how strongly the idea of a human sacrifice as a foundation of the social order is rooted in the religious subconscious.

When people in the highlands of Chile and Peru have dreams about offering a sacrifice on a certain mountain, there is a long-established tradition behind it. At Yunguyo, where Clemente Limachi was ritually decapitated, I was told that the local shamans "talk to the devil," who frequently tells them to sacrifice their sons. Like Abraham, they have supernatural inspiration to perform a human sacrifice. The only differences are that God, not the devil, speaks to Abraham, and an angel comes and stops Abraham's sacrifice.

But if a spiritual being demands human sacrifice, how can the listener determine if it is God or the devil?

And can we really be sure it was an angel, rather than a later editor, who halted Abraham's hand?

Many scholars think Abraham actually sacrificed Isaac. To begin with, there's no hint of criticism for the institution of human sacrifice in the Abraham-Isaac story. God is perfectly within His rights in demanding Abraham's only son. Furthermore, Abraham knows exactly where to go on his three-day journey to the "land of Moriah." And he knows exactly what to do.

In the Holy Land, too, the tradition of child sacrifice was an ancient necessity that followed carefully prescribed patterns. The Pontifical Museum of Jerusalem contains the skeleton of an infant whose head was violently severed from its body some five thousand years ago, before it was buried in a jar underneath a house near the Dead Sea. There's another infant in a similar jar right next to the first. The caption below the exhibit reads:

> The necropolis at Ghassul has not yet been excavated, but a few dozen infant burials have been found in the town area [such as these two]. They were invariably under house floors and were quite possibly foundation sacrifices as encountered elsewhere in the ancient Near East.

The story of ritual infanticide as the foundation stone of a culture has many parallels, including the mundane foundation sacrifice for buildings and houses, a nearly universal custom. The peasants around Lake Titicaca who distrusted the new bridge on the Ilave River because there were no infants buried in the pillars share a conviction common to primitive people of Ghassul, near the Dead Sea.

Aside from the matter-of-fact acceptance of God's right to demand a human sacrifice in the Genesis story of Abraham and Isaac, there are other textual clues that Isaac did not escape death. One is that, although Abraham and Isaac both set out together, after the sacrifice only Abraham and his men return. "Abraham went back to his men, and together they returned to Beersheba; and there Abraham remained" (Genesis 22:19). So it seems that the angel, or editor, who interfered with the original sacrifice forgot, momentarily, to put Isaac back in the script.

Additional proof for this appears in the oral tradition of Judaism, the Midrash. Hebrew scholars like Hyam Maccoby and M. J. Bin Gorion believe some of these Midrashic stories recall a pre-Biblical layer of folklore, and they use them as clues about the story line of the original account of Abraham and Isaac. One story tells how Abraham wounded Isaac and spilled a dangerous amount of his blood. Others describe how Abraham slew Isaac and burned his body to ashes. Later Isaac miraculously returned to life.[3]

Notice how similar this is to the many child sacrifices at the origins of other religions. Cronus, the Titan who fathers the Greek gods, kills his divine children; then Zeus forces Cronus to disgorge them, bringing the gods of the Greek pantheon to life. The Hero-Twins of Mayan lore consent to be sacrificed by the gods, then are resurrected after their bones have been ground into powder and tossed into a river. The Dogon god Nommo returned to life in similar fashion, but only after his father had secured universal benefits for creation by sacrificing his offspring and spreading Nommo's body throughout the heavens. Significantly, the Dogon people trace their descent from Nommo. So, in the Midrashic version of Isaac's death, fiery dissolution and reincarnation follow the ancient script of the Divine Child sacrificed by the Father God, a Divine Child who subsequently comes back to life and is revered as the archetypical ancestor.

"There can be little doubt that the original story of Abraham and Isaac was one of actual human sacrifice," writes rabbinical scholar Hyam Maccoby, a fellow at Leo Baeck College, London.

Like other nations, the Israelites traced the foundation of their tribe to a foundation sacrifice. The paradox that Isaac was the promised and miraculously born child through whom the perpetuation of the tribe was to be secured, and yet at the same time the inevitable victim of the sacrifice, was one that could be solved in various ways, but in any case it is typical of the dilemma of founding a city or a tribe. The device of having twin-founders, one of whom is sacrificed (as in the case of Romulus and Remus, variants of the same name) is one way of solving the dilemma. Another way could be that the next child born could be given the same name as the child sacrificed, thus being regarded as the resurrected or reincarnated lost one. But the success of the new tribe could only be assured by complete surrender to the will of the god. . . .[4]

There is always a bitter note to any demand for a human sacrifice. What would we think of a powerful feudal lord, say, who ordered his vassals to sacrifice their firstborn to him? Even if he relented at the last moment, such behavior is a paranoid loyalty test at best, and sadistic bullying at worst. From our perspective, we can't conceive of a God who would be pleased by human sacrifices, or animal sacrifices, either. By our definition of God, any human sacrifice is satanic.

But Satan and God are sometimes interchangeable terms in the human-sacrifice debate. Curiously, on the last day of the annual Mecca pilgrimage—the spiritual experience of a lifetime for devout believers in Islam—Muslims stone a pillar where they believe Satan tempted Abraham *not* to sacrifice Ishmael. This strange role reversal, where Satan is stoned for tempting Abraham to *spare* his child, seems to say, "Anyone who stands in the way of this horrible but necessary action is, by definition, Satan."

Yet it wasn't until I traveled to Mount Gerizim, sacred mountain of the ancient Samaritan community, that I heard a different version of the original story of Abraham and Isaac, one that points to the separation of God and Satan in the deep recesses of oral tradition.

"This is God's mountain," Etamar Brahim Cohen, my Samaritan guide, tells me, as we stand together on the peak of Mount Gerizim, surveying the sweeping desert that dwarfs the city of Nablus and turns its painted mosques into toy towers. "We don't believe in Jerusalem or Mount Moriah."

There are only a couple hundred Samaritans left today; their continuing dilemma is avoiding kinship restrictions on intermarriage while maintaining their religious identity. It's hard to believe this tiny group of look-alikes, many of whom have red hair, are all that's left of the once-splendid Kingdom of Israel. The Samaritans claim descent from three of the twelve tribes of the northern kingdom, which was destroyed by the Assyrian ruler Sargon in 722 B.C. The Assyrians took most of the Samaritans into exile, but some remained behind, like the remnant left in Judea following the conquest of Jerusalem by the Babylonians in 587 B.C. The Samaritans rebuilt their own Great Temple on Mount Gerizim in 322 B.C., and they have had an unbroken line of High Priests for twenty-three hundred years, giving them the oldest hierarchical succession in Judaism.

"Why did God want Abraham to sacrifice his only son?" I asked Etamar. "It seems like such a terrible thing to want him to do."

"It wasn't God who asked Abraham to sacrifice Isaac," Etamar answered.

"It wasn't?"

"No, it was a bad angel, the *milhaj*," he said. "You remember how two angels appeared to Abraham when they told him God was going to destroy Sodom and Gomorrah? One of the angels spoke, and one of them didn't. The angel who didn't speak was not a good angel. So, when the two angels went back to God, the silent one finally spoke. 'I would like to test Your servant Abraham,' he told God. And God replied, 'Go ahead. Test him any way you like.' So it was that angel, or messenger, who told Abraham to sacrifice his only son. God stopped the sacrifice. But it wasn't God's fault."

Etamar was pleased to see my surprise at this version of the Akedah, one that exculpated God. "That's part of our oral tradition. But it's not written."

This concept of the "bad angel," or *milhaj*, introduces a demonic slant to the Akedah at the same time that it lets God off the hook. The fearsome Yahweh splits into a figure more like God/Satan. Although the split is not fully developed, God's responsibility is attenuated. This is one way of dealing with the paradoxical problems posed.

Curiously, the Samaritans believe Isaac was nearly sacrificed on Mount Gerizim, not Mount Moriah.

"This is where Abraham tried to sacrifice Isaac," Etamar says, pointing to a small enclosure at the highest point of Mount Gerizim. "The Torah says Abraham went to 'the land of Moriah,' not to Mount Moriah. This land around here is called Moriah."

Poor Isaac died a thousand deaths—at Mount Moriah, Mecca (as Ishmael), and now Mount Gerizim. Etamar is quite adamant in arguing the case for Mount Gerizim, pointing out that his mountain has a privileged view over all of Israel. "You can see snowcapped Mount Hermon from here on a clear day," he says. "And you can also see the lights from Tel Aviv on the coast." He also claims that Mount Gerizim has a more ancient tradition to back it up. Moses himself commanded Joshua to perform a complex ceremony on top of Mount Gerizim as the very first act of the Jewish people in the Holy Land (Deuteronomy 11:29). "And archaeologists have found a Canaanite temple going back at least three thousand years on this mountain," he adds.

Etamar's argument in favor of Mount Gerizim fell on receptive ears, since all of his criteria reminded me of Antonio Beorchia's guidelines for locating high-altitude Inca sanctuaries: (1) It should be a very commanding peak; (2) there should be sight lines to other snowcapped mountains and water sources; (3) local legends ascribing ancient rituals to the mountain are a good clue to archaeological ruins. Whenever the Incas entered a new territory, they built altars on the highest mountains, just as Joshua did on Mount Gerizim. In both cases the invaders aimed at subordinating the local mountain gods—whose older cult on Mount Gerizim is attested by the Canaanite temple—to the conquering tribe's new deity.

In the Andes, both shamans and mountains are frequently identified with serpent spirits, who have power over water. Moses had direct conversations with God on the sacred mountain of Sinai, and one of his guardian spirits seems to have been a snake. Moses' first miracle was turning his staff into a snake (Exodus 4:2–4). This magical serpent-staff devoured other serpents, turned all the waters of Egypt to blood (Exodus 7:8–25), and later made water emerge from a rock on Mount Horeb (Exodus 17:5–7).

While *yatiris* in Yunguyo, Peru, use live snakes to cure patients, Moses also created a healing cult to a snake idol: "So Moses made a bronze serpent and erected it as a standard, so that when a snake had bitten a man, he could look at the bronze serpent and recover" (Numbers 21:8–9). This bronze serpent survived in Jewish worship until the reign of King Hezekiah (719–691 B.C.), who "broke up the bronze serpent that Moses had made; for up to that time the Israelites had been burning sacrifices to it" (2 Kings 18:4). This is a frank admission that, in the very heart of orthodox Yahwism, and until a very late date, serpent worship ascribed to Moses continued unabated. Up until the second century B.C., Yahweh was still represented with serpent legs. In Bolivia, the *tiu* of Mount Illimani is both a man and a serpent; Tiu Illimani seduced a virgin, Bernadita, who bore him a son with serpent legs and a human torso—like the drawings of Yahweh. According to mythologist Joseph Campbell, this serpent, which Moses revered, was originally the protagonist of the Garden of Eden story, and was called by the Sumerians "the Lord of the Tree of Life."[5]

Northrop Frye believes a giant sea monster—Leviathan or Tiamat—was originally behind the Bible's Genesis saga. The creation of the firmament in the Book of Genesis (Genesis 1:6–8) parallels the Babylonian hymn of *Enuma elish*, where the dry earth emerges from watery chaos when a sea serpent is sliced in half.[6] Although he knew nothing of the hidden story behind Genesis, Angelino Limachi told me that the universe emerged from primal darkness and flood when the giant snake, Mount Kapia, was chopped into pieces.

"The creation results from the dragon's death," Frye maintains, "because the dragon *is* death, and to kill death is to bring to life."[7] But the serpent is lord of both life and death because the serpent, whose flashing tongue and fearsome strike are like lightning, who lives near water, who emerges from his hole with the first rains, and whose flowing body is a living stream, is also "the lord of waters."[8] In the desert of Israel, as in the barren Andean highlands, life and death depend on fickle mountain torrents, whose twisting waters rush down like so many serpents. Since the snake deity, who lives inside the mountain and owns all of these waters, is believed hungry for warm blood, it yields its precious waters only in exchange for blood. When shamans perform mountaintop holocausts, they pour the blood onto the ground, creating sanguinary trickles, which, as they seep into the parched earth, imitate the movement of the desperately needed mountain rivers. There's an exquisite Moche ceramic vessel which portrays this transubstantiation—a man is decapitated on a mountain peak, and his blood flows down into a stream.[9] The prophet Isaiah also sings about the transformation of sacrificial blood into saving water: "On each high mountain and each lofty hill shall be streams of running water, on the day of massacre when the highest in the land fall" (Isaiah 30:25–26). Isaiah's Yahweh is as anxious for blood and fat as the Tiu Illimani:

> The Lord has a sword steeped in blood,
>   it is gorged with fat,
> the fat of rams' kidneys, and the blood of lambs and goats;
>   for he has a sacrifice in Bozrah,
>   a great slaughter in Edom. . . .

and the land shall drink deep of blood
and the soil be sated with fat.

—Isaiah 34:6–8

Isaiah equates killing the people of Edom to animal sacrifices on Yahweh's "day of vengeance" (Isaiah 34:8). Yahweh, with his sword, resembles the Moche warrior-priest who presides over the immolation of victims.

Since Moses' original purpose was leading the Jews on a pilgrim feast to worship God on Mount Sinai (Exodus 3:12), it's not surprising that he stayed near Mount Sinai until he died. We know that Himalayan and Andean shamans are attached to the mountains where they've had revelations. When Joshua led the Jews into the Promised Land with an elaborate mountaintop ceremony atop both Mount Gerizim and Mount Ebal, he was trying to transfer the authority of Mount Sinai to the highest peaks in the Promised Land. For Abraham, "the mountain of the Lord" was a hill somewhere in Moriah. For Moses, the mountain of the Lord was Mount Sinai; for the northern kingdom of Samaria, following the tradition of Joshua, it became Mount Gerizim; for the rulers in Jerusalem the Lord's mountain was their local Mount Moriah. Other communities had other mountains dedicated to Yahweh. Today, Máximo Coa thinks the Lord's mountain is a pointed peak northwest of Puno where he goes to perform penance after committing a human sacrifice. Yahweh's growth from a local to a regional to a world-conquering mountain deity is the most remarkable success story in the history of weather gods.

The imposing presence of Mount Gerizim, compared with the much lower Mount Moriah (which has sight lines neither to Mount Hermon nor to the coast), must have created an embarrassing problem for the Kingdom of Judah. Maybe that's why the prophet Isaiah decided to elevate Mount Moriah, predicting that, in the future messianic kingdom, the Temple Mount would rise, like the Mapuche Tren Tren, above all others:

> In days to come
> the mountain of the Lord's house
> shall be set over all other mountains,
> lifted high above the hills.
> —Isaiah 2:2

The shamanic strains in Isaiah's oracle hint at a more primitive mountain mythology, one common to all peoples' Mountain of the Gods.

Moses himself was not averse to human sacrifice. In fact, it is at the heart of the most crucial event in Moses' life—when he spoke to God in the burning bush on Mount Sinai and received his commission to free the Hebrews. God's final instruction to Moses was:

> Then tell Pharaoh that these are the words of the Lord: "Israel is my first-born son. I have told you to let my son go, so that he may worship me. You have refused to let him go, so I will kill your first-born son."
> —Exodus 4:22–23

Moses immediately set out to give Pharaoh God's message, accompanied by his wife, Zipporah, and their son. But on the way to Egypt something frightful occurred:

> And it came to pass on the way at the lodging place, that the Lord met him, and sought to kill him. Then Zipporah took a flint, and cut off the foreskin of her son, and cast it at his feet; and she said, "Surely a bridegroom of blood art thou to me." So he let him alone. Then she said, "A bridegroom of blood art thou, because of the circumcision."
> —Exodus 4:24–26

The meaning of these verses has eluded most Biblical commentators except Hyam Maccoby. How Moses' encounter is interpreted depends on who the "he" is who is trying to kill "he." But unless you posit the existence of a big fellow named Yahweh who walks into the inn to kill Moses or his son, the only two males in this situation are Moses and his son. It makes absolutely no sense for God to kill Moses, whom He has just chosen as His messenger. And Zipporah definitely wards off some adult male who is trying to murder her infant. She does this by circumcising her son and throwing the bloody skin from his penis at that potential killer, whom she addresses as her "bridegroom of blood" (or "bloody husband" in the King James version). Since Zipporah was married to Moses, not Yahweh, it seems inescapably clear that Moses was trying to kill his son, but that this horrible deed was connected with Moses' role as Yahweh's representative. Hyam Maccoby, a remarkable scholar whose acclaimed and controversial work shows human sacrifice to be a continuing, though disguised, theme in many Biblical episodes, offers the following revision of this difficult passage:

> And it came to pass on the way at the lodging place, that the Lord afflicted him (with divine madness), and he (Moses) sought to kill him (the child). And Zipporah took a flint, and cut off the foreskin of her son, and cast it at his (Moses') feet; and she said, "Surely a bridegroom of blood art thou to me." So He (God) withdrew from him (Moses—i.e. the fit of madness left him). Then she said, "Bridegroom of blood for the circumcision."[10]

This translation makes sense in light of the momentous undertaking Moses is beginning. He needs a child sacrifice to ensure success. God's message to the Egyptians is full of the sacrificial motif, demanding as He does the whole nation of Israel as His "first-born," and threatening to kill the Pharaoh's first-born children if Israel isn't freed. Apparently Zipporah's decision to give a symbolic offering of the child's penis skin is acceptable instead of child sacrifice, and Maccoby sees this as the real inauguration of the Hebrew rite of circumcision. Zipporah introduces a fundamental religious reform in Judaism, and she does so to save her son. But the Bible editors tried to hide this by making her encounter with Moses almost unintelligible.

"It has never been the official doctrine of Judaism that circumcision is a substitute for human sacrifice," Maccoby writes. "The story of Zipporah, indeed, gives the female too great a role to be acknowledged in patriarchal Judaism as it eventually developed, a part as great as Athene in the acknowledgement of Zeus."[11]

This was not, however, a completely isolated instance in Moses' life. Once, during an epidemic that killed twenty-four thousand Hebrews, Moses commanded the ritual slaying of "the leaders of the people," a practice that involved exposing their dead bodies "before the Lord in the full light of day, that the fury of his anger may turn away from Israel" (Numbers 25:4). On another occasion, Moses offered to sacrifice himself to blot out Israel's sins (Exodus 32:30–35). God refused the offer. Human sacrifice was not something Moses rejected out of hand during crises—either for himself, his fellow leaders, or even for his son.

If Moses considered human sacrifice to be acceptable under extreme circumstances, it's not surprising that his disciple Joshua practiced it during his long war of conquest in Israel. Joshua chose a victim by lot to expiate a disastrous defeat at the hands of the people of Ai; after making the unfortunate man, named Achan, repeat a ritual speech of responsibility for the defeat, the whole community stoned him to death. They erected a stone mound over his body and named the place "the Vale of Achor," in Achan's honor (Joshua 7).

This sacrifice instantly boosted Israelite morale, resulting in the defeat of the Ai. Then Joshua slaughtered the inhabitants of Ai, with special attention to its king; he hanged the king from a tree until sunset, then cut him down and, as with Achan, erected a burial mound: "Over the body they raised a great pile of stones, which is there to this day" (Joshua 8:29). According to the Hebrew law of *herem*, every man, woman, and child of captured cities had to be slaughtered, along with all their animals. This slaughter was seen as a sacrifice to Yahweh, thanking Him for providing victory.

Enforcement was very strict. When King Saul spared the life of the Amalekite King Agag—even though he killed every other Amalekite—the prophet Samuel was furious. Samuel cursed Saul and told him he would lose his kingship as a result. Then the prophet "hewed Agag in pieces before the Lord at Gilgal" (1 Samuel 15:33).

This kind of ritual killing "before the Lord" was typical for all peoples of Palestine of 1000 B.C. A Moabite stele from about 830 B.C. tells how, when a Moabite king captured the Israelite town of Nebo, he killed seven thousand men, women, and children as a holocaust dedicated to Astarte-Chemosh.[12]

This same god Chemosh, or Kemosh, figures in another battle between Israel and the Ammonites, a tribe who wanted to recapture their lands lost to Joshua. In desperate straits, Jewish elders approached a warrior named Jephthah, whom they offered to make Judge of Israel if he could stave off the Ammonites. Although Jephthah accepted the challenge, he was inspired to promise God an unusual sacrifice in exchange for victory: "the spirit of the Lord came upon Jephthah. . . . Jephthah made this vow to the Lord: 'If thou wilt deliver the Ammonites into my hands, then the first creature that comes out of the door of my house to meet me when I return from them in peace shall be the Lord's; I will offer that as a whole-offering' " (Judges 11:29–31).

The vow worked, and Jephthah won a great victory over the Ammonites. But when he returned home, his daughter, his only child, was the first creature to greet him. She came out dancing and playing the tambourine to celebrate her father's triumph. So Jephthah had to fulfill his vow by sacrificing her, a fate that his daughter courageously accepted. It's sad that we don't even know her name. She has gone down in the history of martyrs simply as "Jephthah's daughter."

Although Jephthah's vow of sacrificing the first "creature" to come out of his door makes the story slightly ambiguous, this was part of an unambiguous Iron Age custom of sacrificing children in exchange for military success. King Mesha of Moab immolated his son on the walls of a besieged Moabite city (2 Kings 3:27). Agamemnon sacrificed his daughter Iphigenia to gain favorable winds for the Greek fleet heading to Troy. Idomeneus, one of the Greeks coming back triumphantly from Troy, made a vow almost identical to Jephthah's—to sacrifice the first creature he meets onshore. It turned out to be his own son, whom he killed. The Greek Meander likewise swore he would sacrifice the first people who congratulated him on a military victory in Anatolia. This unfortunate group consisted of his mother, wife, and son.[13]

Perhaps all these vague vows, followed by "chance" encounters with members of the military leaders' immediate family, were carefully choreographed in advance. In any case, they followed a ritual formula well known in the ancient world.

And well known to the Incas, too. The Incas offered child sacrifices to secure military victories, as they did to ensure many other undertakings. Caque Poma's offering of his daughter, Tanta Carhua, has many features in common with the offering of Jephthah's daughter. These include:

1. Human sacrifice was a path to political promotion for men. Both Jephthah and Caque Poma are competing for political supremacy in their tribes. Jephthah's sacrifice, and the military victory it brings him, secures his promotion to Judge of Israel; Caque Poma's offering of his daughter likewise gets him the chieftanship of Ocros, Peru. If you wanted to be a leader, you were expected to sacrifice your children during crises.

2. Both victims are young virgin girls.

3. Both girls died heroically. Jephthah's daughter says, "Father, you have made a vow to the Lord; do to me what you have solemnly vowed, since the Lord has avenged you on the Ammonites, your enemies" (Judges 11:36). Tanta Carhua says, "You can finish with me now, because I could not be more honored than by the feasts which they celebrated for me in Cuzco."

4. Both sacrificed girls became saints whose graves attracted pilgrims from far and wide. Tanta Carhua's grave on top

of Mount Aixa served as a focus for shamanic divination, crop fertility rites, and healing invocations. In the case of Jephthah's daughter, "It became a tradition that the daughters of Israel should go year by year and commemorate the fate of Jephthah's daughter, four days in every year" (Judges 11:40).

When I started reading the Bible in Chile and Argentina after being in contact with Andean human-sacrifice practices, I was struck by how human sacrifice in the Bible also followed drought patterns, as it still does in the Andes. In the mid-1940s and the early 1980s there was an upswing in the practice of child sacrifice in Peru because of severe droughts. During these life-threatening dry spells, human sacrifices are frequently made on Andean hills and mountains; I've been told that in some cases the hand of a victim is left sticking out of the ground on the mountaintop, as a supplication for rain. In light of this, the following incident from King David's reign, c. 1000 B.C., recorded in the second book of Samuel seemed significant.

There was a three-year famine in Israel, apparently caused by a drought. At this difficult time normal prayers and sacrifices couldn't move Yahweh to send rain. This prompted King David to consult Yahweh about the causes of the famine. Yahweh answered: "Blood-guilt rests on Saul and on his family because he put the Gibeonites to death" (2 Samuel 21:1–9). King Saul had been dead for decades when this famine occurred. But the consequences of his massacre of the Gibeonites were believed, in the voice of the shamanic oracle David received, to have upset the balance of nature long afterward and caused the terrible drought.

So it's not too surprising that, when King David asked the Gibeonites what he could do to satisfy their demands against Saul, they requested seven of Saul's male descendants, to sacrifice them "before the Lord in Gibeah of Saul" (2 Samuel 21:6).

King David immediately agreed. He gave the Gibeonites two

of Saul's sons born to Rizpah, a concubine of Saul, and five of Saul's male grandchildren. Pathetic as the fate of King Saul's progeny was, the case of Rizpah, mother of two victims, is more tragic:

> . . . and they flung them down from the mountain before the Lord; the seven of them fell together. They were put to death in the first days of harvest at the beginning of the barley harvest. Rizpah daughter of Aiah took sackcloth and spread it out as a bed for herself on the rock, from the beginning of harvest until the rains came and fell from heaven upon the bodies. She allowed no bird to set upon them by day nor any wild beast by night . . . and thereafter the Lord was willing to accept prayers offered for the country.
> —2 Samuel 21:9–14

The key detail here is that the victims were sacrificed "in the first days of harvest at the beginning of the barley harvest." Normally animal sacrifices accompanied the harvest festival. But this is a special harvest sacrifice, one designed to end the famine—and the drought responsible for it—by bringing rain. So Rizpah's vigil continues until "rains came and fell from heaven upon the bodies." The belief that the exposed bodies of the victims can move the heavens to merciful rain also has an Andean corollary in the up-stretched hand of human sacrifices left visible on Peruvian mountaintops during droughts. Only after the saving rains fall does King David order the bones of the seven victims to be gathered together and buried along with those of King Saul and Jonathan. Then they're all interred together at a new tomb that confirms their status as martyred heroes.

And so the famine ends.

This ritual is predicated on the power of mountaintops to bring rain. The harvest festivals of the Mapuches likewise take place on sacred hills that have "power to call for water." Just as Moses worked water miracles on Mount Sinai, making water emerge from a rock, so the Gibeonites had their own "mountain of Yahweh" where they practiced rain magic. We don't know exactly which peak it was. But, wherever it was, the principle is grounded in the same ecological observation: Rainclouds gather around peaks, storms break out, and streams flow down mountain slopes. So the best place to end a drought-induced famine is on the mountain of Yahweh. And the best sacrifice for the Gibeonites was a Yahwistic *capacocha*, a royal sin offering accomplished with princes of the royal blood. The message from the Bible is that this human sacrifice worked.

King David also advanced his political goals with this sacrifice. By choosing to sacrifice seven male descendants of Saul, David eliminated seven dangerous rivals to himself and his own male successors. At the same time, David cemented good relations with the Gibeonites, a member of the growing Jewish federation. Exchanges of noble victims among Andean peoples was also a form of diplomacy. Thus the Peruvian town of Ocros sent child sacrifices to Lake Titicaca, Chile, and Cuzco, apparently to secure good will. The Gibeonites would have been grateful for David's extravagant holocaust.

The rain offering of the Gibeonites was a complex affair, one that combined fertility rites, diplomacy, scapegoating, and political assassination. King David's solution to the three-year drought was a masterpiece of crisis management.

The prophet Elijah also faced a three-year drought, one that he ended with a spectacular mountaintop rain ritual that included human sacrifice. The scene of Elijah's historic competition with the priests of Baal was a mountaintop in the Carmel range of northern Israel. It is called El Muhraqa, "the Place of Sacrifice."

Carmel's pine-covered peaks afford beautiful vistas of the Mediterranean on the western side; in the northern distance the eternally snowcapped Mount Hermon stands out. Its coastal location and its sight line—to a permanent water reservoir on the horizon—meet the significant criteria for a site for rain magic.

Apparently Elijah, King Ahab of Israel, and the prophets of

Baal all thought so, too, because after three years of drought King Ahab called together 450 priests of Baal, four hundred priests of the goddess Asherah (Astarte), and the lone Elijah for a momentous rain-making competition on El Muhraqa. Here, in front of a huge multitude, Elijah issued his resounding challenge to the priests of Baal:

> Bring two bulls; let them choose one for themselves, cut it up and lay it on the wood without setting fire to it, and I will prepare the other and lay it on the wood without setting fire to it. You shall invoke your god by name and I will invoke the Lord by name; and the god who answers by fire, he is God.
>
> —Kings 18:23–24

The 450 priests of Baal tried all day to cause a fire to consume their bull-offering miraculously. They slashed themselves with knives, causing blood to flow on the ground. But Baal didn't answer.

Then Elijah's turn came. First he repaired "the altar of the Lord," which had been torn down. Then he erected twelve standing stones around the altar, representing the twelve tribes of Israel. He proceeded to dig a big trench around the entire altar, a trench "big enough to hold two measures of seed; he arranged the wood, cut up the bull and laid it on the wood. Then he said, 'Fill four jars with water and pour it on the whole-offering and on the wood.' " The people poured water until "water ran all round the altar and even filled the trench."

Finally, the miracle happened:

> Then the fire of the Lord fell. It consumed the whole-offering, the wood, the stones, and the earth, and licked up the water in the trench. When all the people saw it, they fell prostrate and cried, "The Lord is God, the Lord is God." Then Elijah said to them, "Seize the prophets of Baal; let not one of them escape." They seized them, and Elijah took them down to the Kishon and slaughtered them there . . . .
>
> —1 Kings 18:38–40

Immediately after the slaughter of the prophets of Baal, Elijah informed King Ahab, "I hear the sound of coming rain." Ahab then partook of a sacramental meal, while Elijah went up the mountain again; near the top, he assumed a crouching prayer position with his hands covering his face and his head between his knees. While the prophet remained in this uncomfortable prayer posture, Elijah's assistant looked toward the sea for signs of rainclouds. Elijah ordered him to repeat this action seven times. The seventh time, Elijah's helper spotted a tiny cloud coming from the sea. Then a heavy downpour broke, and the three-year drought ended.

Who was sacrificed on the Place of Sacrifice? Obviously, two bulls were killed at the start. What's revealing about the bull sacrifices of Elijah and the priests of Baal is that they're nearly identical. They take place on the same mountain, and they follow exactly the same procedures. The only difference is that Elijah's sacrifice is consumed by a supernatural fire. The people of Israel were understandably confused about the differences between Yahweh and Baal. Without special miracles like this, there didn't seem to be any distinction between the deities.

What's even more revealing is that the bull sacrifice, miracle or no miracle, did *not* end the three-year drought. The drought ended when the 450 priests of Baal were killed by Elijah. But they weren't killed on the mountaintop; Elijah, Ahab, and the crowd made a long trek (at least half an hour's walk) down to the river Kishon. Why not just dispatch them, together with the bulls, on the mountain? The answer depends on understanding the ritual spot selected for killing the prophets of Baal. The more accurate text of the Jerusalem Bible says that "Elijah took them down to the wadi Kishon, and he slaughtered them there" (I Kings 18:40). *Wadi* is often translated as "river" or "gorge." However it's rendered, wadis were traditional places for human offerings. The people of Judah were in the habit of "sacrificing children in the wadis" (Isaiah 57:5, Jerusalem Bible).

Elijah's entire rain ritual is remarkably similar to Andean practices. The Mapuches believe that every sacred mountain, Tren

Tren, is connected to the ocean and to distant snowcapped peaks, as Carmel is to the Mediterranean and Mount Hermon. At the same time, each Tren Tren has its own, more local source of water—a stream running nearby, or a pool of fresh water. Often shamans sacrifice to the streams and pools at the feet of sacred mountains, as well as at the mountaintops. These sacrifices routinely consist of chickens or sheep. But bull sacrifices to water sources often occur during droughts. And the water from these streams or pools is carried in jars to the mountaintops for rain magic, even as water from the Kishon was probably carried to fill Elijah's deep trench on top of El Muhraqa.

During difficult drought years, there's yet another feature that corresponds to Elijah's procedure—shamans dig a trench near the water source by the mountain, to see if the trench will fill up with water. If the trench fills with water, rain is assured; if not, it's believed the drought will continue. So Elijah's deep trench around the altar of Yahweh was filled with water to attract rain by sympathetic magic known all over the world.

When Juan Cheuquecoy, a Mapuche shaman, challenged Father Luis to a rain contest in 1944, Cheuquecoy invoked the power of a pool of water, Agua del Gato (The Cat's Water). He sacrificed animals and prayed for rain with water offerings taken from this pool. Cheuquecoy's victory over the Catholic priest is recounted with many dramatic details, some of them as improbable as Elijah's mountaintop miracle. But the moral is that the Mapuche blood sacrifices were superior to the Roman Catholic Mass, which had only the symbolic offerings of bread and wine. According to Felipe Painén, when Cheuquecoy finished praying, "the sky turned black and you could hear Manquián [the Mapuche sea god]'s cat purring. Whenever it's going to rain, you hear Manquián's cat purring: *lullull*. . . .Then it rained very hard."

The ocean god's cat is an immense spirit that supposedly controls rainfall; whenever rain is coming, the cat is heard as the sound of the north wind, from where most storms come. Once again, in an exact parallel to Elijah's procedure, the sound of rain came only after the shaman Juan Cheuquecoy finished his sacrifices and prayers at the pool below a sacred hill.

At Lago Budi meteorological phenomena are bound up with a feline entity, Manquián's Cat. But further inland from Lago Budi I've found two groups that sacrifice bulls during droughts, and who each identify the bull's lowing with storm sounds and rushing water. For both of these groups, streams and waterfalls have to be replenished by bull sacrifices, and those sacrifices should be accompanied by the bull's lowing, to bring rain and rushing water.

Was the "sound of coming rain" that Elijah heard after slaughtering the priests of Baal at the Kishon River somehow related to a bull sound?

Baal, consort of Astarte, was a bull. He controlled rain as the Canaanite thunder god. The bull was also a symbol for Yahweh, who was worshipped as a bull by Jews at Bethel and Dan (1 Kings 12:28–30), who sacrificed to golden calves. They believed these golden calves were the gods that brought the Israelites out of Egypt. So there was an ancient tradition that Moses had adored the golden calf, just as he had revered the bronze serpent. The presence of bullhorns on the altar of the tabernacle hinted at the earlier association of Yahweh with a bull. The bullhorns in the tabernacle were smeared with the blood of animal sacrifices (Exodus 29:12), and could also be seized by a person in need of sanctuary (1 Kings 1:50). Thus the bullhorns were the almost tangible presence of Yahweh.

The complete name for Baal is Baal-Hammon. *Hammon* is "sound." Thus Baal-Hammon is "Baal sound." Could the Baal sound have been a bull sound, too? Perhaps rainmaking rites, to both Baal and Yahweh, equated the bull's deep, powerful lowing with the sound of thunder and rushing water, as the prehistoric bullhorns at Cullen Bog, Ireland, once did, and as Mapuche drought rituals still do today. This may be why Elijah claims to have heard "the sound of coming rain" following his slaying of bulls and priests to Yahweh on El Muhraqa.

Some may think it sacrilegious to accuse Elijah of performing a human sacrifice, let alone 450 human sacrifices, and still less to a Yahwistic bull-spirit. After all, Elijah is welcomed to the Passover Seder every year by observant Jews. The Carmelite monks have adopted him as a patron and turned him into a Catholic saint. But the shamanic figure capable of ending a three-year drought in a torrent of blood would probably upset his modern admirers as much as he would be upset by them. Because if "Saint Elijah" returned to El Muhraqa and found his stone altar to Yahweh, built of twelve magical uncut mountain rocks, where he sacrificed bulls, torn down and replaced by the Catholic temple, built with cement, where the only offerings were bread and wine . . . Well, he'd probably want to sacrifice the monks down at the Kishon River, too. I suspect Juan Cheuquecoy's victory over the Roman Catholic Mass would have pleased the old Elijah more than the monastery named after him.

Personally, I think that understanding Elijah's killing of the prophets as a desperate ritual act to end a drought makes him far more understandable than to assume he killed them because of . . . what?

Because they sacrificed bulls?

Because they worshipped on mountaintops?

Because they practiced human sacrifice?

Since Elijah made bull holocausts on mountaintops, and since he believed human sacrifices could relieve droughts, the exact differences between Elijah and the priests of Baal are hard to fathom. At an earlier period, tribal identity went hand in hand with a deity— Chemosh for the Ammorites, Yahweh for Jephthah's Jewish coalition—with their territorial struggles being a battle between their guardian gods as well. In this case, however, King Ahab and most people in the northern kingdom worshipped both Baal and Yahweh, probably considering them different names for the same god, so the tribal equation had broken down. Elijah objected to this syncretism and wanted to restore the exclusive sovereignty of Yahweh. But water magic, blood sacrifice, and mountaintop invocations are similar to the fertility rites of other Canaanite people.

Second century B.C. amulets bearing Jewish symbols:
Yahweh with serpent features.

One of the most insistent laments of the Bible's Book of Kings is that the Hebrews "erected hill-shrines, sacred pillars, and sacred poles, on every high hill" (1 Kings 14:23) in Israel. Each of these hill-shrines had its own seer or prophet. Some hill-shrines had whole groups of prophets, who practiced divination and sacrificial rites, cured illnesses, and carried out familiar shamanic functions without ever paying homage to the Temple in Jerusalem. Thus the Kingdom of Judah, like the Kingdom of Israel before it, faced entrenched mountain worship that was based on prehistoric habits so deeply ingrained that they differ only slightly from similar cults found all around the world.

But a group of Jewish sages chose deliberately to distort and consciously uproot these age-old customs, in one of the most radical religious reforms ever known.

⊡ 20 ⊡

THE BIRTH OF HELL

Hell was born just outside the walls of Jerusalem, in the Valley of Ben Hinnom. The prophet Jeremiah dubbed this "the Valley of Slaughter" (Jeremiah 19:6) because so many children were immolated here in a deep pit known as the Tophet— "Place of Fire." Even kings of Judah burned their sons and daughters at this Tophet. Eventually, the sacrifices ceased. But the memory remained, as the Valley of Ben Hinnom was turned into Gehenna, the Hebrew word for "hell," where sinners suffered the eternal torment of fire.

Having heard so much about hell in Catholic grade school— and seen frightening pictures of children consumed in these flames—I wanted to see the actual spot where the dreadful notion began. I expected something awful in "the Valley of Slaughter," so I was taken aback by its beautiful, deep ravines and verdant olive groves, just outside the white, turreted walls of Jerusalem's Old City. It looked more like paradise than hell.

"If this is hell, then hell is a pretty nice place," archaeologist Gabriel Barkay told me.

Barkay, a professor at Tel Aviv University, admires the valley for its topography and its rich past. "The valley has gotten a bad name because of the burning which went on at the Tophet here," he says. "Jeremiah equated this place with the kind of activity which goes on in hell—bodies burning forever. But you have to remember that those who performed these sacrifices regarded their activities as wholly innocent."

There's direct Biblical testimony that child sacrifice continued until the seventh century B.C. at the Tophet in the Valley of Ben Hinnom. The prophet Jeremiah says, "they have built a shrine of Topheth in the Valley of Ben-hinnom, at which to burn their sons and daughters" (Jeremiah 7:31). King Ahaz of Judah worshipped at this Tophet. "He also burnt sacrifices in the Valley of Ben-hinnom; he even burnt his sons in the fire according to the abominable practice of the nations whom the Lord had dispossessed in favor of the Israelites. He slaughtered and burnt sacrifices at the hill-shrines and on the hill-tops and under every spreading tree" (2 Chronicles 28:3–4). King Manasseh likewise "made his son pass through the fire" (2 Kings 21:6). According to most Bible translations, these child immolations were made to the terrible god Moloch.

Although Moloch has become one of the great demons of Judeo-Christian literature, there's strong evidence that Moloch was not a demon at all but simply the name for child sacrifices dedicated to Yahweh. This new understanding comes from Phoenician settlements in Sicily and North Africa, where Tophets, like that outside of Jerusalem, have been excavated. The Phoenicians were close relatives to the Hebrews—the Bible refers to the Phoenician coastal peoples as Canaanites. They spoke a mutually intelligible language, and the Hebrew alphabet, like all modern alphabets in the Western world, came from the Phoenicians. So did the fire sacrifices of the Jerusalem Tophet.

Curiosity about Yahweh's sacrificial Tophet leads one to Carthage, near the city of Tunis, North Africa. Here there is a pleasant, overgrown garden, shaded by pomegranate and fig trees, which once served as the Carthaginian Tophet, the most prolific known place of child sacrifice in the ancient world. The wild growth of weeds is rivaled by the abundance of sacrificial stelae, popping up everywhere, with their stick-figure representations of Baal-Hammon and Tanit-Ashtarte. Queen Dido of Tyre brought these familiar gods from the Phoenician homeland, much of which is now a part of Israel, when she founded Carthage about 800 B.C.

A UNESCO archaeological team uncovered hundreds of urns filled with the cremated bones of children and sacrificed animals, often mixed with beads and good-luck amulets. Many of these jars were buried under the pointed limestone stelae, with their dedications to Tanit and Baal-Hammon. One stela records a priest in long, flowing robes, holding a child in the act of sacrifice.

The Carthaginian Tophet has many layers, the bottom level dating back to 750 B.C. At this earliest period, animal sacrifice was more frequent than later, although it never constituted more than a third of all ritual killings here. The most primitive burial urns and stelae show wider variety in color and design. Later, as the number of human sacrifices increased along with Carthage's burgeoning population, the burial urns became a uniform, nondescript orange color, and the stelae were also standardized. There are some twenty thousand urns in all.

Archaeologists Lawrence Stager and Samuel Wolff concluded that the Carthaginian Tophet is "the largest cemetery of sacrificed humans ever discovered."[1]

But in spite of the many written accounts of child sacrifice at Carthage, coupled with the physical evidence, some scholars don't admit that child sacrifice occurred here. The connection between the Jerusalem Tophet and the Carthaginian Tophet is what makes the issue so controversial. One of the most disconcerting pieces of epigraphic evidence is that the Carthaginian sacrifices were called "mulk offerings." There was no Moloch god at Carthage or any other Phoenician settlement. The implication is that the proper translation of *mlk* (the Hebrew text of the Old Testament doesn't have vowels, which makes the translation so difficult) should be "human sacrifice," not a deity named Moloch. If this translation is accepted—and a large number of Biblical scholars now favor it—it would mean similar rituals of child sacrifice took place as part of orthodox Yahwism, perhaps on a large scale. "A lot of traditional Bible scholars are getting angry about this," says one of the anthropologists who excavated the Carthage Tophet. "They don't want to face the skeleton in Judeo-Christianity's closet."

But the skeleton comes alive and does an ecstatic dance of death in one of Isaiah's greatest poems, a religious song meant to accompany a human sacrifice at the Jerusalem Tophet. Isaiah began preaching in Judah at almost the exact time that the first sacrificial urns were planted in the Carthaginian Tophet.

> Such shall be your song,
> As on a night a feast is celebrated
> With gladness of heart,
> As when one marches in procession with the flute,
> To enter the mountain of Yahweh,
> To the Rock of Israel.
> Yahweh has made heard the crash of His voice,
> The down-sweep of His arm he has displayed,
> With hot wrath and flame of consuming fire,
> Cloudburst and flood and hailstones.
> Yes! At the voice of Yahweh
> Assyria will cower—
> With His staff He will beat him.
> Every passage of the rod of His punishment
> Which Yahweh will lay upon him
> Will be to the sound of timbrels and lyres;
> With battles of offerings He will fight against him.
> For his Topheth has long been prepared,
> He himself is installed as a victim [*molek*].
> Yahweh has made its fire-pit deep and wide,
> With fire and wood in abundance.
> The breath of Yahweh,
> Like a torrent of sulphur,
> Sets it ablaze!
>
> —Isaiah 30:29–33[2]

What's amazing about Isaiah's song is its explicit ritual content, and the undeniable authorship of Yahweh in the torture and immolation of the Assyrian victim, who is probably the great Assyrian conquerer Sennacherib. The Assyrians were threatening the existence of Judah during Isaiah's lifetime, and they succeeded in annihilating the northern kingdom of Samaria (Israel proper). These verses served as the centerpiece of Paul Mosca's Ph.D. thesis at Harvard in 1975, "Child Sacrifice in Israelite and Canaanite Religion." The translation used above is borrowed from Mosca, with a few slight changes. It is more explicit than the New English Bible or any other popular text, because Mosca translates *mlk* as *molek* that is, sacrificial "victim." In most traditional renderings of these verses, *mlk* was translated *melek*—king. Perhaps Mosca is right in suggesting that Isaiah was creating a deliberate pun, since, in this nocturnal rite, the victim (*molek*) is the Assyrian king (*melek*). But even if this technical term is rejected, Isaiah's poem is clearly about a ritual killing. According to Mosca's analysis of Isaiah's poem, "we begin with the fire—the lightning—of Yahweh's storm theophany and end with the fire of ritual sacrifice."[3] All of the mountain god's weather powers—over lightning, thunder, hail, rain, and wind—become weapons by which Yahweh conquers Sennacherib and then sacrifices him. Thus, the roles of storm god, warrior, and sacrificer converge in this frightening portrait of Yahweh, just as they do in the mythologies of the fierce Andean mountain gods.

It can be argued that Isaiah is speaking allegorically, that these verses are really nothing more than a war song. But, given the exact parallels between Isaiah's war song and the known human-sacrifice rituals of other Canaanite peoples, it is an allegory the Assyrians would have taken literally. Isaiah's Tophet sacrifice takes place at night, around a deep fire-pit, to the sound of music, just as the Phoenician rites did. The main difference between the Tophet ritual extolled by Isaiah and the human sacrifices practiced by the Phoenicians is that Isaiah's victim is offered to Yahweh, whereas the Phoenician victims are given to Tanit and Baal.

Significantly, Isaiah didn't criticize his contemporaries, Kings Ahaz or Manasseh, both of whom sacrificed their children at the Jerusalem Tophet. Paul Mosca concludes from his study of Isaiah 30:27–33 that "the rite of the Jerusalem Tophet—though in hindsight viewed first as unorthodox (Deuteronomist) and finally as idolatrous (Jeremiah and Ezekiel)—was, in fact, part of the official Yahwistic cultus. Isaiah himself seems to have had no particular objection to Yahwistic 'passing into the fire.' "[4]

Isaiah's views of the Tophet and those who sacrificed there are in stark contrast to the later authors of Chronicles and Kings, who saw Ahaz following "the abominable practice of the nations." The difference between Isaiah and Jeremiah is even greater since, while Isaiah praises the Tophet as Yahweh's liberating weapon against the Assyrians, Jeremiah blames the Tophet for the fall of Jerusalem, which he ascribes to Yahweh's anger at idolatrous human sacrifice. Between the time of Isaiah's ministry in the early seventh century B.C. and Jeremiah's preaching in the early sixth century B.C., Jewish thinkers radically redefined Yahwism and suppressed human sacrifice.

Until this time, Yahweh had been worshipped by shaman-prophets on "every high hill" in Israel. But King Josiah of Judah chose to destroy all the hill-shrines in one of the most drastic religious reforms in history. "He brought in all the priests from the cities of Judah and desecrated the hill-shrines where they had burnt sacrifices, from Geba to Beersheba, and dismantled the hill-shrines of the demons. . . . He desecrated Topheth in the Valley of Ben-hinnom, so that no one might make his son or daughter pass through the fire in honour of Molech" (2 Kings 23:8–10). Josiah also razed the hill-shrine at Bethel erected by Abraham, and went throughout Samaria to slaughter "on the altars all the priests of the hill-shrines" (2 Kings 23:20).

Apparently this reversal of age-old custom caused great consternation. When an earlier king, Hezekiah, attempted to suppress some of the hill-shrines, he was accused of destroying Yahweh's legitimate places of worship. (Ironically, the Assyrian King Sennacherib made this accusation against Hezekiah [Isaiah 36:7].) But Hezekiah's grandson, King Josiah, cleverly rewrote history to make Moses the author of his sweeping reforms, whose effects were to fill the temple's coffers with contributions from all over Judah at the expense of the once-independent local shamans. Obviously, the High Priest was one of the principal beneficiaries of this centralization. And it was the High Priest Hilkiah (father of the prophet Jeremiah) himself who, while collecting tribute from all over Judah and Israel, "discovered the book of the law of the Lord which had been given through Moses" (2 Chronicles 34:14), which revolutionized the rules of Hebrew worship.

No one had ever heard of this book of Moses before, so Josiah had to consult a prophetess about its authenticity. She wisely confirmed the divine origin of the newly discovered book. Not surprisingly, the High Priest's book of Mosaic law (perhaps Deuteronomy) supported Josiah's reforms to the letter. One of the most transparent anachronisms of the new rules was the requirement that all hill-shrines be destroyed outside of Jerusalem. Moses built such altars himself, and gave instructions to Joshua to build more of them. Another anomaly in these new teachings is Moses' repeated attacks on human sacrifice, although, as we've seen, Moses attempted to sacrifice his own son, sacrificed a group of leaders to avert an epidemic, and once offered to sacrifice himself. By the new "book of Moses," the old Moses was a heretic.

But with the new book of Moses the human-sacrificial rites that once defined the most sublime degree of piety became abominations. And the Valley of Ben Hinnom, or Gay ben Hinnom, where the Jerusalem Tophet received these sacrifices, became a synonym for "hell," Gehenna, a word that worked its way into several languages.

Josiah's methods were drastic but effective. With the help of Hilkiah, Jeremiah, and other reformers, he succeeded in eradicating human sacrifice for perhaps the first time in history. Animal sacrifices continued at only one place, the Great Temple on Mount Moriah. Although this centralized power in the hands of the Jerusalem priesthood, it had the paradoxical effect of reducing the influence of blood sacrifice outside of the Great Temple. Instead, a new breed of rabbis, or lay teachers, arose. At their local synagogues they created the conception of an ethical God, one bound as much by His covenant as the Jews were bound to Him. Within a remarkably short time—six or seven centuries—the wrathful Yahweh of Isaiah, a storm god burning with desire for revenge and human sacrifice, had become the God of Hillel, whose maxim was "What is hateful to you, do not do to your fellow man. This is the entire Law; the rest is commentary."[5] Human sacrifice was inconceivable for Hillel's God.

Thus we have a precious still shot of cultural evolution in the making: a new book is written and ascribed to Moses, and a new path of religious thought unfolds. The Bible is a portrait of sacrificial thinking in various stages of growth. Like the Aztecs and the Incas, who both evolved solar cults to co-opt the local mountain gods, the Hebrews reworked sacrificial mythology, a conscious adaptation of the oldest rituals to changing circumstances. No society has existed without some form of sacrificial myth and ritual. But, whereas both the Incas and the Aztecs made human sacrifice even more prominent, in the fantastic panoply of the Incas' empire-wide *capacocha* offerings and the elaborate mass slayings of the Aztec state, the Jews made a unique decision to abolish human sacrifice as the centerpiece of culture. The Romans, Greeks, and Hindus diminished its importance, replacing it gradually (though never completely) with symbolic human sacrifices. But the Jews evolved a system in which the concept of human sacrifice was inherently abhorrent.

Still, these remarkable reforms came at the cost of another type of violent suppression—an internalization of sacrificial fear. Anyone who disobeyed the new rules would go to Gehenna, the hell where they would burn forever, as the bodies once burned in the Tophet.

The prophet Jeremiah vividly depicted this unquenchable fire, and it became a part of popular religion. Apparently only a drastic inhibition like this could free people from the captivity of human sacrifice. Ironically, the means of liberation was the old method of ritual death itself, projected into a nightmare: what men had practiced from the beginning of time became a punishment meted out by God for all eternity.

Gehenna and the burning that went on there became identified with the demon Moloch. As we've seen, this great demon was also born from changing attitudes toward the Tophet fire-pit, since the original *molek* was just a pious human-sacrifice offering. "Thus, between the Josianic reform and the closing centuries of the pre-Christian era, we may catch a glimpse of the rarest of all events, the birth of a god—a god whose cult had, happily, long since been abandoned."[6]

Gehenna burned itself into the Christian Gospels: "It is better to enter into the kingdom of God with one eye than to keep both eyes and be thrown into hell [Gehenna], where the devouring worm never dies and the fire is not quenched" (Mark 9:47–48). Here we see the Tophet wedded to the serpent, which Jesus calls the "devouring worm." Originally Moses set up a bronze effigy of this serpent (Numbers 21:9), which was worshipped until King Hezekiah tore it down six centuries later (2 Kings 18:4). But now the serpent has been changed into the devil, just as the Mapuche leviathan Cai Cai Filu and the Aymara mountain serpent were converted to "devils" by Christian missionaries. And just as Cai Cai Filu and the monster snake on Mount Kapia are thought to be ravenously hungry for human flesh, here, too, the Christian serpent demon is pictured devouring people. One of the reasons that Aymara shamans can easily adapt satanic rituals to their own practices of mountain worship is that Satan, "that serpent of old" (Revelation 12:9), is an ancient relative of their snake god on Mount Kapia.

In spite of John Milton's vivid picture of the blood-smeared Moloch in *Paradise Lost*, there was no demon Moloch, just as there was no Paradise lost.

No serpent spoiled the Garden of Eden.

Eden belonged to that old serpent. And Eden, as the children buried beneath the lovely, overgrown garden in Carthage know too well, raged with the fires of hell. The process by which the fantasy of Eden became the nightmare of hell claimed its own victims, too. It's no accident that the fifth-century theological battles over this man-made hell took place near Carthage, spearheaded by Saint Augustine and the African bishops who followed him. Together they enforced a new doctrine that any infant who died without baptism would go straight to hell—a teaching meant to intimidate pagan parents into surrendering their age-old custom of dedicating newborn children to Tanit, who by this time was called Dea Caelestis.[7] Such Tanit dedications were symbolic, though the Church Father Tertullian claimed that child sacrifice in North Africa secretly continued well into the Christian era.

Julian of Eclanam, an Italian bishop, ridiculed Augustine's doctrine of hell, asking him: "Tell me then, tell me: who is this person who inflicts such punishment on innocent creatures. . . . You answer: God. God, you say! God! He Who commended His love to us, Who has loved us, Who has not spared His own Son for us. . . . He is the persecutor of newborn children; He it is who sends tiny babies to eternal flames."[8]

Julian's question "Who is this person who inflicts such punishment on innocent creatures?" is a profound one. Does God send babies to hell? Or is Augustine's God, as Julian suggests, really a demon in disguise? Peter Brown, one of Augustine's biographers, says that, "Augustine had always believed in the vast power of the Devil: God had shown His omnipotence most clearly in restraining this superhuman creature."[9]

Julian, however, suspected that Augustine had given this superhuman devil power so vast that Satan had become more than God's equal. Originally, Satan was God's messenger, a messenger with the unpleasant job of testing God's faithful servants, as Satan tests Job, for instance. The Samaritan folktale about the *milhaj*, or bad angel, testing Abraham through the sacrifice of Isaac puts another divine messenger in a similarly ambiguous position. But Satan's new role as Moloch—king of the eternal realm of hell and recipient of burning children—usurped Yahweh's former position as the warrior-priest who presided over the Jerusalem Tophet and the immolation of child victims. Not surprisingly, Satan soon acquired the horns, serpents, and magical staff that were once the possession of the storm god Yahweh on Mount Sinai. The devil who grew out of these mythological distortions is a direct descendant of Yahweh the mountain god, just as the *tiu* of Illimani springs from the defamed mountain deities of the Andean past.

As we've seen in the Andes, each new victim of sacrifice becomes another guardian spirit in the sacrificer's army of spiritual slaves. And since Satan was capturing all unbaptized souls in his Gehenna—along with a great many Christian souls as well—his legions were constantly increasing, and his power, quite naturally, grew to fantastic proportions in both popular religion and formal theology. Julian of Eclanum accused Augustine of being a Manichaean heretic—a believer in a divided universe where the powers of darkness were greater than the powers of light.[10] Julian contrasts the God 'Who has not spared His own Son for us" with the God who consigns tiny children to flames, as though the two figures were irreconcilably opposed to each other. But it seems to me that the God who is willing to sacrifice His own child through the agony of crucifixion is precisely the same figure who throws the children of others into hellfire. Both act as Lords of the Sacrifice, deriving their enormous powers, like Jephthah or the Inca ruler, from the ritual deaths of children.

God the Father's sacrifice of Jesus is a divine parallel to King Ahaz's immolation of his own son in the Jerusalem Tophet. This type of child sacrifice, outlawed by King Josiah in the seventh century B.C., was revived as the centerpiece of Christian faith.

⧉ 21 ⧉

CALVARY AND CAIN

It doesn't take long to walk from the gleaming Dome of the Rock on Mount Moriah to Calvary, the nearby hill where Jesus was crucified. Triumphant Crusaders built the Church of the Holy Sepulcher here; a stone chalice in the middle of a large, dimly lit hall marks what medieval Christians believed was the center of the earth, just as the great Rock of the Foundation on Mount Moriah defined the world's center for Judaism. Instead of the luminous Muslim mosque, where, as in Judaism, no graven image is allowed, the shadowy Church of the Holy Sepulcher presents the shocking figure of a man nailed to a cross. In contrast to the austere beauty of mosques and synagogues, the familiar crucifix looks strange indeed: a scene of torture as a focus of worship.

Some think it is a different world—a more primitive, pagan world. "What's always struck me about Christianity is that it's not, as it claims to be, a continuation of Judaism," I was told by Hyam Maccoby.

According to Maccoby, "the whole tendency of the Jewish system was to *reduce* the importance of sacrifice." But in Christianity the centuries-old sublimation of sacrifice, particularly of human sacrifice, "disappears as if in a sudden bout of psychosis.

405

We are back at a primitive level at which the abyss opens and panic requires a victim. It is not surprising under these circumstances that the human victim reappears, after so many centuries of animal substitution."[1]

Maccoby looks at the Old Testament with the same unflinching scrutiny he applies to the Christian Gospels. He fully recognizes that Biblical editors have covered up the original role of human sacrifice in the Akedah and in many other instances, including Moses' attempt to kill his son, discussed earlier. Maccoby's work demonstrates that no one can dismiss human sacrifice as an unpleasant sideline to the great stories of the Bible. But it's precisely because Biblical editors chose to conceal the human-sacrifice myths embedded in the core of the Old Testament that "a large part of the Hebrew Bible constitutes a campaign against human sacrifice."[2] He claims that, unless you understand the Old Testament as a continuous, carefully conceived diatribe against human sacrifice, you won't be able to grasp how incredibly discontinuous the New Testament is, and why the Christian message flies in the face of a painful cultural evolution away from sacrifice toward personal responsibility. Thus Maccoby sees Christianity mistakenly claiming to fulfill the promises of Judaism, when, in fact, it turns back the clock: the New Testament is older than the Old.

I've presented some cases of human sacrifice in the Old Testament, largely based on my first hand research in the Andes. But Hyam Maccoby is the master sleuth of human-sacrifice detective work. In his book *The Sacred Executioner*, Maccoby unravels some of the most tangled murder mysteries in the Bible, using human sacrifice as a paradigm. After reading it, you will never again think of Adam, Cain and Abel, Lamech, Noah, or Enoch, among others, in the same light.

Maccoby is short, white-haired, sixtyish, soft-spoken, unassuming, and comfortably burrowed in among books at his suburban-London study.

There are numerous signs of his growing notoriety all around us. There is a British TV show about his latest work, *The Myth-*

maker: Paul and the Invention of Christianity; a BBC production, with an all-star cast including Christopher Lee, of a play Mr. Maccoby wrote concerning a Jewish-Christian theological debate in the Middle Ages; a book, *The Origins of the Holocaust: Christian Anti-Semitism,* the proceedings of a panel discussion over Mr. Maccoby's controversial claim that anti-Semitism is the inevitable result of the Christian Gospels and their sacrificial ideology. That panel, sponsored by the City University of New York, brought together Rabbi Marc Tanenbaum, one of America's most respected religious leaders, and Eugene Fisher, executive secretary of the U.S. Catholic Bishops' Secretariat for Catholic-Jewish Relations, among others. Even his detractors have to concede that, as Rabbi Tanenbaum puts it, "Professor Hyam Maccoby's provocative thesis represents the beginning of an exceedingly important debate."[3]

Although Maccoby has done much of his work in one room, his results have the impact of a vast archaeological expedition through all the layers of Judeo-Christianity's subconscious. "When I look at a text I like to look for bits that stick out like a sore thumb, that go against the grain of the narrative," Maccoby says. "It's kind of like an archaeological dig."

Maccoby has formidable tools to dig with. As a classics student at Oxford he acquired proficiency in Greek and Latin; later he became a respected literary critic, specializing in T. S. Eliot. One of his advantages lies in an ability to see the Bible as a complete story, with a plot behind the seemingly patchwork narrative. He approaches the Bible as a literary critic, using the tools of anthropology, archaeology, linguistics, and sociobiology, but always keeping his eye on the plot.

Maccoby feels that he has broken a Biblical code, a secret cipher covering up the primitive meanings of many Old Testament myths. Central to his deciphering is a figure he calls "The Sacred Executioner," who appears again and again, with different names and in different places, but always with a deadly function.

Maccoby considers a variety of sacred murders from the Hebrew, Egyptian, Scandinavian, Roman, and Christian traditions that fit the following pattern: someone commits a murder that is enormously beneficial for society. Often the murder isn't presented as a human sacrifice. But there is a hidden motive, seen from the fact that

> a city will be founded, or a nation will be inaugurated, or a famine will be stayed, or a people will be saved from the wrath of the gods, or a threatening enemy will be defeated. Such good consequences are exactly the results that were hoped for by the performance of human sacrifice. If the slaying is blamed on an accident, then nobody will be blamed; but more usually the slaying is attributed to malevolence on the part of the slayer. In this case, the hidden character of the story is betrayed by the equivocal nature of the punishment meted out to the slayer. He will be cursed, but not put to death; he will acquire special magic powers; he will be driven out of society, but special pains will be taken to ensure that he survives. By taking blame for the deed he is performing a great service to society. . . .[4]

The first example on Maccoby's list is the Cain and Abel story. Ostensibly, this story is the first account of a homicide, a brutal, envy-driven action. Cain is angry because Abel's animal sacrifices, the firstlings of his flock, were accepted by God, whereas Cain's vegetable sacrifices were not. So Cain kills Abel in a jealous rage. God responds, not by killing Cain, which is what one would expect, but by banishing him to be "a vagrant and a wanderer on earth" (Genesis 4:13). In fact, God accords a special mark of protection to Cain, so that no one will kill him: "if anyone kills Cain, Cain shall be avenged sevenfold" (Genesis 4:15).

The sacrificial context of this story is enough to arouse suspicion. The story seems to say, "If you restrict yourself to vegetable sacrifices, without offering the firstlings of your flocks, then human sacrifice will be necessary."

God's curse was less effective than it first appears. Instead of going into permanent banishment, as the curse ordains, Cain goes and founds a city, which he names after his son Enoch. Thus Cain is a respectable patriarch, the first city-dweller in the world, and his mythical status is similar to that of Romulus, who also killed a brother, Remus, when he founded Rome. Moreover, Cain's descendants go on to become the inventors of music, metallurgy, and animal husbandry—inventions typically ascribed to godlike culture heroes in every primitive society. If it weren't for God's (unfulfilled) curse against Cain, one would conclude that the murder of Abel somehow secured great blessings for Cain and his tribe.

The disproportionate role of Cain in the Biblical story poses a literary puzzle, and an ethical problem, parallel to the overshadowing stature of Satan in *Paradise Lost* (which, incidentally, Milton patterned closely on the story of Cain). Maccoby brilliantly resolves this puzzle by suggesting that Cain, not Adam, was the archetypical ancestor, the First Man of the tribe that first told the Genesis story.

So the question arises: was there any tribe with a mythical hero named Cain?

The Hebrews didn't trace their ancestry back to Cain, whom the Bible treats as a murderer. But the Hebrews were in close contact with the Kenites, a tribe whose founder was called Cain (Numbers 24:22). Many Biblical experts have posited a profound influence by the Kenite tribe on the Hebrew Bible, since Moses was living with his father-in-law, Jethro, a Kenite priest (who, interestingly enough, was also called Cain, according to the Septuagint Bible) at the time when God spoke to Moses on Mount Sinai. Jethro actually founded the Jewish Sanhedrin when he gave Moses very detailed instructions about collective leadership (Exodus 18:14–26); Jethro's daugher, Zipporah, apparently inaugurated infant circumcision as a substitute sacrifice to save her son from Moses (Exodus 4:24–26). So there's evidence of Kenite influence in two of Judaism's most distinctive features.

Maccoby argues that the Kenites traced their genealogy from a supreme patriarch named Cain, and that the most plausible explanation for the inordinate, and otherwise inexplicable, importance of a murderer like Cain in the Bible's creation story is that Cain's murder was part of a very different Kenite saga in which Cain was the hero. The primal homicide, condemned in the Hebrew Bible, was originally the salvific event which secured urban life, metallurgy, music, and animal husbandry for humanity. A seemingly senseless homicide paved the way for civilization. Progress was bought for a price.

Part of the price was Abel's death. But collective guilt was a larger, more enduring penalty. One way of coping with it was by banishing the sacrificer, who himself became a second victim, condemned to be a perpetual outcast, like Cain. This idea survives in the most solemn Jewish festival, the atonement sacrifice of Yom Kippur. Two goats are brought to the Temple and lots are cast between them. One goat is slain for the sins of the people; the other is banished into the wilderness as atonement for the slain goat. The first goat was offered "for the Lord"; the other was given to the desert demon Azazel (Leviticus 16:8–10). Maccoby believes the two goats were originally human victims—one killed, like Abel; one banished, like Cain.

But choosing a Sacred Executioner is only one way of attenuating sacrificial guilt. Many human-sacrifice rituals required a victim to break a taboo symbolically, to justify his death. When Joshua had lots cast to choose a victim from his army following a defeat at Ai, the unlucky soldier, Achan, assumed responsibility for the military disaster by publicly confessing to having committed a contrived crime. African kings likewise violated tribal laws just prior to being sacrificed, again disguising the religious act as a political one. When a bull was slain at the Athenian New Year's celebration, the Athenians waited until the bull munched on cakes placed in front of it; unfortunately, the cakes belonged to Zeus, so the bull was killed for stealing the god's food. This was called "the Bouphonia," which translates into a general principle of "the comedy of innocence," by which people try to avoid responsibility for sacrificial killing.[5]

By keeping all of these artifices in mind, Maccoby exposes

hidden layers of many myths. It is a new way of looking at old problems. One test of any proposed paradigm is how successfully it explains data that previous paradigms failed to cover. By this standard, Maccoby's Sacred Executioner theme is remarkably effective in clearing up inscrutable Bible passages. Another test is a paradigm's predictive power. And this is where I find Maccoby's approach most convincing.

Thousands of miles from Hyam Maccoby's study, the Aymara shaman Máximo Coa intuitively restored the Genesis myth of the ancient Kenites: "Cain was strong, while Abel was weak. Cain, the strong one, killed Abel, the weak one, and that's why humanity is descended from Cain." This appears to be pure invention on Máximo's part. The Bible says that humanity descended from the virtuous Seth, Adam and Eve's third son (Genesis 4:25–26), since all of Cain's progeny supposedly died out after the great Flood. Máximo and Maccoby, however, see things differently. Maccoby claims that Seth is a colorless name which could be translated as "he who was added," while Seth's supposed descendants are really just a jumbled-up version of Cain's lineage.[6] Máximo Coa says that Seth "was so good that God let him enter the Garden of Eden once again, where the guardian angel didn't forbid him entrance, as he had to Adam and Eve." Seth was so good, in Máximo's creation saga, that he was no good at all—Seth left no children and, in fact, ceased to exist as a human being. Hyam Maccoby thinks Seth was a clumsy editorial insertion, a man who never existed in the colorful Kenite story.

In a way, Máximo is related to the Kenites. This tribe collectively converted to the Hebrew faith, and became a religious elite called the Rechabites, who served in the Temple like the Levite priests.[7] The Rechabites were admired for their asceticism, since they refused to live in anything but tents and abstained from alcohol. "We have drunk no wine all our lives . . ." the Rechabites told the prophet Jeremiah. "We have not built houses to live in, nor have we possessed vineyards or sown fields" (Jeremiah 35:8–9). This sounds like Máximo, who said, "I don't have a house, nor the smallest piece of land." Máximo also claimed he didn't drink alcohol.

"Máximo is a sort of Kenite or a Rechabite," Hyam Maccoby observed. "Listening to him is like being present at that powerful, seminal moment when new myths are created."

Like Cain, Máximo is "a vagrant and a wanderer on earth" (Genesis 4:13). And he wanders for the same reason Cain did: he is a sacred executioner, who has to atone for the sin of human sacrifice. Just as the scapegoat, who stands for Cain, was thrown off a high mountain as a sacrifice to Azazel, so Máximo retires to a high mountain after performing a human sacrifice, where he does penance for his sin. Máximo apologizes to the victim's soul, saying, "We've given you to the *tiu*. But it wasn't for any other purpose." He also apologizes to the Christian God. "Lord, I have sinned," he prays. "It wasn't because I wanted to do it; it was because this *apu*, Your holy mountain, was so desirous of this sacrifice."

"The scapegoat expelled into the wilderness is under the protection of Azazel, the desert demon who is a mountain god, just as Máximo is under the protection of his *tiu*," Maccoby says.

Máximo also permanently atones for his human sacrifices through ascetism and suffering. "God has punished me," he says, pointing to his lame knee. He is proud of this punishment, however, and brags that his lame leg is his "passport"; he also calls it the "cross" he is carrying. Thus, Máximo's lameness is another sacrifice which helps his patrons and protects him from the forces of law and order. His lame leg is quite literally his mark of Cain.

Perhaps the coincidence between Máximo Coa's and Hyam Maccoby's interpretations of Genesis is no more than a mere curiosity. But I think that, whatever the original Genesis story may have been, anthropological evidence supports the thesis that Cain, the killer, was our real collective ancestor. In very primitive tribes, where there are no written laws or strong social hierarchies, homicide takes a terrible toll. Among the aboriginal Yanomamo Indians of the Amazon, 30 percent of the adult males are murdered and 44 percent of the surviving men have participated in a killing, according to a twenty-three-year study recently published by anthropologist Napoleon Chagnon. Those who kill have more wives and offspring than nonkillers because the main purpose of interclan warfare is the acquisition of wives, and aggressive groups scare rivals away.[8] Among the Dyak of Borneo, a young man had to obtain at least one trophy head "before he could even contemplate marriage."[9] If Cain killed, then Cain was "strong" and left lots of offspring, while the "weak" Abel died out. Máximo's deduction has the cool logic a sociobiologist might employ; when his passionate delivery is put aside, the Book of Genesis according to Máximo reads like a corollary to Charles Darwin's theory of the survival of the fittest. Máximo enacts the rituals and embodies the myths that Hyam Maccoby has decoded.

Maccoby helped me see how myth and ritual are entwined in the Mapuche legend about Juan Manquián, the sea god worshipped at Lago Budi. Manquián is a powerful being who controls rain, fish, crops, and wealth in general. He is sometimes described as the ocean's minister, or Prime Minister. At one time, however, Juan Manquián was just a mischievous fifteen-year-old boy who liked to make fun of people. One day he went for a walk by the ocean and he saw a small waterfall, known as "The Girl's Water," which empties into the Pacific near Lago Budi. He laughed at the waterfall and said, "You look like you're pissing into the ocean."

Juan Manquián was extremely rude to say such a thing to the spirit of the waterfall. And since all water spirits are connected to the ocean, the ocean decided to punish Manquián for his bad joke. When Juan Manquián tried to walk away from the ocean, he found that his feet were stuck.

Manquián desperately cried to his friends for help. Several came and tried to pull him out. He remained stuck. Then his friends brought oxen, but the oxen couldn't budge Manquián either. Finally, a great *guillatún* celebration was convened, with all the people around Lago Budi participating. They sacrificed animals to the sea god; they prayed loud and long. But nothing could free Juan Manquián from the ocean's curse. In the end, Juan Manquián nobly accepted his fate. "Don't pray for me anymore," he told the crowd of Mapuches who had come to save him. "I belong to the ocean. This is my place." From that moment onward Juan Manquián was converted into a stone pillar, and he became one with the ocean god. Today he is worshipped almost indiscriminately with the ocean.

When I described to Maccoby the sacrifice of five-year-old José Luis Painecur at Cerro Mesa in 1960, he was struck by the parallels between the Manquián myth and the ritual death at Cerro Mesa. José Luis Painecur was offered to the ocean during a special *guillatún* ceremony, where hundreds of Mapuches supplicated the ocean to withdraw its waters and let them live. His arms and legs were cut off, and he was placed in the sand, "like a stake," until the waves came and carried him away. In this case, José Luis Painecur screamed for help, not from the ocean, but from his "friends" and relatives. He did not gracefully accept his fate.

The Manquián myth and the brutal sacrifice of José Luis Painecur are almost opposites, but both begin with a young boy screaming for help, develop into full-fledged *guillatún* ceremonies with sacrifices to the all-powerful ocean, and end with a boy stuck in the sand like a pillar or a stake. The Manquián myth is a muddled memory of a blood ritual, one that absolves all participants of responsibility for their sacred crime.

"The distancing devices here are beautiful," Maccoby said. "At the Athenian New Year's festival, the knife was held responsible for the bull's slaying. In this Mapuche myth, the ocean was held responsible for the boy's death.

"The Manquián myth also helps you to understand certain parts of the human sacrifice ceremony where the little boy was killed in 1960," Maccoby suggested. "You say his arms and legs were cut off and he was placed in the sand like a stake. In a sense, they cut off his arms and legs to make him into a stone pillar, like Manquián. So they tried to make him into a representative of the ocean, in order to control the wild flood. The boy's sacrifice at Cerro Mesa was actually an enactment of the Manquián myth."

According to Maccoby, people must hide the truth about human sacrifice in order to deify their victim. Juan Manquián had become a demigod. But the Mapuches would have trouble praying to a god if, every time they thought of him, they also thought, "This is the boy whose arms and legs we gruesomely cut off while he begged for mercy." With a relationship like that, the Mapuches would expect a curse from Juan Manquián, not unlimited wealth and blessings. It would be traumatic even to remember him, just as it is traumatic and divisive for people at Lago Budi to deal with any of the facts surrounding the sacrifice of 1960.

Nonetheless, the people of Lago Budi have shifted all the blame for the sacrifice of José Luis Painecur onto Machi Juana, who is their Sacred Executioner. Although everyone else considered that the sacrifice was necessary, and that it saved their lives, they nonetheless hated Machi Juana. "Dirty old shit of a *machi*" was the way one old woman described Machi Juana, even though that woman's own father had actually been the tribal chief who really controlled the event, in conjunction with the male ritual leader. Machi Juana did not initiate the sacrifice of José Luis Painecur, but she accepted the blame for it. In doing so, she became a strange, taboo figure, who acquired immense power in other people's minds. Other shamans carried out special investigations to see whom she was magically murdering, and what crops she was ruining. Yet she also played the chief female role at the annual *guillatún* festival, making her taboo and sacred at the same time.

"This is an extremely interesting kind of splitting," Maccoby said, when I told him about Machi Juana. "Sometimes she is sacred, and sometimes she is accursed. This is the first time I've come across that kind of duality. Normally the Sacred Executioner is either sacred or accursed, depending on the attitude of the society toward human sacrifice. It's quite extraordinary."

In the Mapuche mythology, then, we have three distinct

human-sacrifice stories, with three different approaches to guilt, all based on exactly the same ritual offering to the ocean. The first is the creation story itself, a straightforward human sacrifice by the primal couple, the Mapuche Adam and Eve, on a sacred mountain, to preserve human life from the rising ocean. There's no guilt attached to anyone at Lago Budi for this remote death. So there's no need to disguise it, either. The boy's cries have been muffled by the distance of time.

Manquián is closer to home. He was sacrificed at The Girl's Water, a specific point on the coast. His Christian name, Juan, shows Spanish influence, and the fact that Christian missionaries from the sixteenth, seventeenth, and eighteenth centuries reported no stories about Manquián suggests the sacrifice was recent—perhaps, as the story goes, about a hundred years ago. The proximity of the crime, in time and space, as well as the need to be on Manquián's good side, forces a revision of the facts.

There's no chance for such a polite approach to the brutal sacrifice of José Luis Painecur in 1960. Everyone knows where and why he was killed; most people know how he was killed, with all the gory details; and, worst of all, people know how many hundreds participated. It was a communal act, and even those who weren't alive or didn't go to Cerro Mesa feel both the benefits from the sacrifice and the guilt it brings. Here only the most direct distancing device could work—the Sacred Executioner is the solution. Machi Juana embodies the collective guilt.

And this is an important corollary of human sacrifice mythology: No one can live with deicide. Someone else has to be blamed. It can be an accident. Or God's will. Or the fault of the victim. In many instances, a malevolent Sacred Executioner, like Cain or Machi Juana, is blamed. Sometimes these devices are jumbled up.

But if no one can live with deicide, another corollary is that no one can live without it. In one way or another, every culture has a human sacrifice hidden in its invisible foundations. And this is the great paradox of so many religions: A sacrifice is absolutely essential to save the world. But the bloodshed should be blamed on someone else.

Faced with this universal dilemma, we can appreciate the innovative approach of the Hebrew Bible, where the preferred method of dealing with human sacrifice is by denying it or by translating the human killing into an animal offering. This is the message in the Abraham and Isaac story, the Paschal lamb offerings, and the New Year's scapegoat sacrifice. Judaism was able to do this because it denied, as a first principle, the possibility that God could die, or that sacrificed victims could become gods. Yes, Isaac, Jephthah's daughter, and others do become cult figures. But the whole thrust of the reform is to disguise the true nature of their deaths. When this proved impossible, as in the case of Jephthah's daughter, the compilers made the story as equivocal and accidental as possible, and took the added precaution of eliminating the victim's name, to diminish her cultic attraction.

Having seen how the Mapuches and Hebrews dealt with sacrificial guilt, we're prepared to examine a question that is crucial to Western culture: Jesus' sacrifice on the cross. The issue is not whether Jesus was really sacrificed or not. Clearly, the Romans crucified Jesus as a criminal. What interests us is how Jesus' death functions as a sacrifice. Catholic theologian Saint Thomas Aquinas wrote, "It is clear that Christ's passion was a true sacrifice."[10]

The Gospels present Jesus' crucifixion in a direct, unembarrassed way that resembles the original Mapuche creation myth. But the appalling facts of the horrible ordeal, including flogging, mockery, and final nailing to the cross, are more like the mind-wrenching details of the 1960 sacrifice of little José Luis Painecur, which Mapuches reveal at Lago Budi only as a terrible secret. The role of the sacrificers, on the other hand, is as inverted as in the story of Manquián. So Christianity has a most complex approach to sacrifice. Maccoby calls Christianity "the supreme example" of human-sacrifice ideology.

Although Christianity has obvious parallels with Mapuche and other primitive mythologies, it differs drastically from the Old Testament. For, if the Old Testament is an exercise in hurriedly dumping bodies in unmarked graves, Christianity uncovers the victim and places him right on the altar. Why doesn't Christianity follow the Old Testament's sacrificial thinking?

In the first place, Jesus' death is indispensable to Christian salvation. Without Jesus' *via dolorosa* the world is unredeemed and we're all damned to eternal hellfire. So, between these two agonizing alternatives, Christians prefer Jesus' death. But Jesus is God, not God's minister, like Manquián. Remember that Manquián, like most sacrificial victims in primitive religions, was promoted to the level of demigod *after* his death. According to the Apostles' Creed, however, Jesus was "begotten, not made, one in Being with the Father, through Him all things were made." Jesus is God from the Beginning. He is as Absolute as the God of Abraham, Isaac, and Jacob. But who is powerful enough to kill Almighty God?

The only answer is God Himself. God the Father. Jean Eudes, an eighteenth-century Roman Catholic priest and canonized saint, mulled this fact over, with depressing results:

> God willed that His Son suffer inconceivably cruel and horrible torments; not only that He suffer them but that He die the most shameful and atrocious death of all possible deaths! Oh, how severe is the will of a Father regarding His Son! How strange and terrible it is![11]

Only God the Father could ordain the death of His Son. In practical terms, apart from the sophistication of doctrine, this contradicts the Christian teaching that God is love, and that God the Father loved His Son above all else. A few saints like Jean Eudes may grapple with this dilemma, but for mundane Christianity the real question is "Whom are we going to blame for killing Jesus?"

It's inconceivable that anyone would accept real blame for an atrocious deicide like Christ's crucifixion. Such guilt is unpardonable, unthinkable, and, ultimately, unbearable. On a cosmic plane,

God the Father is to blame for Christ's death. On the plane of redemption, all sinners are theoretically to blame. But on the practical level, Jews are to blame. They are the Sacred Executioners *par excellence.*

Hyam Maccoby has devoted much of his life to answering two questions: (1) How did Jesus really die? (2) How did the Christian religion really begin? His conclusion is that, whereas the Old Testament is a book that turns ancient human sacrifices into animal offerings, the New Testament is an exercise in converting a political crucifixion into a cosmic sacrifice.

More has been written about Jesus in the last twenty years than in the previous two thousand. "There is no historical task which so reveals a man's true self as the writing of a Life of Jesus," Albert Schweitzer wrote in *The Quest of the Historical Jesus.*[12] Marxists see Jesus as a Marxist; homosexuals see him as a homosexual; Christians see him as a Christian; and Jews see him as a Jew. Many scholars have thrown up their hands and dismissed the task as hopeless. Rudolf Bultmann, one of the leading New Testament theologians of the century, concluded, "Whoever prefers to put the name of 'Jesus' always in quotation marks and let it stand as an abbreviation for the historical phenomenon with which we are concerned is free to do so."[13]

Maccoby disagrees. "I think that's a convenient cop-out," he says. "Christian scholars started seeing that Jesus and the whole Jerusalem Church were looking much too Jewish, so they just said, 'Let's give up. We're never going to get to the bottom of this.'"

This may just prove the point—Maccoby's insistence that Jesus was a thoroughly Jewish figure is another example of everyone's seeing himself reflected in Jesus. But it's a fact that Jesus was born a Jew. He was circumcised and presented at the Temple as a first-born Jewish boy. He began his career at a synagogue by reading from the Hebrew Scriptures during a Jewish service, and continued to teach that the covenant of Moses was valid throughout his public life. He did not preach to Gentiles, and he specifically instructed his disciples to seek out only "the lost sheep of the house of Israel"

(Matthew 15:24). On his two encounters with Gentiles recorded in the Gospels, Jesus presumed the superiority of the Jewish people over them. He even referred to Gentiles as "dogs" in an encounter with a Syro-Phoenician woman (Mark 7:26–28), though he seemed more sympathetic toward Samaritans. Jesus was addressed as Rabbi. And he came from the tough hinterlands of Galilee, hotbed of resistance to the unpopular Roman rule.

Knowing that Jesus was a practicing rabbi who regarded Mosaic law, including temple sacrifice, as valid, we may find it a surprise that he deliberately allowed himself to be killed in order to replace Mosaic law with a sacrificial cult to his own person. Given the cultural context of first-century Judaism, this would be a reversal at least as radical as Josiah's seventh-century-B.C. suppression of human sacrifice.

Maccoby tries to get to the bottom of the Jesus mystery by looking for more "sore thumbs," pieces of evidence in the Gospel narratives that go against the grain of the story, particularly as it relates to Jesus' passion and death. The Gospel accounts of Jesus' trial, appearance before Pilate, and crucifixion ring several alarms simply on the basis of what we know about guilt-shifting devices in sacrificial stories.

According to the Gospels, the High Priest and the Sanhedrin accuse Jesus of blasphemy, and Pilate, forced by the enraged Jewish mob, tries to spare Jesus, who is a pacifist with no political ambitions. Pilate is naturally sympathetic to this unfortunate victim of Jewish fanaticism. "I can find no case against him," Pilate says (John 19:6). He offers to release Jesus, but the crowd demands Jesus' death. "Crucify him!" they shout. "Crucify your king?" Pilate asks plaintively. "We have no king but Caesar," the vicious crowd answers (John 19:15). Pilate offers to let Jesus go free, but the crowd insists. "His blood be on us, and on our children" (Matthew 27:26). Pilate washes his hands of Jesus' blood, and finally gives in.

How does this story compare with the historical data we have about Roman Palestine? Pilate was one of the most brutal governors in the history of the Roman occupation. He was eventually fired by the Romans because of a massacre he perpetuated against the Samaritans. His keen interest in Jesus' fate goes against the grain of everything we know about him from historical sources such as Josephus, Tacitus, and Philo. Pilate was what we would call today "a hanging judge." But in those days the distinctly Roman form of execution, reserved for political rebels and slaves, was crucifixion. So Pilate was a crucifying judge. Roman law did not, however, permit someone to be crucified because he violated some principle of Jewish theology. Blasphemy against Jewish dogma was not a crucifiable offense; it wasn't any kind of offense at all. So it is very curious indeed that Pilate crucified the apolitical Jesus for blasphemy.

Here we see a strange inversion taking place: the kind Roman governor wants to save the rabbi from the Jewish crowds who, until just a few days before, had adoringly followed the rabbi. Unfortunately, the kind governor can't stave off the blood-mad crowd, who assume responsibility for the death of the God-man in such unequivocal fashion that they appear to realize his divine status consciously, but want to murder him anyway. They are almost demons. The saddened Roman leader, who goes on to become a saint in one Christian country, commands that Jesus be flogged and crucified. On top of the victim's cross he orders that a sign be placed: "King of the Jews" (John 19:19). The Gospel version presents a Roman governor who kills a Jewish Messiah—a common enough event in Roman Palestine. But then we're subjected to a magical sleight of hand, and told to believe the opposite of what we see happening. The cruel, omnipotent governor is not to blame; the Jews are the villains. This reversal of reality flies against common sense and historical fact, although it corresponds exactly to what we would expect from a Roman Church mythology, based on universal guilt-shifting devices.

The Gospels themselves contain clues that contradict their overall message. Luke begins his Gospel with a personal note, saying that he "has gone over the whole course of these events in detail" and is prepared to give "authentic knowledge" about the formative period of Christianity. There's a touch of the historian here, someone who has documents at hand. Luke narrates a whole section in the Acts of the Apostles in the inclusive "we," and it's generally accepted that he traveled with Paul, making him an eyewitness to events. Analyses of both Luke's Gospel and the Acts have confirmed their stylistic and thematic unity, giving rise to the term "The Double Lukan Work."[14] Moreover, the Jerusalem School for Study of the Synoptic Gospels has concluded that the Gospel According to Luke translates better into Hebrew than any of the other Gospels, leading scholars there to suggest that Luke had access to a now lost Hebrew manuscript, a deduction that Maccoby reached independently from textual clues.[15]

In Luke's Gospel, the High Priest's accusation against Jesus is different and more detailed than in the other Gospels: "We found this man subverting our nation, opposing the payment of taxes to Caesar, and claiming to be Messiah, a king. . . . His teaching is causing disaffection among the people all through Judaea. It started from Galilee and has spread as far as this city" (Luke 23:2–5).

Since Galilee was where Judas of Galilee ignited a huge tax revolt against the Romans in A.D. 6, this accusation would have aroused Pilate's utmost interest. Judas of Galilee was also a Messiah, and the Romans killed him, too.

The High Priest's accusation makes it clear that Messiah simply meant "king" to the Jews. It did not mean "Son of God" in the Christian sense. All Jews considered themselves sons of God.

But the Jews had definite expectations about what the Messiah would do and where he would do it. The prophet Zechariah predicted that the Messiah would come into Jerusalem on an ass (Zechariah 9:9), then go to the Mount of Olives, where a divine miracle would split the mountain in two, and the foreign oppressors would be destroyed (Zechariah 14:4–7). Jesus followed this script closely. He rode into Jerusalem on an ass, to a messianic display that included shouts hailing "the coming kingdom of our father David" (Mark 11:10). Jesus was hardly pacific when he overturned the

tables in the Temple, belying the Christian belief in his other-
worldliness.

And there is another passage from Luke's Gospel which hints
at something even more violent. At the conclusion of the Last
Supper, just prior to going up the Mount of Olives, Jesus tells his
disciples, whoever "has no sword, let him sell his cloak to buy one."
His disciples then brought out two swords. "It is enough," Jesus
said (Luke 22:36–38).

Why would Jesus give a speech about swords immediately
before going to the Mount of Olives unless he expected a confron-
tation with the Romans, of the kind envisaged by Zechariah?

If Maccoby is correct, Jesus was neither a militarist revolutionary, as Marxists and liberation theologians would like, nor a
detached mystic who deliberately seeks his own death, as Christians
would make him out. Rabbi Jesus was obviously no military genius—anyone who thought two swords would be "enough" against
the ultra-efficient Roman military machine was sadly mistaken. At
the Mount of Olives, Jesus offered only symbolic resistance to the
Romans, hoping that God would call the heavenly legions into
action. In effect, Jesus was trying to force God's hand. Jesus tried
to entice the Shekinah—the presence of God—down upon the
Mount of Olives, in a world-changing event. It was the supreme
leap of faith.

"Jesus was a type of Messiah well known in Israel in the first
century," Maccoby maintains. "He believed that God would work
a great miracle against the Romans on the Mount of Olives, and
that this would usher in both freedom for Israel and a messianic
era of peace for the whole world. Two other would-be Messiahs,
one called Theudas and the other known as 'The Egyptian,' had
similar hopes. 'The Egyptian' also led a group of followers up to
the Mount of Olives in expectation of a similar miracle, which had
been prophesied by Zechariah."

There's strong evidence that Jesus' own contemporaries also
saw him as a mystical militant like Theudas or The Egyptian. In
the Acts of the Apostles, Peter and leaders of the early Nazarene

sect in Jerusalem were brought before the Sanhedrin. The High Priest, a Sadducee and Roman sympathizer, wanted to execute them. But the majority of the Sanhedrin were Pharisees, who often opposed the Sadducees, as they did on this occasion, sparing the lives of these key followers of Jesus. Gamaliel, the Pharisee leader, makes a statement about Jesus and his followers that challenges many Christian assumptions about the early Church:

> "Men of Israel, be cautious in deciding what to do with these men. Some time ago Theudas came forward, claiming to be somebody, and a number of men, about four hundred, joined him. But he was killed and his whole following was broken up and disappeared. After him came Judas the Galilean at the time of the census; he induced some people to revolt under his leadership, but he too perished and his whole following was scattered. And so now: keep clear of these men, I tell you; leave them alone. For if this idea of theirs or its execution is of human origin, it will collapse; but if it is from God, you will never be able to put them down, and your risk finding yourselves at war with God."
>
> —Acts 5:35–39

Gamaliel doesn't even hint that Jesus may have preached anything heretical against Judaism. The whole thrust of the argument is that Jesus, like the other would-be Messiahs, was involved in a political struggle against the Romans, who, in fact, put Theudas and Judas of Galilee to death as they had Jesus.

"Like Gamaliel, who was one of the great founders of the rabbinical tradition, Jewish scholars for the past three centuries have been regarding Jesus in a friendly way," Hyam Maccoby says. "My work is a continuation of this Jewish school that identifies Jesus as a Jewish teacher, one who was in no way a heretic or the founder of a rival religion." Some prominent Christian scholars are moving in the same direction. Oxford historian E. P. Sanders concluded in his recent book, *Jesus and Judaism,* that "it is difficult to find any substantial conflict between Jesus and the Pharisees."[16]

It's evident from Luke's Acts of the Apostles that the early Nazarenes were very devout Jews. He writes that "they kept up their daily attendance at the temple" (Acts 2:46). The impression is one of utmost zeal in the performance of Temple duties, where animal sacrifices took place daily. If the early Nazarenes regarded Jesus' death on the cross as the ultimate salvific act, replacing the Torah, they couldn't have countenanced these Temple sacrifices. There's no sign of any ritual that would have set the Nazarenes apart from orthodox Judaism.

Yet the Gospels claim that Jesus instituted such a rite during the Last Supper, when he changed the bread and wine into his own body and blood (Mark 14:22–24).

By instituting a cult of his own body and blood, making himself the Paschal lamb, Jesus would have reversed a thousand years of Biblical writing and rewriting. The communion ritual reinstates the human sacrifice that the ram on Mount Moriah replaced.

⊡ 22 ⊡

WEREWOLVES
AND THE EUCHARIST

I attended a Roman Catholic Mass at a Franciscan chapel on Mount Zion, very close to where Jesus supposedly celebrated the Last Supper. There's a black metal sculpture of the Last Supper behind the altar, in which Jesus stands, upright and tall, holding the sign of peace, which is also the first piece of communion bread. There are eleven smaller men around him, some arguing, some eating, some grasping the towering God-man, and one crouching figure, face down, set off from the rest.

The Mass is concelebrated by two Italian priests, young, friendly men who are leading a pilgrimage of college students and adults from Milan. "As we gather together to celebrate these Sacred Mysteries, let us call to mind our sins," one of the priests intones. The readings come from the Gospel accounts of the Last Supper:

> During supper he took bread, and having said the blessing he broke it and gave it to them, with the words: "Take this; this is my body." Then he took a cup, and having offered thanks to God he gave it to them; and they all drank from it. And he said, "This is my blood, the blood of the covenant, shed for many."
>
> —Mark 14:22–24

One man begins crying, not a quiet sobbing to himself, but a terrible, public wail, like a teakettle letting off steam—a high-pitched whine that penetrates a collective nerve. Another student comes over to comfort him. But eventually he has to be carried off, uncontrollably weeping. For a moment it looks as though the emotion is going to catch on. A woman starts crying, too. Things teeter on the edge, when, mercifully, several people burst out laughing, which helps to bring back an embarrassed *status quo*.

There's something frighteningly direct about someone's giving his body and blood for you. One wonders how the apostles took it so calmly, without any comment whatsoever, when even today the full force of the original idea can provoke both catharsis and hysteria.

"The Passover Feast was a spring festival," the Italian priest says. "The pagans also had a spring festival, when they celebrated the coming of a new cycle of growth in nature, the birth of the sun in Aries." Having made the parallel, however, the priest quickly disavows its implication. "The Eucharist is completely different from the Pagan celebrations. It is unique, holy, public and eternal, something which goes beyond the rites of the pagan temples."

Hyam Maccoby thinks the real story is a complicated mix of pagan ceremony and a Jewish meal.

Maccoby, along with other Jewish scholars, like Pinchas Lapide, places Jesus' triumphant entry into Jerusalem on Palm Sunday in the fall, not the spring as the Gospels have it.[1] This is because the cry of the multitude, "Hosanna! Blessings on him who comes in the name of the Lord!"(Mark 11:9), and the use of palm branches are both taken from the Feast of the Tabernacles, the harvest festival celebrated after Yom Kippur. "There are no green palm branches in March to celebrate Palm Sunday," says Maccoby. "They don't get leaves until the fall." In addition, Jesus attempted to eat fruit from a fig tree prior to the Palm Sunday episode, which is also impossible in spring.

There is something wrong with the chronology of Jesus' last week on earth.

And there is something wrong, from a Jewish standpoint, in deliberately arranging your own death, as Jesus was apparently doing. Suicide wasn't permitted. Even the defenders at Masada violated Jewish law in their collective self-destruction. What's worse, from a Jewish perspective, is that drinking the blood of any animal was strictly prohibited. So even the symbolic imbibing of human blood would have aroused violent antipathy.

Maccoby believes that the Gospel According to Luke opens an unexpected vista on the original Last Supper. Unlike Mark and Matthew—whose Last Supper narratives are virtually identical regarding the Eucharist—Luke presents a strange problem to Bible scholars:

> Then he took a cup, and after giving thanks he said, "Take this and share it among yourselves; for I tell you, from this moment I shall drink from the fruit of the vine no more until the time when the kingdom of God comes." And he took bread, gave thanks, and broke it; and he gave it to them, with the words: "This is my body."
>
> In the same way he took the cup after supper, and said, "This cup, poured out for you, is the new covenant sealed by my blood."
>
> —Luke 22:17–20

Luke has placed *two* cups of wine into the communion rite. Only the second one, inserted at the end of the Last Supper, almost as an afterthought, has anything to do with Jesus' blood. This is a glaring contradiction, one that the New English Bible has solved by eliminating the second cup altogether. The New Spanish Bible is following the same course. When I spoke to Juan Mateos, director of the New Testament Project for the New Spanish Bible, he told me, "The second cup of wine, where Jesus says, 'This cup, poured out for you, is the new covenant sealed by my blood,' was taken from Paul and inserted. We're suppressing it."

In the amended version of Luke, then, there is only one cup of wine, and it is not a communion cup at all. It is simply a messianic toast to the coming of "the kingdom of God." And if there's one area where a broad consensus of New Testament scholarship exists, it is the agreement that, by heralding "the kingdom of God," Jesus was talking about the kingdom of God *on earth,* by which he meant a complete transformation of life on earth into the messianic age. The prophet Zechariah predicted this new age would commence following a miracle on the Mount of Olives, to which Jesus and his disciples repaired with their two swords after the Last Supper. In light of this Jewish expectation, this final toast showed extraordinary optimism, not resignation to a sacrificial death.

Again, Luke includes a detail that unravels the whole story. His more historical approach to the life of Jesus apparently made it painful for him to suppress some of the original material he had at hand. He follows the Pauline mystical revision of Jesus' life, but occasionally leaves in older layers of the Jesus narrative which contradict the Pauline myth. We've seen this in his version of Jesus' trial, where the accusation against Jesus wasn't blaspheming but claiming the kingship and inciting a tax revolt against the Romans. It occurs in Jesus' inexplicable interest in acquiring swords before going up to the Mount of Olives, and again in Gamaliel's speech before the Sanhedrin, revealing that the leading Pharisee of the day didn't consider Jesus to be anything but a Jewish Messiah. Finally, it appears at the institution of the communion rite, the one ceremony that absolutely set Christianity apart from Judaism, by the clumsy insertion of two communion cups at the Last Supper, one borrowed from Paul, the other . . . from the real story? Luke's sense of guilt about suppressing the facts made his hand waver at times—a tremble that, seen through Maccoby's microscope, reveals the hairline fractures in Christianity's foundation myth.

But where did Paul get the communion ritual?

This is one of the least considered and most crucial questions in Christianity. The first groups to practice the communion ritual were Paul's Gentile converts—no mention of such a rite appears among the Jerusalem Nazarenes, who attended the Temple on Mount Moriah each day. And since all four of the Gospels were written after Paul's Epistles, it's long been assumed that Paul heavily influenced the Gospels. Indeed, the first reference to the communion ritual comes, not from any of the Gospel writers, but from Paul himself, in the First Letter to the Corinthians:

> For this is what I received from the Lord, and in turn passed on to you: that on the same night that he was betrayed, the Lord Jesus took some bread, and thanked God for it and broke it, and he said, "This is my body, which is for you; do this as a memorial of me." In the same way he took the cup after supper, and said, "This cup is the new covenant in my blood. Whenever you drink it, do this as a memorial of me."
>
> —1 Corinthians 11:23–25, Jerusalem Bible

The statement "for this is what I received from the Lord" has a shamanic ring to it. Paul often claims special revelations from God as the source of his Christology, not any teaching from the other apostles or from any human being. He's very insistent on this point throughout his brilliant and embattled career. "I must make it clear to you, my friends, that the gospel you heard me preach is no human invention. I did not take it over from any man; no man taught it me; I received it through a revelation of Jesus Christ" (Galatians 1:11–12).

Paul sees himself as Christ's special medium to the world: "The life I now live is not my life, but the life which Christ lives in me" (Galatians 2:20). Paul contemptuously dismisses anyone who attempts to criticize his teachings:

> For the Spirit explores everything, even the depths of God's own nature. Among men, who knows what a man is but the man's own spirit within him? In the same way, only the Spirit of God knows what God is. . . . A man gifted with the Spirit can judge the worth of everything, but is not himself subject to judgement by his fellow-men. For (in the

"But when he talks about Jesus, he also identifies Jesus, and sees himself as a Christ-figure. So Paul is like a novelist who loses himself among his own creations, sometimes identifying with the hero and sometimes with the villain."

Máximo gets lost in the same kind of artistry, enacting one role after the other like a one-man repertory theater. His two most compelling creations, however, are his "Jesus" persona and his "Tiu" personality. Actually, these are mergers with the victim (Jesus) and the Sacred Executioner (the Tiu) similar to Paul's flitting between his roles as persecutor and partner of Jesus. "Every Sacred Executioner sees himself as both a Christ-figure and a Christ-killer," Maccoby says. The contrast between Máximo's kindly consolation of a poor woman next to the cross at Mount Azoguini, and his fiendish laughter about her suffering and symbolic offering of her to the Tiu is the most dramatic example of Máximo's split personality.

Paul's inquisitorial second nature is never far removed from his Christ-role, either. He accuses his rivals, probably representatives of the Jerusalem Nazarene movement, of being "sham-apostles, crooked in all their practices, masquerading as apostles of Christ. There is nothing surprising about that; Satan himself masquerades as an angel of light" (2 Corinthians 11:13–15). Anyone opposing Paul is Satanic, blinded by dark forces. "You stupid Galatians! You must have been bewitched" (Galatians 3:1).

Paul was the first to see the opportunity for blaming Christ's death on the Jewish people as a whole. He did this by penetrating the human sacrificial meaning behind the selection of Israel as God's "chosen" or "firstborn" people. This was always a dangerous designation. In the Andes, the Incas designated Tanta Carhua as an *aclla*, or "chosen," of the Sun. Even today, I've heard female victims referred to as "the chosen ones." If anyone is "chosen" for the Tiu around Yunguyo, it means that the shamans have thrown coca leaves to find which person the Tiu wants sacrificed, and the leaves have come up whole next to that person's name. Such lotteries were also known in ancient Israel. Being Yahweh's "firstborn" also had sacrificial connotations, as Yahweh demanded all firstborn creatures as offerings. Northrop Frye writes that "It seems clear that God's statement 'Israel is my son, even my firstborn' (Exodus 4:22) confers a highly ambiguous honor, raising the possibility that Israel is being chosen either as a sacrificial victim, to be passed over and sent into exile, or even both."[4]

Paul seems to imply both fates when he compares the Jews with Ishmael, Abraham's son who is driven into desert exile (Galatians 4:22). He also tells his gentile disciples: "In the spreading of the Gospel they [the Jews] are treated as God's enemies for your sake" (Romans 11:28). Maccoby writes that this phrase of Paul's "sums up the role of the Jews in the Christian myth as the Black Christ who assumes the burden of guilt for the bloody deed without which there would be no salvation."[5] At the same time, however, Paul says that when the Jews finally convert to Christianity it will mean the resurrection from the dead (Romans 11:15–16), a sign of the millennial age. So the Jews are both cursed as sacrificial scapegoats and marked with special power, like Sacred Executioners everywhere.

Máximo's attitude toward the Jews is more overtly Manichaean than Paul's. Máximo inveighs against the Jews with hysterical enthusiasm, but only after giving his carefully calculated motives for doing so: "Now, ignorant people think that the devil killed Jesus. That's a lie! The devil, the Tiu, didn't have anything to do with the death of Jesus. It was his own cousins, the Jews, who abused and killed him." Máximo emphasizes that *"all* the people of Jerusalem shouted, 'Crucify him! Crucify him!' "

All the Jews have to be blamed in order to cover up the fact that the Tiu, whom Máximo calls Mallku Mallku Mallku, really "mistreated Jesus more than all the others." Thus, Máximo has two wildly divergent accounts of Jesus' death. In one of them, all the Jews are to blame. In the other, Jesus meekly submits to the Tiu, healing his ear, which Peter had cut off, and telling Peter to put away his sword. "Don't be rude to the Tiu, Peter," Jesus says.

"With patience, with my suffering, with my precious blood alone, I am going to buy this world." Then Mallku Mallku Mallku— whose name marks him as the highest expression of the mountain god—happily goes back to tormenting Jesus. Aymara folktales confirm Máximo's second version of Jesus' death. According to one story, the Tiu is really the third member of a Holy Trinity consisting of Jesus, Mary, and the Tiu himself. But in this Aymara version of the Holy Trinity, it is the Tiu who sacrifices Jesus, not God the Father. Once the Tiu kills Jesus, all the Tiu's friends "came out and set to feasting, jumping about, drinking, and shouting for joy."[6]

Jesus' death is a great relief to all the mountain gods. From the standpoint of the Aymara natives, Jesus' poverty and suffering are necessary, but only as a prelude before getting on with the important work of enjoying wealth, just as Máximo re-creates Jesus' Passion before requesting money from the rich Tiu. Máximo contradicts his own thesis that the Jews are to blame for Jesus' death, making it transparently obvious that the Tiu is behind it all. In the same way, Paul's device of treating the Jews as "enemies" is also a way of disguising the fact that the being who kills Jesus is either a devil stronger than God or a God who is a devil. The real killer of Jesus is both a God and a devil—he is the Tiu of Mount Sinai, a formidable mountain spirit whom the rabbis had tried to kill off, and whom Paul resurrected from the dead.

It's interesting to contrast Paul and Jesus at the critical moments of their lives when they were on trial. When he is brought before the High Priest, Pilate, and King Herod, Jesus is silent, resigned, and defenseless. But when Paul is brought before James, the brother of Jesus and head of the Jerusalem Nazarene movement, and accused of abrogating Jewish laws and customs in favor of a new religion, Paul consents to perform a temple ritual, including animal sacrifice, to prove his loyalty to Judaism (Acts 21:21–26). In fact, at this point in his career Paul considers the law of Moses an unnecessary anachronism, since it has been replaced by the new covenant of Christ's sacrifice. But he keeps these views to himself and pretends to be an ordinary Jew. Like Máximo, Paul has one set of teachings for his inner circle of disciples, and another, ostensibly orthodox one for the authorities.

Later, when he is tried before the High Priest and the Jewish Sanhedrin, Paul doesn't even wait to hear his accusers. He immediately starts defending himself: "My brothers, I have lived all my life, and still live today, with a perfectly clear conscience before God." This is too much for the High Priest, who knows all about Paul's past, so he orders an attendant to hit Paul on the mouth. Paul instantly curses the High Priest: "God will strike you, you whitewashed wall!" When the attendants ask Paul if he is trying to insult the High Priest, Paul gives an outrageous response: "My brothers, I had no idea that he was High Priest." Then, before Paul can be charged with disturbing the peace with heretical teachings against the law of Moses, Paul announces: "My brothers, I am a Pharisee, a Pharisee born and bred; and the true issue in this trial is our hope of the resurrection of the dead." This wins the sympathy of the Pharisees, who believe in the resurrection of the dead, so they acquit Paul over the High Priest's protests (Acts 23:1–10).

The real issue at Paul's trial was whether or not Paul was spreading a new religion (Acts 21:28). But Paul cleverly distorted the charges against him to divide the Sanhedrin. Clearly, Paul didn't practice the Christian doctrine of turning the other cheek—he curses the High Priest who orders him struck on the mouth. Exaggeration, self-aggrandizement, curses, sarcasm, and outright deception were all part of Paul's tactics at this difficult juncture of his life.

If you want to start a new religion, survival is the first rule. Máximo is a firm practitioner of this principle. When Máximo was jailed in 1981, he turned the tables on his accuser, Paulino Chipana, the uncle of Nieves Chipana, by accusing Paulino of having sacrificed Nieves. Máximo later went free through a large bribe. Paul was also saved from the High Priest because the Roman governor of Palestine "had hopes of a bribe from Paul" (Acts 24:26). Since Paul had raised substantial amounts of money from his gentile converts for charitable purposes, Maccoby thinks it's likely that Paul did bribe the Roman governor.

Although Paul is known for his doctrine of salvation through faith alone, few people have been so resourceful at outwitting their many enemies as Paul was. In this sense, Jesus was Paul's opposite, not his double. Jesus apparently had such faith in God that he went up to the Mount of Olives hoping to provoke a cataclysmic miracle. Paul was too practical to make such idealistic miscalculations. Paul's faith is more like Máximo's. Máximo claims that thieves leave him alone because he knows "the great magical science." Then he adds, "I also carry a pistol with me." Paul went to Jerusalem placing his faith in God—but also armed with money, Roman citizenship, and a willingness to tell his enemies exactly what they wanted to hear, and, failing that, to improvise divide-and-conquer strategies along the way. If "humanity is descended from Cain," as Máximo and sociobiology tell us, new mythologies are also made by the "strong" survivors, rather than the victims.

Religious revolutionaries often resort to what Joseph Campbell calls "mythological defamation." This is "terming the gods of other people demons, enlarging one's own counterparts to hegemony over the universe."[7] Thus far, we've seen three instances of mythological defamation which altered the Bible. The first case was Moses'—or his followers'—decision to seize the Kenite myth of creation, but to change Cain from the heroic First Man to an accursed villain. The second time this occurs is when Josiah and Hilkiah massacred the Jewish shamans, destroyed their serpent and bull idols and made "Moses" justify their actions in a new book that converted the old gods into demons. Paul's strategy was also to pin his new myths on a "Jesus" of his own invention, one who created a communion ritual that the Jerusalem Nazarenes had never heard of, while turning the Jews, the heroes of the Hebrew Bible, into demonic Sacred Executioners.

Admirable though their determination, inspiration, and boldness may be, the decisions of these reformers had unexpected consequences. Josiah not only killed the Jewish shamans, he, along with Jeremiah and other radicals, also had to vilify virtually every Jew who had been practicing ancestral fertility rites for centuries. And when the Babylonians conquered Jerusalem not long after these drastic changes, the only explanation Jeremiah could come up with was that God was punishing the Jews in a special way because of their long idolatry. Of course, this was nonsense. If anything, people must have suspected that God was punishing Jews for the unprecedented suppression of mountain-fertility cults and human sacrifice. But that was precisely the conclusion Jeremiah wanted to refute, so he depicted the Jewish past in the most condemnatory way possible, turning the innocent worshipers of past generations into virtual demons, and the Jewish nation into a particularly hateful one in God's eyes: "I have done this to you, because your wickedness is great and your sins are many. . . . Men call you the Outcast, Zion, nobody's friend" (Jeremiah 30:15–17).

Paul and his disciples were able to use these diatribes in their restoration of human sacrificial myth and ritual, conveniently turning the Jews into the Outcast punished for Christ's death. So Jeremiah's propaganda *against* human sacrifice became Pauline ammunition in favor of it. In the end, the Jews became the outcasts accused of murder, fulfilling the role of Cain, in a strange, circular path that made them partners in the destiny Moses inflicted on the Kenite First Man. The survival of Cain's haunting presence mocks all efforts to denigrate him, a lesson in the extraordinary, subterranean power of myths, and of the devastating consequences of mythmaking gone awry.

To understand how the Jewish people wound up in this predicament, we have to examine the complex sources behind Paul's mythology. If Paul claims all his teachings are a direct "revelation," as traditional shamans always do, there's good reason to question this. Machi Juana likewise claims that no one taught her anything— that she learned everything directly from God. I believe Machi Juana does have formidable intuitive abilities. But her prayers and sacrifices closely follow ancient shamanic customs. In the same way, Paul's communion ritual can be traced to Oriental mystery religions.

The cult of Attis was one of the most popular of the Greek mystery cults. Knowing this, we come to a fact that is key to the development of Christianity: the cult of Attis was particularly strong in Saint Paul's home town, Tarsus, in Asia Minor. Every spring, thousands celebrated the violent death of the god (by castration), followed by his burial and triumphant resurrection. A few ecstatic devotees usually castrated themselves in the process. Jocelyn Godwin, a professor at Colgate University, makes the following comparison between Jesus' passion and that of Attis:

> . . . the spring rites would begin on 15 March with the entry of the "reed-bearers," whose exact significance is uncertain. A week later, at the equinox proper, was the "entry of the tree," the evergreen pine under which Attis died and which was revered and mourned as a symbol of the god himself. It is impossible to ignore the associations with Jesus' entry into Jerusalem surrounded by palm-bearers, and his bearing of the cross or tree which became his chief symbol. And this is not all: on 22 March the tree, decked with funereal purple, was laid to rest in the temple of the Mother as in a sepulchre. The next day was one of vociferous mourning, and on the day following, the "day of the blood," the Mother's worshippers would whip themselves and some of them, carried away by ecstasy, would perform the irreversible act. With the dawn of 25 March came the day of rejoicing for some— convalescence for others—as Attis' resurrection was celebrated.[8]

So, whereas Jesus' Passion doesn't work in a Jewish chronology, it fits perfectly with the cult of Attis—the triumphal entry into Jerusalem around the time of the spring equinox, the agonizing death a week afterward, followed by a resurrection three days after the god's death. What's even more revealing about this tie-in, however, is that the Attis cult, like other mystery religions, featured a communion meal, in which members partook of food representing the resurrected god.[9]

Written sources attest to Attis' popularity in Asia Minor, and recent archaeological digs have uncovered vases with Attis' resurrection depicted on them, in plentiful quantities, at Tarsus.

"The discovery of these vases is important," Hyam Maccoby says, "because it shows that Paul was exposed to the dramatic Attis rites while growing up in Tarsus."

Walter Burkert has analyzed the origins of the mysteries in *Homo Necans*. The popular mysteries of Attis, Mithras, and Dionysus all involve killing a victim and eating the body in a sacred initiation. He argues that this is the re-enactment of a primitive hunting rite. Arcadia, which became a synonym for paradise, is a good place to start looking for this ancient legacy, at the festival of Zeus the Wolf on Mount Lykaion, the Wolf Mountain.

According to Greek legend, Lycaon, the first king of Arcadia, killed his grandson, Arkos, cut up his body, cooked it in a tripod kettle used for animal sacrifices, and served the cannibalistic dish up to Zeus. This legend had a ritual counterpart that was re-enacted every year atop Mount Lykaion at the Pan-Arcadian Festival, though it was done secretly and at night. Anyone who ate of the human meat was supposedly transformed into a "wolf" and had to enter a special clan, and they all lived in exile together for nine years. If they didn't eat any more human flesh during these nine years, the "wolves" were allowed to rejoin normal society.

Similar stories about human-flesh food and blood wine at Icha, Lake Titicaca, emphasize that such food is delicious—more delicious, in fact, than any other food—but should not be eaten. There's an obvious conflict in this: if something is delicious, you want to eat it. In the Greek legend, some hint of this attraction remains— the child's flesh is served up to Zeus, making it a kind of ambrosia of the gods. The Aztecs, too, believed that flesh from sacrificed victims could bestow part of their spirit on the eaters. And there's good evidence that a magical potion made of human flesh, called Borfima, was the main goal of many sacrificial slayings by the Human Leopard Society in Sierra Leone, Africa. So the notion of imbibing the precious spirit substance of a sacrificed victim is attested to in many cultures, and the Christian communion ritual shares their central theme. That is why Aymara natives have no trouble understanding the Catholic rituals and why they suspect Catholic priests of hoarding human fat to make communion hosts.

Both ancient Greece and the present-day Andean peoples have stories about bloodsucking entities who are mixed up in this kind of flesh-eating. Should we dismiss all these stories as fiction, or is there a deeper reality toward which they point?

The most obvious meaning of the werewolf transformations is the taboo surrounding human sacrifice. Anyone who ate the flesh of the sacrificed child in the secret ceremony atop Mount Lykaion had to live in banishment for nine years, cut off from Arcadian society like a wolf in the forest. This is a typical way of describing the ritual impurity and temporary banishment from society incurred by a person who carried out a human sacrifice. What at first sounds like a weird, impossible literary invention of men turning into wolves was actually a standard feature of primitive society. This says that no human being is to blame for the sacrifice—it was the wild, wolflike urge to kill that came out, in a fit of madness, among some of the participants at the ritual. The wolf is responsible.

But who are the wolves?

"There is no doubt that werewolves existed, just like leopard and tiger men, as a clandestine *Männerbund*, a secret society, wavering between demonic possession and horseplay, as is common in such a *Männerbund*," Burkert writes. "In Europe, there is at least one case of a 'werewolf' on record in sixteenth century Livland. There, the werewolvish activity consisted for the most part of breaking into other people's cellars at night and drinking any beer found there. More dangerous and perhaps more ancient were the bands of leopard men in Africa, who conspired to assassinate others and practice cannibalism."[10]

The metamorphosis into an animal form is one of the most universal magical powers attributed to shamans, and the "spirit" of a powerful and dangerous animal like the wolf or the leopard was held to confer special powers and dangerous status on any individual who possessed it, or was possessed by it.

Animal-costumed *Männerbunde* also existed in the Andes. The Jesuit extirpator of idolatry, J. de Arriaga, found such a cult on the Peruvian coast in the early seventeenth century. Arriaga punished seventy-three shamans for macabre sacrifices of both children and adults. These shamans, called *brujos* by Arriaga, were organized into a clandestine society with a well-defined hierarchy of "captains" and "soldiers." They entered houses at night when people were sleeping, and stealthily cut people with their fingernails to extract blood, which they sucked, causing the person whose blood had been stolen to die in a few days. Because of their method of sucking their victims' blood, these sacrificers were called the "suckers." Supposedly, these "suckers" also cooked human blood and transformed it into meat, which they ate at secret gatherings. Arriaga claims that "at these meetings the devil appeared sometimes in the shape of a lion, other times as a tiger, and . . . they furiously adored him."[11]

Arriaga's blood "suckers" closely resemble the Aymara *liqui-chiri*. A *liquichiri* is someone who assumes an animal shape to enter houses at night and suck sleeping people's fat. The unsuspecting person always dies a few days later. Of course, this is a euphemism for human sacrifice, when the victim's fat and blood are removed for ceremonial purposes. What Arriaga adds to our understanding of contemporary practices is that some ancient Peruvians really did don animal costumes for their human sacrifices and they had a quasi-military organization like those of the Arcadian wolf-men and the African leopard societies. Perhaps these sacrifices were once made in the presence of a warrior-shaman who was "adored" as one of the feline gods of the Andean pantheon.

It's of particular interest that Arriaga's feline-worshippers supposedly used their fingernails to extract blood from victims during nighttime sacrifices. They were probably trying to imitate a prowling puma, or a jaguar, who claws his prey to death, thus turning their sacrifice into a ritual hunt much as the African leopard-men did. In a curious parallel, Inca priests used their fingernails to cut the throats of guinea pigs for a divinatory rite. Another ritual,

known as *Huacarpaña*, "consisted in blood offerings, extracted with
the fingernails, through clawings, of children and animals."[12] It
would be hard to cut a guinea pig's throat or to claw much blood
from a child, unless the priest's fingernails were exceedingly long
and specially sharpened for this purpose. There must have been a
crucial importance attached to these priestly "claws" that may well
be a holdover from what had once been a full feline disguise, such
as that used by the principal lion or tiger man of the coastal
"suckers."

In all these examples, magical power adheres to behaving like
the sacred animal, whose fearful strength and unpredictable violence make the animal-man into a ceremonial killer and an exile
from normal society, at least so long as the animal frenzy, contrived
around the sacrificial act, seizes him. In Africa, among the initiates
of the Human Leopard Society, the leopardlike roaring, stalking,
and killing of a victim had to go on outside the village, in the forest,
and at night. In Greece the wolf rituals were also at night, and
anyone who ate human flesh—or its ritual simulation—became an
outcast. Again, we see the distinguishing features of the Sacred
Executioner pattern: those who commit the sacrifices become simultaneously taboo and very powerful, hated and needed. Society,
which is blessed by the sacrifices, shifts the blame for the necessary
bloodshed on outsiders, who are banished, if only in their animal
forms, and if only for the short time it takes them to get out of
their costumes.

Burkert's great contribution to sacrificial anthropology is placing these animal transformations into an evolutionary perspective.
He sees these werewolf and leopard *Männerbunde* as the missing
link of cultural evolution—memories of the decisive step when the
first humans organized themselves into hunting bands, thus copy-
ing the strategy of the wolf and placing themselves for the first
time beyond the lethal reach of the leopard. To early hominids,
wolves and leopards embodied superhuman capabilities, particularly in their ferocious hunting skills. By organizing armed hunting

bands, man made his most critical evolutionary decision, one that set humans above all other species and turned other species into man's food.

"You are what you eat" is particularly true of evolution. By choosing to kill in hunting groups, men acquired plentiful protein sources, but difficult social choices. The violence of the human wolfpack had to be curtailed when it came to women and—particularly—children. The myriad myths about child sacrifice and cannibalism, Burkert proposes, stem from the great threat infanticide and cannibalism posed to human survival. After all, it's much easier to kill helpless humans than to go on long, dangerous hunts. Only in certain contexts could men kill. Hunting was one. Warfare, another. Sacrifices, of animals and humans, provided a very special occasion when the great taboo could be lifted. Although we think of human sacrifice as gratuitous violence, it began as a means of restricting violence to a carefully controlled arena, thus banishing it from the rest of domestic life. Sacrificial ritual restricted killing to a few occasions a year, and taught, through male initiation procedures, that violence belonged to the hunting group as a whole, whose success depended on cooperation and hierarchy.

Another consequence of killing for a living is guilt. Animal killing also produces anguish in the aggressor, and a need to shift the blame. "The greatest danger to life is the fact that man's food consists entirely of souls," an Eskimo shaman said, neatly summing up the hunter's dilemma.[13]

Much sacrificial ritual is an apology to the animals for the unforgivable but unavoidable act of killing them. One way of making amends was to see the animal victim as a god, whose death in the hunt was followed by his resurrection, permitting him to be hunted again. This shows the anxiety arising from the conflict between the need to kill and the fear the food source will be exhausted. Animal gods peopled the ancient world, as did men, dressed in animal skins, performing religious rituals. There is this constant confusion: animals who are people, people who are animals, and gods who are both.

"You saved us by shedding blood," the Mithraist priest says to Mithras the bull, whose body and blood were ritually eaten by initiates of this mystery religion. "By dying you restored our life," Catholics pray before eating the body and blood of Jesus. Like Mithras, the god-bull, Jesus has an animal aspect, "the Lamb of God . . . who takes away the sin of the world" (John 1:29). Thus the Christian communion commemorates the great, primal sin of killing animals for a living. By the animals' flesh and blood, man survived: "By dying you restored our life." We have lost sight of our origins, so we see Holy Communion only as a "mystery," a great paradox. But Burkert concludes that "what has become a mystic paradox had been just fact in the beginning."[14]

Burkert believes these animal transformations must be understood as relics from *Homo necans*, man the hunter-killer. I've found this to be the most satisfactory explanation so far for the strange animal characteristics surrounding human sacrifice in the Andes. I can see no reason why agricultural water rituals should have such bloodthirsty gods as recipients, or why the executions themselves should be stylized as hunts.

The final stage of every Mapuche *guillatún* requires the men to ride around the victim in closing circles, until all converge in a screaming frenzy to make the kill. This is not a strictly agricultural ritual. Remember that the most closely guarded secret about José Luis Painecur's sacrifice at Cerro Mesa involved the actions of two naked men, armed with archaic spears, whom Machi Juana called "my black sheep." They performed a wild, threatening dance, waving their spears at the ocean, home of the leviathan serpent, Cai Cai Filu, who is also a predator, rising out of the depths to search for human blood. The men, equated with sacrificial animals themselves, threaten the god and feed him at the same time. Content, Cai Cai Filu returns to the depths.

The Aymara mountain gods, with their serpent and feline aspects, are equally ferocious, and just as hungry for human flesh. I believe that the popular obsession with human fat in the Aymara vampire myths stems from its regular use and exchange in the relatively recent past. Llama fat is still bought and sold for many magical and healing purposes. Human fat must have had similar uses, but it would have been more precious. The basic use for animal and human flesh is indisputable: to feed the blood-addicted *tius*, who have the powers and appetites of vampires.

The age-old end of sacrificial ritual is to banish these blood-thirsty monsters from human society. Fear of the great predators and serpents still lurks in the race memory. But the greatest fear is of the greatest predator—man in wolf's clothing, the *Homo necans* himself. The recurrence of vampires and werewolves points to the need to exorcise perpetually the killer within us. When the deranged Christian Evangelists at Vista Hermosa drove a stake through the heart of seven-year-old Hernán Edgardo Cofre, they were desperately trying to exorcise that vampire ancestor, not knowing that it was they, not the boy, who were possessed by it.

Thus, in an evolutionary sense, there's a basis for that cliché-ridden horror film scenario: whenever the hero holds up the crucifix, the vampire cringes and retreats out the window. Sacrificial ritual, in Burkert's view, is the primary check against the animal in man. He accords Christian ritual a primary role in preserving Western civilization:

> In the storm of history it was always those societal organizations with religious foundations that were finally able to assert themselves: all that remained of the Roman Empire was the Roman Catholic Church. And here, too, the central act remained the incredible, one-time and voluntary sacrifice in which the will of the father became one with that of the son, a sacrifice repeated in one sacred meal, bringing salvation through admission of guilt. A permanent order thus arose—cultural progress that nonetheless preserved human

violence. All attempts to create a new man have failed so far. Perhaps our future chances would be better if man could recognize that he still is what he once was long ago, that his existence is defined by the past.[15]

Ironically, killing other species for a living forced human society into limiting violence more effectively than any other species has done. Harvard sociobiologist Edward O. Wilson says that, if we consider the hour-by-hour observation of other species, "the murder rate is far higher than for human beings, even taking into account our wars."[16] With more and more sophisticated killing technologies, more and more restrictions had to emerge. Sacrifice is the most powerful restraint. When a community performs human sacrifice, all the survivors get an unequivocal message: "If you don't conform to the rules, this can happen to you."

Both Burkert and René Girard credit sacrificial ritual with man's sublimation of primitive aggression. "Even the most violent rites are specifically designed to abolish violence," writes Girard in *Violence and the Sacred*.[17]

Hyam Maccoby disputes the necessity of sacrifice as the keystone of culture.

"Burkert has a very despairing viewpoint, although it's obviously a very profound one," he says. "He believes you can't have civilization without this human sacrifice at the center. Of course, almost all communities are, in fact, based on this type of sacrifice. But the Jewish community is not—it is one community that has tried to steer clear of this pessimism, this basic notion of original sin, which in Burkert's view is the genetic urge for violence. Now, you can't ignore this fact. You just can't pretend it isn't there, with a kind of illusory, rose-colored vision. In Judaism there is a sacrifice of Isaac. You can't falsify the brutality of existence. But Jews try to transform it, to go through it, to turn this undeniable fact into something more hopeful. The basic Jewish question is: how can we set up a community that is not based on human sacrifice?"

Given this fundamental preoccupation with overcoming

human-sacrifice ideology, it is one of the great paradoxes of history that the Jews are the people most identified with a human sacrifice, one that is simultaneously a deicide. In Christianity, Jesus is "true God and true man." He is also "the Lamb of God . . . who takes away the sin of the world." And Christianity also has ravening wolves, represented by the Jews screaming for Jesus' blood. Indeed, the "Jews," like Bultmann's "Jesus," should be placed in quotes, for they cease to resemble human beings in their macabre, blood-thirsty transformation. The idea that the Jews were cursed by God for killing Jesus begins in Paul's writings, evolves in the Gospels, and reaches its culmination in medieval mythology, where the Jews are actually vampires who need human blood to survive, full heirs of the werewolf legends from Mount Lykaion, kin to the blood-thirsty creature that came to kill Hernán Edgardo Cofre at Vista Hermosa.

In the old mystery-religion rites, the sacrificed god was killed by the impersonal powers of nature, masked as fierce beasts. The werewolves and the child god on Mount Lykaion jointly enacted the cyclical birth and death of the seasons and of all living things. In the case of Jesus, however, his one-time salvific act was ladened with an urgency unknown in the pagan rites, and so his killers acquired an absolute wickedness foreign to the more tolerant mystery cults. By making the Jews the collective Sacred Executioner in Jesus' death, and by psychologically modeling them after the bloodthirsty werewolves of Greek folklore, the gospel writers turned what might otherwise have been just another story into an ongoing historical tragedy. People might doubt whether Jesus had ever existed in the way Christians claimed, but no one could deny the existence of the outcast Jews. The Jews became the most tangible proof of the Christian myth.

The Gospel According to John, which contains some of the most moving poetry in world literature, also contains the most venomous anti-Semitism. Catholic theologian Rosemary Ruether makes this embarrassed admission about the Fourth Gospel:

"The Jews," for John, are the very incarnation of the false, apostate principle of the fallen world, alienated from its true being in God. They are types of the carnal man, who knows nothing spiritually. . . . Because they belong essentially to the world and its hostile, alienated principle of existence, their instinctive reaction to the revelation of the spiritual Son of God is murderousness. What they do recognize is that in Christ their false principle of existence has been unmasked and comes to an end. So whenever the light breaks through in their presence, they immediately seek to "kill him." In this murderousness they manifest their true principle of existence.[18]

Pinchas Lapide, a Jewish scholar of the New Testament, remarks that "an Eskimo whose knowledge of Christianity came solely from the Fourth Gospel would, on the basis of such texts, have to conclude that for some unexplained reason Jesus had strayed into the company of treacherous, unbelieving, murderous Jews whose spitefulness would sooner or later cost him his life."[19]

One Mapuche shaman I spoke with didn't know much about Christianity, but he seemed to attribute almost as much importance to the diabolical Jews as to Jesus himself. Perhaps the most amazing thing was his identification of the Jews with the power Nenmapu, the Lord of the Earth. This is sometimes a collective term for ancestral god-spirits who live on snowcapped volcanoes and control floods, landslides, earthquakes, and lava flows. In pre-Christian Mapuche beliefs, these volcano deities were usually the most powerful spirits in the Mapuche pantheon. But when I spoke to Machi Antonio Paineo, these former gods had already converted to Judaism: "The spirit of Nenmapu wanders on the volcano. These spirits have all usurped the power of Almighty God. These are false gods. The volcano is where the Jews live, the enemies of Jesus Christ."

Antonio Paineo lives in an isolated valley, across a stream and at the foot of a tall mountain, where not even ox carts can safely travel. He told me that he's never seen a Jew in his life—except on the volcano, in his shamanic visions. For him the Jews are simply creatures of cosmic power and evil, similar, in fact, to those of John's Gospel, whose spirit he has apparently imbibed from Christian missionaries.

Mapuches don't know much about the fine points of Christian theology, but they immediately grasp the dualism of the Christian message. "Yes, bad people made Jesus suffer a lot on that mountain," Machi Clara Huenchillán told me. "And that's why we all have such good luck now."

The good luck brought to us from Jesus' torment depends on the bad people's doing their job—and doing it well. This is also true in the local Mapuche sacrifice of José Luis Painecur, where the "bad" Machi Juana is blamed for performing the act that brought good luck, and life itself, to the whole community. According to Antonio Paineo's thinking, Machi Juana works for the "Jews" on the volcano. She's in touch with them from her station on Cerro Mesa.

Machi Juana is the "Jew" of Lago Budi. Perhaps the oddest thing about Machi Juana is that even her fiercest detractors, like Machi Antonio Paineo, don't want her to die. "God is not going to let Machi Juana Namuncura die for a long time," Paineo said. "He's going to keep her poor as a flea until she's very old, maybe ninety years old, as punishment for that boy she killed. And so that everyone will see her punishment."

"Old age and suffering are characteristics of the Sacred Executioner," Maccoby told me. "The Sacred Executioner bears the guilt of society, so it would be a great loss if the Sacred Executioner were allowed to die. The Sacred Executioner is supposed to suffer infinitely. This is exactly how Christianity treats the Jews—the Jews have to bear the guilt for Christ's death to the end of time. The medieval myth of the Wandering Jew embodies this concept. According to the story, there is a Jew who pushed Christ when he was carrying the cross, so, as punishment, that Jew can't die until the Second Coming of Christ. He has to wander around the world as an outcast, like Cain, for his participation in Christ's death. He's become immortal, and he can't even kill himself, though he often tries. If he did, the community would have to suffer instead.

"The Wandering Jew is symbolic of Christianity's ideal for the Jew: someone who willingly accepts being hated, because by doing so the Jew performs a great service for society. The Jews are necessary for the Christian religious economy. But I, and most Jews, repudiate that role."

Although the Wandering Jew is a burdensome image, Maccoby doesn't consider it the worst Christian myth about Jews. Far more dangerous were the blood-libel stories, in which Jews were blamed first for capturing Christians and crucifying them at the Passover, and later for sacrificing and eating the flesh of Christian children. The first ritual-murder accusation surfaced in Norwich, England, where Christians accused Jews of crucifying an apprentice named William on Easter Eve, 1144, as a mockery of Christ's passion. Mob violence against the Jews in England followed, as did the canonization of Saint William of Norwich, whose only act of sanctity, it seems, was to die of an epileptic fit.

But the ritual-murder accusation flourished thereafter, resulting in pogroms and persecutions in which tens of thousands of Jews were tortured and killed. A series of popes and Catholic prelates denounced this insanity, beginning in 1247 with Pope Innocent IV. In a letter to the bishops and archbishops of Germany and France, Innocent IV wrote, "Nor shall anyone accuse them [the Jews] of using human blood in their religious rites . . ."[20]

In spite of such letters, the ritual-murder accusation became more frequent as time went on. "Whenever a corpse was found the responsibility for the death was assigned to the Jews.[21] Pope Gregory X commanded all Jews imprisoned on blood-libel charges to be released, noting, "It sometimes happens that certain Christians lose their Christian children. The charge is then made against the Jews by their enemies that they have stolen and slain these children in secret, and have sacrificed the heart and blood."[22]

Why the obsession with Jews and human sacrifice? The advance of civilization did not diminish the problem. From the seventeenth to the early twentieth century the ritual-murder accusation became the single greatest cause of suffering among Jewish people in Poland and Russia. "This absurdity provided the spark which led to the outbreak at Yelisavetgrad, on April 27th 1881, of the wave of pogroms which stained the last years of the old Russian Empire, constituting one of the greatest tragedies of the sort in the recent history of the human race."[23] Between 1887 and 1891 at least twenty-two pogroms occurred in Europe. In 1911 a young man's death in Kiev, Russia, again set off the ritual-murder charge, igniting anti-Jewish killings that aroused worldwide condemnation and drove many Russian Jews to emigrate.

In almost every case the court systems rejected the ritual-murder accusations, the pontiffs opposed them, great men spoke out, and yet they were powerless to stop what became, in some parts of Europe, a growing fixation with Jews and cannibalistic human sacrifice. Of course, this was a neat inversion of reality. The Jews did not have any religious rituals involving Christian flesh and blood. But Christians did—in the body and blood of the crucified Christ himself. The Jews didn't need to crucify anyone at Eastertime. But Christians did—because without Christ's crucifixion their salvation was in jeopardy. It's no accident that the greatest hysteria against Jews in Christendom focused on the supposed Jewish responsibility for rituals that Christians themselves were performing. Jews became the continuing partners of Jesus in the Christian Passion Play: for allegedly torturing, killing, and eating Christians, they were tortured and killed.

Bernard Lewis, a professor of Near Eastern history at Princeton, argues, in his 1987 book *Semites and Anti-Semitism,* that the differing treatments of Jesus' crucifixion in the Christian Gospels and the Muslim Koran account for profoundly different attitudes and treatment of Jews in Christian Europe and the Muslim world. The Koran says that the Jews failed in their attempt to murder Jesus. "But they did not kill him, nor crucify him, but only a likeness of him that was made to appear to them. . . . Certainly, they did not kill him, but God raised him up to Himself."[24] Thus the Koran makes the Jews powerless, nonthreatening. The Jews never had as much freedom or mobility in Muslim countries as they enjoyed in many parts of Europe, but neither were there the deranged outbursts against them that occurred in some Christian countries. Muslims had no terrible pogroms or blood-libel stories until modern times, when such traditions were imported from Europe. The Muslims could afford to treat the Jews as unimportant infidels.

But Pauline Christianity had no such option. By blaming the Jews for Christ's death, Christianity made the Jews frighteningly strong, since only an immense power could kill God. In fact, Paul associates the Jews with "the god of this passing age" (2 Corinthians 4:4), a term for the Gnostic Demiurge, the great evil god who rules over earth until the world is redeemed. There's a close connection between Paul's "god of this passing age" and the Mapuche shaman's vision of the Jews as the Nenmapu, "the Lord of the Earth." Máximo Coa also has a *tiu* who runs the world in opposition to the Christian God. Interestingly enough, Máximo denounces the Jews only in front of the Christian cross; when he moves over to the *tiu*'s idol, he says, "The *tiu* loves the Jews a lot—that's why the Jews are all millionaires." In all these cases the Jews are rivals of God and Good. Like Machi Juana, the Jew as Sacred Executioner is as much feared as hated, and the conspiracy theories about the Jews are like immense blowups of the exaggerated stories of Machi Juana's malefic powers.

Christianity places enormous importance on the Jews. Millennial movements have long believed that Christ's second coming can't occur until the Jews convert—or are killed. Nazism has been considered such a millennial movement. The Third Reich was supposed to last a thousand years; but before this new age could come, Hitler foresaw a cosmic battle between himself and the Jews. In this struggle, Hitler was sometimes compared to Christ, while the Jews were his mortal enemies. "The Jews crucified Jesus," Hitler said; "therefore they are not worthy of life."[25]

Although Hitler may have initially profited politically from his endless scapegoating of the Jews, by the early 1940s Hitler was diverting valuable resources from a life-and-death struggle on two fronts to the irrational goal of killing Jews. But perhaps that's the wrong way of looking at the Holocaust. "World War II makes a lot more sense if you see it not primarily as a Nazi war of conquest but as a way to purify the world by killing Jews," says John Roth, a Holocaust expert at Claremont McKenna College. "From the perspective of Nazi logic, it didn't matter so much if they failed to conquer Europe—at least they would succeed in what they saw as a kind of cosmic sacrifice, or excision, of the Jews, which was more important to them. I think Hitler viewed himself as a Sacred Executioner of sorts. The Nazis held a mystical belief that the Holocaust was a ritual of purification."

"Why is there this wave of hatred, this scarlet thread that reaches from Golgotha to Auschwitz?" asks Pinchas Lapide.[26] His question contains a hint of the answer—the scarlet thread was the sign of Cain carried by the scapegoat banished into the wilderness each year at Yom Kippur. The Jews were also marked by this scarlet thread, carrying the sign of Cain for Christianity, living in perpetual wandering as punishment for the death of Christ.

This scarlet thread turns into a river of blood, the torrent of the Holocaust, under Hitler's insane direction. But, as the Holocaust Memorial in Jerusalem shows, the Holocaust began with the Nazi version of blood-libel stories, those inverted human-sacrifice parables. At the entrance to the Holocaust Museum, as the very first exhibit, there are samples of Nazi propaganda. One prominent piece is a cartoon of a hideously caricatured Jew—grotesquely fat, with a peninsular nose, dark-skinned, and obscenely rich. This monster offers candy to two fair-haired German children. A German woman next to me read the caption and explained, "The cartoon says, 'I'll give you candy but you have to come with me.' He's going to kidnap the children."

Outside there is a monument to the largest child-kidnapping operation in world history—a memorial to the one and a half million Jewish children who perished in the Holocaust.

There is something more terrible than death here. Perhaps it's a sense of godforsakenness, the great void you feel in the face of this tragedy. *How could God let this happen?* Perhaps Abraham asked himself the same question on the way to Mount Moriah: *What kind of God is this?* Jesus put the question to his Father more directly: *"Eli, Eli, lema sabachthani?"* "My God, my God, why hast thou forsaken me?" (Matthew 27:46).

Many people cry as they walk around the memorial. They give voice and tears to a black stone statue of a woman, holding her head between her hands, grieving over a pile of small gray stones. People come and add new pebbles to the pile, as though adding to the numberless children. The statue is called *The Silent Cry*. She has no name, but everyone gives her one. She is Rizpah, mourning for her sons on the Mountain of Yahweh. Or Mary on Mount Calvary.

The little mound of stones in front of the Mother keeps growing, making this the only time I have actually seen the fabled Mountain of the Gods rise; and if a stone were added for each victim in the history of sacrifice, I suppose the pile would have grown until, in fulfillment of prophecy, it really was "set over all other mountains, lifted high above the hills" (Isaiah 2:2).

I added a few pebbles myself, thinking, as I carefully balanced them on the precarious pile:

This one is for the Inca child of Mount Plomo.

This is for José Luis Painecur of Cerro Mesa.

This one is for Tanta Carhua of Mount Aixa.

This is for Clemente Limachi of Mount Santa Bárbara.

Many others came to mind—Abel, the first victim; the original Isaac; Achan, for whom Joshua erected a pile of stones; Jesus on Calvary and his millions of brothers who perished in the Holocaust. Then I said the Holocaust memorial prayer for all of them, and for all of us who, in one way or another, feel bound up with all of them.

Exalted, compassionate God, grant perfect peace in Your Sheltering Presence, among the holy and pure, to the souls of all our brethren, men, women, and children who were slaughtered and burned. May their memory endure, inspiring truth and loyalty in our lives. May their souls be thus bound up in the bond of life. May they rest in peace.

And let us say: Amen.

NOTES

CHAPTER 1
THE UNSPEAKABLE SACRIFICE

1. Walter Burkert, *Homo Necans*, p. 85.
2. Nigel Davies, *Human Sacrifice*, pp. 31–33.
3. Burkert, *Homo Necans*, p. 35.
4. Arthur A. Demarest, "Overview: Mesoamerican Human Sacrifice in Evolutionary Perspective," pp. 228–45.
5. Aubrey Burl, *The Stonehenge People*, p. 125.
6. Ibid., p. 215.
7. Aubrey Burl, "The Recumbent Stone Circles of Scotland," p. 70.
8. Burl, *Stonehenge People*, p. 216.
9. Personal inverview, March 1986.
10. Personal interview, January 1984.
11. Linda Schele and Mary Ellen Miller, *The Blood of Kings*, p. 14.
12. Erik Eckholm, "Secrets of Maya Decoded at Last, Revealing Darker Human History," *The New York Times*, May 13, 1986.
13. Hyam Maccoby, *The Sacred Executioner*, p. 97.
14. René Girard, *Violence and the Sacred*, p. 300.
15. A. C. Bhaktivedanta, *Bhagavad-Gita As It Is*, p. 96.
16. Sören Kierkegaard, *Fear and Trembling*, p. 82.
17. Arthur Koestler, *Darkness at Noon*, pp. 183–84.
18. Alberto Green, *The Role of Human Sacrifice in the Ancient Near East*, pp. 97–108.
19. Davies, *Human Sacrifice*, pp. 73–98.
20. Mary Karen Dahl, *Political Violence in Drama*, pp. 2–3.
21. Steven Kull, "Nuclear Arms and the Desire for World Destruction," p. 583.

CHAPTER 2
THE INCA CHILD

1. Grete Mostny, "La momia del Cerro, El Plomo," p. 60.
2. Pierre Duviols, "La capacocha," p. 19.
3. María Rostworowski de Diez Canseco, *Estructuras andinas del poder*, pp. 130–79.
4. María Rostworowski de Diez Canseco, *Historia del Tahuantinsuyo*, p. 16.

5. R. T. Zuidema, "Shafttombs and the Inca Empire," p. 141.
6. Ibid., p. 142.
7. Duviols, "La capacocha," p. 13.
8. Zuidema, "Shafttombs," p. 141.
9. Ibid., p. 143.
10. Ibid., pp. 138–39.
11. Arthur Demarest, "Overview: Meso-american Human Sacrifice in Evolutionary Perspective," p. 239.
12. Zuidema, "Shafttombs," p. 145.

CHAPTER 3
THE AMATEURS TAKE OVER

1. Rogelio Díaz Costa, "Practicas religiosas en el incanato, en relación con la 'momia' del cerro el Toro," pp. 124–67.
2. Gerald Taylor, *Ritos y tradiciones de Huarochiri*, p. 373.
3. Antonio Beorchia, "El enigma de los santuarios indígenas de alta montaña," p. 83.
4. Thomas Zuidema, "Shafttombs and the Inca Empire," p. 162.
5. Jorge Checura Jeria, "Funebría incaica en el Cerro Esmeralda," pp. 77–78.
6. Ibid., p. 78.
7. Ibid., p. 83.
8. Johan Reinhard, "Las montañas sagradas," p. 54.
9. Zuidema, "Shafttombs," p. 134.

CHAPTER 4
HUNTING FOR MUMMIES

1. Antonio Beorchia, "Veladero: Un nevado rebelde," *El Diario de Cuyo*, March 15, 1987, sect. 2, p. 6.

CHAPTER 6
THE SORCERESS AT LAGO BUDI

1. Valencia Durán, Corte de Nuevo Imperial, October 2, 1962, p. 84.
2. María Mardones Montenegro, "Proceso seguido en contra de Juana Catrilaf

por el delito de homicidio de Antonia Millalet," *Juris prudencia*, Vol. III, July–August 1955, Chile, p. 85.

CHAPTER 9
HOUNDING THE HOLY FATHER

1. Johan Reinhard, *The Nazca Lines*, pp. 14–21.
2. Mayo Calvo, *Secretos y tradiciones Mapuches*, pp. 83–84.
3. Louis Faron, *The Mapuche Indians of Chile*, pp. 10–11.

CHAPTER 11
LAKE TITICACA

1. *Diario la República*, March 3, 1986.
2. Interview with Sergeant Gilberto Torres Soto, September 10, 1986, Puno, Peru.
3. Henri Favre, "Tayta Wamani: Le Culte des montagnes dans le centre sud des Andes péruviennes," p. 131.

CHAPTER 12
THE SNAKE MOUNTAIN

1. Julio María Elías, *Copacauana—Copacabana*, p. 27.
2. Ibid., p. 25.
3. Ibid., p. 47.
4. Antonio Beorchia, "El enigma de los santuarios indígenas de alta montaña," on jacket.
5. Elías, *Copacauana*, p. 26.

CHAPTER 13
BLACK MAGIC

1. Hans van den Berg, *Diccionario religioso Aymara*, p. 78.

CHAPTER 15
TRACKING THE SACRED EXECUTIONER

1. Antonio Beorchia, "El enigma de los santuarios indígenas de alta montaña," pp. 135–43.

2. *La clavícula del hechicero, o El gran libro de San Cipriano*, pp. 76–81.

3. Manuel Vargas, "The Carnival of Oruro," p. 172.

4. Lupe Andrade S., "Nuevos hallazgos en Tiahuanaco," *Ultima Hora* (La Paz), December 11, 1988, p. 8.

5. Evan Hadingham, *Lines to the Mountain Gods*, pp. 167–70.

6. Gerald Taylor, *Ritos y tradiciones de Huarochiri*, pp. 371–73.

7. Michael Harner, *The Jivaro*, pp. 134–169.

CHAPTER 16
THE GOOD SEED

1. Manuel Vargas, "The Carnival of Oruro," p. 171.

2. Evan Hadingham, *Lines to the Mountain Gods*, p. 166.

3. Joseph Campbell, *Primitive Mythology*, pp. 444–52.

4. *The Popol Vuh*, trans. Dennis Hedlock, p. 159.

CHAPTER 17
THE SOULS CRY OUT

1. Christopher Donnan, "Unraveling the Mystery of the Warrior-Priest," p. 551.

2. *The African Guardian* (Lagos, Nigeria), May 23, 1988, reprinted in "World Report," *Insight*, June 20, 1988, p. 42.

3. Francisco Paca Pantigoso, "Pobladores toman justicia por sus manos y matan ladrón en Puno," *Diario la República*, October 16, 1988, p. 5.

4. Richard Ellman, *Oscar Wilde*, pp. 563–64.

CHAPTER 18
THE HIDDEN GOLD MINE

1. Thomas Zuidema, "Shafttombs and the Inca Empire," p. 146.

2. *El gran libro de San Cipriano*, p. 57.

3. Ibid., p. 64.

4. Antonio Beorchia, "El enigma de los santuarios indígenas de alta montaña," pp. 135–43.

5. Ibid., pp. 161–64.

6. Ibid., pp. 65–66.

CHAPTER 19
THAT OLD-TIME RELIGION

1. Zev Vilnay, *Israel Guide*, p. 139.

2. Hyam Maccoby, *The Sacred Executioner*, p. 99.

3. Ibid., p. 83.

4. Ibid., p. 75.

5. Joseph Campbell, *Occidental Mythology*, pp. 9–31, 274–75.

6. Northrop Frye, *The Great Code: The Bible as Literature*, p. 146.

7. Ibid., p. 188.

8. Campbell, *Occidental Mythology*, p. 10.

9. Christopher Donnan, *Moche Art and Iconography*, p. 110.

10. Maccoby, *Sacred Executioner*, p. 89.

11. Ibid., p. 96.

12. Donald Harden, *The Phoenicians*, p. 111.

13. Alberto Green, "Human Sacrifice in the Ancient Near East," p. 162.

CHAPTER 20
THE BIRTH OF HELL

1. Lawrence E. Stager and Samuel R. Wolff, "Child Sacrifice at Carthage," p. 32.

2. Paul G. Mosca, "Child Sacrifice in Israelite and Canaanite Religion," pp. 201–202.

3. Ibid., p. 208.

4. Ibid., p. 212.

5. Irving M. Bunin, *Ethics from Sinai*, vol. 2, p. 112.

6. Mosca, "Child Sacrifice," p. 240.

7. Peter Brown, *Augustine of Hippo*, p. 23.

8. Cited in ibid., pp. 391–92.

9. Ibid., p. 395.
10. Ibid., pp. 393–97.

CHAPTER 21
CALVARY AND CAIN

1. Hyam Maccoby, *The Sacred Executioner*, p. 106.
2. Hyam Maccoby, *The Mythmaker*, p. 110.
3. Marc Tanenbaum, *The Origins of the Holocaust*, p. 53.
4. Maccoby, *Sacred Executioner*, p. 7.
5. Walter Burkert, *Homo Necans*, p. 42.
6. Maccoby, *Sacred Executioner*, pp. 18–19.
7. Ibid., pp. 57–73.
8. Napoleon A. Chagnon, "Life Histories, Blood Revenge, and Warfare in a Tribal Population," p. 985.
9. Nigel Davies, *Human Sacrifice*, p. 171.
10. Thomas Aquinas, *Summa Theologica*, 3a, 38, 3.
11. Jill Haak Adels, ed., *The Wisdom of the Saints*, p. 9.
12. Albert Schweitzer, *The Quest of the Historical Jesus*, p. 4.
13. Rudolf Bultmann, *Jesus and the Word*, p. 14.
14. Josep Ruis-Camps, *El camino de Pablo a la misión de los paganos*, p. 13.
15. "Who Was Jesus?," p. 40.
16. E. P. Sanders, *Jesus and Judaism*, p. 318.

CHAPTER 22
WEREWOLVES
AND THE EUCHARIST

1. Pinchas Lapide and Ulrich Luz, *Jesus in Two Perspectives*, p. 41.

2. Hyam Maccoby, *The Mythmaker*, pp. 172–82.
3. Ibid., p. 183.
4. Northrop Frye, *The Great Code: The Bible as Literature*, p. 186.
5. Maccoby, *Mythmaker*, p. 203.
6. Manuel Vargas, "The Carnival of Oruro," p. 172.
7. Joseph Campbell, *Occidental Mythology*, p. 80.
8. Jocelyn Godwin, *The Mystery Religions*, p. 112.
9. *Encyclopaedia Britannica*, "Mithras," 1957, vol. 15, p. 623.
10. Walter Burkert, *Homo Necans*, p. 88.
11. Pierre Duviols, *Cultura andina y represión*, p. lxx.
12. Rogelio Díaz, "Prácticas religiosas en el Incanato, en relación con la 'momia' del Cerro El Toro," pp. 136–37.
13. Burkert, *Homo Necans*, p. 22.
14. Ibid.
15. Ibid., p. 82.
16. Barbara Burke, "Infanticide," p. 31.
17. René Girard, *Violence and the Sacred*, p. 103.
18. Quoted in Hyam Maccoby, *The Sacred Executioner*, p. 145.
19. Lapide and Luz, *Jesus in Two Perspectives*, p. 71.
20. S. Grayzel, *The Church and the Jews in the Thirteenth Century*, pp. 113–14.
21. Cecil Roth, ed., *The Ritual Murder Libel*, p. 21.
22. Ibid.
23. Ibid., p. 16.
24. Bernard Lewis, *Semites and Anti-Semitism*, p. 120.
25. Lapide and Luz, *Jesus in Two Perspectives*, p. 75.
26. Ibid., p. 59.

BIBLIOGRAPHY

Ardrey, Robert. *The Hunting Hypothesis: A Personal Conclusion Concerning the Evolutionary Nature of Man.* New York: Atheneum, 1976.

Beit-Arieh, Itzhaq. *Edomite Shrine: Discoveries from Qitmit in the Negev.* Jerusalem: Israel Museum, 1987.

Beorchia, Antonio. "El enigma de los santuarios indígenas de alta montaña." *Revista CIADAM* (San Juan) 5 (1987).

Bhaktivedanta, A. C. *The Bhagavad-Gita As It Is.* Los Angeles: Bhaktivedanta Book Trust, 1975.

Bouysse-Cassagne, Thérèse, with the collaboration of Philippe Bouysse. *Lluvias y cenizas: Dos pachacuti en la historia.* La Paz, Bolivia: HISBOL, 1988.

Brandon, S.G.F. *The Fall of Jerusalem and the Christian Church.* London: S.P.C.K., 1951.

———. *Jesus and the Zealots: A Study of the Political Factor in Primitive Christianity.* Manchester, England: University of Manchester Press, 1967.

———. *The Trial of Jesus of Nazareth.* London: B. T. Batsford, 1968.

Brown, Peter. *Augustine of Hippo.* Berkeley: University of California Press, 1969.

Bunin, Irving M. *Ethics from Sinai.* New York: Philipp Feldheim, 1964.

Bultmann, Rudolf. *Jesus and the Word.* New York: Charles Scribner's Sons, 1958.

Burke, Barbara. "Infanticide." *Science* 84 (May 1984): 26–31.

Burkert, Walter. *Homo Necans: The Anthropology of Ancient Greek Sacrificial Ritual and Myth.* Berkeley: University of California Press, 1983.

———. René Girard, and Jonathan Z. Smith. *Violent Origins: Ritual Killing and Cultural Formation.* Ed. Robert G. Hamerton-Kelly. Stanford: Stanford University Press, 1987.

Burl, Aubrey. "The Recumbent Stone Circles of Scotland," *Scientific American* (September 1982): 66–72.

——. *The Stonehenge People*. London: J. M. Dent & Sons, 1987.

Cabeza Monteira, Angel. "El santuario de altura inca Cerro El Plomo." Graduate Thesis, University of Chile, 1986.

Calvo, Mayo. *Secretos y tradiciones Mapuches*. Santiago, Chile: Editorial Andrés Bello, 1980.

Campbell, Joseph. *The Masks of God: Primitive Mythology*. New York: Viking Penguin, 1988.

——. *The Masks of God: Occidental Mythology*. New York: Viking Penguin, 1988.

Chagnon, Napoleon A. "Life Histories, Blood Revenge, and Warfare in a Tribal Population." *Science*, February 26, 1988, pp. 985–92.

Checura Jeria, Jorge. "Funebría incaica en el Cerro Esmeralda." *Estudios Atacamenos* (Iquique); reprinted in *Revista CIADAM* (San Juan) 5 (1987): 77–81.

Cohn, Norman. *The Pursuit of the Millennium*. New York: Harper Torchbooks, 1961.

Cona, Pascual. *Testimonio de un cacique Mapuche*. Santiago, Chile: Pehuen Editores, 1984.

Dahl, Mary Karen. *Political Violence in Drama*. Ann Arbor: University of Michigan Research Press, 1987.

Davies, Nigel. *Human Sacrifice: In History and Today*. New York: William Morrow, 1981.

de Avila, Francisco. *Ritos y tradiciones de Huarochiri del siglo XVII*. Trans. José Arguedas. Mexico City: Siglo Veintiuno Editores, 1975.

Demarest, Arthur. "Overview: Mesoamerican Human Sacrifice in Evolutionary Perspective." In *Ritual Human Sacrifice in Mesoamerica: A Conference at Dumbarton Oaks*, October 13–14, 1979, ed. Elizabeth H. Boone. Cambridge, Mass.: Harvard University Press, 1984, pp. 227–47.

Donnan, Christopher. *Moche Art and Iconography*. Los Angeles: UCLA Latin American Center Publications, 1976.

——. "Unraveling the Mystery of the Warrior-Priest." *National Geographic*, October 1988, pp. 550–55.

Duviols, Pierre. "La capacocha: mecanismo y función del sacrificio humano, su proyección geométrica, su papel en la economía redistributiva del Tawantinsuyo." *Alpanchis* (Cuzco) 9 (1976): 11–57.

——, ed. *Cultura andina y represión*. Cuzco, Peru: Centro de Estudios Rurales Bartolomé de las Casas, 1986.

El gran libro de San Cipriano. Buenos Aires: Editorial Faquir.

Elías, Julio María. *Copacauana—Copacabana*. Tarija, Bolivia: Editorial Offset Franciscana, 1976.

El pequeño libro de San Cipriano. Lima, Peru: Editorial Mercurio.

Ellman, Richard. *Oscar Wilde*. New York: Alfred A. Knopf, 1988.

Faron, Louis. *Hawks of the Sun: Mapuche Morality and Its Ritual Attributes*. Pittsburgh: University of Pittsburgh Press, 1964.

———. *The Mapuche Indians of Chile*. Prospect Heights, Illinois: Waveland Press, 1986.

Favre, Henri. "Tayta Wamani: Le Culte des montagnes dans le centre sud des Andes péruviennes," Colloque d'études péruviennes. (Aix-en-Provence), no. 61, pp. 121–40.

Freud, Sigmund. *Moses and Monotheism*. Trans. Katherine Jones. New York: Alfred A. Knopf, 1939.

Friedman, Elias. *El-Muhraqa: Here Elijah Raised His Altar*. Rome: 1985.

Frye, Northrop. *The Great Code: The Bible as Literature*. New York: Harcourt Brace Jovanovich, 1983.

Ghiglieri, Michael. "War Among the Chimps." *Discover* (November 1987), pp. 66–76.

Girard, René. *Violence and the Sacred*. Baltimore: John Hopkins University Press, 1977.

———. *Job: The Victim of His People*. Trans. Yvonne Preccero. Stanford: Stanford University Press, 1987.

Godwin, Jocelyn. *The Mystery Religions*. New York: Harper & Row, 1981.

Grayzel, S. *The Church and the Jews in the Thirteenth Century*. Philadelphia: Dropsie College, 1933.

Green, Alberto Whitney. *The Role of Human Sacrifice in the Ancient Near East*. Missoula, Montana: Scholars Press, 1975.

Haak Adels, Jill, ed. *The Wisdom of the Saints*. New York: Oxford University Press, 1987.

Hadingham, Evan. *Lines to the Mountain Gods: Nazca and the Mysteries of Peru*. New York: Random House, 1987.

Harden, Donald. *The Phoenicians*. New York: Pelican Books, 1980.

Harner, Michael. *The Jivaro: People of the Sacred Waterfalls*. Berkeley and Los Angeles: University of California Press, 1984.

Harris, Marvin. *Cows, Pigs, Wars and Witches: The Riddles of Culture*. New York: Vintage Books, 1974.

Hayward, Robert. "The Aqedah." In *Sacrifice*, ed. M. F. C. Bourdillon and Meyer Fortes. New York: Academic Press, 1980.

Heider, George C. *The Cult of Molek: A Reassessment*. Sheffield, England: Journal for the Study of the Old Testament Press, 1985.

Hernández Príncipe, Rodrigo. "Idolatría del pueblo de Ocros cabeza de esta comunidad." In *Cultura andina y represión*, pp. 461–76. Cuzco, Peru: Editorial Bartolomé de las Casas, 1986.

Hocquenghem, Anne Marie. *Iconografía mochica*. Lima, Peru: Pontificia Universidad Católica, 1987.

Hsia, R. Po-chia. *The Myth of Ritual Murder: Jews and Magic in Reformation Germany*. New Haven: Yale University Press, 1988.

Isbell, B. J. *To Defend Ourselves: Ecology and Ritual in an Andean Village*. Austin: University of Texas Press, 1978.

Kauffmann Doig, Federico. *Manual de Arqueologia Peruana* (7th ed.). Lima, Peru: Iberia, 1980

Kierkegaard, Sören. *Fear and Trembling*. Harmondsworth, England: Penguin Books, 1985.

Koestler, Arthur. *Darkness at Noon*. New York: Bantam, 1981.

Krahl, Luis, and Oscar González. "Expediciones y hallazgos en la alta cordillera de la provincia de Coquimbo (Cerros Las Tórtolas y Doña Ana), 1956–1958." *Anales de Arqueología y Etnología* (Mendoza) 21 (1966): 101–29.

Kull, Steven. "Nuclear Arms and the Desire for World Destruction." *Political Psychology* 4: 3 (1983): 563–91.

La Magia Blanca. Lima, Peru: Editorial Mercurio, 1981.

La Magia Negra. Lima, Peru: Editorial Mercurio, 1988.

La Magia Roja. Lima, Peru: Editorial Mercurio, 1988.

Lapide, Pinchas, and Ulrich Luz. *Jesus in Two Perspectives* Minneapolis: Augsburg Publishing House, 1985.

Leiva Orellana, R. Arturo. "Rechazo y absorción de elementos de la cultura espanõla por los araucanos en el primer siglo de la conquista de Chile (1541–1645)." Thesis, University of Chile, 1977.

Lewis, Bernard. *Semites and Anti-Semitism*. New York: Norton, 1987.

Lyon, Patricia J. "Female Supernaturals in Ancient Peru." *Ñawpa Pacha* (Berkeley) 16 (1979): 95–140.

Maccoby, Hyam. *Revolution in Judea: Jesus and the Jewish Resistance*. London: Orbach and Chambers, 1973.

———. "The Parting of the Ways." *European Judaism* 1 (1980) 17–21.

———. *The Sacred Executioner: Human Sacrifice and the Legacy of Guilt*. New York: Thames and Hudson, 1982.

———. *The Mythmaker: Paul and the Invention of Christianity*. New York: Harper & Row, 1986.

———, et al. *The Origins of the Holocaust: Christian Anti-Semitism*. New York: Columbia University Press, 1986.

Mardones Montenegro, María. *Proceso seguido en contra de Juana Catrilaf por el delito de homicidio de Antonia Millalet*. *Jurisprudencia* L11 (July–August 1955): 85–102.

Medina, Alberto, Francisco Reyes, and Gonzalo Figueroa. "Expedicion al Cerro El Plomo." *Arqueología Chilena* (Santiago) 4 (1958): 43–83.

Mocsa, Paul G. "Child Sacrifice in Canaanite and Israelite Religion." Unpublished Ph.D. dissertation, Harvard University, 1975.

Mostny, Grete, ed. "La momia del Cerro El Plomo," *Boletín del Museo Nacional de Historia Natural* (Santiago, Chile) 27:1 (1957).

Murphy, Cullen. "Who Do Men Say That I Am?," *The Atlantic Monthly* (December 1986), 37–58.

Oakland Rodman, Amy. "Pre-Columbian Cultures of Bolivia." In *An Insider's*

Guide to Bolivia, comp. Peter McFarren, Teresa Prada, and Ana Rebeca Prada. La Paz, Bolivia: Fundación Cultural Quipus, 1988, pp. 99–110.

The Popol Vuh: The Mayan Book of the Dawn of Life. Trans. Dennis Tedlock. New York: Simon & Schuster, 1985.

Prochaska, Rita. *Taquile: Weavers of a Magic World*. Lima, Peru: Arius, 1988.

Reinhard, Johan. "Las montañas sagradas: Un estudio etnoarqueológico de ruinas en las altas cumbres andinas." *Cuadernos de Historia* (Santiago) 3 (1983): 27–62.

———. *The Nazca Lines: A New Perspective on Their Origin and Meaning*. Lima, Peru: Editorial Los Pinos, 1985.

———. "Chavín and Tiahuanaco: A New Look at Two Andean Ceremonial Centers." *National Geographic Research* 3 (1985): 395–422.

Rius-Camps, Josep. *El camino de Pablo a la misión de los paganos: Comentario lingüístico y exegético a Hechos 13–28*. Madrid: Ediciones Cristiandad, 1984.

Rojas Vilchez, Raúl. " 'Sacrifican' a campesino en Puno," *Diario La República* (Lima, Peru), March 3, 1986, p. 14.

Rostworowski de Diez Canseco, María. *Historia del Tahuantinsuyo*. Lima, Peru: Instituto de Estudios Peruanos, 1988.

———. *Estructuras andinas del poder*. Lima, Peru: Instituto de Estudios Peruanos, 1983.

Roth, Cecil, ed. *The Ritual Murder Libel and the Jew: The Report of Cardinal Lorenzo Ganganelli*. London: Woburn Press, 1934.

Rowe, John H. "Inca Culture at the Time of Spanish Conquest." In *Handbook of South American Indians*, Vol. 2. Washington, D.C.: Smithsonian Institution, pp. 183–330.

Sanders, E. P. *Jesus and Judaism*. Philadelphia: Fortress Press, 1985.

Schele, Linda. "Human Sacrifice Among the Classic Maya." In *Ritual Human Sacrifice in Mesoamerica: A Conference at Dumbarton Oaks*, October 13–14, 1979, ed. Elizabeth H. Boone. Cambridge, Mass,: Harvard University Press, 1984, pp. 6–48.

———, and Mary Ellen Miller. *The Blood of Kings: Dynasty and Ritual in Maya Art*. Fort Worth, Texas: Kimbell Art Museum, 1986.

Schobinger, Juan, ed. *La "momia" del Cerro El Toro*. Mendoza, Argentina: 1966.

———. "Breve historia de la arqueología de alta montaña en los Andes meridionales." In *La "momia" del Cerro El Toro*, pp. 11–27.

Schweitzer, Albert. *The Quest of the Historical Jesus*. London: A & C Black, Ltd., 1936.

Scobie, Alistair. *Murder for Magic: Witchcraft in Africa*. London: Cassell, 1965.

Stager, Lawrence E., and Samuel R. Wolff. "Child Sacrifice at Carthage: Religious Rite or Population Control?" *Biblical Archaeology Review* (January/February 1984), pp. 31–51.

Tanenbaum, Marc. "A Response to Professor Maccoby's Thesis." In *The Origins of the Holocaust: Christian Anti-Semitism*, ed. Randolph L. Braham. New York: Columbia University Press, 1986.

Taylor, Gerald. *Ritos y tradiciones de Huarochiri: Versión paleográfica, interpretación fonológica y traducción al castellano.* Lima, Peru: Instituto de Estudios Peruanos, 1987.

Urton, Gary. *At the Crossroads of the Earth and the Sky.* Austin: University of Texas Press, 1981.

Valencia Durán. *Proceso, Rol. No. 24.228, a fin de investigar el delito de homicidio perpetrado en la persona de Luis Quimén Painecur.* Juzgado del Crimen de Nuevo. Imperial: October 2, 1962.

Van den Berg, Hans. *Diccionario religioso Aymara.* Iquitos, Peru: CETA-IDEA, 1985.

Vargas, Manuel, "The Carnival of Oruro." In *An Insider's Guide to Bolivia*, comp. Peter McFarren, Teresa Prada, and Ana Rebeca Prada. La Paz, Bolivia: Fundación Cultural Quipus, 1988, pp. 169–72.

Velasco de Tord, Emma. "La K'apakocha: Sacrificios humanos en el Incario." *Etnohistoria y Antropología Andina* (Lima) (1978): 193–99.

Vilney, Zev. *Israel Guide.* Jerusalem: Hamakor Press, 1973.

"Who Was Jesus?," *Time*, August 16, 1988.

Wilber, Ken. *Up from Eden: A Transpersonal View of Human Evolution.* Garden City, N.Y.: Anchor Press/Doubleday, 1981.

Wilhelm de Moesbach, Ernesto. *Voz de Arauco.* Villarrica, Chile: Imprenta San Francisco, 1959.

Zuidema, Thomas. "Shafttombs and the Inca Empire." *Journal of the Steward Anthropological Society* 9:1–2 (1978): 133–79.

INDEX